Antoine

Life of Napoleon

Vol. 4

SALZWASSER
VERLAG

Antoine Henri Jomini, H. W. Halleck

Life of Napoleon

Vol. 4

Reprint of the original, first published in 1864.

1st Edition 2022 | ISBN: 978-3-75259-248-1

Verlag (Publisher): Salzwasser Verlag GmbH, Zeilweg 44, 60439 Frankfurt, Deutschland
Vertretungsberechtigt (Authorized to represent): E. Roepke, Zeilweg 44, 60439 Frankfurt, Deutschland
Druck (Print): Books on Demand GmbH, In de Tarpen 42, 22848 Norderstedt, Deutschland

LIFE OF NAPOLEON.

VOLUME IV.

LIFE

OF

NAPOLEON

BY BARON JOMINI

"Je fus ambitieux; tout homme l'est, sans doute;
Mais jamais roi, pontife, ou chef, ou citoyen,
Ne conçut un projet aussi grand que le mien."

VOLTAIRE, *Mahomet.*

TRANSLATED FROM THE FRENCH.

WITH NOTES,

BY H. W. HALLECK, LL.D.

IN FOUR VOLUMES.—WITH AN ATLAS.

VOL. IV.

NEW YORK

1864.

CONTENTS.

VOL. IV.

CHAPTER XVIII.—*Continued.*

CAMPAIGN OF 1812 IN RUSSIA.

FROM THE EVACUATION OF MOSCOW TO END OF CAMPAIGN.

CHAPTER XIX.

SPRING CAMPAIGN OF 1813.

FROM THE DECLARATION OF WAR BY PRUSSIA TO THE GENERAL COALITION.

CHAPTER XX.

AUTUMN CAMPAIGN OF 1813.

FROM THE RENEWAL OF HOSTILITIES TO THE RETREAT ON THE RHINE

CHAPTER XXI.

CAMPAIGN OF 1814.

FROM THE RETREAT ON THE RHINE TO THE ABDICATION OF FONTAINEBLEAU.

CHAPTER XXII.

CAMPAIGN OF 1815.

FROM NAPOLEON'S RETURN FROM ELBA TO HIS EXILE TO ST. HELENA.

LIST OF MAPS

TO ILLUSTRATE

JOMINI'S LIFE OF NAPOLEON.

VOL. IV.

CHAPTER XVIII*.

CAMPAIGN OF 1812 IN RUSSIA.

PART II.—RETREAT FROM MOSCOW.

Napoleon finally determines to retreat—Attack on Murat—Departure from Moscow—Retreat on Borowsk—Position of the two Armies—Battle of Wiasma—Approach of Winter—Conspiracy of Mallet and Lahorie—Disaster of Krasnoi—Desperate Efforts of Ney—New Difficulties of the Retreat—March of Kutusof on Elvira—Projects of the Russians—Battle of the Beresina—Remarks on this Passage—Continuation of the Retreat—Napoleon departs for Paris—Motives of this Departure—General Causes of the Failure of this Campaign—Continuation of the Retreat under Murat—He resigns the Command to Eugene—Final Refuge of the Army behind the Elbe—Summary of the Campaign of 1812 in Spain—The English destroy the Bridge of Almaraz—Capture of Salamanca—Wellington enters Madrid—His unsuccessful Siege of Badajos—He retires into Portugal—Operations in the East of Spain—Conclusion.

Napoleon finally determines to retreat.—The time necessary for a reply from St. Petersburg to my overtures having passed, it was evident that the enemy did not desire peace. As our occupation of the salient point of Moscow had not produced the desired effect, and as the winter-season was rapidly advancing, it was now absolutely necessary to regain the line of the Borysthenese, in order to cover our communications. It was impossible to pass the winter amid the ruins of Moscow. On the thirteenth of October there was a light fall of snow. This was a powerful spur in hastening our departure. I hoped to be in motion by the twentieth of October. On the fifteenth the hospitals were evacuated, the sick being sent to Smolensko. The snow of the thirteenth was followed by fine weather.

* Continued from Vol. III.

Attack on Murat.—On the eighteenth of October Ney's corps entered Moscow preparatory to beginning the retreat, and while I was passing it in review the news came that Murat was exposed to a total defeat: a heavy cannonade had been heard all the morning, and the alarm had already reached Moscow. In fact, the Russians, certain that Murat was not in sufficient force to resist their entire army, had conceived a project to destroy him. It had been verbally agreed to avoid a war of outposts, until an answer to my proposition could be received; but Kutusof had rejected every proposal for an armistice, saying that he had no authority to make one. Murat was over-confident and off his guard, and our soldiers, unaccustomed to a repose which they regarded as a forerunner of peace, did not think there was any danger of their being troubled. Benningsen, at the head of two-thirds of the Russian army, thought to carry away our van-guard at Winkowo. The false direction of one of his columns accelerated his attack, and prevented the success of his plan. Nevertheless Murat was compelled to yield to superior forces, and, although he escaped a total defeat, we lost considerable baggage, several cannon, and many brave men.

Departure from Moscow.—I left Moscow on the nineteenth of October, while Lauriston went to seek the expected reply from St. Petersburg: Murat, at the same time, defiled by the left to disengage himself from the presence of the enemy. I, at first, took the road to Taroutina, but, at Troitzkoje, I inclined to the right by the road to Kalouga in order to reach Borousk and Malojaroslawetz before Kutusof could be informed of my intention. If we should gain this last city before him, nothing could prevent our reaching, if not Kalouga, at least Joucknow, to take the road to Elnia.

We left Moscow with a train equal to the army of Darius.

My forces numbered about eighty thousand combatants, and some fifteen thousand convalescents; we had some six hundred pieces of cannon, and two thousand carriages for the artillery. To diminish my train as much as possible I had preserved only such of my lighter bridge equipages as might be necessary in urgent cases. As we could not rely upon regular distributions, each company formed an equipage of two or three carts for the transportation of such provisions as it had collected from the ruins of Moscow, and from the surrounding villages. To these equipages were added those in which, under the pretext of carrying provisions, they concealed the illicit booty which the soldiers, and even the officers, had found in the deserted cellars and stores of Moscow. In order the better to conceal this booty, they pretended that these carts contained clothing, &c., to protect them from the cold. The officers not serving with troops had also each their cart or *britscha* for the same purposes, and under the same pretext. There were almost as many wagons as combatants: never did a modern army present such a spectacle; and it was with such *impedimenta* that we were about to make the most delicate and difficult retreat ever undertaken by an army.*

I was forced to tolerate these abuses, as they were almost our only resource. Our train diminished daily, and the wagons emptied of their provisions served for the transportation of our sick and wounded, or for barricades against the enemy's light troops. Our numerous body of horses con-

* The people who accompanied the army in its retreat from Moscow were mainly Jews, Germans, and Italians who had remained there, notwithstanding the orders of the Russian authorities for its entire abandonment on the approach of the French. Knowing that, for this disobedience, they would be given up to the barbarity of the Cossacks, on the return of the Russians, they were obliged to join the French in order to save their own lives. A large portion of these families, however, were murdered by the Cossacks, or perished from cold and hunger, during the retreat. It is estimated that sixty thousand perished in this way.

sumed all the forage on the way, and gradually diminished for the want of food. The traces which we left behind us attested that *great enterprises perish from the very greatness of the preparations required for their success.*

Mortier remained at Moscow with seven or eight thousand men. He was to cover our communications till our march was well begun, and then to blow up the Kremlin, destroy the public buildings, and evacuate the place.* He was to rally the remains of Junot's troops at Mojaisk, and follow my army on the first favorable opportunity.

Retreat on Borowsk.—Although I had determined to follow the route to Borowsk, I first marched on the old road to Kalouga, in order to deceive the Russians, and enable the king of Naples to collect his scattered troops. On the twentieth, the viceroy, who formed my van-guard turned to the right in order to reach, at Bykassowo, the road from Borowsk on Malojaroslawetz, which, on the twenty-third, was occupied by our troops. I was exceedingly impatient to reach Borowsk where I could learn whether Kutusof had got wind of our departure, and had taken any measures to

* The task assigned to Mortier was a most difficult one, and few of his friends ever expected to see him again. Napoleon embraced him in taking leave, and said to him frankly, yet sadly: "I rely on your good fortune. Still, in war, we must sometimes make part of a sacrifice." In addition to his danger from hosts of the enemy who surrounded him, he had to destroy an immense amount of military munitions left behind. Thousands of barrels of powder were collected in the vaults, and halls and appartments of the Kremlin. On abandoning the place a slow match was attached to this mine. "The Cossacks, eager for plunder, rushed within the deserted halls. Suddenly the majestic fabric was raised into the air. The earth shook under the feet of Mortier. The explosion, in most appalling thunder peal, startled the army in its midnight bivouac. From the darkened and sulphurous skies there was rained down upon the city a horrible shower of fragments of timber, rocks, shattered weapons, heavy pieces of artillery, and mangled bodies." It should be remarked that while preparing to destroy these magazines, Mortier and his division was hotly pressed by the enemy around the Kremlin, and a single spark from his own or the enemy's fire, must have destroyed him and all his men. His success was complete, but almost miraculous.

intercept our march on Kalouga. Here also I was to be joined by Murat, and from here I proposed to push forward Eugene in the direction of Malojaroslawetz. Our future safety depended upon our reaching this point before Kutusof, which, if he had not heard of our departure, was still possible, although three days had been spent in insignificant movements by which we had gained only ten leagues on our line of march. The twenty-third I departed on a gallop for Borowsk, which place Eugene had occupied the night before, and where Murat had already arrived. Nothing being perceived of the enemy except reconnoitering parties on the left, Eugene received orders to march on Malojaroslawetz, and to occupy that city with his advanced guard, as soon as possible. We now had every reason to think that we should reach, without obstacle, the new road from Smolensko by Elnia (Jelnia).

Belluno had been ordered to occupy that place by the division of Baraguay d'Hilliers which consisted of about ten thousand men of the provisional regiments, or recruits, destined for the different regiments of the army. I also directed the governor of Wiasma to send a movable column of three or four thousand men with estafettes in the direction of this new road.

The numerous parties of the enemy on the left denoted some important movement. At Borowsk I learned that Mortier, with powder found in the mines of the Kremlin, had blown up a part of its buildings, and especially its arsenal, and on the twenty-third, had taken the road to Mojaisk, carrying with him General Wintzingerode, who had ventured alone with his aide-de-camp into the streets of Moscow. I hardly thought that Kutusof could debouch in time on Borowsk: but Eugene, who did not understand my projects, and who was occupied with the enemy on his left, advanced too slowly; he did not fear an engagement, but thought that I might be attacked, and if so, that it would be necessary for him to return to take part in the engagement.

But one of those fortuitous events, which seemed connected with this fatal campaign, now defeated my designs. Kutusof, hearing of Eugene's march on Borowsk, but not supposing that we were retreating, had projected a plan to strike the fourth corps-d'armée, as he had Murat. Doctorof, with twenty-five thousand men was directed to accomplish this object. On approaching Borowsk he encountered our army, but supposed it nothing more than Eugene's corps. The partisan Seslavin, getting wind of our approach, informed Doctorof of it, but that general was incredulous. The bold Cossack, piqued at his report not being believed, advanced even to the gates of Borowsk, and captured an officer of the Young Guard, who confirmed his story. Doctorof's chief of staff hastened to Taroutina, to announce to Kutusof that I had left Moscow, and that all my army was on the road to Kalouga: at the same time, the corps which had been sent to surprise Borowsk, directed its march on Malojaroslawetz. This fortuitous incident produced the most grave consequences; for the Russian army, which would have remained quiet at Taroutina, had it not been for this accidental receipt of the important news of my retreat, raised their camp on the twenty-fourth, and also directed their march on Malojaroslawetz. On the morning of the twenty-fifth, Doctorof reached that city, and expelled our detachment; but the viceroy soon arrived with his whole corps, and retook the place. An obstinate combat followed, and continued all day. The viceroy sustained himself with glory against a superior force. The Russian corps, which successively arrived, continually reënforced the engaged troops. Seven times was the burning city taken and retaken; but its ruins finally remained in the hands of the viceroy. We lost the brave Delzons, and Pino and two of Eugene's aides were wounded. Toward night my army also reached Malojaroslawetz. Davoust sustained Eugene with two divisions which established themselves on the flanks of the fourth corps, so as to enable it to maintain its position.

We were now masters of this city, or rather of a funeral pile covered with dead; but we were none the further advanced towards the accomplishment of our object. Kutusof had taken position at some distance and still barred our passage. To force this barrier it would have been necessary to give battle to an army which had already established itself on the very communication which we wished to open; or to give battle for the purpose of effecting a lateral retreat. But such a course seemed to me the less prudent, as it was not indispensable, the road to Wereya being still open in our rear. The chance appearing to me too hazardous, I renounced the project of piercing my way to Kalouga, and decided to regain the road to Wiasma,—the only way which was now open to me. During the twenty-fifth, the two armies remained in position, almost within cannon range of each other. But, on the twenty-sixth, I took the road to Borowsk.

Every thing in this retreat seemed to be at the caprice of fortune; for, at the very moment that I renounced the intention of piercing the enemy's lines, Kutusof, on his side, fearing to risk a general battle, ordered a retrograde movement. I was soon informed of this, but persisted in my resolution, which was certainly a fault. I had a consultation with my officers, and all, even to the stoic Mouton, were of the opinion that it was necessary to regain the Niemen by the shortest and least difficult rout. Thus, instead of taking the direct road to Medyn and Joucknow on Elnia, driving before us the cavalry which still barred the way, I returned by Wereya on Mojaisk.

Respective Position of the two Armies.—Our chances of a retreat were now most unfavorable, as may readily seen by examining the respective position of the parties. The Russian army reached Taroutina with sixty thousand old soldiers and twenty thousand irregular troops ; but while there, it had been reënforced to ninety thousand regular soldiers and thirty thousand militia and Cossacks. The Cossack cavalry, though unfit for battles, is intelligent, enterprising, and indefatigable. There are no European horses, nor even Russian, that can rival those of the Don, in enduring fatigue and privations ; and, in our present situation, this militia was even more useful to the enemy than the *élite* regiments of the guard.

Our line of retreat now lay on a single isolated road ; while the enemy's army had a road, even shorter than ours, that led obliquely on Wiasma, Smolensko, Krasnoi, and Kopys. We had now not more than fifteen thousand horse, and at the end of two weeks not over five thousand, with which to make reconnoisances in front, and to protect our flanks and immense parks. My infantry numbered from sixty to sixty-five thousand brave men ; but what could they do against an enemy who, by the lateral direction of his line of operations, could select his time and attack us in the most critical position, either in front or rear ? If we had taken the road to Elnia, the enemy would have followed us only in rear, and we should not have been exposed to parallel attacks on our line of retreat, thus daily compromising our safety.

Having regained the great road to Smolensko, I continued to follow it. Our only object now was to escape as soon as possible across this desolated country. To avoid inconvenience in the march, I divided my army into four corps, which followed each other at about half a day's distance. I began the march with my guards ; then came successively the corps of Ney, the Viceroy, and Davoust. The latter formed the rear-guard.

Kutusof sent, in pursuit of us, his Cossacks and an advanced guard of twenty-five thousand men, under the orders of General Miloradowitsch, who overtook our rear-guard on the first of November, near Gjath. The main body of the Russian army marched directly on Wiasmá, with the intention of cutting off our retreat. We, however, reached that city before the Russians. I passed through the city, directing Ney to await there the arrival of the Viceroy and Davoust, who might otherwise be cut off. The event justified the necessity of this precaution.

Battle of Wiasma.—On the third day of November Miloradowitsch executed very skillfully a forced march parallel to the great roads, and debouched on that road between Wiasma and Federowskoe. The viceroy had already reached Wiasma, but Davoust had not yet passed Federowskoe. The circumstance was critical; but the viceroy accomplished everything by the vigor of his resolution. He immediately turned back and assailed the Russians, who, hemmed in on the other side by the troops of Davoust, were obliged to decamp in haste, and open a passage to those in rear. My two corps now fell back on Wiasma closely followed by the Russians who had received a reënforcement.

Seeing us in retreat, the enemy redoubled his energy, and drove our rear-guard from Wiasma and across the river of that name. This affair, which we might regard as a victory, since we repelled and defeated the enemy, cost us about five thousand men *hors de combat*. It might, however, have had disastrous consequences for us, if the main body of the Russian army, which had already reached the road from Wiasma to Joucknow, had acted with decision; but Kutusof, who feared to engage in a general battle, had stopped at Bykowo, three leagues from Wiasma, and sent forward only a heavy detachment of cavalry. This was held in check during the battle by the corps of Ney. The operations of Kutusof on this occasion have been criticised.

In a tactical point of view they were certainly faulty, for if his sixty thousand men encamped at Bykowo, had driven Ney from Wiasma, he would have destroyed the half of my army: but on the other hand, as he was certain of our retreat to the Niemen, he deemed it more safe not to risk a battle, but rather to build for us a *bridge of gold!*

Approach of Winter.—Having escaped this imminent danger my army continued its retreat on Smolensko. Our march was becoming every day more difficult; the provisions which we brought from Moscow were exhausted; our horses were dying from starvation; this forced us to leave much of our artillery: winter now succeeded to an extraordinarily fine autumn. Ney who now commanded the rear-guard complained of the disorder which was daily increasing among our men. My eagles, formerly the emblem of triumph, had now become to our faithful soldiers only a talisman for privation and suffering. Death seemed the inevitable fate of those who still pressed around them with courageous resignation.

Conspiracy of Mallet and Lahorie.—Fate seemed resolved now to heap upon me every misfortune. As if those which had arrayed themselves before our eyes here, were not sufficient, it prepared in France the overthrow of my throne by a simple state's-prisoner! On the sixth of November, within a day's march of Smolensko, I heard of the conspiracy of Generals Mallet and Lahorie,—the most singular, perhaps, in the history of the world.

General Mallet, more renowned for his exploits of gallantry than for his feats of arms, was an ardent demagogue; but not a partisan of the Bourbons as some have since pretended. His conduct had compelled me (for the last four years) to shut him up in prison. He had afterwards been transferred, on account of ill health to a *maison de santé*, where he was on parole. Here this ardent adventurer conceived the bold project of overthrowing my government. He had heard of our arrival in Moscow, and of the burning of that city. Foreseeing the result of the campaign or thinking that I would be so much occupied at eight hundred leagues from Paris as not to be able to check his designs, he escaped on the night of the twenty-third and twenty-fourth of October, presented himself at the barracks, announced my death, and, supplied with a forged order from the staff of the place, he demanded a detachment in the name of the provisional government which had just assumed the reins of state. At the head of his troop he flew to the Conciergerie, and released General Lahorie, former aid-de-camp of Moreau; this officer with a detachment of a hundred men, marched to the house of the minister Savary, arrested him and sent him to prison in his own place, while he installed himself as minister in the place of Savary. Mallet had gone to the residence of General Hullin, commandant of Paris, whom he hoped also to replace. Finding him more disposed to resistance, Mallet fired a pistol at him and wounded him; but Colonel Laborde, having recognised Mallet as an escaped prisoner, seized hold of him, and struggled with him till the guard could secure his person. The troops now saw that they had been deceived, and returning to the office of police, they seized Lahorie just as he was being measured for a minister's coat, and carried him back to the Conciergerie.

The senate, called together by the archchancellor, met just in time to learn the arrest of these insane conspirators, who, on being tried by a military commission, received the reward due to their rash attempt.

If this movement had been delayed till the news of our disastrous retreat had reached Paris, the result might have been different. We should not have escaped so cheaply, if, taking example from Prince Edward, a Bourbon prince had landed at Havre at the same time that they installed a provisional government at Paris. I communicated this news only to a small number of my officers, and I was convinced, from the effect which it produced on them, that the fragile nature of my power astonished them more than the misfortunes that were hanging over us.

Renewed Disasters in the Retreat.—On the seventh of November, the cold began to be more serious, and developed with frightful rapidity the germs of dissolution which had already appeared at Wiasma. We had left Moscow with more than ninety thousand men ; but not half this number was under arms at Dorogobuje. We now had only two marches to make before reaching Smolensko ; we were about to receive the hand-mills which had been sent from Paris, and for the want of which our soldiers had been obliged to live on boiled rye. I hoped to find here provisions and a sufficient shelter to enable us to reëstablish order. The division of Baraguay-d'Hilliers, coming from France with reënforcements for the regiments, had been cantoned on the road to Elnia which we were about to reach. The sight of these soldiers, in order and in discipline, would be calculated to produce a beneficial influence upon our veterans. I moreover trusted to the firmness of Ney to have time to effect the reorganization of the army. But a crowd of circumstances combined to destroy these frail combinations and deceitful hopes.

Flank March of Kutusof on Elnia.—Kutusof had left to his Cossacks the care of pursuing us, while he himself, with the main body of his army, marched parallel to the great road by Elnia. This plan was the more advisable on his part, as it took his army over a more fertile country while, at the same time, it threatened my line of retreat, and forced me to hasten my march without giving my troops any repose. His vanguard thus fell upon Liakowo in the midst of the division of Baraguay-d'Hilliers, and carried off Augereau's brigade, after an insignificant combat.

I arrived at Smolensko on the ninth, and the remainder of my army on the thirteenth. We had looked upon this place as the Land of Promise, and as the termination of all our misfortunes. But how greatly were we deceived. This city, which in the summer had appeared to us so charming, and whose environs, especially on the south side, seemed so rich and prolific in grain, now presented only deserted houses filled with the sick and dying, and destitute of magazines! The presence of Belluno's corps for two months in the vicinity, the garrison of the place, the fifteen thousand sick and wounded, and the passing troops, had consumed sixty thousand rations per day,—an immense supply, sufficient for my whole army of Italy, but which had here been consumed as fast as it arrived. Thus, instead of the supplies which I had expected, I found at Smolensko only scenes of desolation. My army arrived in disorganized bands; three days of severe cold weather, though in no way extraordinary, had sufficed to break up, in a great degree, our organization, and to cause us to abandon nearly two hundred pieces of artillery.

On leaving Dorogobuje, the viceroy's corps took the road to Doukowchina which he had followed in our advance, but in a very different attitude. Closely pursued by the five thousand horse of Platof, he found himself closed in on the Vop, a stream scarcely perceptible in the summer, but now so swollen by the rains as to be fordable only in certain places. The bridges had been destroyed, and the steep banks of the river were now covered with snow and ice. After numerous efforts Eugene succeeded in crossing with a few pieces and his infantry, who were obliged to ford the stream with the water up to their shoulders; but the artillery and baggage were lost. The half famished remains of this corps reached Smolensko at the same time with the rear-guard of Ney.

Plan of the Russians to cut off Napoleon's Retreat. — I was greatly relieved by the arrival of these two corps, but still there was the most urgent necessity for an immediate march. The enemy now exhibited as much activity as audacity, and almost everywhere gained an ascendency over my lieutenants.

Wittgenstein, coöperating with the corps of Steinheil to cut off St. Cyr's retreat on the Dwina had attacked him at Polotsk ; St. Cyr and Wrede had repelled his attack, it is true, but not finding themselves in condition to sustain a second assault, they abandoned Polotsk and fell back on Czereya. Wittgenstein had followed in pursuit as far as Zeasnicki on the Oula. This circumstance had forced Victor to leave Smolensko in order to rally the wrecks of Oudinot ; the two marshals had established themselves at Czereya, in order to hold Wittgenstein in check ; his army, reënforced by the militia of St. Petersburg and the troops of Finland, now numbered not less than seventy-five battalions and thirty-eight squadrons, without including the Cossacks. Tschighagof had also taken the offensive on Minsk and the Bug, with one hundred and two battalions and one hundred and sixteen squadrons.

The corps of Schwartzenberg and Reynier, seeing themselves opposed by superior numbers, after the junction of Tormassof and the army of Moldavia, instead of adopting Minsk as the pivot of their operations, recrossed the Bug and based themselves on Warsaw, thus renouncing all coöperation with my army. In consequence of this grave error, Admiral Tschighagof left Sacken to observe the Austrians, and prepared to advance with the rest of the army of Moldavia on Minsk, where he could coöperate with Wittgenstein so as to establish a formidable mass on our rear. On the other side the grand Russian army, already established on the road to Poslaw, was ready to intercept the route to Mistislaw and menace that to Krasnoi.

Napoleon retreats on Krasnoi.—It was now necessary to hasten our retreat before this last hope should be closed against us. I left Smolensko with my guards on the fourteenth. The viceroy, Davoust, and Ney followed at the distance of a day's march. The latter reënforced by the fresh troops of the garrison of Smolensko blew up the walls of that city, and departed, as my rear-guard, on the seventeenth. This march, with columns in echelons, at a considerable distance, and across a desolate country where no subsistence could be procured, has been the subject of criticism ; and I must confess that a retreat by wings, in three columns, by parallel roads, would have been more advantageous. If I had foreseen the event of Krasnoi, I should have descended the Dnieper by the right bank by Katana as far as Doubrowna or Orcza, thus placing that river between my army and the enemy. It is certain that this resolution would have saved us many cruel losses. But, as our maps of the country were defective, and we had no knowledge of the existence of practicable roads in that direction, I could not venture upon such an uncertainty.

We had already sustained immense losses ; our artillery was reduced one half, and our cavalry entirely ruined. Even the horses which had survived the effects of hunger and fatigue, were not properly shod for the ice, and there was no iron in the country to supply this deficiency. From Wiasma to Orcza there are numerous little hills, and the streams had cut for themselves deep beds. These steep slopes of the road were so covered with ice that our horses could not draw our pieces and caissons ; our men were continually obliged to assist in moving these loads, and every day a large number of carriages were abandoned in the road. The pen of history can never fully describe the misfortunes of this retreat; the horrors suffered by our army exceed the most exaggerated stories of fiction.

Battle of Krasnoi.—It was now scarcely possible that we could reach Krasnoi without encountering the enemy. In fact, the advanced guard of Miloradowitsch appeared, on the fifteenth, between that city and Korytnia. I reached Krasnoi with the main body of my guards; but the rear of the column had to sustain an unequal combat. The next day the viceroy found Miloradowitsch in a position commanding the great road, and closing the passage. He attempted to cut his way, sword in hand, but failed. The enemy thinking him lost beyond hope, summoned him to surrender. But the viceroy was not a man to be easily discouraged: while his rear-guard amused the Russians with demonstrations of an attack on the great road, he escaped with the main body between that road and the Borysthenese. He reached Krasnoi in the night, if not without loss, at least with glory, for he had saved the greater part of his corps. On the same day, the sixteenth, Kutusof also arrived before Krasnoi, and established himself within a short distance of the city on the road to Roslaw.

My situation was now critical. Davoust and Ney were still in rear, and if I suspended my retreat till they came up, the enemy might prolong himself by the left, and easily intercept our only line of communication. But it seemed a hard extremity to abandon the half of my army to the Russians. I therefore determined to brave the danger, and wait at Krasnoi, at least till the arrival of Davoust. But to remain here inactive would only embolden the enemy; I therefore resolved to act on the offensive. On the morning of the seventeenth I caused the village of Ouwarowo to be assailed by Mortier, and marched there myself at the head of the Old Guard. The combat was continued with varied success until the arrival of the first corps. Kutusof, fearing the result of a general battle, and trusting to cold and hunger to effect the destruction of my army, had directed Miloradowitsch not to compromise himself for the sake of opposing the march of Davoust. This general, menaced with an attack, fell back on the right of the army, and did not again reach the great road, till the troops of the marshal had entirely passed. The Russian van-guard now made a vigorous attack upon our left, while Kutusof detached the greater part of his army to turn Krasnoi, to debouch on the road between that city and Liady, to turn our right, and thus entirely cut us off. On learning the march of this column, I felt that I had not a moment to lose, and ordered an instant retreat. Our rear-guard experienced a considerable loss, but the main body of the army was saved. We passed the night at Liady, and the next day continued our retreat on Doubrowna and Orcza.

I think I acquired some glory in this affair of Krasnoi. Perhaps my march in echelons on a single road may be criticised; but the impartial historian will say with what resolution I disengaged successively the corps of Davoust and Eugene. Marching on foot through the snow, and supporting myself with a cane while crawling up the slippery slopes of the road, I myself directed the columns which drove back the enemy.

Happy would I have been, if like the Emperor Julian, I had here encountered death, which I desired! But since the invention of gunpowder there are no combats hand to hand, as in antiquity, with the sword and buckler of the Romans; and I found no Parthian to terminate my career.

Desperate Efforts of Ney.—I had taken the road to Orcza, with the deepest regret at the necessity of abandoning Ney in order to save the rest of the army; he seemed lost beyond hope. But to our utter astonishment this brave general succeeded in saving his eagles and the élite of his corps. On reaching Krasnoi on the evening of the eighteenth, he found the Russian army established in a position commanding the great road; after admirable but unsuccessful efforts to dislodge the enemy, he found himself completely cut off. But taking council from his own courage alone, he put himself in march with about three thousand men on Gousinoe, where he crossed the Borysthenese on recently formed ice. The first battalion succeeded in reaching the right bank, but the ice broke with those in rear, and many were drowned. The remainder of this corps and the stragglers from the rest of the army, finding no chance of retreat, were compelled to surrender. Ney had succeeded in crossing the river only to fall into the midst of the Cossacks of Platof. The enemy had a good battery of artillery, while Ney had not a single cannon, nor a single cavalry soldier. His soldiers were destitute of munitions and could scarcely discharge their fire-arms; but having recourse only to their own valor and their bayonets, they finally succeeded, after some severe combats, in joining us at Orcza, on the night of the twentieth and twenty-first. My joy was so much the greater as I had regarded them as lost. Ney was saluted by the whole army, as the most intrepid of its chiefs.

New Difficulties to be Encountered.—The affairs of Krasnoi had cost me one-half of my combatants, and I now had to devise means for saving the remainder, which was no easy matter. The first thing to be done was to renounce the system of echelons on single roads, for a march by parallel columns; but how could we expect to do this with two thirds of our soldiers reduced to a disorderly mob? Moreover, the roads from Orcza to Wilna were intercepted by Wittgenstein, and Admiral Tschighagof might advance on the line of the Beresina, so as to close the roads from Orcza to Minsk. On leaving Smolensko, I had ordered Oudinot to place himself at Bohr, so as to reconnoitre the road to Minsk, and, at the same time, had directed Victor to try what resistance Wittgenstein was likely to oppose to our march on Wilna. On the fourteenth, Victor attacked the Russians at Czasniki, but, finding them solidly based on the Oula, he returned to Czereya.

At Doubrowna I learned that Tschighagof had advanced on Minsk, while the garrison of that place had fallen back on Borisof; and it was to be feared that Dombrowsky, who was blockading Bobrouisk had not been able to gain the *tête-de-pont* of the Beresina. I hesitated at Orcza what course to pursue. Should I advance against Tschighagof with all my remaining forces, or direct my march against Wittgenstein so as to form a junction with Belluno? If I advanced in the direction of Polotsk, might not Kutusof unite with the army of Moldavia and anticipate me at Wilna?

Hoping still, by forced marches, to anticipate the admiral on the Beresina, I gave my troops but a single day's repose at Orcza, and, on the twenty-first, I resumed our march on Cokrano. Oudinot's corps was now to form the van-guard, and that of Victor the rear-guard. I reached Tolocsin on the twenty-second, and Bohr the next day. I here found it was necessary to open a passage sword in hand, as the Russians had anticipated us on the Beresina. The admiral had entered Minsk on the seventeenth, and on the twenty-first his advanced guard attacked and carried the intrenchments of the *tête-de-pont* of Borisow before Dombrowski, who had just arrived from Boronisk, had been able to establish himself. The next day the admiral passed the Beresina. His advanced guard at Bohr was defeated and completely routed on the twenty-third by Oudinot's corps. The admiral had merely time to repass the Beresina, and destroy the bridge of Borisow.

This success was therefore useless, and my position more critical than ever. I called to me a general officer who had indicated the existence of a direct road from Jembin to Molodeschno; I imparted to him my embarrassment and my projects. Reasoning on the principles of war, I thought to fall, as at Castiglione and Ratisbon, on the armies that annoyed me the most. I thought to unite my guard and remaining forces to Belluno's corps, and, with these fifty thousand men, to attack Wittgenstein, drive him back on the Dwina, form a junction with Macdonald, and retake the road to Wilna. This general objected that this manœuvre, perfectly correct under any other circumstances, would now be accompanied with numerous inconveniences. It was objected:

1st. That the country of Lepel and the upper Beresina was covered with marshes, the dikes of which Wittgenstein, with his one hundred and fifty pieces of cannon, could defend till Kutusof came to his assistance;

2d. That the destitute condition of our army would not permit us to delay the retreat;

3d. That, by taking the direction of the Dwina, we should expose ourselves to be attacked in rear by the united forces of Kutusof and the admiral, before we could finish with Wittgenstein;

4th. That, as the road to Minsk was occupied by the enemy, it would be more prudent to take the road from Jembin on Molodeschno, for, if we found that closed, we could then take the passage of Vileika. Both of these roads, and especially that from Jembin, passed through a fertile country which had not yet been laid waste.

But these peremptory reasons were not sufficient to deter me from my plan; I still adhered to a manœuvre which might procure us glorious results, and rescue us from the hands of the enemy. I called another general who had been sent the day before by Belluno, and who might have more positive information respecting the positions of Wittgenstein. His opinions only tended to confirm those of the other officer, and, urged by the advice of Murat and Eugene, I finally relinquished my project. I, therefore, left on the twenty-fourth, for Lochnitsa, and, on the twenty-fifth, collected all my forces at Borisow, except Victor's corps. This last, pursued by Wittgenstein, also moved on Lochnitsa, instead of taking the road to Baran so as to cover our march.

Passage of the Beresina.—Never had my situation been so desperate as now. Hemmed in on the right and left, and in rear, by superior forces, I found myself arrested in front by a river difficult to cross, and defended by an entire army. And it was with soldiers half dead with hunger and cold that I now had to overcome obstacles that would have frightened the best organized army in the world. Fortune seemed resolved to heap upon us every possible calamity during this fatal retreat. The cold, so severe on our arrival at Smolensko as to close the Dnieper, suddenly moderated after my arrival at Krasnoi; a thaw of two days broke the ice, and the Beresina was much swollen. This was a double misfortune. If the river had been frozen sufficiently to enable us to pass with cannon, we should have crossed in twenty-four hours in sufficient force to crush Tschighagof, without even the trouble of building a bridge.

This river, on the contrary, was now greatly swollen and filled with large masses of floating ice, so as to render the construction of our bridges not only difficult, but almost impossible. But, as I could not command the elements, it was necessary to take my part and redouble my efforts to overcome the immense obstacles which both nature and the enemy opposed to my passage.

The forces which I had brought from Moscow did not exceed fifteen thousand combatants including the guards, and the corps of Belluno and Oudinot amounted only to about the same number. In our front disputing this difficult passage, was Tschighagof with twenty-eight thousand men; on our right Wittgenstein and Steinheil with twenty-five thousand men, and on our left Kutusof with fifty thousand. I felt that I could effect this passage only by a surprise; and to do this it was important to make demonstrations on several points in order to deceive the vigilance of the enemy. Oudinot displayed the heads of his columns in the direction of Oucholoda, toward the Lower Beresina, while the other detachments in silence ascended the river toward Wesselowo. These demonstrations produced the desired result; the admiral prolonged himself by his right toward the road to Igoumen. We profited without delay by the false movement to effect the passage above Borisow. On the night of the twenty-fifth and twenty-sixth, we moved from Borisow to Studenka, where we arrived on the morning of the twenty-sixth. General Aubry had constructed a bridge of poor materials for infantry, while General Eblé, with the sappers and pontoniers, erected a trestle bridge, for the passage of all arms. This bridge, eighty toises in length, was constructed with admirable rapidity by our brave sappers, who precipitated themselves into the water up to their shoulders, notwithstanding the severe cold and the enormous masses of ice that floated in the Beresina. One-half of these intrepid men perished in their devoted efforts to save the army. Nothing could diminish their ardor. The vanguard of General Tschoplitz hastened to oppose itself to our projects; as this might prevent the construction of the bridge, the cavalry of Corbineau swam the river with their horses, and were supported by a battalion of sharp-shooters, who crossed on a raft. The enemy was repelled, but he soon succeeded in reëstablishing himself so as to command the debouch. As soon as the bridge of plank was finished, Oudinot's infantry crossed over and drove Tschoplitz to Strakow, a league from Borisow; being reënforced by Pahlen at this place, he resumed the offensive. But Oudinot, taking advantage of a piece of woods, succeeded in maintaining his position. Our brave soldiers seemed convinced of the importance of this combat, and every one redoubled his energy; Frenchmen, Poles, Swiss, Croates, covered themselves with glory, and the enemy was held in check the whole evening. Thus far everything had gone for the best; but it was still necessary to secure the road from Jembin, which crossed a marsh, over which was a kind of dyke with three bridges of one hundred toises each. If the enemy should destroy these, the ice not being sufficiently strong to supply their place, all would be lost. Oudinot was ordered to send in haste a detachment, which fortunately arrived there in time to secure the road. In the meantime the remainder of our broken troops and the corps of Belluno, approached Studzianka. Ney crossed in the night with the Poles and a division of the Young Guard, amounting in all to not more than twenty-five hundred men; he was to unite with Oudinot, and he put himself at the head of the few forces which we could oppose to Tschighagof. I crossed with my head-quarters after noon, and the passage continued a part of the night and all day of the twenty-seventh. It could only be effected slowly, the trestle bridges having broken twice, on account of the muddy bed of the stream and the masses of floating ice. Tschighagof thus gained time to return to Borisow with the two divisions which he had taken in the direction of Ouscha; but, instead of marching directly against Oudinot, he remained opposite Borisow, and sought to communicate with Wittgenstein. Belluno's corps had left that city in the night of the twenty-sixth and twenty-seventh, to march to Studzianka leaving Parthouneaux's division to guard Borisow until noon, as much to draw the attention of Tschighagof as to afford a momentary check to Wittgenstein.

This detachment was unfortunate ; hardly had the division returned to Borisow when it was announced that it was cut off. As soon as Parthouneaux learned that Wittgenstein had established himself at Staro-Borisow between him and Belluno, he attempted to effect his escape. There are two roads leading from Borisow to Studzianka, one of which was closed by Wittgenstein, while the other was still open. Unfortunately, Parthouneaux took the one occupied by the enemy. Ignorant of the enemy's force, he attacked him with bravery ; but, after useless efforts, he fell into the hands of the Cossacks and was taken prisoner. The next morning his division, numbering about three thousand men, besides some four thousand stragglers from other corps, surrendered to the enemy. A battalion which at the same time took the other road, succeeded in effecting its escape. The taking of Borisow enabled Tschighagof to establish a bateau-bridge so as to communicate with Wittgenstein ; he was now reënforced by Jermolof and Platof.

The enemy combined, for the twenty-eighth, a simultaneous effort on the two banks of the river, and the result was calculated to decide the fate of our army. Wittgenstein prepared to attack Belluno by the left bank, while the admiral marched at the head of his divisions on Stakhow. We anticipated him by attacking his advanced guard, which we drove back on Stakhow, notwitstanding a glorious resistance. Ney threw a division of Doumerc's cuirassiers into the woods which were occupied by the Russian chasseurs ; they made great havoc in the enemy's ranks and captured between twelve and fifteen hundred prisoners. The enemy was driven back, but, after a bloody combat which continued till after ten o'clock at night, they succeeded in holding Stakhow. The brave Generals Zayonschek and

Legrand were wounded and the remains of the second corps fell, covered with the laurels which they had won within the last two days.

In the mean time Victor had made a no less glorious resistance against the attack of Wittgenstein. He first bravely disputed, with only seven or eight thousand men, the heights which border the avenues of Studzianka, but finding that he was likely to be surrounded, he concentrated his forces near the bridges. The Russians now crown the heights with their batteries and pour in a heavy fire upon the multitude of sick and wounded and stragglers, and the innumerable quantity of carriages which had collected here for the purpose of crossing the river. This confused mass of men, horses and wagons, rush with such impetuosity to the bridges, that three-quarters of them are either trampled under foot or precipitated into the river.

The piercing cries of these wretched beings, as they are thrust forward to inevitable death by their own countrymen, in their haste to escape the murderous fire of the enemy's batteries ; the horrible aspect of the thousand women who have followed in the train of the army, as they are trampled under foot by the flying columns, or driven into the river, or mutilated by the enemy's artillery ; caissons and shells exploding in the midst of this straggling mass ; the bed of the Beresina covered with the wrecks of broken carriages and the bodies of the dead ; all together formed a scene of desolation without parallel in the annals of history !

The firmness of Belluno saved the remains of this multitude, by affording them time to escape by the bridges ; but they had the greatest possible difficulty in opening a passage through the broken carriages, and the dead bodies of men and horses. The cannonade continued till night, and it was not till the morning of the twenty-ninth, that Belluno passed the Beresina with three thousand men who remained to burn the bridges.

Remarks on this Passage.—Had it not been for the misfortune of Parthouneaux, we might have prided ourselves on this famous passage. It was a fine spectacle to see eight or nine thousand men, under Ney and Oudinot, repelling the three divisions of Tschighagof, while on the other side, Belluno's eight thousand men were gloriously contending against the efforts of Wittgenstein. And in what a situation did our soldiers sustain this desperate combat? A prey to famine and cold, surrounded by the enemy, six hundred leagues from their country, without hope of escape from destruction, destitute of munitions, and seeing nothing but disorder around them, they nevertheless fought and died like heroes! The Russians, on the contrary, inured to the climate, well furnished with supplies, fighting for their own firesides, encouraged by success far surpassing their hopes, with a large army ready to sustain them; having a numerous cavalry, and well-served artillery; in a word, certain that success would secure for them rich trophies, fought under advantages immensely superior to ours.

But it must be confessed that these advantages were in some degree counterbalanced by several fortuitous circumstances. In the first place, through a misunderstanding, one half of Wittgenstein's corps remained in rear, so that that general could not act upon Belluno with the desired vigor. Again, the numerous stragglers in the train of our army, though useless as combatants, deceived the enemy respecting our numbers, and made him more cautious in his operations. Moreover Tschighagof, being a sailor by profession, was not accustomed to military operations on land, and his cavalry could not act with advantage in the woods, while the same obstacle assisted in covering our infantry, and concealing their numbers. But it must not be supposed from these remarks, that I wish in the slightest degree, to depreciate the glory won on that memorable occasion. I merely wish to present a true picture of the relative circumstances, in order that posterity may do justice to all. With respect to the circumspection of Kutusof which has been so much criticized, it is certain that if he had acted with more celerity and audacity, he would have overtaken us. But it must be remembered that, like most of the Russian generals, he overestimated our numbers, and was compelled by political considerations to spare the remains of his army. It was important that Russia should be able, on her return to the Niemen, to exhibit a considerable force in order to detach Prussia and Austria from our alliance.

Continuation of the Retreat.—But let us return to the remains of my army. The sad victory which we had just gained was glorious, but it did not ameliorate our situation; it did not avert, but merely retarded our ruin. It was necessary to continue our retreat, although the exhausted condition of our troops rendered them incapable of any longer enduring the fatigues and privations to which they were exposed. To crown our misfortunes the cold, which had moderated for some days before, now set in with redoubled severity; and the enemy, piqued at having allowed us to escape at the Beresina, pursued us with renewed energy. Our march from Jembin to Smorgoni completed the dissolution of our army.

Napoleon departs for Paris.—I was deeply affected by the disasters of my troops; but I felt that, as a sovereign, I was bound to act for the salvation of the entire nation, rather than for the few. I could do nothing more for this army; but the interest and destinies of a great people reposed on me; my duty to this people now required that I should return to France, and organise the means of repairing this great disaster. I, therefore, at Molodeschno, on the fifth of

December, gave the command of the remains of my army to the king of Naples, and set out for Paris.

Motives of this Measure.—My detractors have loudly declaimed against this departure. If I had been the grandson of Louis XIV., and my natural successor had been in France, ready to mount the throne, I should not have hesitated to share the fortunes of my companions in arms; for my presence in France would not have been necessary to save the empire. But what could I do with thirty thousand half starved and half frozen men, six hundred leagues from their own country, fighting against all Germany, and with a Russian army in their rear? Ought I to augment the trophies of the enemy by my own capture, merely for the purpose of remaining with an army which must necessarily pass beneath the Caudine forks? I left with only two officers, and returned three months after with three hundred thousand men, of which there existed only the skeleton when I first put foot on the French territory. This fact alone should forever silence the critics who make war only in the salons of the capital. Who besides myself could have raised this army, and organised a new train of six hundred pieces of artillery, which appeared triumphant in the fields of Lutzen and Bautzen?

General Causes of the Disasters of this Campaign.—But before passing to the discussion of this memorable resurrection, let us review the principal causes of the failure of my expedition into Russia. Some of my partisans have attributed the ill-success of the campaign entirely to the premature and excessively cold weather; this is not true. The cold weather did not begin till the seventh of November, and was not excessive, for, until our arrival at Krasnoi it varied from 3° to 8°, and after the twentieth, it continued to thaw till our arrival on the Beresina. There was no time when the ice on the Dnieper would bear infantry. This cold did not exceed that of the Eylau campaign, but then we were in a country abundantly supplied with resources, whereas, in 1812, there were no means of supplying our most pressing wants. Our numerous columns became disorganised, and it required a week's halt in some intrenched camp well stored with magazines to enable us to recruit our men and reorganise our regiments. We expected to find such a camp at Smolensko, but failing in this, our only other asylum was on the Vistula, and our army was destroyed before it could reach it. The cold was quite supportable previous to our arrival on the Beresina, and then we had left only fifty thousand combatants out of the three hundred thousand which I had led to the banks of the Dwina and to Moscow. The true causes of this catastrophe were :—

1st. I did not intend in commencing the war to advance further than Smolensko, the first campaign ; but the difficulty of procuring supplies for two hundred and fifty thousand men in that devastated and sparsely populated country ; and more especially the erroneous statements of Murat that he had cut up the Russian army on the Louja, induced me to advance too far into the interior.

2d. I hoped to fight a decisive battle between Wilna and the Dwina, but was unable to bring the enemy to a general action. If I could have found another Austerlitz or Friedland in the plains of Lithuania, all Europe would have been subject to my power.

3d. Jerome neglected to profit by a favorable opportunity to destroy Bagration.

4th. The Poles of Wolhynia and Podolia, did not second my projects with the ardor I expected. If the corps of Poniatowski had been sent into these provinces instead of the Austrians, a better result would probably have been produced.

5th. Lithuania, from the failure of the crops the previous

year and the requisitions of the Russians, did not afford us the resources I anticipated. I neglected no means to repair the evil, and ordered hand-mills from Paris to grind the rye which we found in the country ; but they arrived too late to be of any great use.

6th. The cattle which I had purchased in Poland and Galicia did not reach us in time, and moreover, were insufficient to supply our wants. And the immense magazines which I had collected at Dantzic could not be transported to Smolensko in sufficient quantities for the support of such an immense army. I had organised thirty-four battalions of the train, each battalion conducting one hundred and fifty four-horse wagons. Twenty of these battalions followed my army, making a provision train of twelve thousand horses, carrying four millions of rations. But this was merely sufficient for fifteen days ; whereas it required four times this number for regular distributions, inasmuch as my depôts were twenty-five days' march in rear of the army. The convoys required fifty days to go and return. To obviate this difficulty, I ordered boats from France to transport my magazines up the Niemen and the Wilia ; and where the water was too shallow in the latter stream for navigation, I directed rafts to be constructed. What more could I do ? *Great enterprises into distant countries, says Montesquieu, perish from the very extent of the preparation required to secure their success.*

7th. I remained two weeks at Wilna, whereas I ought, by the first of July, to have pushed on against the main army to Gloubokoe and Polotsk, or to have directed my march on Minsk against Bagration. Had I profited by the false direction of the principal army of the enemy toward Drissa, to turn their left and throw them back upon the Baltic, the destruction of their army would have been certain. But the difficulty of obtaining provisions, and the fear that Bagration might defile on my rear in order to regain Drissa, induced me to make the halt at Wilna, which eventually cost us dearly.

8th. Murat failed to do any thing with his thirty thousand horse to harass and cut up the enemy in his retreat.

9th. At Borodino we were ignorant of the existence of Touckzof's corps toward Oustitza, which modified the effect of the first plan of attack. We failed to throw a sufficient mass against the enemy's left, by the old road to Smolensko, and, for reasons already given, my reserve did not come into action at the most opportune moment.

10th. It was unfortunate that I did not pursue the enemy still further than Moscow; it was a choice of evils, it is true, but perhaps he would have accepted battle at Taroutina, and, if victorious, I would have been master of the rich provinces of Kalouga; if the enemy had continued his retreat to the Wolga, I should have had a more favorable line of retreat by Roslaw. But the fear of penetrating further into the enemy's country induced me to halt at Moscow.

11th. We had no good maps of the country, and knew not the position of the practicable roads; while the enemy profited by his superior knowledge in this respect.

12th. Turkey signed the treaty of peace at the moment when I expected her to renew the war with vigor; and Bernadotte at the same time deserted my cause, and allied himself with the Russians. This double incident changed the chances of the war. Sebastiani or Andreossi should have been sent to Constantinople, six months sooner, with money, to induce the divan to continue the war with Russia.

13th. The enemy had greatly improved in the art of war. After the camp of Drissa his operations were conducted with skill; and the concentration of his forces on the Beresina, ordered by the Emperor Alexander, was one of the finest military movements of the age.

14th. I committed a capital fault in not uniting the corps of Macdonald, Oudinot, St. Cyr, and Victor under a single chief, possessing vigor and skill. These hundred thousand men united, might have destroyed Wittgenstein, and secured my line of retreat.

15th. Finally, I was deceived in the military character of the Emperor Alexander, as well as in the efforts of the Russian nation to sustain him.

Some writers, instead of looking at the natural causes of our disasters, have preferred to attribute them to supernatural means, like the manna of the desert, and the closing of the waters of the Red Sea. These writers can see no fault in my operations, and no merit in those of our adversaries. Never have they rendered me a worse service than in depreciating the actions of my opponents; they thus tarnish my own glory and that of the French army, for that glory consists in having surmounted unforeseen obstacles. The Russians certainly effected a retreat of three hundred leagues without having their army cut to pieces, and without leaving us any trophies. Barclay and Bagration, after being separated by a hostile force of three hundred thousand men, again effected their junction in spite of all our efforts: Wittgenstein, though opposed by three marshals with a force twice his own, maintained a threatening attitude during the whole campaign; and the army, defeated at Borodino, was again in condition to dispute our passage at Krasnoi:—how could all this have happened if my enemies did nothing but commit faults? Again, how could men possessing no talents or merit collect their scattered forces, and concentrate them with troops from Finland and the Pruth, late in the autumn, on the Beresina, to dispute the passage of that river? Undoubtedly they were favored by a thousand advantageous circumstances, but it would be unjust to refuse them the praise which they deserve.

Undoubtedly the Russians committed some great errors, especially in the first period of the campaign ; their primitive position, their direction on Drissa, and their retreat from Smolensko, are the most prominent. It is true also that Kutusof might have done more, for, in his place, I certainly should not have failed to destroy the army that left Moscow; but his circumspection did not prevent his making skillful manœuvres ; these manœuvres were the result of the instructions of Alexander or of his staff, and it would be unjust to say that they were without merit. It is ridiculous to say that our disasters were in no way due to the Russians : it is true that they were not the result of any great victories gained ; but in the second period of this campaign, the generals, the army, the government, and the nation, all did their duty.

But if my admirers have been unjust towards my rivals, my personal enemies have not been less so towards me. My conduct in this campaign was not below the renown which I had previously gained. I did not venture into an inhospitable country without due preparation. But the immense distance to be passed over, and the enormous preparations required to support so large an army, all turned against me. My forces were prudently disposed of in echelons, and no point was needlessly exposed ; if I ventured much, it was only after having taken every precaution which human foresight could suggest to secure the success of my operations. But let us return from this digression, and conclude the operations of my lieutenants after my return to Paris.

Continuation of the Retreat under Murat.—In leaving Molodeschino I resigned the command of my army to Murat, giving him Berthier as his chief of staff, (major-general). The former, of a rash and chivalric character, had not any more than the other the will of iron suited to such difficult circumstances. My departure became the signal of new disasters, still more terrible than any which preceded them. The cold increased to thirty degrees, and even the birds fell dead to the earth! In the three marches from Smorgoni to Wilna more than twenty thousand men fell by the way-side; and the remainder, half dead with cold and hunger, threw themselves into Wilna like a troop of madmen. This flourishing city contained immense resources; a part of our magazines had been brought here from Königsberg, and the Duke of Bassano had collected here supplies from all Lithuania; but the disorder was so great that it was impossible to make regular issues; a part was given up to pillage, and the remainder left, untouched, to the enemy. Wittgenstein and Tschighagof pressed close on our rear, while Kutusof followed within two days' march. The division of Loison, which had opened the passage, and was echeloned on the road, now formed the rear-guard. The intrepid Ney who had successively commanded the whole army, was still charged with sustaining here the shock of the enemy. Although composed of fresh and robust soldiers, Loison's division lost, in these three days, two-thirds of the men present, and there were scarcely five thousand men left before Wilna to oppose the Russians. Ney fought with resignation and courage, but his feeble force could not prevent the enemy's partisans from penetrating into the suburbs of the city. Sixty thousand half-famished men had quartered themselves in the hospitals, magazines, and private dwellings; by feeding on heavy half-baked bread they had contracted diseases not less fatal than the severe cold. In two days Wilna was but one vast lazaretto. Those who could drag themselves along, left at the sound of the enemy's cannon.

Two leagues from Wilna is the mountain of Ponary whose steep and icy slope became, for our horses and the remains of our artillery and baggage-train, a true barrier of iron. All our remaining carriages were here abandoned;

our treasure was divided among our soldiers who, loaded down with gold, half-famished with hunger and half-dead with cold, took in mournful despair the road to Kowno. The Emperor Alexander, having returned to his army in order to gather the fruits of his plan of campaign, entered Wilna amid scenes of desolation exceeding even the romantic description of fiction. He halted here to afford succor to the twenty thousand dying men who filled the city, and to provide for the wants of his own army which now began to suffer as much as ours. His columns continued the pursuit on Kowno.

The severe cold had closed the Niemen so that it could be readily crossed with artillery. This circumstance, which would have been so favorable to us on the Beresina, now became fatal to our army, which had scarcely six thousand men capable of firing a gun. The Cossacks reached the Niemen at the same time with the wreck of our forces, and threatened the debouches of the bridge. Each one sought for himself an issue; some took to the woods of Wilkowisk, and the road to Warsaw, while the greater number, with Murat and his head-quarters, took the road to Königsberg; Ney, who had been left in the city with a rear-guard of only five hundred combatants, found on evacuating the town, that the enemy were in possession of the bridge across the Niemen. Valiant as Achilles, and strong as Ajax and Diomede, this hero seized a musket, and throwing himself upon the enemy with forty brave men, cut his way through the ranks of his astonished foes.*

* Abbott thus describes Ney's final retreat, and crossing of the Niemen:

"On the twelfth of December, the French arrived at Kowno, upon the banks of the Niemen. On the thirteenth, they crossed the bridge, but about thirty thousand in number. The 'Old Guard' was now reduced to three hundred men. They still marched proudly, preserving, even unto death, their martial and indomitable air. The heroic Ney, through miracles of suffering and valor, had covered the rear through this awful retreat. The march from Viasma to

Murat has been reproached for having taken the road to old Prussia and thus exposing himself to be thrown into the sea; but the hope of being reënforced by the garrison of

the Niemen had occupied thirty-seven days and nights. During this time, four rear-guards had melted away under his command.

"Receiving four or five thousand men, the number would soon be reduced to two thousand, then to one thousand, then to five hundred, and finally to fifty or sixty. He would then obtain a fresh supply to be strewn in death along the road. Even more perished from fatigue and the cold than from the bullets of the enemy.

"In the following way he conducted the retreat. Each afternoon, at about five o'clock, he selected some commanding position, and stopped the advance of the Russians. His soldiers then, for a few hours, obtained such food and rest as was possible under such circumstances.

"At ten o'clock he again resumed, under cover of night, his retreat. At daybreak, which was about seven o'clock, he again took position, and rested until ten o'clock. By this time the enemy usually made his appearance. Cautiously retiring, Ney fought them back all day long, making as much progress as he could, until five o'clock in the evening, when he again took position.

"In order to retard the advance of the Cossacks, powder and shells were placed in the wagons which it was found necessary to abandon, and a long lighted fuse attached. The Cossacks, observing the smoke, dared not approach until after the explosion. Thus, for more than a month, by night and by day, Ney struggled along against blinding storms of snow and freezing gales, with his ranks ploughed by the shot and shells of the enemy.

"At Kowno, Marshal Ney collected seven hundred fresh troops, and planting a battery of twenty-four pieces of cannon, beat back the enemy during the whole day, while the army was defiling across the bridge. As these troops melted away before the fire of the foe, he seized a musket, and with difficulty rallied thirty men to stand by his side. At last, having seen every man safely across the river, he slowly retired, proudly facing the foe.

"The bullets flew thickly around him; still, he disdained to turn his back upon the foe or to quicken his pace. Deliberately walking backward, he fired the last bullet at the advancing Russians, and threw his gun into the stream. He was the last of the 'Grand Army' who left the Russian territory.

"General Dumas was seated in the house of a French physician, on the German side of the river, when a man entered, enveloped in a large cloak. His beard was long and matted, his emaciated visage was blackened with gunpowder, his whiskers were singed by fire, but his eyes beamed with the lustre of an indomitable mind.

"'At last I am here,' said he, as he threw himself into a chair. 'What, General Dumas, do you not know me?'

"'No,' was the reply; 'who are you?'

"'I am the rear-guard of the Grand Army, Marshal Ney. I have fired the last musket-shot on the bridge of Kowno, I have thrown into the Niemen the last of our arms, and I have walked hither, as you see me, across the forest.'"

Königsberg, and of getting supplies in that rich country, and the idea of basing himself on Dantzic, are the excuses which he gave in justification of his resolution.

Including the Prussian contingent, Macdonald had still twenty-four thousand men. In my march on the Beresina I had employed every means in my power to send him orders to move on Wilna and Kowno; but Wittgenstein, after the passage of the Beresina, had forced him to take the road to Königsberg.

Being abandoned on his march by the Prussian corps of York, and his right wing being turned, Macdonald was fortunate in gaining Königsberg with the Polish division, which he afterwards directed on Dantzic to reënforce the garrison.

Murat, after having also directed the division of Heudelet on Dantzic, cantoned twenty thousand men behind the Vistula, his right on Thorn, and his left in the direction of Elbing. But the defection of the Prussians rendered the position untenable, and exposed our communications: the enemy had only to present himself on our right flank, in order to throw these wrecks on Dantzic. In fact, the Russians attacked Eugene's head-quarters at Marienwerder, and, through the negligence of the out-posts, succeeded in penetrating into the place. The alarm was given, and Eugene at the head of a few brave men, opened a passage; but more than a thousand prisoners fell into the hands of the enemy. The extreme left of our cantonments retired into Dantzic, while the right, composed of Bavarians, entered Thorn: fifteen thousand men directed their march on Posen, forming echelons on the road. The Russians satisfied themselves with Bromberg and Elbing.

Continuation of the Retreat under Eugene.—Seeing that there was no further hope of effecting the reorganization of the army, and convinced of the defection of Prussia, Murat resolved to return to his kingdom, without waiting for my permission. He left Posen on the seventeenth of January, in spite of the remonstrances of the viceroy, who represented to him the irregularity of his conduct both as a marshal of France and as my lieutenant. Blinded by the hope of preserving his throne, he departed under the name of one of his aids-de-camp, and left to Eugene the care of continuing the retreat.

The viceroy remained ten days at Posen to restore more order to his columns; and the Russians, arrested by the fortifications of Thorn and Dantzic, also halted behind the Vistula. Rapp, who commanded at Dantzic, had collected an army of more than thirty thousand men, but at least ten thousand of these were invalids. Nevertheless, it was a considerable army, and I hoped that, under the protection of these formidable ramparts, it would afford occupation for the enemy. But it was unable to take the field, and did not equal my expectations.

The Russians waited for the opening of navigation to besiege the place, causing it to be observed, first by General Lewis, and afterwards by the duke of Wurtemberg. General Barclay was left before Thorn, with two divisions of grenadiers, and a siege-park, afterwards organized by the Prussians, enabled them to form a regular attack.

The defection of General York was soon followed by a convention which neutralized the Austrian corps of Schwartzenberg. This marshal, in leaving to Tschichagof the field free to march on the Beresina, had entitled himself to the gratitude of our enemies: he had fallen back on Warsaw, and stipulated with the Russian generals an armistice, which, it is true, enabled Reynier to retire, but which, at the same time, neutralized the Austrian army, and permitted the enemy to pursue us to the last extremity.

Kutusof, not trusting to the continuance of this neutrality, left Sacken to observe him; but he had sufficient troops besides this to destroy the wrecks of the forces of the viceroy, who redoubled his efforts to find some place of refuge.

Twenty thousand French and their allies, mutilated by the frost, and fifteen or sixteen thousand men still capable of bearing arms, pursued by an army of sixty thousand active men, inured to the climate, thus dragged themselves along from Wilna to the Oder, through a hostile population.

His Army finally takes Refuge behind the Elbe.—This sad, but glorious, retreat is a phenomenon in history; and one hardly knows at which to be most astonished,—the great disasters which befell our army, or the final return of the viceroy to the Elbe. Except a warm engagement near Kalisch between Reynier's corps and the Russians, there were no further military events worthy of notice. The arrival on the Oder of fifteen thousand fresh troops from Italy, under General Grenier, enabled Eugene to retire in good order behind the Elbe. A new campaign was now about to open.

But diplomatists were in the mean time coolly discussing the best means of profiting by my disasters in the North; and, as if to give them additional hopes, fortune had been but little less fatal to my armies in Spain than on the banks of the Beresina.* We will give a brief summary of our affairs in the Peninsula.

* "Many attempts," says Thiers, "have been made to reckon up the losses suffered by France and her allies in this Russian expedition, and although such a calculation is as impossible as terrible, some idea of the truth may, nevertheless, be attained. The total force of the army, intended to act from the Rhine to the Niemen consisted of six hundred and twelve thousand men (with the Austrians, six hundred and forty eight thousand), and one hundred and fifty thousand horses. Of these five hundred and thirty three thousand had passed the Niemen, of whom there remained, under the Prince Schwartzenberg and Reynier, about forty thousand Austrians and Saxons, fifteen thousand Prussians and Poles under Marshal Macdonald, and some isolated troops, numbering about thirty or forty thousand.

"Of the remaining four hundred and thirty-eight thousand, about one hundred thousand had fallen into the hands of the Russians; and, according to

Summary of the Campaign in Spain.—While my troops were triumphant at Tarragona and Valencia, the Cortes of Cadiz were planning the basis of their constitutional edifice. The liberals or *communeros*, were in the majority, and they excelled even the extravagance of our constitutent assembly. Their intentions were no doubt pure, for they imitated revolutionary France even to excluding the members of their constitutent assembly from the first elections to the legislative body. Nevertheless, their principles were not pleasing either to the grandees or the high clergy ; and the opposition of the latter was the more decided as the Cortes, following my example, had ventured to strike at the abuses of the Church. Joseph had made pacific overtures to the Cortes, and the disasters of Tarragona and Valencia had somewhat shaken their courage ; the more reasonable of the Spaniards began to reflect, that, if England should deliver their country, they would become still more dependent on the cabinet of London, than Godoy had ever been on that of France. They, therefore, thought that they might obtain a preferable result

this calculation, therefore, about three hundred and forty thousand would have perished: but this happily was not the case, for a certain number of men who had deserted their ranks at the commencement of the campaign, had gradually rejoined their country across Poland and Germany. Nevertheless it can be no exaggeration to say, that in the course of the campaign about three hundred thousand men fell beneath the enemy's fire and the severity of cold and want."

M. Laurent de l'Ardèche, Vol. II., p. 166, estimates the loss of the French army during the Russian campaign at three hundred and fifty thousand men, more than sixty thousand horses, a thousand cannon, and nearly twenty thousand wagons and carriages. He also says that, including the population of the abandoned cities, who perished for want of food and shelter, the loss of the Russians must have far exceeded that of the invaders.

Large numbers of women and children, when driven from their homes by their own countrymen or the Cossacks, in pursuance of the orders of the government to lay waste the country as fast as the French advanced, perished, in the fields and forests, from hunger, fatigue, and exposure. In some places the road-sides and plains were covered with the unburied dead of the Russian inhabitants. Had their own government permitted these people to remain in their homes, very few of them would have been molested by the French.

by treating with my brother, and thus become the arbiters of their own future. Joseph offered to recognize their constitution with certain indicated modifications, and they decided to send deputies to Madrid to treat on these bases; and these deputies were actually on their way, when the disastrous battle of Salamanca entirely changed the face of affairs.

The English had redoubled their efforts during this campaign, the retreat of Massena and the success of Wellington and Beresford serving as a stimulus to incite them.

They recruited in Germany from the prisoners of war, and even from the malefactors; anything seemed good enough to oppose us.

In making this statement I must not be accused of undervaluing their army, for their own parliamentary debates prove that they sought criminals in the bottom of the prisons to incorporate them in the regiments employed in the Peninsula.

The taking of Ciudad-Rodrigo and Badajos, as glorious for Wellington as discreditable to the two generals who permitted these disasters to take place, began to show the extent of our danger. It was thought that the English general, able in a war of positions, but wanting enterprise in an open country, had taken these posts only the better to secure his line of defense in Portugal. They expected that he would now trouble our two armies in Estremadura, but they did not attach to these events the importance which they deserved.

On the approach of the war in Russia, I had recalled all my guard from Spain, as well as the legions of the Vistula and several skeletons of dragoon regiments, destined to form lancers; I had, moreover, withdrawn many men of the *élite* to complete the Old Guard, and dissolved what has been called the "Army of the North." Nevertheless, our forces in the west and south amounted to one hundred and thirty thousand men; Soult had forty-five thousand in Andalusia; and Marmont nearly as many toward Salamanca. Souham guarded old Castile with twelve thousand men; Joseph, with his guard and the army of the centre, held La Mancha, the banks of the Tagus, and Madrid. Independently of these forces, divisions of occupation were stationed in Navarre, in the Asturias, in Leon, and in Biscay. On deciding to march against Russia, I at first had the intention of concentrating all my forces behind the Ebro; but the important successes of Suchet in the kingdom of Valencia and the destruction of Blake's army, animating our hopes in the Peninsula, caused me to change my plan and to persist in guarding Andalusia.

Wellington's Anglo-Portuguese army had been increased to more than seventy-five thousand men, and the Cortes had finally given him the general command of the Spanish army of sixty thousand men. Moreover, the natural advantages of his position were very great. Our line of operations, extending from Bayonne to Cadiz, was more than two hundred leagues in depth. Portugal was like an impenetrable fortress, placed on the flank and centre of this line, while the fortifications of Ciudad-Rodrigo and Badajos served as advanced works to the main bulwark. Wellington, departing from such a base, was certain to act with advantage against an enemy who was obliged to occupy a whole kingdom and to secure himself against a multitude of Spaniards, little formidable in line, but continually harassing our posts with indefatigable activity. As it was impossible, on account of the guerrillas, to form any system of regular magazines, the French could not remain long together in large masses, and, their positions being greatly extended in order to cover their supplies and their line of retreat, they were exposed to attack on every side.

Wellington saw the advantage of his position, and at last took the offensive. He had three plans from which to choose: first, to move to the right on Soult; second, to debouch at the centre on Madrid; third, to operate at the left on Marmont. By operating at the south Wellington would draw there the principal masses of the French, and only the more completely effect the invasion of Spain. But in going to the north he would draw Soult in that direction, and thus deliver over the south of Spain to the junta of Cadiz. If the French should commit the error of attempting to guard Seville instead of going to the support of Marmont, then the latter would be defeated, and, as the line of retreat on Bayonne lay in that direction, a victory on the Douro would be certain to cause the evacuation of half of the Peninsula, and even of the capital. This was too evident to escape my penetration; but deceived in the character of their chief, I hoped that the English would not venture to commit their troops far from Portugal. I, however, gave a *carte blanche* to Joseph and Jourdan, who thought, like myself, that they could face the danger.

The English destroy the Bridge of the Tagus at Almaraz.— Conformably to his plan of operations, Wellington debouched from Portugal in the month of May. In order to retain Suchet in the east and prevent reënforcements from being sent to Joseph, Wellington requested the landing of ten thousand English and six thousand auxiliaries from Minorca on the coast of Catalonia. The general wisely commenced his operations by destroying the great bridge of Almaraz across the Tagus, in order to cut off all communication between the armies of Soult and Marmont. This bridge was not only secured by a well-constructed *tête-de-pont*, but also by the little fort of Mirvales which closed the gorges through which passes the road to Truxillo. Hill succeeded in turning this fort by ascending the rocks of Manaderos with all the necessary implements for an escalade. The officer who commanded the foreign battalion in the *tête-de-pont*, allowed himself to be surprised on the eighteenth of May, and the detachment which guarded a part of the works on the right bank basely fled; its chief was condemned to death, but the evil was without remedy. After this important *coup-de-main*, Hill returned to Badajos. Soult and Marmont each sent divisions to sustain the place, but the bridge and great depôt of munitions had been destroyed, and, as the enemy had also disappeared, our troops returned to their respective quarters.

Taking of Salamanca.—Wellington, having completed his preparations, crossed the Tormes at a ford, on the seventeenth of June, invested Salamanca and established himself in observation at San Christoval. Marmont, having collected his forces, presented himself there on the twentieth, but not venturing to attack the enemy, he retired again after two days' manœuvering, and asked for reënforcements from Joseph, and from General Caffarelli, who was commanding in Castile. The three small forts constructed to cover Salamanca, being warmly battered, surrendered on the twenty-fourth, Marmont then fell back on the Douro between Toro and Tordesillas, where he was joined by Bonnet's division from the Asturias; his force now numbered between forty-two and forty-five thousand. Wellington followed him with at least an equal army. Joseph, indecisive like all mediocre men, first declared that he could not detach any reënforcement from Madrid, and that the marshal must do all he could to sustain himself. Caffarelli also replied that he was hard pressed by the insurgents of Navarre and the Asturias. The marshal, judging that it was necessary at whatsoever cost to drive the enemy back into Portugal, resolved to take the offensive as soon as he was joined by Bonnet's division. After making new demonstrations on Toro, he fell back to the left on Tordesillas, passed the Douro, and advanced against the extreme right of the English.

After some manœuvres intended to deceive his adversary, Marmont collected the mass of his forces behind the hills of the Arapiles, and resolved to drive the English from these heights, from which place he hoped to operate with advantage on their right, if they remained in position, or to cut them up if they attempted to retreat.

General Maucune had orders to carry this post with the advanced guard. This valiant soldier executed his task with audacity, but afterward advanced with too much precipitancy into the plain beyond. Marmont ascended the eminence to ascertain the state of affairs, and just as he saw the enemy, instead of retreating, making preparations to assail with advantage, his arm was broken by the bursting of a shell. It was now necessary to sustain this division, and to attack the second hill opposite the enemy's centre. The battle was thus begun in a disadvantageous situation. The wounded marshal resigned the command to Clausel, but all the experience of this brave general could not remedy an affair so improperly begun. Maucune was separated from the rest of the line by half a league, and Wellington moved one Spanish and four English divisions and all his cavalry on the point where we were most exposed to his attacks. Imitating the example of Frederick at Rosbach, or rather mine at Austerlitz, he waited till our left was well separated, then ordered Beresford to attack the heights of Arapiles, and directed, by an oblique march, the half of his army on the extreme left. Taken in front and flank this wing was thrown on the centre which evacuated the Arapiles in pretty good order, but was finally involved in the defeat of the left.

Foy, who commanded our right, thought to assist the centre by a lateral movement, but was assailed by the enemy's left and reserve, and succeeded with difficulty in covering the retreat. This defeat which cost us eight or nine thousand men *hors-de-combat*, was calculated to decide the fate of Spain. The consequences were the more to be deplored as they destroyed the hope of effecting an arrangement with the Cortes, or of securing the pacification of the Peninsula. I was the more displeased with this result, as Joseph had changed his mind in relation to reënforcing Marmont, and marched with his guard, his reserve and part of Caffarelli's troops on Segovia to rejoin the army of Portugal.

This circumstance prejudiced me against this imprudent marshal, as it seemed that he had compromised our safety on account of his jealousy and the desire to decide the question before the approach of my brother. But as it was not absolutely certain that he knew of the vicinity of the king, I only replaced him in the command, and directed that he should not even be informed of this until the recovery of his wounds. I had an old affection for my companion in arms; he and Junot had been the first of my aids-de-camp. The loss of Spain is, however, to be dated from this catastrophe, and posterity will decide whether it was the fault of Joseph or of Marmont.

Wellington enters Madrid.—The military results of this campaign were, for us, as unfortunate as its political consequences. The broken army of Marmont retired to Burgos; Clausel did not even deem it prudent to hold Valladolid, for fear of being obliged to accept a new battle. Wellington, getting possession of that city on the thirtieth of July, caused the army of Portugal to be observed by two divisions, and on the fifth of August marched on Madrid by Segovia. Joseph, on hearing the loss of the battle of Salamanca, and not being able to unite with Clausel without danger, retired by Guadarama on Madrid, evacuated that capital after having thrown his baggage in the Retiro, and fell back with the army of the centre behind the Tagus, and urged Soult to send him twenty thousand men from Andalusia. This unfortunate army of the south caused all our embarrassments, and, nevertheless, was the resource to which it was always necessary to resort. As Soult could not, without compromising his army, send half of it to the king, he proposed to Joseph to fall back on him, to hold Andalusia, and give me time to send reënforcements into the north of Spain to drive out the English. This project would have been good, if I had been tranquil at Paris ; but as I was then in Moscow, it was therefore exceedingly objectionable.

Joseph, listening to better advice than that of Soult, ordered him to abandon Andalusia, and join him at Valencia, where he retired with the troops of Count d'Erlon. Hardly had he left his capital when the English general entered there in triumph (August 12th). The intoxication with which he was received soon gave place to very different feelings, when it was known that he had levied a contribution on that city of ten millions !

The Retiro had been fortified for the last two years, to serve as a depôt : its enceinte was a double line ; the first line was too extended, and required too many forces for its defense ; the second was too confined, and its garrison was exposed to the fire of the besiegers. The garrison being too weak to defend the first line, Wellington carried it at the first onset ; he then bombarded the second, which was surrendered by the commandant a few hours after, with censurable precipitation. They captured here one hundred and eighty pieces of cannon and rich stores.

Wellington has been blamed for going to Madrid for a triumph instead of pursuing the wrecks of Marmont's corps. It is very certain that a second victory over Clausel would have driven his army to the Pyrenees, and have greatly embarrassed Soult and Joseph in the south But the English general relied much upon the moral effect which the taking of the capital would produce upon the already flagging courage of the Spaniards.

On the reiterated orders of the king, Soult determined to sacrifice the immense works which his army had erected around Cadiz, and, on the twenty-fifth of August, took the road to Grenada and Lorca on Yecla, after having effected, at Huesca, his junction with the corps of Count d'Erlon; he conferred with Joseph and Suchet at Almanza, and then immediately directed himself on the Tagus by the road from Alicante to Madrid. Ballesteros, who had fought against him with so much constancy during the whole summer, did not trouble his retreat which he might have done, either by operating on the flanks, or by the direct road from the Sierra Morena to Madrid. It appears that he had been ordered into La Mancha to act under the orders of Wellington; but his pride revolted at serving under another, and he preferred to let our columns escape unmolested. The Cortes broke him of his command, and banished him to Ceuta.

Wellington's unsuccessful Siege of Burgos.—In the mean time Wellington had left Madrid to return to the north against Clausel, who had just resumed the offensive against the divisions left in observation near Burgos, and had already advanced on the Douro to disengage Toro and Zamora. Wellington left General Hill, with three Anglo-Portuguese divisions, to guard Madrid, and marched anew against Burgos at the head of four divisions and the Spanish army of Galicia. General Souham (to whom Clausel, who was sick with his wound, had given the command), fell back on Briviesca, a formidable position on the principal spur of the Pyrenees which covers the left bank of the Ebro. The English general, though destitute of his park of heavy artillery, determined to attack the castle of Burgos, hoping that what could not be effected by his large field-pieces and howitzers, could be accomplished by subterranean warfare, and sapping the foot of the walls with his miners.

General Dubreton, who commanded the garrison, was a man of head and heart. He executed many sorties with success, on the trenches; nevertheless the breaches were finally made practicable, and the assault given; but it completely failed. Our great depôts were in a kind of intrenched camp between the castle and the old donjon. Wellington now redoubled his efforts, giving a new assault on the eighth of October, but with the same ill-success as before: and finally, on the twenty-second, he raised the siege after a loss of thirty days and three thousand men.

He retires into Portugal.—Two circumstances decided Wellington to retreat. First the approach of Souham to El Olmo, his army being reënforced by General Caffarelli with two divisions of infantry, and a brigade of cavalry. The second was the march of Soult on Aranjuez and Madrid, threatening to cut off his line of retreat by Portugal. The English army immediately retired behind the Douro, but not without considerable losses in the combats which its rear-guard had to sustain against our light cavalry and the divisions of Foy and Maucune, especially at Celada, Villadrigo, and Villa-Muriel. Wellington, after blowing up the fine bridges of Zamora, Toro, and Tordesillas, regained Salamanca.

Joseph and Soult, after driving Hill from Madrid, also took the road to Salamanca, and on the tenth of November our three armies united on the Tormes. They still numbered eighty thousand foot-soldiers and ten thousand horse. Although worn out with a fatiguing and ill-directed war, the idea of avenging the defeat of Salamanca had revived their enthusiasm; and the soldiers loudly demanded to be led against the enemy. Soult, to whom the king had given the command, wished to profit by this feeling to act on Wellington's line of retreat; but he was delayed by the difficulty of crossing the Alba, and the English general, taking advantage of a terrible rain and fog, effected his retreat towards Ciudad-Rodrigo.

Wellington was now driven back to the position from which he had started; but his operations had resulted in the deliverance of all the south of Spain;—Grenada, Seville, Andalusia, Cadiz, and Alicante; and he had acquired a marked ascendency over my generals. This campaign, although slow and measured, did honor to Wellington. The choice of his strategic direction was wise, and his tactical dispositions, skillful. Nevertheless it must be confessed that, with an army of seventy-five thousand men assisted by ten millions of Spaniards and Portuguese, full of fervor for their cause, and with only a fraction of our own force to oppose him, he was bound to accomplish some important results. The thirty days lost at Burgos certainly militate against him; and he has been justly blamed for giving Clausel time to reform the army which had been defeated at Salamanca.

Secondary Operations in Catalonia, &c.—In the east the war does not offer the same interest as in the former campaigns. General Suchet, satisfied with the taking of Valencia and Peniscola, and annoyed by the unfortunate expedition of Montbrun, rested on his laurels. General Decaen, with Lamarque and Maurice Mathieu, kept up an active contest with the Catalonians who, under Lascy, threatened at the same time Tarragona, Barcelona, Gerona, and Tortosa. The distance of Suchet's troops had revived the war-like ardor of the intrepid mountaineers of Monserrat, Manresa, Reuss and Vicque. Maurice Mathieu encountered Lascy, on the twenty-third of January, on the heights of Alta-Fulla, routed his army, captured all his artillery, and took near two thousand prisoners. Decaen carried the mountain of

Olot, drove Sarsfield on Centelles, and explored the whole country to Barcelona.

But these successes did not destroy the activity of the insurgent parties in Catalonia, and it was only with the greatest care on our side that we could maintain Barcelona, and keep its garrison supplied with provisions. After completing the organization of Valencia, Suchet made a reconnoissance of Alicante. Joseph O'Donnel had organized a corps of eight or nine thousand men to cover the environs of the city, and Suchet was soon convinced that the place was too strong to be taken without a regular attack. At this epoch the English made known their intention of landing ten or twelve thousand Anglo-Sicilians under General Maitland on the eastern coast of Spain. On hearing this I united the corps of Catalonia, Aragon, and Valencia under the orders of Suchet. While the English squadron was making demonstrations at the mouth of the Xucar, O'Donnel thought to surprise and destroy General Delort at Castella (July 22d). This intrepid officer, without fearing the enemy's numbers, and taking advantage of an injudicious movement of the Spanish cavalry, threw himself on his adversaries with the twenty-fourth dragoons and his cuirassiers, captured their artillery, sabred and dispersed their infantry, and returned with more prisoners than he himself had soldiers. This brilliant exploit of eighteen hundred Frenchmen against nine thousand Spaniards crowned the expedition of Suchet. The Irish General Elliot succeeded O'Donnel in the command, but was not more fortunate than his predecessor. Not venturing to land in the midst of our troops, Maitland debarked near Alicante, and again threatened Castella.

Suchet was at this time obliged to shelter the columns of Joseph, who returned from Madrid with the burlesque cortège of a fugitive court. The contrast between the army of

Aragon, well-clothed and equipped, and the army of the centre, undisciplined, destitute of everything, and serving as a mere escort to the thousand carriages of the grandees of Spain who shared the fortunes of the king, formed a picture worthy the pencil of Calot. As soon as he could get rid of this embarrassment, Suchet resolved to again menace Alicante. Maitland, on his side, sought to get possession of Denia ; but Duncan's brigade was repulsed, and Suchet, to threaten the enemy in his position, pushed forward Harispe's division even under the cannon of Alicante.

In the mean time the war in Catalonia continued without material change. The bands of Eroles, Milans, Rovira, and Sarsfield, distinguished themselves by their boldness and activity, and our convoys had great difficulty in getting supplies into Barcelona. It required all the talents of Decaen, Lamarque, and Maurice-Mathieu, and all the constancy, bravery, and resignation of their soldiers, to drive Lascy from Vicque. The bands of Aragonese, although less enterprising than the Catalonians, continued to harass the division which had been left to guard that province.

Conclusion.—The news of the retreat from Moscow, and the terrible bulletin that announced my return to Paris, was calculated to precipitate the ruin of our affairs in Spain, and revive the confidence and enthusiasm of our enemies. In fact, the disasters of the Russian expedition destroyed the *morale* of our army which was more fatigued by the character of the war than discouraged by the chances and perils of battle.

But it is time to close this brief outline of the campaign of 1812 in Spain, and return to the dispositions which I made to save France from the dangers that threatened her on all sides.

CHAPTER XIX.

SPRING CAMPAIGN OF 1813.

General State of Europe—Mission of Bubna—Amicable Protestations of Austria—Napoleon's Preparations for a new Campaign—Eugene behind the Elbe—Prussia declares against Napoleon—March of the Allies on the Elbe—They enter Saxony—Negotiations with Austria—She declares an armed Mediation—Napoleon rejoins his Army—He advances on the Saale—Organization of his Army—Levy in Mass in Prussia—Movements of the Allies—Position of their Armies—Napoleon effects his Junction with Eugene—He directs his March on Leipsic—Project of the Allies—Battle of Lutzen—Remarks on this Battle—Pursuit of the Allies on Dresden—Eugene sent to organize an Army in Italy—New Negotiations—Another Mission of Bubna—Napoleon accepts the Proposition of a Congress—Caulaincourt's Proposition to Russia—Napoleon repairs to Bautzen—Fortified Position of the Allies—Ney's March to turn this Position—Combats of Weissig and Königswarth—Ney debouches on Klix—Battle of Bautzen—Remarks on this Battle—Nesselrode's Reply to the Overtures of Caulaincourt—Combats of Reichenbach and Haynau—The Allies throw themselves on Schweidnitz—Armistice of Neumark—Combat of Luckau—Treaty with Denmark—Third Mission of Bubna—Negotiations of the Allies at Reichenbach—Metternich at Dresden—His Interview with Napoleon—Envoys to the Congress of Prague—Napoleon meets his Empress at Mayence—Military Projects of the Allies—Negotiations at Prague—Summary of Operations in Spain—Battle of Victoria—Suchet's Operations in the East of Spain.

General State of Europe.—Europe was not less astonished at my reverses that it had been at my successes. I had just lost that army which had been the terror of the world ; and my enemies might now hope to conquer the remainder, for the relative proportion of forces was changed. I was not to be deceived respecting the sentiments which now agitated Europe, for I foresaw that, the first moment of surprise being passed, I should find against me a formidable league, of which I now only heard the smothered cries of joy.

Mission of Bubna.—The moment of defeat is certainly an unfavorable time for concluding a treaty of peace. Austria, however, hoping to derive greater advantages from her alliance with me than from any which she could form with my enemies, interposed to mediate a peace.

General Bubna was sent to me, on the part of that court, to assure me of its benevolent dispositions. In his official language Bubna spoke only of the good offices of the cabinet of Vienna for the reëstablishment of peace, and was most prodigal in his protestations and assurances of the wish of his government for the maintenance of our alliance. But in the salons, and in private conversations, he let it be understood, that, as a return for these dispositions, his government expected the retrocession of some of its provinces, and particularly of Illyria. This desire was perfectly natural, and I should not have hesitated to gratify it, if I had known precisely what my father-in-law wished ; that is, what he was disposed to do for me, and what price he set upon this assistance. We were reciprocally distrusting each other for want of a frank and open explanation. It was evident that Austria would profit by her situation to recover a part of her lost power ; but to attain this object by honorable means, it was essential that she should not hesitate to declare herself. Her situation, however, was somewhat embarrassing, for she had only a single alternative ; she had either to maintain our alliance and seek to obtain from me concessions sufficiently important to reëstablish the equilibrium between us, or to break the alliance and declare herself in favor of my enemies.

The first of these seemed the most advisable course to pursue, although it was no easy matter to dictate conditions to one of my character, and, moreover, my father-in-law could not, with very good grace, say to me : *I am your ally, and you must give me your provinces.* Austria, therefore, preferred to show how necessary she was to me, and thus induce me to explain what I would be disposed to do for her. I, on the contrary, wished to gain time, being persuaded that under any circumstances I could make better terms after gaining a battle. I formed a just estimate of my resources and felt confident that, in two or three months, I could beat the enemy and drive him behind the Vistula, thus regaining my European preponderance.

The second plan was not less embarrassing for Austria than the other; for, if my preponderance had appeared excessive and threatening, there were also equal reasons for fear, if that preponderance should pass entirely into the hands of Russia. Moreover, an ally is not to be instantly converted into a public enemy; time and the formalities of negotiations are required to accomplish this.

Under all the circumstances, I determined not to voluntarily offer myself to be despoiled, but to wait till I could ascertain the exact intentions of the cabinet of Vienna; in the mean time seeking to obtain from Austria some formal declaration respecting the continuance of our alliance. As Bubna only spoke of the desire of his master to intercede for peace, I reiterated to him all the assurances which he could desire, and confirmed them by my direct correspondence with my father-in-law. The reports which reached me from Vienna were, however, daily becoming more alarming. Lord Walpole, the secret envoy of England, promised, it was said, to Austria ten millions of pounds sterling, Illyria, and even the kingdom of Italy, if she would declare against me. Thus a power, which had not a single battalion to dispose of, was generously offering to give away vast provinces on the continent, to which not the shadow of a title had yet been acquired.

Amicable Protestations of the Cabinet of Vienna.—Nevertheless, the protestations of Metternich were so positive that

I was for a time deceived. I saw in his proffer of good offices only a sincere desire on the part of Austria to interpose between the contending parties, and thus increase her own importance. How could I fail to believe a minister who said to mine on the fourteenth of February, "that my alliance with Russia was an alliance of war, imposed by victory, and ought from its nature to be dissolved; but on the contrary that the alliance with Austria reposed on the most permanent interests; that Austria had herself voluntarily sought this alliance, and that if she now had it to make over again she would make it upon precisely the same basis; that if it did not already exist, she herself would now solicit it, for a half century had demonstrated the advantages of the one precisely similar which had been negotiated by Prince Kaunitz in 1756."

Nor did the cabinet of Vienna confine itself to these protestations; it announced, the middle of March, that Prince Schwartzenberg, as chief of the auxiliary corps, was coming to Paris to receive my orders; and Metternich spoke of bringing one hundred thousand, instead of thirty thousand men, into the field, if the enemy should still refuse to make peace. The letter announcing the return of Schwartzenberg was certainly remarkable:

"His presence at Paris has, under the circumstances, been deemed necessary by the Emperor of Austria for the reciprocal interests of the two courts. As an embassador and chief of the auxiliary corps he will be of service to Napoleon, in the negotiations, if they are commenced, or in receiving his orders for the coming campaign, if, contrary to the dearest wishes of the Emperor of Austria, it becomes necessary to continue the war."

At the same time M. de Floret communicated, by the orders of his court, the overtures of the cabinet of Vienna to England and Russia; and also the views of the Emperor of Austria on the events that were transpiring in Prussia. "The personal sentiments," said to be, "of the Emperor of Austria are most strongly opposed to measures like those resorted to by Prussia. He blamed, in the strongest terms, such defection; his sentiments were most unequivocally in favor of continuing the alliance; and his zeal was both strongly and truly in favor of peace,—a peace less necessary for France than for Austria herself. Such were the declarations of the agents of the cabinet of Vienna. It had explained its views in the same way, it was said, at Berlin, at Wilna, and at London. "Their course of conduct was *purely Austrian*, and they wished *to place France in her true attitude*, which was not to fear the continuance of the war, nor to oppose the negotiation of peace."

My minister of foreign affairs, however, distrusted these fine protestations, and proposed to me to restore Ferdinand to Spain, and the Pope to Rome.

It was thought that by this means I might voluntarily accomplish what Europe would perhaps sooner or later impose by force; and, moreover, that I might in this way obtain an additional force of one hundred thousand men to assist me in Germany, and thus show to Europe that I renounced both Spain and Rome, the better to maintain my ascendency in the north. I consented to the restoration of the Pope, and went myself to Fontainebleau, under the pretext of a hunting party. I saw the Pontiff, and frankly proposed to him to forget our spiritual and temporal quarrels, offering him the restoration of Rome, provided he would maintain the independence of the Gallican Church. A new concordat was signed to this effect on the twenty-fifth of January. But the restoration of Ferdinand was a different matter. The new retreat of Wellington into Portugal, notwithstanding the victory of Salamanca, gave me hopes of still maintaining our power in the Peninsula. I preferred to risk my throne, rather than to surrender the maritime interests of France. They could not regard the restoration of the Pope as the result of fear, for I could have nothing to apprehend from that quarter ; but the return of Ferdinand might give my enemies an exaggerated idea of our embarrassments.

Energetic Preparations for a new Campaign.—During the interval of these negotiations, I was making every preparation to resume an imposing attitude on the Oder. The disasters of Moscow, instead of discouraging me, had animated me with new ardor ; I felt equal to the exigency of the occasion, and France shared my confidence and my energy Never did a people present a more noble and lofty character. Instead of mourning over our losses, we thought only of the means of repairing them ; in three months I accomplished my object. This fact alone is sufficient to confound the declamations of those intriguers who triumph only in the disasters of their country. France, it is true, showed herself great in misfortune ; but if there was in the whole of my career a single moment which merits the admiration of posterity, it was this, beyond all doubt.

In less than three months, more than six hundred pieces of cannon and two thousand caissons were on the road to the Elbe ; the cohorts of the first ban were formed into regiments of the line ; the number of these regiments was increased to one hundred and fifty by the creation of twenty new *cadres ;* the newly levied conscripts filled up the old *cadres.* The depôts of the regiments in Spain were completed and organized as provisional ; the *cadres* of one hundred battalions were drawn, for this purpose, from the army in Spain, their soldiers being all transferred to the battalions which remained with that army. I increased the number of the regiments of the Young Guard to sixteen, so as to incite among the conscripts a rivalry to get into these corps ; which then passed as the *élite* of my army, but which in reality were inferior to the ordinary regiments of the camp at Boulogne. They were not wanting in courage, but in the habit of enduring fatigues, privations, and dangers; in a word, they wanted the force of discipline and experience.

The *personnel* of the artillery was reorganized by means of the companies of cannoneers, which had been attached to each cohort of the bans: seventy of these companies were sent into Germany. I had six fine regiments of well-disciplined marine-artillerists; these were withdrawn from the ports, and also sent into Germany. These brave men did not object to the loss of their prerogatives, while I directed them to act as infantry.

A small number of these companies, however, were required to complete the artillery of the guard. The reorganization of cavalry was more difficult. I, however, remounted, in Hanover, the squadrons which had lost their horses in Russia; I levied a part of the postillions, and the sons of postmasters, and of the mounted guards of the forests; I also formed guards of honor in order to stimulate the proud and warlike youth of the country. The gensdarmerie also offered me a resource; two thousand officers and non-commissioned officers of this corps d'élite left their residences to aid me in forming the *cadres* of our young cavalry. The order, regularity, and activity which marked the fusion of all these heterogeneous elements constitute, perhaps, the most remarkable trait of my administration.

I thus re-appeared, at the opening of the campaign, as formidable as ever, at least in numbers. The enemy was surprised at the sudden return of our eagles. The army which I commanded, and especially the cavalry, was less warlike than that of Boulogne; but the heritage of glory gave it confidence, and I led it to the field against the enemy without hesitation.

I had a great task before me: it was necessary to reëstablish our military ascendency, and to resume a contest which had been so near its termination. I still held Italy, Holland, and most of the fortified places of Germany. The army of Spain, though defeated at Salamanca, had soon regained its supremacy by the concentration of its forces ; it had again confined Wellington to Portugal, and with the exception of Andalusia and Galicia, still occupied nearly all the peninsula. A reënforcement of thirty thousand conscripts ought to enable it to maintain its position. I had, therefore, lost but little ground ; it was only the prestige of my invincibility that was gone : it still required well-combined efforts on the part of my enemies to overthrow me, and these efforts might fail for want of union. England, however, redoubled her activity, and Prussia was preparing to make war *en masse*. The levies ordered by Russia in 1812 were collecting from all quarters into Poland to complete the organization of her army. Austria, convinced that the moment for pronouncing was approaching, armed herself with all possible activity. The princes of the Confederation, compelled by their own weakness to follow the strongest party, marched with hesitation under my flag. But my declared enemies, and doubtful allies caused me less inquietude than the secret societies which were formed for the overthrow of my power. These societies were organized in Bavaria, Saxony, and Wesphalia, while agents of the coalition were preaching a crusade against me in every part of Germany.

Eugene behind the Elbe.—While I was preparing my forces for a new contest, Eugene completed his long and difficult march from the Vistula to the banks of the Elbe. Prince Schwartzenberg in consequence of the convention with the Russian generals, had left General Frimont to march back his corps into Austrian Galicia. Poniatowski, by a subsequent convention, had retired without arms across the Austrian territory to rejoin me on the Elbe. Eugene, although reënforced by Grenier, had been obliged to garrison the places of the Oder, and brought for the defense of the Elbe only twenty thousand men, exclusive of the Saxons who were destined for the garrison of Torgau.

Prussia declares against Napoleon.—Prussia, after having disapproved the defection of York, sent to me, first, Prince Hatzfeld, and then General Krusemarck, to claim the reimbursement of the ninety millions of francs which she said we owed her for supplies furnished to our army. If I had had to deal only with Frederick-William, I should have retained him in my alliance by restoring a part of his lost provinces, and by paying him the money which he claimed: but I knew that he would be induced by the feelings of the army and of the nation to declare against me: in fact, his cabinet was even then negotiating with Russia. I thought it useless to deceive Krusemarck, and told him plainly that I was not disposed to supply arms to my enemies. The Prussian government now no longer concealed its hostility: a treaty of alliance was signed with Russia, on the twenty-seventh of February, at Kalisch, and the two sovereigns soon after met at Breslau to concert their political and military operations. Russia promised to bring one hundred and fifty thousand men into the field, and Prussia eighty thousand as a *minimum*, and double that number if circumstances permitted. It was agreed to make an appeal to the people and princes of Germany, and to strip of their territories all those who did not join in the coalition. A committee was formed, first, under the presidency of Kotschubey, and afterward of Stein, for inciting and directing the *levée en masse*. It is also said that a secret convention was signed, near the close of March, stipulating for the assistance of Austria.

March of the Allies on the Elbe.—The Russian army, having passed the Oder and the Rohr, moved its headquarters to Bunzlau, where Kutusof, already aged and broken down by the fatigues of the campaign, died of an epidemic fever which prevailed in the army, and also in the countries through which they passed. Count Wittgenstein succeeded him in the command, and directed a part of his army with Blucher on Dresden, and the remainder, with the corps of Bulow, Kleist, and York, by Frankfort on Berlin. Eugene, finding himself unable to defend the Spree against the united armies of Prussia and Russia, fell back from Copenick on Wittenberg, and Augereau, who had at Berlin only a few conscripts, evacuated that capital on the approach of the allies, and followed the retreat of the army behind the Elbe.

Eugene, informed of the reënforcements which were approaching, thought to defend the line of that river; Belluno, with two new divisions which afterward formed the second corps-d'armée on the Saale, covered the space between Magdebourg and the confluence of that river. Davoust, with a part of the eleventh corps, defended the interval between Torgau and Dessau; while Reynier was to secure Dresden with Durutte's division and the wrecks of the Saxons and Bavarians. As it was less important to guard this line than to assemble the scattered forces, I directed him to concentrate toward Magdebourg. Davoust and Reynier, after some difficulty with the citizens who opposed the blowing up of some of the arches of the bridge of Dresden, left the Saxons at Torgau, and descended the river with their few remaining troops. I had also directed on Magdebourg the regiments of infantry formed by the cohorts of the first ban. This reënforcement of twenty-four thousand men, under the orders of Lauriston, increased the number of combatants in the vicinity of the city to fifty thousand. Vandamme went to command a corps-d'armée formed of the cohorts in the departments of the mouths of the Elbe and the Weser.

The Allies enter Saxony.—The enemy continued to advance with excessive confidence; Count Wittgenstein and the Prussians, under Bulow, entered Berlin: the first, leaving Count Woronzof to mask Magdebourg, passed the Elbe in the environs of Dessau; and Blucher, with the corps of Silesia and that of Miloradowitsch, debouched by Dresden. At the approach of the enemy's columns, the king of Saxony left for Ratisbon; but afterwards, on the invitation of Austria, returned to Prague, where he was at the same time more secure and nearer to his states. The cabinet of Vienna was making every effort to enclose this prince in her toils: it sought to induce him to unite his destinies with those of Austria, with the hope of acting the mediator. Such a step was directly opposed to our treaties, and to the statutes of the Confederation of the Rhine, and consequently could not be approved by the principles of morality. A model of virtue and loyalty, this prince at first resisted all those insinuations: but finally, drawn on by the hope of contributing to the general pacification, and of saving his country from the disasters of war, he declared that he would follow in every respect the course which Austria might pursue. Such was the condition of affairs in Germany when I was prepared to resume the contest, and to take the initiative in the new campaign.

Continuation of Negotiations with Austria.—In the mean time Austria continued to speak of peace, reproving the defection of others, and protesting her fidelity to the alliance of 1812.

If she negotiated with Russia and England, it was, she said, only for us and with us; and she communicated to me all her correspondence. Nevertheless, the news from Vienna was very different from these fine official protestations. Public opinion at Vienna was the same as at Berlin. All official notes were of the most pacific character; but confidential overtures indicated other and different intentions. They manifested the wish that I should renounce the protectorate of the Confederation of the Rhine, and also my projects respecting the Duchy of Warsaw. But the cabinet did not present these as its own conditions, but as those expected by the allies. It protested its own disinterestedness, but let me understand that it expected the restitution of Illyria. I determined a little late, and, perhaps, too indirectly, to sound the views of the Austrian cabinet, by authorizing the Duke of Bassano to hold out the offer of Silesia; so as to see whether Austria placed her hopes elsewhere than in the results of a coöperation with France. Silesia had been taken from Austria by Frederick the Great; it was a valuable province; and as Prussia had declared against me, it would be necessary to punish her severely. But instead of being satisfied with this acquisition, the cabinet of Vienna manifested the most opposite views by laying down as a principle that Prussia was to be reconstructed in proportions even greater than in 1806.

As the correspondence of my ambassador at Vienna, Count Otto, seemed too much in the views of Austria, I thought it prudent to replace him with M. Narbonne, a shrewd courtier, capable of penetrating the mysteries of that cabinet. His reports soon confirmed my fears. The Prince of Schwartzenberg, announced for more than a month, did not arrive; and it was evident that Austria merely wished to gain time to increase her forces. She expended her paper-money, regardless of the depreciation produced by large issues, provided it furnished her with battalions.

As I was about to join my army, I took leave of Bubna, charging him with a letter to my father-in-law, in which I repeated what I desired to do for peace, and the means which seemed best calculated to lead to negotiations. My position was so delicate that I could not do anything abruptly. If I provoked Austria to formal declarations which proved unfavorable, I would thus accelerate the crisis which I wished to avoid. I was preparing to strike decisive blows in Germany, blows calculated to secure her fidelity, and procure me an honorable peace, independent of her arbitration.

Schwartzenberg finally reached Paris just as I was leaving to join my army. I merely asked him if the Austrian contingent was still at my disposal. On receiving his affirmative answer, I left him to complete his negotiations with the Duke of Bassano. My minister used all his diplomacy to draw the Austrian negotiator further towards an alliance than the other desired. But the object on both sides was to gain time, and all the negotiations of Bubna, Floret, and Schwartzenberg, tended only to that object. And so long as Austria remained in her present line of conduct, it was not good policy for us to push matters, for I felt assured that a victory in Saxony would retain her under my flag.

Austria declares an armed Mediation.—The negotiations of Narbonne at Vienna finally drew from Austria the avowal that she intended to offer an armed mediation, that is, to make herself the arbiter of peace. Schwartzenberg soon received new instructions. In a note as long as it was obscure, in which he spoke with affectation of *the Jacobin ferment which threatened the stability of thrones, of the disinterestedness of the emperor for his monarchy, and of his solicitude for the general repose*, he let it be understood that, in order to obtain new sacrifices from the Austrian people, his master could not announce a formal intention of uniting his forces to those of France, but that he wished merely to show himself in arms in order to obtain peace. But notwithstanding its general ambiguity, this note contained some protestations very amicable for France; for it *avowed the partiality of Austria for us, as we sincerely desired peace.* Quieted by these new assurances, we thought that Austria really intended to act the part of a friend, when the fit occasion should arrive. However, Metternich and even the emperor himself, in their conferences with Narbonne, advanced a little farther. They spoke already of the independence of the Confederation of the Rhine, the dissolution of the Duchy of Warsaw, the restitution of Illyria, the reconstruction of the Prussian monarchy, as conditions which would be demanded by our enemies, and which it would be difficult for a mediator to refuse. This new state of things gave rise to two questions: would Austria break our alliance, by declaring herself the mediating power? would she leave me her contingent? On the first point Metternich did not fail to make the most positive assurances: "The alliance," he said, "continued; Austria would instantly contract it, if it did not already exist; she would persist in it; and would change in no respect its conditions. This alliance was based on interests too identical, too inherent in the nature of things and too invariable in their character, to be influenced by either reverses or successes." With respect to the contingent, he said, that, in order to preserve the appearance of impartiality, the cabinet of Vienna could take no active part in the war; it was enough for her to be secretly inclined in our favor, without having its mediation rejected by my enemies on account of her furnishing me with troops.

Napoleon returns to his Army.—During these discussions, I left Paris to rejoin my army. As my enemies were not yet prepared I wished to profit by the occasion to resume the offensive and recover our glory. The Russian army which had pursued us to the Elbe was broken by the winter campaign. Having left some corps before Dantzic, Thorn, Modlin, Zamosc, and Custrin, and another to occupy Poland and follow Poniatowski, it now scarcely numbered sixty thousand combatants. For the moment, Prussia could not unite with it more than fifty thousand combatants. By uniting the cohorts of the first ban, which I had very fortunately organized in 1812, and amalgamating a levy of one hundred and twenty thousand conscripts with the remains of my army which had returned from Russia, we could count on two hundred and fifty thousand men, and concentrate them on the enemy before he could collect an equal number. I resolved to profit by this circumstance. My enemies have not failed to attribute this to personal ambition, and to accuse me of having lost this opportunity to restore the peace of the continent! Was it more proper for me to now submit to the yoke and implore the good-will and support of the cabinet of Vienna, or to first beat the enemy while still inferior in numbers, to finish my armaments, and then subscribe to an honorable and advantageous peace?

He advances on the Saale.—On the twenty-fifth of April, I arrived at Erfurth, where I found my guard reorganized. Ney's corps assembled at Weimar numbered forty-eight thousand; Marmont's corps at Gotha, numbered not less than twenty-five thousand; Bertrand, who commanded about the same number from Italy and Wurtembourg, was already at Saalfeld, and Oudinot, with as many at Cobourg. I was thus again at the head of one hundred and forty thousand men, exclusive of the viceroy, who, with forty thousand combatants, was under the cannon of Magdebourg, and of Belluno and Davoust on the Lower Elbe. Independently of these forces, Augereau was directed to organize at Wurzburg a small army for the three-fold purpose of imposing on Austria, observing Bohemia, and maintaining Bavaria. I had as yet only eight or ten thousand cavalry, those who had escaped on foot from Russia were waiting in different parts of Germany for their horses. But this arm is far less important in gaining a victory, than in deriving the full advantage from success. I had sufficient means for opening the campaign, especially as the chances were in our favor, and as the enemy exposed himself to our blows. I therefore, did not hesitate.

Organization of the French Army.—My army was at this time organized into twelve corps:

1st corps,	*Vandamme*..........	3	divisions,
2d "	*Belluno*,.............	2	"
3d "	*Ney*,................	5	"
4th "	*Bertrand*,...........	3	"
5th "	*Lauriston*,..........	3	"
6th "	*Marmont*,...........	3	"
7th "	*The Saxons*, at Torgau,		
8th "	*Poniatowski*,		
9th "	*The Bavarians*,		
10th "	*Rapp*, at Dantzic,		
11th "	*Macdonald*,..........	3	divisions,
12th "	*Oudinot*,............	3	"

Augereau's army at Wurtzburg was composed of five divisions of infantry; its battalions arrived in June and July.

Levy in Mass in Prussia.—No sooner had the king of Prussia pronounced for the enemy than his council took every measure in their power to incite the people of Germany against us. The ordinances of April 21st, directing a *levée en masse*, promised to make every city a Saragossa, and every village a funeral pile. The good Saxons, Silesians, and Westphalians, were to transform themselves into ferocious Aragonese: *liberty* could not be too dearly purchased! They go still farther, and proclaim *equality!* Old honors have been effaced by the disgrace of bearing a foreign yoke! The new genealogical trees are to date from 1812, and no one is to hold public office who has not served one year in the War of Independence! It must be confessed that these measures were not calculated to favor the permanent interests of sovereigns, however advantageously they might assist the accomplishment of their temporary objects. A civilized people is not easily satisfied with the mere hopes of an ideal liberty. The desire to crush my power made the sovereigns forget the danger of exciting popular passions.

Movements of the Allies.—But as these proclamations produced little effect, without the support of the bayonet, the allies resolved to pass the Elbe, and spread, with impetuosity, over the country between that river and the Rhine. Tettenborn entered Hamburg at the head of a few hundred Cossacks, without opposition; Westphalia and Hanover, more exasperated than in 1809, were only waiting for the signal to rise; and Denmark on being summoned declared against us. It was important to prevent the fatal consequences of these irruptions. Pushing rapidly on Hamburg the corps of Vandamme, formed of the garrisons and depôts of the Lower Rhine, I sent Marshal Davoust to command in that important part of the theatre of war.

Position of their Armies.—On the other side, the army of Wittgenstein marched on the Saale with the same assurance which had proved so fatal to the Prussians in 1806. This general had just been placed, by the sovereigns, at the head of the combined forces. He was with thirty thousand men between Dessau and Halle. Blucher had collected twenty-five thousand men at Altenbourg; and Miloradowitsch was at Chemnitz, with fifteen thousand Russians. The Russo-Prussian reserves were advancing from Dresden on Leipsic; the corps of Bulow and Woronzof were masking Magdebourg, and covering Berlin against the viceroy. The divergent direction of all these corps showed that the enemy arranged his operations more with reference to giving force to his proclamations, than to opposing a formidable army.

Napoleon effects his Junction with the Viceroy.—As it was important to effect a junction with the viceroy, with the least possible delay, I resolved to advance immediately. I arrived at Naumbourg on the twenty-eighth of April, and, the next day, Ney entered Weissenfels, after driving back the Russian van-guard of cavalry; Marmont reached Kösen, and Bertrand, Dornbourg; Oudinot had not yet passed

Saalfeld; but the viceroy, after having ascended the left bank of the Saale, arrived at Mersebourg. Count Wittgenstein marched parallel with Eugene on the right of the Saale and the Elster, and concentrated his forces on Leipsic; Blucher filed by his right, and marched on Borna; while Miloradowitsch and the reserves advanced in the direction of Altenbourg.

Napoleon directs his Forces on Leipsic.—Having secured my junction with the viceroy, I resolved to march on Leipsic, with the intention of attacking the enemy wherever I should meet him. My affairs required a victory, and my superiority in numbers now gave me promise of success. On the first of May the Russian advance-guard, which we encountered at the defile at Ripach between Weissenfels and Lutzen, was thrown on Pegau, after an engagement which, except for the death of Marshal Bessières, was unimportant. This veteran and faithful general was here killed by a musket-ball: a sad end for an old warrior who had survived so many battles, to die in a petty skirmish of a rear-guard.*

* Thiers thus describes Bessières' death:

"At daybreak Marshal Ney's troops advanced upon the vast Lutzen plain, formed in squares, which were accompanied by artillery, and preceded by numerous tirailleurs. Arriving at the brink of a long and deep ravine, called the Ripach Ravine, from the name of a village which it traversed, the squares broke for the purpose of passing it, and when it had been crossed, reformed and continued their advance. The division Souham held the foremost place; marching with an excellent bearing, and had just deployed, when Marshal Bessières, who usually commanded the cavalry of the guard, and should not consequently have been where he now was, advanced a little to the right, for the purpose of being better able to observe the enemy's movements, and suddenly fell dead, struck by a bullet in the breast.

"It was the second time, alas! that this brave man had been hit on the battle-field by Napoleon's side, the first time being at Wagram, where a bullet had struck him, but only caused a contusion. His death on the present occasion caused, in spite of the general confidence, a painful foreboding in more than one heart.

"He was a valiant man, of a lively Gascon temperament, but possessed of a fine intellect, and of a courage which frequently led him to express to Napoleon useful truths both impressively and opportunely. Napoleon loved and

My army was now in echelons from Naumbourg to Leipsic. Lauriston's corps and the army of the viceroy formed the head, between Leipsic and Marckranstedt; Eugene and the corps of Macdonald occupied the latter of these towns; my guards and head-quarters were established at Lutzen, which was covered on the side towards Pegau by Ney's corps; Marmont arrived at Poserna, and Berthier was in march for the same point; Oudinot, still further in rear, marched from Jena to Naumbourg. On the morning of the second of May, the viceroy continued his movement on Leipsic. I wished to follow at his right on Marckranstedt. Impatient to learn whether the enemy would abandon to us the important strategic point of Leipsic, the centre of all the great communications of northern Germany, I set out with my guard to ascertain whether any opposition would be made: the enemy, however, was preparing to surprise me on another side.

Project of the Allies.—The allies, recovering from the excessive confidence inspired by the reports of their couriers, now saw that mere demonstrations, by the head of their columns, were not sufficient to drive us from Germany. They heard with astonishment of my return on the Saale with a powerful army, but, considering the reports of my strength to be exaggerated, they still hoped, by concentrating their own masses, to beat in detail our hastily levied conscripts, who were now assembling by twenty different

esteemed him, and felt a sincere pang of sorrow at his loss; but then exclaiming, 'Death comes nigh us!' pushed forward to watch the march of his young soldiers, and experienced in the spectacle a satisfaction equal to that felt by Ney two days before; beholding his conscripts repelling again and again the repeated charges of the enemy's cavalry, and strewing the ground before them with three or four hundred killed and wounded foemen.

"The troops halted at Lutzen, and Napoleon went to visit the monument of Gustavus Adolphus, who had been struck down on this plain, as Epaminondas, in the bosom of victory, and gave orders that a monument should also be raised to the memory of the Duke of Istria, killed on the same ground."

routes; it was not supposed that these forces could contend with the old bands of Russia and the troops of the *élite* which Prussia had reorganized within the last six years. Supposing the corps of Ney, Marmont, and Mortier, much less than they really were, the allies resolved to attack them on the march, so as to prevent their junction. This project seemed the more admissible for the allies, as they hoped by it to draw over to their side Saxony, which was disposed to abandon our cause. The king, it is true, retired at the approach of the allies, but the people, acted on by the emissaries of the *Tugenbund*, were uncertain, and might carry over their sovereign in spite of himself. Already a tacit convention had neutralized the Saxon corps of General Thielmann under the cannon of Torgau, and the enemy was negotiating with Prague to obtain its adhesion to the coalition.

Stimulated by these powerful motives, and deceived respecting the numbers of our troops, the allied sovereigns resolved to take the offensive and manœuvre against my extreme right. With this object Wittgenstein had left only a corps of five thousand men to defend Leipsic, and had united between Zwenkau and Pegau a mass of seventy thousand men, composed of his own army, the corps of Blucher, and the allied reserves. With this mass he resolved to pass the Elster and march on Lutzen, so as to assail in rear my army which he supposed to have filed on Leipsic. Miloradowich directed himself on Zeits to cover the flank and communications of the allies during their operations beyond the Elster.

Battle of Lutzen.—It was extremely important for us to sustain ourselves at Lutzen, as the possession of that place by the enemy would enable him to cut my army in two. Wittgenstein debouched on that city on the morning of the second, but instead of finding here my extreme right, he encountered the centre of my army. This manœuvre of the enemy, although it failed in its object, was certainly worthy of praise; so little was I expecting to be assailed on this side, that I had taken with me Marshal Ney, leaving his corps without its chief. It would be difficult to say what would have been the result if the enemy had made good use of his twelve thousand superb cavalry, for Ney had not six hundred horse with which to oppose them. While Wintzingerode paraded his squadrons before Tournau, and the Prussians were losing time in forming, Ney's troops ran to arms; the four French divisions were in echelons in the villages which covered Lutzen on the side toward Pegau and Zwenkau. The fifth, composed of German troops, covered their left. The first division composed entirely of conscripts, eighteen years of age, was attacked at eleven o'clock, and, seconded by the division of Girard, sustained the combat with glory. The troops being arranged in echelons, the attacks were successive and partial, which was favorable for our new troops. The Prussian brigades of Klux and Ziethen advanced on Goeschen; that of Roder served as a reserve; Dolfs' cavalry was directed on Starsiedel, with the hope of turning the columns of Ney. York's corps and the Russian division of Berg formed the second line. The Russian corps of Prince Eugene of Wurtemberg was in column of march to the left, where the cavalry of Wintzingerode deployed. There was no unity of action in this first effort; Souham and Girard, after having disputed Gros-Goeschen and Rahna, were forced to fall back on Klein-Goeschen, which Souham also abandoned.

At the sound of this violent attack Ney left me to fly to the head of his troops; I also returned to Lutzen with my guard, and directed Eugene to renounce his march on Leipsic and join the contest. Officers were also sent to Marmont, directing him to hasten into line on the right of Ney, and to Bertrand directing him to fall upon the enemy's flank.

Ney, having reached his corps about noon, assembled his divisions, and threw those of Souham, Girard and Brenier on Klein-Goeschen, thus dislodging the Prussians. This vigorous blow retards the operations of the allies and gives time for the corps of the right and left to come to the assistance of the centre. Marmont, having reached the field during this interval, prolongs the right of the army which the enemy sought to gain, and debouches toward Starsiedel, without troubling himself with the numerous cavalry which Wintzingerode deployed in the fields of Kobson, or that of the Prussians which afterward formed between this first village and Rahna. These squadrons finally advanced to the charge; the divisions of Campans and Bonnet, formed in squares, repel them; they several times renew the attack, but our brave regiments oppose an impenetrable front; a single battalion is broken by the Russian cavalry.

But this first reënforcement has not yet restored the equilibrium in our favor; for Blucher has at the same time ordered York's corps and the Russian division of Berg to enter into the first line and retake the villages of Rahna and Klein-Goeschen which Ney had just gained. The shock now becomes more general and more serious. Ney is forced to fall back behind Kaya, which he defends with all the vigor of which he is capable. The enemy throws himself with impetuosity on this village; twice is Ney driven out; and a final effort of Berg's division secures its momentary possession to the allies. Our young soldiers surpass my hopes in this obstinate contest; but, more brave than experienced, they suffer severe losses. I arrive at this point the moment when Ney is preparing a final effort to regain Kaya with the division of Ricard. I order Count Lobau to put himself at the head of this troop, while the marshal conducted his other divisions to assist him. This movement is executed with the rapidity of lightning; Count Lobau penetrates into Kaya with that steadiness for which he is so distinguished ; he is warmly supported by the divisions of Brenier, Girard and the remains of Souham which Ney leads back to victory. A terrible combat is engaged between this village and Klein-Goeschen where the enemy debouched with all his united means. Girard and Brenier fall like heroes at the head of their young soldiers, whom they persist in leading to the fight, although severely wounded. Girard cries to his men : "*Soldiers this is the day for France ; let us avenge the defeat of Moscow or die.*"

The enemy now felt that victory would escape him unless Blucher was more effectively sustained. For this purpose Wittgenstein moved from the left to the right the corps of Prince Eugene of Wurtemberg which had at first marched in the opposite direction. One of these divisions debouched from Eisdorf beyond the Flosgraben, and pushed the division of Marchand ; the other reënforced Berg at Klein-Goeschen ; this village was again carried, and Ney for a third time driven behind Kaya. The arrival of the grenadier corps and the Russian guard which the allied sovereigns were awaiting with impatience, might decide the battle against us. The moment was decisive ; I threw on Kaya the two divisions of the Young Guard which returned and debouched from Lutzen, followed by the Old Guard and all my cavalry. The enemy was driven back to Klein-Goeschen.

Here a new scene is developed. Seeing the inutility of his efforts against the centre, Wittgenstein prepared to strike on the left of Ney ; the corps of grenadiers under the orders of Konownitzin, had just arrived on the field of battle ; its two divisions debouched by Eisdorf and Gros-Goeschen. This movement which might have been decisive if all my troops had been engaged, did not have the success which the allies expected ; I had taken measures to provide for this event. Eugene had received the orders of which I have already spoken ; but seeing Lauriston's columns engaged in the faubourgs of Leipsic, and thinking he ought to leave them to occupy that city, he hastened to Macdonald's corps and directed it on Kitzen. The arrival of these three fresh divisions decided everything ; the victory was no longer doubtful. Konownitzin and the Prince of Wurtemberg vainly sought to defend the village of Eisdorf ; being attacked on all sides they were forced to abandon it. The allies now saw their right turned, while Ney and Marmont pressed them in front towards Goeschen, and Lauriston, master of Leipsic, prepared to push Kleist in the direction of Connewitz, and Bertrand, debouching at the opposite extremity, at the head of Morand's division, turned the left of the allies by Gosserau and Pobles. Seeing the danger of their position, they now abandoned the four burnt villages and fell back behind Gros-Goeschen where the arrival of the Russian guards enabled them to maintain their position.

Darkness even did not terminate the battle. The scouts of Marmont advanced in the dusk beyond Starsiedel, and gave the alarm to the Prussians. A night combat ensued in which the enemy was at first repulsed. Blucher then put himself at the head of his reserve of cavalry and executed a rash charge. Some squadrons penetrated between our lines, and our troops, being unprepared for the attack fell into disorder ; this was still further increased by a *hourra* of the Cossacks on the ambulances in rear of our line. But this attack was attended by no serious consequences ; our troops soon recovered from their surprise and made Blucher pay dearly for his isolated and ill-conceived enterprise ; his squadrons did not regain their line without considerable loss.

Remarks on this Battle.—The day had been bloody without being decisive. Ney's corps alone had lost twelve thousand men and five hundred officers *hors-de-combat*, and we had gained neither trophies nor results. The number of men wounded in the hand was so great that our young conscripts were accused of self mutilation in order to avoid the fatigues of the war. Perhaps this resulted from their being unaccustomed to the use of weapons. The accusation was, nevertheless, of sufficient importance to merit an examination.

This battle, having been unforeseen, had produced no important results. I therefore determined to renew it the next day in order to complete the defeat of the enemy, if he committed the fault of remaining on the left of the Elster. To obtain still greater results, I ordered Lauriston, who had entered Leipsic during the battle and driven Kleist on Wurtzen, to leave only a detachment in the city and with the mass of his corps to march along the left bank of the Elster, so as to threaten the enemy's bridges.

But Wittgenstein, having already perceived the danger of his position, profited by the night to recross the river. The following day the allied army continued its retreat in two columns on Dresden and Meissen; Wittgenstein with the Russians took the road to Altenbourg and Chemnitz; I caused him to be pursued by Bertrand and Oudinot. Blucher took the direct road to Colditz; I myself followed him with Marmont, the guard, and the corps of Macdonald, commanded by the viceroy. Ney, with the third and fifth corps, took the road to Leipsic on Torgau, from which place he was to act in concert with the Duke of Belluno who was leading the second corps from Magdebourg on Wittemberg. Davoust and Vandamme at the head of the first corps again entered Hamburg.

Pursuit of the Allies on Dresden.—Although the pursuit was made with activity, yet, for want of cavalry we obtained no results. We overtook the rear-guard of Blucher on the Mulde where it was much cut up; but the fresh corps of Miloradowitsch appeared to cover the retreat, and conducted itself with that cool bravery and steadiness so characteristic of the Russian army, and which results from their fine military institutions and severe discipline. The viceroy engaged in three successive combats, at Elsdorf, Nossen and Wilsdruf; he pushed the enemy, but did not succeed in cutting him up. The Russians recrossed the Elbe on the seventh, at Dresden, and the Prussians at Meissen. Finally, on the eighth of May, we arrived before the capital of Saxony; Miloradowitsch blew up the bridges, burned the magazines, and prepared to defend the new town which is situated on the right of the Elbe. I made a reconnoisance of the advantageous heights of Priesnitz; a bridge of boats was thrown across here under the protection of eighty pieces of the guard, and two battalions of voltigeurs crossed on rafts. As at Essling, a sudden rise of the Elbe threatened the security of our bridges; but the army had not yet passed; and even if they had commenced the passage, the enemy would not have been prepared to attack us. Our troops, in their impatience, used long beams to build over the two arches of the stone bridge which had been blown up by the enemy; finally the approach of night decided the Russian general to begin his retreat. Dresden was now in our possession, and its magistrates came out to meet me. I reproached them for the conduct of the inhabitants in Eugene's retreat, and on the approach of the enemies of their sovereign, and pardoned them only on condition of their sending a deputation to their king to solicit his return.

The information which reached me after I entered this capital was far from agreeable: On the one hand, I learned that General Thielmann, the governor of Torgau, had been several times at the head-quarters of the allies, and Ney informed me that he refused to open the gates of the place to my troops. This revelation indicated the use which Austria expected to make of her influence and her mediation;

this state of uncertainty could not continue. I therefore immediately detached my aid-de-camp, Montesquiou to Prague; he was the bearer of dispatches demanding to know of the King of Saxony, if he was still a member of the Confederation of the Rhine, and what treaty had released him from the engagements which he had contracted. This brave and loyal prince answered by coming himself to Dresden on the twelfth of May, having previously forwarded a formal order to receive us at Torgau. Thielmann, being enraged against us, abandoned his sovereign and passed into the service of Russia. The Saxon troops, again placed under the orders of Reynier, formed, with Durutte's division, the seventh *corps-d'armée*. Nevertheless, this difficulty lost us five days in the pursuit, and Ney did not cross the Elbe at Torgau till the thirteenth.

Eugene sent to organize an Army in Italy.—The political horizon began to lower in the direction of Austria: I, therefore, resolved to send Eugene into Italy where he might be more useful to me in case of a rupture. The most pressing orders had been sent there to replace the French troops which had been withdrawn, and to form again the Italian army, which the cruel losses in Catalonia and Russia had almost destroyed.

Negotiations between Bassano and Schwartzenberg.—While I was thus marching to new victories, I had left the Duke of Bassano and Schwartzenberg at Paris to discuss our reciprocal interests. Although my minister had the same confidence as myself in the success of our military operations, and although he would have preferred to discuss directly the question of peace, yet under the circumstances his mission was naturally limited to ascertaining the intentions of Schwartzenberg, without making any offers himself, at least not until after the first events of the campaign. It was important to ascertain what were the intentions of my enemies, and what the limits assigned by Austria to the sacrifices required of me; and at the same time to avoid any formal declaration which might be immediately changed by the results of a victory. As Bassano and Schwartzenberg had been negotiators of my family-alliance, an intimacy had sprung up between them favorable for a frank explanation. In one of their conferences in which Bassano sought to ascertain the influence which my marriage might exercise on Austria, Schwartzenberg replied that *policy had concluded that marriage, and that policy might break it again.* It was evident from this that the considerations of kindred were, in Austria, to be made subordinate to the interests of the cabinet. Bassano pretended not to notice the remark, and turned the conversation to matters of less importance. He immediately informed me of the fears which this conference had excited in his mind, concealing, however, the threatening words, lest the anger excited in me by them might interfere with the negotiations. "It is necessary," he wrote to me, "to hasten the treaty with Austria, and to profit by her present hesitation to draw more closely the ties of blood and policy which now connect the two powers." A few days afterwards Prince Schwartzenberg communicated dispatches from London, in which Baron Weissenberg announced the ill-success of his overtures. "Austria," said he, "is very far from submitting the peace of the cabinet to the caprices of England. The zeal of the cabinet of Vienna will not diminish, and she will soon take a very peremptory step towards the allied powers to bring them to final explanations." The mission of Prince Schwartzenberg closed with these new assurances. He had just left Paris when the renewal of hostilities was followed by the battle of Lutzen.

New Mission of Budna.—On arriving at Dresden I learned the departure of Schwartzenberg, and the opinions formed from these conferences by my minister respecting the question of a general peace. Great events were now to be decided: it was natural to hope that my victory at Lutzen would reëstablish my relations with Austria. Unfortunately the results of this victory were not sufficiently decisive to influence Austria as was desired. Metternich, informed at the same time of the too frank explanations of Schwartzenberg and of my victory at Lutzen, felt that he was about to be compromised; he trembled lest I might profit by the occasion to have a reconciliation with Russia. The consequences might thus become still more important than the battle itself. It was not impossible but that I might have a frank understanding with the Emperor Alexander, as at Tilsit; I flattered myself that I would have found him disposed to a reconciliation, if I sacrificed to him the Duchy of Warsaw. The wily diplomat hastened to send to him Count Stadion, and to dispatch to me by Budna a letter from my father-in-law. The same protestations as before were here renewed, in nearly the same terms. *The mediator,* wrote the emperor, *is your sincere friend: it is important to place on an immovable basis your dynasty, whose existence is now inseparably connected with that of his own.*

In the absence of the Duke of Bassano, I directed Caulaincourt to confer with this envoy, whose language differed a little from that of his sovereign. Budna confessed that the alliance was suspended at least in some of its articles, but when pressed to specify what these were, he pretended that on this point he had no precise instructions. There was every reason to believe that the first of the articles referred to was that of the guarantee of the territories. In that case it was important to know what changes were expected in the state of things guaranteed in March, 1812. Although Budna had no instructions on this subject, it was understood from him that Austria hoped for Illyria, a part of Galicia, and the Innviertel; and that the allies required the dissolution of the Confederation of the Rhine, and of the Duchy of Warsaw. These were rather given to be understood than positively asserted; they, however, were only a repetition of what had already been said to M. de Narbonne at Vienna. Austria proposed a congress for explaining herself more categorically. Coming to me, as they did, immediately after my brilliant victory, these ambiguous and exacting propositions wounded my feelings, and in a moment of displeasure I remarked that "*if Budna annoyed me with such pretensions, I would treat at any price with Russia, and then have an explanation with these Austrians!*" These words were foolishly repeated by my imprudent admirers, and, coming to the ears of my father-in-law, were calculated to prejudice him against me, and to favor the inclinations of his cabinet in favor of my enemies.

Proposition for a Congress accepted.—The reports which reached me from all directions were of a nature to destroy my last illusions. With an extraordinary refinement of address, Austria sought to paralyze my allies. "She appeared in Denmark, in Saxony, in Bavaria, in Wurtemberg, and even at Naples, as a friend of France, who only wished for peace; *she negotiated with them to discontinue their military preparations, as being both ruinous and useless, for, if I consented to treat, she was ready to put one hundred and fifty thousand men in the scales in my favor!*"

During the few days which had just passed, events were pressing beyond the Elbe, where the enemy were concentrating at two days' march from my head-quarters; I left for Bautzen to cut the knot, so artistically formed by Austria. However, without rejecting anything, I answered Budna: "Austria can, if she pleases, renounce the alliance; I shall not be wounded by it; I fear nothing so much as half-way measures, the common resource of irresolution and weakness; I accept the proposition to assemble a congress at Prague, and if the other powers accept it, I am willing to facilitate a treaty of peace by concluding an armistice."

Bubna transmitted my proposition directly to Stadion at the head-quarters of the allied sovereigns, and, in his letter, *he did justice to the pacific dispositions which I manifested, notwithstanding my victorious attitude.* On my part, I wrote to my father-in-law to renew the sentiments which I felt towards him; but I declared *that, as a good Frenchman, I would rather die, arms in hand, than to subscribe to conditions presented at the point of the sword. I was ready to negotiate, but not to receive the law.*

Caulaincourt's Propositions to Russia.—Bubna left for Vienna with these assurances. On my side, I wished to profit by the occasion which the proposition of an armistice presented, to send Caulaincourt to the Emperor Alexander; he received the order on the eighteenth of May. I preferred to give the advantages of peace to a noble and chivalric enemy, rather than to these traders in mediation, who subjected everything to selfish calculation, and coolly counted the price of defection. The instructions which I gave to Caulaincourt, dated at Hartha, May 19th, sufficiently attest the sentiment which animated me. They contain these words: "His Majesty does not reject the possibility that new circumstances and new combinations may induce him to return to his system with Austria; but, in the present situation of affairs, such is not his thought. His intention is to negotiate with Russia a peace which may be glorious for that power, and which may pay Austria the price of her bad faith, and the political fault she has committed against the alliance of 1812, by drawing together Russia and France. If the convention made for Poland, after the peace of Vienna, had been accepted, with some changes in the terms, there would have been no bitterness, and no war. The Emperor Alexander will readily reply to these arguments by referring to the radical vice of the existence of the Duchy in respect to Russia; which will naturally lead, after much mystery and reserve, to the following proposition, of which the secret will be previously asked of him, in case he should not accept it:

"To limit the existence of the Confederation of the Rhine to the Oder, drawing a line from Glogau to Bohemia: this will give to Westphalia an increase of one million five hundred thousand souls. Prussia will have in compensation the Duchy of Warsaw with the territory of Dantzic, except a small *arrondissement* for Oldenbourg; Prussia will then acquire four or five millions of inhabitants, Dantzic, Thorn, Modlin, and all the Vistula. She will become complete, and will form, for Russia, a new frontier which will cover her, and form for her a great security, inasmuch as Prussia, having her capital near to her, will be in her system. France and Russia will be separated by three hundred leagues, with a respectable power between them. The king of Prussia, having his capital at Warsaw, Königsberg, or Dantzic, will be in the Russian system. Thus France and Russia, having nothing more to fear from each other, will easily place themselves in such relations as naturally to produce a close alliance."

It was also stated in these instructions:

"It is useless to revert to the stipulations of Tilsit, which were directed against England only; whereas now the question is for a general peace, and the Emperor Alexander will sooner or later feel the necessity of adopting a proper system for causing his flag to be respected."

Napoleon goes to Bautzen.—Caulaincourt repaired to the advanced posts and waited, the nineteenth, for an answer to his request for a safe-guard to the head-quarters of the allied sovereigns. In the meantime I did not sleep on vague hopes; military operations were continued; the moment of an inevitable and decisive shock was approaching. My masses were in motion; it was necessary that the armistice should be agreed upon on the twentieth, or that the arena should be left open for new combats; and, to give more weight to my propositions, I flew to the point where my glory and interest called me.

After the passage of the Elbe there was some uncertainty about the enemy's movements: the public rumor announced that the Prussian army had descended the river to join Bulow's corps which covered Berlin, thus separating from the Russians who were said to be fortifying themselves at Bautzen. The fact was that the whole allied army was occupying the superb positions around that city, when the arrival of some reënforcements, among which were two divisions of grenadiers which returned from the siege of Thorn, under the orders of Barclay de Tolly, seemed to encourage them to receive a new battle. I caused them to be observed by the corps of Bertrand, Marmont, Macdonald, and Oudinot. I was expecting, on my side, some fine divisions of cuirassiers and light cavalry, reorganized by Latour-Maubourg, and two divisions of the Young Guard. When these troops had joined me, I went, on the twentieth, before Bautzen. No reply to Caulaincourt's application for a safe-guard had reached the out-posts; it was therefore necessary to resort to the chance of arms, which of all others I feared the least.

Fortified Position of the Allies.—The allies had profited by the ten days' repose to surround their camp with field-works. Their principal position was located on the famous mountains of Klein-Bautzen and Kreckwitz, which had served as a refuge for Frederic the Great after the surprise of Hochkirch, and where, by the strength of his position, he had braved the superior army of the victorious Daun. It is true that the Austrian marshal came from the direction of Goerlitz, and we came from the opposite direction by Dresden. The left, supported on the great chain of the mountains of Bohemia, was but little exposed to an attack; the right, established behind the lakes of Malchwitz, was difficult of access; but by turning it at a greater distance toward Bergern, it might be taken in reverse. However strong it might be on the front and flanks, this position offered two grave inconveniences: it had only one line of retreat, by Wurschen and Hochkirch, on Reichenbach; and as its line of battle rested on the neutral frontier toward its extreme left, it was clear that we should cut off the enemy's retreat, if we could gain the least success at the opposite wing. The army of Wittgenstein was charged with the defense of the left, from Baschutz and Nieder-Kayna to the mountains near Kunitz; that of Blucher held the right, from Malchwitz to Kreckwitz; the centre and reserves were between Litten and Baschutz.

Ney's March to turn their Position.—It will be remembered that Ney had debouched from Torgau with the ten infantry divisions of the third, fifth and seventh corps. If the report of the separation of the enemy's armies were confirmed, I should have left him in the interval between them, and should have assisted him by a movement to the left, throwing myself on the right of the Russians. In every state of the case, I thought it best to place under the orders of this marshal the second corps commanded by Belluno, and to prescribe to him a demonstration on Berlin, causing him to be sustained by the corps of Reynier, who would advance toward Dahme (Sayda). The marshal was to remain with the third corps on the great road from Luckau to Lubben, and to detach only Lauriston from his right on Hoyerswerda, in order to reënforce me toward Bautzen. Ney, attaching too much importance to the movement on Berlin, was about to go there in person; he was, fortunately, prevented from doing so by the news received from Lubben, which announced the arrival of Barclay in the direction of Bautzen. As soon as I learned the concentration of the enemy's forces on this last point, I wished to prolong Ney toward Kalhau and Spremberg. This movement was good to force the enemy from his position without battle, but it was not sufficiently concentric to gain great results. Ney fell back, on the seventeenth, from Kalhau on Senftenberg; he was advised to direct Belluno and Sebastiani on Spremberg, to complete the manœuvre for seizing the only line of retreat of the allies. This movement was not executed, either because Ney feared to isolate this corps too much or that Belluno would march too slowly to arrive in time.

The conqueror of Elchingen then advanced in procession, from the eighteenth, with the third corps in the woods of Senftenberg, preceded by Lauriston, and followed by Reynier and Belluno. Our communications had been troubled by the partisans of Lutzow; many of my orders had been intercepted. Duplicates were sent by messengers, to direct a movement which he had been making for two days.

Combats of Weissig and Konigswartha. — The ground between the Spree and the Schwarz-Elster is cut up by great marshy forests; it is a turf-bog where it is not possible to travel in the autumn or spring except by two narrow roads. Lauriston, detached after the passage of Torgau, had marched, with slow and measured steps, by Dobrilugk; his baggage obstructed the roads. Ney arrived, on the nineteenth, at the middle of his columns at Hoyerswerda, and directed them on Weissig to flank his march and open the road of Königswartha, which he had followed with the third and seventh corps. At the report of his approach, the allies, ignorant of his force and thinking, undoubtedly, that they had to deal only with the corps of Lauriston, conceived the project of fighting him separately, and for that purpose detached against him General Barclay with his corps and that of York.

Informed, on my side, of the arrival of Ney at the environs of Hoyerswerda, I pushed, on the nineteenth, an Italian division of Bertrand's corps on Königswartha, in order to secure the junction. This incident gave place to a double engagement. Barclay, marching to Königswartha, fell upon the Italian division, which was not on its guard, although bivouacked in the middle of the woods; it was surprised and dispersed with the loss of all its cannon and two thousand prisoners. This took place within a league of Ney's advanced guard; Kellerman, who commanded this vanguard, hastened to save the wrecks of the Italians, and Barclay fell back at his approach. York had not been so fortunate; his column encountered the centre corps of Lauriston, and was defeated with a loss of near five thousand Prussians. Maison's division gained the honors of the victory.

Ney debouches on Klix.—These incidents had no influence on the great question; the loss was nearly equal on both sides, and the allies rejoined their army. On the twentieth, Ney debouched at Königswartha on Leichnam and Klix. In order to give the allies no opportunity to molest him, and at the same time to drive them from all the advanced positions which covered their camp, I ordered an attack upon the city of Bautzen and the heights occupied by the left of the Russians. Oudinot and Macdonald carried Dobershau and Strehla, then advanced to Binewitz and Auritz. My right and centre passed the Spree, carried the city of Bautzen, and dislodged the enemy from the heights of Nieder-Kayna and Nadelwitz which covered the front of the intrenched camp. My manœuvre accomplished its object; the allies reënforced Miloradowitsch in the mountains, and Ney concentrated the third and fifth corps behind Klix, ready to strike, the next day, a blow not inferior to either Ratisbon or Friedland in the importance of its results.

Battle of Bautzen.—On the twenty-first of May, at the break of day, the battle was commenced throughout the whole line. We renewed against the left of the allies the demonstration of the previous day. Oudinot wished to pierce by Kunitz on Rachlau; but Miloradowitsch drove him beyond Binowitz; I ordered Macdonald to sustain him; my centre is deployed to impose on the enemy, but not to engage him. Ney crosses the Spree at Klix, places Maison's division as flankers behind the lake of Malschwitz, pushes the two other divisions of Lauriston on Gottamelde, and conducts the entire third corps on the wind-mill of Glein: *these forces afterwards direct their march on the spires of Hochkirch,** and the seventh corps, which was expected about one o'clock, was to act as their reserve. Lauriston was to march by Baruth, and Belgern in the same direction.

This manœuvre was perfect and ought to have produced incalculable results; but several unfortunate circumstances marred its success. I had expected, rather late, to give Ney instructions as to the part which he was to play in this battle. But these instructions did not reach him in time, and were of rather too general a character. At eight o'clock in the morning I had written him a pencil note giving him only a laconic order to be, by eleven o'clock, at the village of Preititz, and to attack the enemy's right. The officer who carried this note made a long detour by Klix in the hopes of finding the marshal there; at ten o'clock he arrived on the heights of Glein which Ney had just taken possession of, much sooner than I had expected.

Thus far all was well: for the directions assigned to the columns of our left on the spires of Hochkirchen accomplished the same object as my order to march on Preititz. It was now only ten o'clock: Preititz being only eight or nine hun-

* The credit of this manœuvre is claimed by Jomini, who was at this time acting as Ney's chief of staff.

dred toises from the heights of Glein, Ney was unwilling to accelerate the attack by an hour. He waited for Reynier's corps, and lost three-quarters of an hour in forming his troops: he then only advanced Souham on Preititz, leaving his three other divisions at the distance of half a league, and the third at the distance of a league. Souham, penetrating the village without support at the moment when Blucher detached Kleist to reënforce Barclay, fell into the midst of these two corps, and suffered severely without producing any result: his division fell back in disorder. Ney caused him to be sustained by his batteries of reserve and the division of Delmas. Finally, near one o'clock, hearing the approach of Reynier's columns which appeared in rear of Klix, the marshal sent three of his divisions on Preititz. Lauriston, who had been engaged towards Gottamelde at the head of two divisions of infantry against a feeble detachment of three thousand men under General Tschaplitz, affirmed that he was opposed by superior forces, and advanced with great caution over the ploughed ground that separated him from the village of Baruth. Men and precious time were thus lost by unreasonable delay. If Ney had operated with decision, as at Friedland, he would have arrived about noon in rear of the enemy's line on the road to Wurschen, between Belgern and Purschwitz; and no one can calculate the immense results of a movement like that which Blucher executed against us at Waterloo.

Success, however, was only postponed, for there was still time at one o'clock to obtain great results. But unfortunately Ney did not appreciate his position. As he penetrated Preititz, Blucher, who found himself assailed in rear, caused some battalions to descend from the heights of Klein-Bautzen with twenty pieces of artillery. These cannon, firing against the flank of the marshal's columns, made him forget the direction of Hochkirch which he had indicated in the morning; and instead of debouching in front on the road to Wurschen, he directed the head of his column to the right, and climbed the hills in rear of Klein-Bautzen, a position which, it is true, commanded the whole field of battle, but which deviated entirely from the manœuvre which had been directed in order to get possession of the enemy's line of retreat. The appearance of twenty of the enemy's squadrons in the plain between Preititz and Purschwitz contributed to induce Ney to adopt this unfortunate movement. He had only six feeble squadrons of cavalry, and feared to expose himself in the plain while Blucher occupied the heights in his rear.

While this was passing at the decisive point of the battle, I brought into action the corps which were to assail the enemy's front. Oudinot, at the extreme right, continued to fight with ardor at the foot of the mountains of Bohemia, against Miloradowitsch and Prince Eugene of Wurtemberg; Macdonald seconded him and maintained the combat toward Binowitz and Rabitz. Marmont and the Duke of Treviso held in check the enemy's centre and reserves on the heights between Kreckwitz, Baschutz, and Jenkwitz. At twelve o'clock Ney's cannon announced that the moment had come for striking at the centre. Soult, at the head of the corps of Bertrand, threw himself from Baschutz on the heights of Kreckwitz where he assailed Blucher in front, at the moment when the latter had weakened his forces in order to defend Preititz. The Duke of Ragusa, placed before the Russian intrenchments of Baschutz, first battered them with his artillery and then prepared for an assault. My Young Guard and eight thousand horse of Latour-Maubourg waited in the ravine of Nadelwitz for me to give them the signal for victory. Blucher, reënforced by York was threatening to repel Bertrand, when I threw this reserve of the *élite* on Litten. Blucher being thus turned on the left by Treviso and Latour-

Maubourg, threatened in reverse by Ney, and assailed in front by Soult, saw the impossibility of resisting these concentric attacks and retired beyond Burschwitz, like a lion pursued by audacious hunters. Marmont then penetrated toward Baschutz, which the Russians could no longer defend without exposing themselves to be cut off.

Ney, advancing at the same instant from Preititz on the hills of Klein-Bautzen found not a single enemy to oppose, but saw them defile by a road to which he had been much nearer than they were only two hours before. This marshal had begun the battle in rear of the allies' camp, and ended it almost in rear of the columns of our centre!

The retreat of the Prussians was protected by Barclay, who, defeated on the heights of Glein, instead of changing front to form a crotchet *en potence*, prepared to place himself in echelons more distant on the heights of Belgern, and thus covered the avenue of Wurschen against Lauriston and Reynier. The latter had not reached the field of battle till near three o'clock; he formed himself in the plain of Cannewitz, and at four o'clock engaged in a warm cannonade against Barclay. Ney supported him with the third corps; Lauriston joined his left, by forming opposite Rackel. At dark Barclay put himself in retreat, and the Saxons entered pell-mell with his rear-guard into Wurschen.

In the mean time the Russian left had fought bravely at the foot of the mountains against the corps of Oudinot and Macdonald; as soon as we were masters of Purschwitz and Litten I ordered Marmont to move from the centre to the right so as to take that wing in reverse and cut it off from the road to Hochkirch. But it was too late; the enemy had begun his retreat and for want of cavalry our troops could not reach the road in time. Night terminated the combat here as at Wurschen.

Remarks on this Battle.—In tracing out the movements

of the different masses on the field of battle, we see that Ney and Lauriston, with eight divisions, contended with Kleist and Barclay who had only twenty thousand men; they ought to have destroyed them, whereas they allowed them to destroy the division of Souham.

If Ney had executed the precise order which had been given to him at eight o'clock in the morning, and had displayed one-half the energy which he exhibited at Friedland, Elchingen, Moskowa, and numerous other occasions, the enemy would have lost the greater part of his army and all his materials; the allies could never have saved their left wing and their cavalry. Austria after such a victory would have ranged herself under my banners, which I would have again carried victorious to the Niemen.

The fate of my empire thus depended upon the faulty movement of the most valiant of my generals; it is just, however, that I should take my own share of the blame. After the left wing under Ney was on the decisive point of the battle, I should have moved there myself with a part of the Old Guard and my reserve of cavalry, or at least have sent to the marshal a more detailed order than the brief pencil note simply directing him to march on Preititz. I should also have instructed him to oblique to the left in the direction of Drehsa, which was the same as that of the spire of Hochkirch. It is true that I had indicated to him this point of Drehsa in my dispatch of the eighteenth, but then he was too far from the field of battle.

If Latour-Maubourg's cavalry, debouching in the morning from Nieder-Gurch by Malschwitz, had been directed to second Ney at Preititz, no doubt we would have captured Blucher's infantry, and I should now be on the throne. But as it was, we took no prisoners and found on the field only a few dismounted cannon; we had again sacrificed twenty thousand men without any important result.

Reply to the Overtures of Caulaincourt.—The next day after the battle we received Nesselrode's reply to the overtures of Caulaincourt; the letter was dated the twentieth and accompanied by a note dated the twenty-first. The Emperor Alexander, already allied with Austria, refused to receive any proposals not coming through that power. It was natural to infer from this that these powers were already intimately connected. This refusal of the Emperor of Russia was dictated by a praiseworthy but exaggerated loyalty; he refused to become the arbiter of the peace of Europe for allies who were far from grateful.

Combats of Reichenbach and Haynau.—The next day I pursued the allies, and rudely assailed their rear-guard which had taken position near Reichenbach. The enemy stood firm: impatient at the opposition, I myself repaired to the vanguard to animate it with my presence: the enemy fled; but I paid dearly for the advantage. A spent ball killed both Marshal Duroc and General Kirgener of the engineers, who were in my rear; Bruyère, one of my old soldiers of Italy, had fallen only a few hours before. Duroc was a man dear to my heart, and his loss greatly affected me.*

* The following is Thiers' account of Duroc's death:

"After the cavalry engagement which had thus taken place on the plain, General Reynier with the Saxon infantry occupied the Reichenbach heights, and Napoleon, considering that sufficient had been now effected for this day, gave orders that his tent should be pitched on the ground the troops then occupied.

"As he was alighting from his horse there arose a cry, 'Kirgener is dead!' On hearing these words Napoleon exclaimed, 'Fortune nous en veut bien aujourd'hui!' But to the first cry immediately succeeded a second, 'Duroc is dead!' 'Impossible!' said Napoleon, 'I have just been speaking to him. It was, however, not only possible, but the actual fact. A bullet, which had struck a tree close to Napoleon, had, in its rebound, slain successively General Kirgener, an excellent engineer officer, and then Duroc, himself, the grand-marshal of the palace.

"Duroc, a few minutes before his death, overcome by a singular feeling of sadness, had said to M. de Caulaincourt, 'My friend, do you observe the emperor? After a series of misfortunes he is now victorious, and should profit

A few hours after, a still warmer combat took place at Haynau. Profiting by my want of cavalry to reconnoitre our line of march, Blucher laid an ambuscade for Ney, who advanced with haste at the head of the fifth corps, and crossed the valley of Weisse, without exploring the heights beyond. The infantry of Lauriston, while about to establish their bivouacs, were suddenly assailed by three thousand horse; Maison and Puthod formed squares; but the cavalry had time to sabre a battalion which was in advance of the others, and to capture several pieces of artillery. Lauriston

by the teachings of misfortune . . . . But see! he is still the same, still as insatiable as ever for war . . . . The end of all this cannot possibly be a happy one.' He had received a cruel wound in his entrails, and there could be no hope that he could survive it. Napoleon hastened to him, took him by the hand, called him his friend, and spoke to him of a future life, where at length they might find rest; uttering these words with a feeling of remorse which he did not acknowledge, but which thrilled the inmost recesses of his heart.

"Duroc thanked him with emotion for these testimonies of regard, confided to his care his only daughter, and expressed a hope that his master might live to vanquish the enemies of France, and then to enjoy repose in the midst of that peace of which the world had so much need. 'As for myself,' he continued, 'I have lived as an honorable man should live; I die as a soldier should die. I have nothing to reproach myself with. Let me again recommend my daughter to your care.' And then, as Napoleon remained beside him, holding his hands, and seeming overwhelmed with serious reflections, he added, 'Go, sire, go; this spectacle is too painful for you.' And Napoleon left him, saying, 'Adieu, my friend. We shall meet again, and perhaps soon . . . !"

"It has been asserted that these words uttered by Duroc, 'I have nothing to reproach myself with,' were an allusion to some unjust reproaches made against him by Napoleon, who in his moments of excitement did not spare even the men whom he esteemed the most. But he rendered full justice to his grand-marshal, who was the second sincere and truly devoted friend whom he had lost during the space of twenty days.

"Napoleon was, indeed, profoundly moved by his loss.

"Leaving the cottage in which the dying Duroc had been placed, he went to sit down upon some fascines near the advanced posts; and there remained, overpowered with grief, his hands lying listlessly on his knees, his eyes wet with tears, deaf to the fire of the tirailleurs, unconscious of the caresses of a dog belonging to one of the regiments of the guard, which frequently ran beside his horse, and now stood before him licking his hands. Such, and so changeable is human nature! So contradictory in its various aspects; so incapable of being judged by any but God alone."

drew upon himself this loss by placing his cavalry (twelve hundred horse) on his left flank, instead of pushing it in advance of his position to reconnoitre the roads.

The Allies throw themselves on Schweidnitz.—The allies had continued their retreat by Lauban, Löwenberg, and Goldberg; I supposed they would repass the Oder, but they left the road to Breslau at Goldberg, and directed themselves by Jauer and Striegau on Schweidnitz. This change of their line of operations gave me some uneasiness: to allow themselves to be cut off from the Oder and Poland, and to throw themselves against the mountains of Glatz, was, on the part of the enemy, a fault so manifest in a military point of view that it could only be accounted for on grounds of political policy, by supposing that the allies were already certain of the accession of Austria to the coalition; but I did not believe that the affair was as yet so far advanced.

Armistice of Neumark. — The allies now proposed an armistice which I accepted for the three-fold purpose of not offending the cabinet of Vienna by a refusal, of enabling myself to ascertain more clearly the intrigues of Austria, and of seeking to effect a new understanding with the Emperor Alexander.

This armistice is perhaps the greatest fault of my life. By consenting to it, I probably lost the only remaining opportunity to restore my former power. By thus yielding to the intercession of Austria, I had inspired her with confidence in her own strength, and thus hastened her decision against me. If, on the contrary, I had continued hostilities, my firmness would have imposed on her; the Russo-Prussian army, turned by its right, overpowered by my superiority, and thrown back into the mountains of Glatz, would there have found its Caudinè Forks, while Austria, intimidated by my success, would not have ventured to offer the allies a free passage through her states. I would have become again master of Europe, dictating peace as a conqueror. Even admitting that Austria had resolved to permit the entrance of the allied troops into her territory, my position would not have been worse than it was in the month of September; for, if my army recruited one hundred thousand men during the armistice, that of the enemy received more than double that number, exclusive of those which Austria organized during the interval.

Combat of Luckau.—At the moment of signing this armistice Marshal Oudinot sustained a slight check at Luckau. I had directed him on that city, after the battle of Bautzen, to attack Bulow's corps which had followed the march of Belluno when he left Wittenberg to join Ney, and thus threatened our line of operations. Bulow was stronger than we supposed, and the Duke of Reggio did not succeed in his mission, which, however, was rendered useless by the armistice.

Treaty with Denmark.—On returning to Dresden, on the tenth of June, I found there an envoy from the king of Denmark, who had left Copenhagen after the battle of Lutzen to form a still closer alliance. Never was a treaty more easily concluded: we had the same interests and the same enemies. An English squadron was before his capital, and had summoned the king to cede Norway to Bernadotte; what other part could Denmark take than to throw herself into our arms? The Duke of Bassano soon concluded with that power an offensive and defensive alliance.

Third Mission of Bubna.—The course pursued by Austria was very different: Bubna also returned to Dresden, but bringing neither the powers nor the instructions which he had sought at Vienna. He announced that England had rejected all the insinuations of Weissenberg; that she had found even the conditions of Luneville too favorable to France. Austria then announced that she had proposed at

London the basis of the treaty of Luneville! Bubna seemed to forget the proposition of a congress; he affirmed that Austria, having a schedule of the pretensions of Russia and Prussia, now wished to know what concessions I would make. Thus showing that the negotiations in a congress was to be carried on through the intermediation of Austria, who would then have at her mercy all the other continental powers. Astonished at this new pretension, I directed the Duke of Bassano to address a note directly to Metternich, to ask for formal explanations.

Negotiations of the Allies at Reichenbach.—The emperor of Austria had just established his court at Gitschin. The Emperor Alexander and the king of Prussia were at Reichenbach and Peterswalde: they had assigned a rendezvous for Bernadotte at Trachenberg, for forming a plan of operations. This prince-royal of Sweden, although allied for a year past to Russia and England, had not deemed it proper to take an active part in the war of 1812. But as they now promised him Norway in exchange for Finland, which had been ceded to Russia in 1809, and as the English had undertaken to put him in possession of that kingdom, he had agreed to bring twenty-five thousand Swedes on the Elbe, and had just landed at Stralsund.

It was at the head-quarters of Reichenbach that the allied powers bound themselves by new engagements through the intervention of England. Russia promised to bring into the field one hundred and sixty thousand soldiers, exclusive of her garrisons; Prussia, one-half that number; while England was to furnish subsidies: neither of the contracting powers was to treat separately.

Count Stadion transmitted these negotiations to the cabinet of Vienna, which authorized him to accede to them, if I should reject the *ultimatum* which would be proposed to me. By a formal convention of the twenty-seventh of June the allies agreed to the mediation of the cabinet of Vienna, having previously stipulated the conditions which should be imposed on me. Thus Austria, who was boasting of her partiality for me, had actually acceded to the coalition against me, previous to the opening of the negotiations!

Metternich repairs to Dresden.—Under these circumstances Metternich deemed it best to come himself to Dresden to try his diplomatic talent in making the formal explanations which I had demanded: he protested his moderation and his love of peace. I well knew what his interests were in carrying on the war; but even if there had been any means left for attaching him to our alliance, I must confess that I did not adopt those most likely to accomplish that object. Supposing myself in the place of the cabinet of Vienna, would I have neglected to profit by the only opportunity which had occurred during the last fifteen years for recovering, by a single stroke of the pen, what had been lost in ten unsuccessful campaigns? under such circumstances would it not have been politic in me to offer Austria advantages sufficient to retain her in my alliance?

The question is difficult to decide. To offer her great concessions on my part might seem a pusillanimous act, and inspire her with contempt for my weakness. The demands which the cabinet afterwards addressed to me through Bubna, were transmitted as the conditions of Russia and Prussia; they seemed to me exaggerated. I exhibited anger, and my threats were repeated; and it is probable that these influenced her ulterior conduct.

The exact epoch at which Austria entered into formal engagements with the allies is not yet known. There, however, is good reason to believe that it was even previous to the battle of Lutzen; for the king of Prussia gives this to be understood in his proclamation to his people on the eighth of May. Upon this date will depend the judgment of posterity respecting her conduct and mine. It was plain that I sought to leave her in the position agreed upon by our reciprocal treaties; and even admitting that it would have been more skillful on my part to have offered her great advantages in the month of January, it must, at least, be confessed that I did not fail in any of my engagements by seeking to conquer and to make peace without recurring to her mediation. My object and my means were equally legitimate.

His Interview with Napoleon.—My interview with Metternich at Dresden completed the breach with the cabinet of Vienna. After some discussion on the interest of different parties and on that of Austria to remain in my alliance, this cunning diplomatist enumerated the concessions which the allies required, and to which I must subscribe, if I wished Austria to declare in my favor. He required not only the surrender of Illyria, but also that of Poland, of a part of Germany and Italy, the restoration of the Pope to Rome, the independence of Spain, Holland, and the Confederation of the Rhine!

What impression ought it to make upon a victorious soldier to require him to surrender, without drawing his sword, all the territory which he had won in ten campaigns and a hundred battles? I must, indeed, have fallen in the estimation of those who could propose to me to abandon countries which the allies could not even threaten; countries which were separated from them by a powerful and victorious army and by numerous formidable fortresses! To make such propositions to me, they must have supposed me more base than the senate of Carthage! My feelings of insulted honor as a man, got the better of my cooler calculations as a statesman, and I replied to Metternich in terms well calculated to make him my mortal enemy. In this I was wrong. I should have sought to separate the Austrian interest from those of Russia and Prussia, and instead of asking Metternich *how much England had given him for making such propositions to me,* I should have told him that Austria had two interests to consult, and that I was ready to satisfy both ;—that it was for her interest that we should remain the arbiters of the continent, and that he had only to enumerate the measures which he deemed best calculated to secure this object. Perhaps the moment for doing this had already passed ; nevertheless, by making the attempt, I should have performed my duty to my throne and to France. On the contrary, by this exhibition of my indignation, I destroyed the only remaining hope of a pacific arrangement. Metternich retired, *convinced that war, though only partially successful, would restore to Austria her lost power, and that this was his only means of saving his honor and serving his master.* But, although war was now fully decided on, Austria still wished to gain time, either to complete her preparations or to determine the bases of her arrangement with the coalition. A congress at Prague was, therefore, agreed upon, and the armistice extended to the tenth of August.

At the moment that Metternich was leaving Dresden, I received the news of Joseph's defeat at Vittoria. This increased the embarrassment of my position, and if England had been included in the proposed treaty I might have accepted the conditions offered ; but to close this war with all the difficulties of my maritime quarrel still on my hands, was too important a step to be hastily taken.

It will be remembered that my threat to make peace with Russia had been reported to Austria. This inconsiderate but laudable frankness, joined to my angry remarks to Metternich, embroiled me with Austria, and perhaps cost me my crown. In 1803, my warmth to Wentworth contributed to involve me in the war with England. The head of a state should treat all foreign ministers with cool reserve, and negotiate with them only through the medium of adroit and skillful agents. They should never be admitted to his intimacy. The abrupt frankness of a soldier is not well suited to affairs of diplomacy.

Napoleon's Envoys to the Congress of Prague.—Hoping that the congress of Prague might afford me means of explaining myself at the same time to Russia, Prussia and Austria, I sent there the Duke of Vicenza and Narbonne. In taking leave of the former, I explained my feelings at the equivocal conduct of Austria; I announced to him that I regarded it as an indignity to reward her by giving her all the advantages of the peace; that I should prefer to see Russia profit by it, as she had purchased these advantages by her heroic devotion, the ravage of her provinces, and the loss of Moscow; in a word, I repeated the instructions which I had given to him when intrusted with a mission to the Emperor Alexander, previous to the battle of Bautzen.

Arrival of the Empress Maria Louisa at Mayence.—The court of Austria had returned from Gitschin to the chateau of Frewald near Prague; I had left for Mayence where the empress then was, and where I had called together some of my ministers to consult upon the measures to be taken for the interior of France on the probable resumption of hostilities. The minister of finance had come to receive the keys to my treasury of reserve in the vaults of Marsan, forty millions of which were now appropriated to the most urgent expenses required in preparation for another campaign.

Some have thought that this interview with the empress was had for the purpose of dictating to her measures calculated to influence the resolutions of the Emperor of Austria. This is erroneous. It is true that I dictated to her a letter to her father, for I saw no wrong in inciting in him favorable sentiments toward us; but to imagine that I reposed the destinies of my empire on such means is too absurd. The empress took no part in state affairs, and I knew too well the character of the Austrian cabinet to suppose that such a measure could be decisive.

Military Projects of the Allies.—Before going to Mayence, I was informed of the military and diplomatic council at Trachenberg, where, since the ninth of July, the allies had been discussing a plan of operations. Austria had designated General Waquant as her commissioner in this council of sovereigns; and young Count Latour was to assist in arranging the plan of campaign in the name of that power. Some wished to form three armies of one hundred and fifty thousand each; the first under Bernadotte and composed of Russians, Prussians, and Swedes, was to operate at the north with Berlin as a centre, and to attack Hamburg; the second under Blucher in Silesia, to advance by Lusace on Dresden; while the Austrians reënforced by fifty thousand Russians and Prussians, were to operate on Dresden by Bohemia. The Emperor Alexander and his generals were in favor of drawing Blucher's army into Bohemia, in order to cover Prague and the line of operations, while the grand army acted by the left bank of the Elbe. This course was more wise, more skillful, and more in accordance with military principles. But it was opposed by Austria, because she was unwilling to see two hundred and twenty thousand foreigners in Bohemia, and by Prussia, who wished to cover Silesia and to have the means of sustaining Bernadotte in case Berlin should be threatened. The plan of three armies was adopted, leaving that of Blucher on the Oder; but the Emperor Alexander insisted on the necessity of reënforcing the grand army at the expense of those of a secondary character, and it was agreed that one hundred thousand Russo-Prussians should move from Silesia into Bohemia, under the orders of Barclay de Tolly, to act in concert with the same number of Austrians by Freyburg and Töplitz on Dresden.

In order to avoid reverses on secondary points, they de-

cided that Blucher and Bernadotte should never accept battle when I moved against them, but that they should resume the offensive as soon as I moved to other points. This well-conceived plan failed to accomplish its object, on account of its faulty execution, and the vigor of my first operations. If I had then known the tenor of their plan, I should not have exhausted myself in vain pursuits of Blucher, but have taken, from the opening of the campaign, the most certain means of striking decisive blows wherever it suited me.

Negotiations at Prague.—In the mean time the negotiations made very little progress at Prague. The choice of ministers to treat with the Duke of Vicenza was unfortunate. Russia had sent M. Anstett, a Frenchman by birth, and my personal enemy; the laws of the empire prohibited any treaty with him. The commissioners appointed to sign the armistice of Neumark had no power to extend it. All the month of July was thus consumed in preliminary discussion. The armistice was finally extended to the tenth of August, which left hardly two weeks in which to arrange the most complicated interests of all Europe. Moreover, difficulties arose about conducting the negotiations, whether in open council, or through a mediator, or by written notes. Each one sought to show his diplomatic knowledge by discussing the forms followed by the congress of Teschen and of Utrecht, and no progress was made. Austria wished every thing to be done by written notes, through her, as the mediator. This made her the arbiter of peace, and prevented all arrangement between France and the other powers. Nothing could justify such a pretension; moreover, Metternich had said at Dresden that Austria had no intention of making herself the arbiter. My negotiator could not yield to such unexpected demands; and Metternich well knew that I was at Mayence, and that no new instructions could be received from me much before the expiration of the armistice. I had supposed that the negotiations would commence by the twenty-sixth of July, and that five or six days would be required for the discussion of the conditions of peace. That time was sufficient for my journey to Mayence. What was my surprise to learn on my return that my plenipotentiaries had not exchanged a single word with MM. Anstett and Humboldt, the plenipotentiaries of Russia and Prussia! A blind man could have seen that no negotiations were possible under such circumstances. I now had but one course to pursue, and I adopted it without hesitation. This was, not to open these negotiations at all, as they had not been commenced, but to demand directly of the mediator what were the conditions necessary for concluding peace. As Caulaincourt was no longer a plenipotentiary in the congress, I directed him, on the sixth of August, to address that question to Metternich, who replied on the seventh. He demanded the restitution of Illyria, the reconstruction of Prussia with her frontier on the Elbe; the surrender of the Duchy of Warsaw, to be partitioned out to Russia, Prussia and Austria; the renunciation of the Protectorate of the Confederation of the Rhine; the guarantee of all the powers, great and small, and that none should be changed without a general consent; the independence of Holland; and the independence of Spain under Ferdinand VII.; the publicity and execution of the last article were to be postponed till the conclusion of a maritime peace, provided that this should be calculated to facilitate that object.

There was nothing new in these sacrifices, except that they were now put in the shape of positive demands. I could not persuade myself that the allies did not wish to trace around me the circle of Popilius, and that all their negotiations consisted in dictating positive conditions to be signed by me without modification; in a word, that it was proposed to force me to comply with the exaggerated pretensions of Metternich. From these harsh conditions I turned my thoughts to the fine field between the Elbe and the Oder, all the keys of which I now held in my power, and was daily augmenting their value by constructing vast intrenched camps at Dresden, and Pirna, and a *tête-de-pont* at Königstein. My confidence was increased by the success of the new levies in France, and the assurances of attachment sent through the prince of Neufchatel by the king of Bavaria. Although desirous of peace, which was much needed by his people, the brave and loyal Maximilian swore *that he would lose his life rather than desert my alliance.*

There were a thousand other circumstances which seemed to ensure me a victory, and which inclined me to reject conditions so harshly imposed.

At Presbourg, Tilsit, and Schönbrunn, time was allowed for negotiation, although interests less general were discussed, and sacrifices less important were required. When Austria yielded me the Tyrol, I was master of her capital and victorious at Austerlitz. When she ceded me Illyria, I was master of Vienna and victorious at Wagram. When I imposed on Prussia the cession of her provinces, I was not only master of Berlin, but also of Königsberg and Prussia. In making these treaties with defeated Austria, two whole months were allowed for negotiation; but now, this power wished to impose, without discussion, conditions much more harsh, upon a general who had just gained two glorious victories! It is customary for a state which has lost ten provinces in a war to sacrifice one-half of these, in order to obtain peace and save the remainder; but it would be a new thing for a state which had lost only Poland, to sacrifice Germany, Holland, and the half of Italy, and her own dignity! I had before declared to my father-in-law that I never would submit to conditions dictated by the sword, and I now could not, without dishonor, subscribe to these propositions. I therefore spent the ninth in weighing these conditions and the consequences of rejecting them. If they could be modified, I might agree to them without dishonor, for they would no longer have the appearance of an imposed *ultimatum*. This desire might have sprung from self-love, but the feeling was natural and laudable, springing as it did from a sense of honor. I, therefore, wrote to the Duke of Vicenza, on the night of the ninth and tenth, that I would accept the *ultimatum*, with the reservation of Trieste and the guarantee of the integrity of Denmark. The reservation of Trieste may seem a small affair to be weighed against a question of peace, but on account of its maritime importance, and for the reasons above given, I determined to make it. The article concerning Denmark was an act of loyalty, but should have been sooner mentioned, if intended to be insisted on.

Perhaps, however, the delay was of little importance; for if they wished peace, the treaty could be signed as well during the ten days' notice of the renewal of hostilities, as before the denunciation of the armistice. The allies thought differently, and as my reply did not reach them till the eleventh, Austria declared the negotiation broken; the Russian and Prussian ministers decamped in the greatest haste, and notice was immediately given of the cessation of the armistice. These facts prove incontestably that the allies preferred war to peace. It must be confessed that in this, as the events proved, they consulted their own interest; but it would be unjust to charge me with the consequences of the rupture.

I, however, was still ignorant of the formal decision of the allies, and their departure from Prague, when Bubna left Dresden to join his court at Gitschin. My minister advised me not to compromise peace by any concealments. Yielding to his solicitations I authorized him to see Bubna, and to give him the formal assurance that I would accept all which was desired by the cabinet of Vienna. Vain hope! The demon of discord had prevailed. The allies had already entered Bohemia, and their numerous columns were approaching Dresden.

Narbonne, being forced to leave Bohemia, returned to Dresden to render an account of the sad result of his negotiation. Caulaincourt, who had a private mission, remained some days for my final orders. He received these orders to accept all the conditions of Austria. But the cabinet of Vienna now replied that it was too late, the commissioners having left. This was a mere pretext, for if Austria, as the arbiter, considered these conditions just and suitable for the general interest of Europe, she could easily transmit them to the other parties who were interested in them. The Emperor Francis had a rendezvous with the Emperor Alexander at Gitschin, on the fourteenth, and did not hesitate to declare that he was resolved to run all the chances of the war: a profession which left nothing to be added, for no one could misinterpret it.

In thus waiting till the last moment before subscribing to the harsh conditions of the allies, I had supposed that, if the armistice should be denounced, the congress would continue till the resumption of hostilities, if not during the war. Those of Westphalia and Utrecht had lasted several years, during which the military operations were continued. The dissolution of the congress and the sudden departure of the plenipotentiaries characterize, better than I could, the resolution of my enemies. I have been reproached for this measure, but it is perfectly evident that this rupture was less my work than that of a coalition, who were anxious to divide my spoils.

Such are the true points from which we must view this important epoch, which decided the fate of my Empire and of Europe. A Mazarin or a Ximenes, remembering the fable of the oak and the reed, would have bent before the storm in the hope of rising again, more strong than ever, when it had past. But self-respect, or rather the honor of the victorious captain prevailed over the cool deliberations of the statesman. What general in my place would have taken a different course?

But we must render unto Cæsar the things which are Cæsar's, and the event proved that, if the conduct of Austria was base, it was nevertheless conformable to her temporary interests. Afterwards, at Frankfort and Chatillon, the same can not be said for her. Before that time it was for me to parry the blow; and if I did not, it would be unjust to impute it either to an excess of presumption or a want of sagacity; I was deceived by the promises of Bubna and Schwartzenberg, and by the insignificant results of my first victories. The world will never agree respecting this negotiation; some will accuse Metternich of felony, while those whom he benefited will praise him to the skies. By an impartial writer, the matter may be summed up as follows:

In the month of January, Austria wished to profit by her advantageous situation to regain her lost territories; but she feared to ask these openly. As it was sufficient for my purposes that this power remained neutral in the early part of the campaign, I did not hasten to retain her in my alliance, by restitutions which could only be made at my own expense. As her indirect overtures through her ministers at Paris and Vienna had not accomplished what she desired previous to the battle of Lutzen, she now sought to obtain it by concert with my enemies. But still preferring to acquire provinces by treaty rather than by incurring the chances of war, she hoped to enrich herself with my spoils, through her character of mediator: when she distrusted the results of this calculation she determined to risk the chance of arms; for she had much to gain and nothing to lose.

The difference in the language of the Austrian cabinet at the two epochs will be regarded by some as a violation of good faith: it must be confessed, however, that the first declarations of Austria may have been honorable, and made to see what effect her insinuations might produce; she may be reproached for not explaining herself more openly, but she may say in excuse that she was deterred from doing so by the fear of irritating me. Some writers, in their desire to enhance my glory and good faith, have overlooked the correspondence of the cabinet of Vienna, or have given it only in a mutilated state. In this it is plainly shown that, after the month of April, Metternich and the emperor gave M. Narbonne to understand that it would be necessary to restore Illyria, renounce the Protectorate of the Confederation of the Rhine, and the Duchy of Warsaw, and finally the restoration of the Prussian monarchy. Nor should it be forgotten that Austria did not dissemble that she would go to war, if I should not accept her conditions as the mediating power. I am far from excusing the conduct of the Austrian cabinet, especially in her attempts to seduce my allies, and, while pretending friendship, to hedge me about with difficulties.

This conduct on her part is the more inexcusable as she had every reason to pursue a course of policy frank and open, and at the same time loyal and strong. Instead of sounding me by the mission of Bubna, Schwartzenberg, and Metternich, she had only to say: "The alliance of 1756 was calculated to make France and Austria the arbiters of the continent; the alliance of 1810 and of 1812, had the same object. This also is what now is desired. But you have reduced us to a secondary part by destroying our influence abroad, and by taking from us our finest provinces, and our only port. It is just that we should profit by the present occasion to regain them; unless we do so our alliance will be odious to our people. Therefore restore to us the frontiers of 1805, and the Tyrol, and renounce the Confederation of the Rhine. Holland may remain in your possession until a maritime peace is made. You can retain Italy, and settle the question of Spain and of England without our interference. Join us in treating, without delay, with Russia and Prussia, on just and moderate terms; let us amicably arrange the question of the Duchy of Warsaw; since the disaster of Moscow this can only be an apple of discord, without the slightest advantage to you. Austria will then bring two hundred thousand men into the field to sustain your cause, and dictate these conditions to your enemies: then we will always be your allies."

I should have immediately subscribed to such conditions, for I should have seen in them the good faith and real interest of Austria; and even if I had not consented to these sacrifices, Austria could then have attacked me openly and honorably, proving to Europe that my ambition had forced her into the war. My position in this affair was less complicated than hers, and my conduct was indisputably more frank. To maintain our treaties, and thus paralyze the action of that power, while I planted my victorious eagles on the Niemen,—such was my object. I should have accomplished it, without violating any of my engagements, if the victory of Bautzen had equaled my expectations. But I failed, by gaining only a half victory, and my conduct seemed rash and even audacious. If the movement of the left wing had been conducted conformably to the order given by Ney's chief of staff in the morning, I would still have been master of Europe. Thus the destinies of nations often depend upon the most insignificant incidents. But it is time to quit the diplomatic arena, and return to military events. Before, however, we continue our relation of the operations of the armies in Saxony, we will hastily review the condition of affairs in Spain.

Summary of Operations in Spain.—Wellington, after having obtained, in 1812, the liberation of Andalusia by his manœuvres on the Douro, and the bold occupation of Madrid, had been forced to raise the siege of Burgos, before the united arms of Soult and Joseph. He had taken up his winter-quarters about Ciudad-Rodrigo, and profited by it to re-enforce his corps. His army, in the spring of 1813, was composed of seventy-five thousand Anglo-Hanoverians and Portuguese. The Cortes of Spain conferred on him the command of all their forces, and took measures to place a corps of fifty thousand Spaniards at his immediate disposition, in the west and north. The evacuation of Andalusia, Grenada, Galicia, Estremadura, La Mancha, and the Asturias, enabled the Cortes to double their levies, and they neglected nothing to incite ardor and patriotism in the hearts of the Spaniards.

Our forces in this part of the theatre of war amounted to about ninety thousand men. Besides these, Suchet had from thirty-five to forty thousand men in the east. Two divisions of dragoons, and twelve thousand of the best troops, had been drawn from the Peninsula to the army in Saxony. Soult also had rejoined me just before the battle of Bautzen. The regiments in Spain were very weak; climate, battles, guerilla bands, assassinations, &c., had cost us many men, and my immediate wants in Saxony had compelled me to draw there, in provisional regiments, the recruits intended for the army in Spain. To disguise our real weakness, we preserved the names of the army of Portugal, the army of the south, the army of the centre, and the army of the north, for skeleton corps not numbering more than fifteen or sixteen thousand men. Reille commanded the army of Portugal, Drouet, that of the centre, Gazan, that of the south, and Clausel, that of the north. Joseph's guard, which was reduced to three thousand Frenchmen, and a thousand

Spaniards, with a feeble Spanish division, formed the reserve.

It will be remembered that after the union of our three armies on the Tormes, Joseph had returned to Madrid, where he hoped to maintain himself by supporting his right on the Douro, and his left on the Tagus towards Toledo. In a military point of view such a position was not defensible; but such is the unfortunate alternative of an army which has, at the same time, to resist organized masses, and to keep in subjection an insurgent population. To subsist their forces in a country which is destitute of the means of transportation or of navigation, *extension* was necessary; whereas, to fight the opposing forces, *concentration* was equally essential. The Anglo-Portuguese army had greatly the advantage in this respect, as they could receive provisions from Lisbon and Oporto by the Douro, which was navigable to near Miranda, and by numerous brigades of mules which carried provisions for a distance of three hundred miles. This enabled them to act against us with united forces whenever they pleased.

Having completed his preparations for resuming the offensive by the end of May, Wellington deemed the decisive point to be the right of the French on the Douro. By obtaining a success here, he threatened our only line of retreat, and a victory like that of Salamanca would throw us back on the Pyrenees. The evacuation of the south had enabled the Junta to raise troops, and assemble a considerable Spanish corps on the Tagus which threatened our left and the capital. The army of Galicia and the Asturias might take the right in reverse, and advance by Bilboa to the defiles of Tolosa. Wellington, favored by these two demonstrations, resolved to pass the Douro, the middle of May, near Lamega, to fall on Zamora, and thus turn all Joseph's system of defense. After having succeeded in this first operation, the English general concentrated his forces at Toro, and continued his march towards Palencia.

Joseph now, for the first time, renounced the defense of Madrid and collected his forces at Burgos. The increasing efforts of the Anglo-Spaniards, the sad effects of our disasters in Russia, and the necessity of seeking the security of the army rather than the preservation of a useless capital, justified this resolution; but it was now necessary to instantly take the initiative against the enemy, or to retire. Joseph prefered to remain on the defensive. But the new demonstrations of the enemy soon forced him to blow up the fort of Burgos and to retire into the plains of Vittoria.

It would be difficult to find a worse place for a battle, under the circumstances in which Joseph was situated. The gulf of Biscay closes the frontier of France and Spain into a kind of gorge between Bayonne and St. Jean-Pied-de-Port. There is but a single road on the west of the Pyrenees, which runs from Madrid to Bayonne. There is another road practicable for cannon, from Vittoria to Pampeluna; whence it runs on one side to the Col-de-Maya, and on the other, to St. Jean-Pied-de-Port, by the valley of Roncevaux, celebrated under Charlemagne by the famous retreat of Roland. To take a position parallel to a road would enable the enemy to occupy a corresponding line, and by the least effort of his left against our right, to intercept our communications. If we add to this that the basin of Vittoria is surrounded by commanding mountains, precisely in the prolongation of the English left, and in the direction of their approach, it will be seen how ill-suited it was for our army. It was necessary either to take the initiative and to attack the enemy wherever he might be found, or to retire upon the Pyrenees. The latter was certainly the wisest plan; for a victory which, before 1812, would have been decisive, would now be of little importance.

Battle of Vittoria.—Joseph's left, under Clausel, remained at Logrono to cover the important road to Pampeluna. A flying corps was sent to Bilboa under Foy, to cover the debouch from that city on St. Sebastian. These two detachments were the necessary consequence of giving battle in a defensive position. In any other country than Spain, it would have been preferable to renounce the road to Bayonne, to retire parallel to the Ebro to Saragossa, so as to join Suchet and fall on Wellington when separated some one hundred and fifty leagues from his vessels and his depôts. The national guards of the south and some battalions of the line would have been sufficient to watch the Bidassoa and guard the place of Bayonne ; and the English general would not have ventured to enter the Pyrenees with one hundred thousand Frenchmen in his rear. This manœuvre had the assent of the best generals in the army ; but Joseph and Marshal Jourdan thought that the spirit of the Catalonians and Aragonese rendered this strategic line unsafe. If it was necessary to base themselves on Bayonne, they ought to have avoided a battle, or at least to have received it on the heights of Salinas. Jourdan, it is said, formed this project, but was overruled by the others, who feared the embarrassment of Joseph's *impedimenta*, and who wished to dispute the possession of Castile. Joseph's camp resembled that of Darius ; he was encumbered with the families and baggage of the unfortunate Spaniards who had taken office under him. A part was sent away the evening before the battle to Tolosa, under the escort of Maucune's division of the army of Portugal ; nevertheless, there still remained much more than the situation of our affairs justified.

The allies passed the Ebro on the fifteenth of June. On the twenty-first they presented themselves before Joseph's *corps-de-bataille*, which was posted parallel to Zadorra and the road. There was sufficient time during these five days to adopt a course suited to the circumstances, but they did nothing. The battle which decided the fate of the Peninsula took place on the twenty-first of June. It was more disastrous than bloody. The left and centre were driven back on Vittoria by Hill and Beresford, who attacked them concentrically toward Ariniz and the bridge of Mamorio, penetrated the interval between them, and thus forced them into a precipitate retreat. The right wing, after having sustained a vigorous combat against General Graham at Gomarra Mayor, near the great road to Bayonne, suffered themselves to be defeated after hearing the loss of Vittoria. An English division, turning the right wing, succeeded in gaining the road before our troops; the alarm immediately spread, and each one hastened to gain, in disorder, the road to Pampeluna, the only one remaining by which they could reach the Pyrenees. The entire column of equipages fell into the hands of the conqueror; cannon, baggage, caissons, in a word, every thing was abandoned, and Joseph arrived at Bayonne in a worse plight than I reached the Beresina. A most scandalous disorder blasted all the laurels of the army of Spain, caused only by a panic terror, like that of the Austrians at Marengo.

Joseph merited many reproaches for his military conduct in this affair; but not those which have been made by his detractors. The fault was not so much in the disposal of his troops, as in his giving battle at all in this position. He should have taken the offensive; or if not, have received battle in the defensive position of Salinas.

The news of this disaster made me regret that I did not evacuate Spain on my return from Moscow. This would have enabled me to assemble one hundred thousand veteran troops behind the Rhine. The Spaniards would never have crossed the Pyrenees, had I abandoned the country to Ferdinand; and Wellington would not, with his English forces alone, have attempted the invasion of France. His theatre of operations would probably have been transferred to Holland or elsewhere.

Operations of Suchet.—In the east of Spain fortune was more favorable. Dissatisfied with the conduct of General Maitland, the English had replaced him with Murray, a chief of staff of much merit. He arrived at Alicante with orders to take the offensive so as to favor the projects of Wellington against the line of the Douro. During the winter the allies had reorganized and reënforced the Spanish army of Elliot. In the month of April, 1813, Murray took position at Castella, with twenty thousand Anglo-Sicilians and Spaniards, and detached some corps to Villena. Between the twentieth and twenty-second of April, Suchet, by a rapid march, enveloped a battalion at Villena, defeated Elliot's corps at Yecla, and the English vanguard in the defile of Biar. This success brought him before Murray's position at Castalla, which he immediately resolved to attack. But as he failed to carry it, Murray made an attack in his turn, but was arrested by our artillery in the defile. Our army returned to Valencia with its prisoners, but did not long remain inactive. Not venturing an attack on our intrenchments, Murray decided to evacuate the east and seek to operate on our communications.

He reëmbarked his troops, and his fleet passed Valencia on the first of June. He again debarked his troops at Salo, where he got possession of Fort San Félipe de Balaguer, and began an attack on Tarragona. Twenty-eight heavy cannon were landed for this purpose.

Hearing of this danger, Marshal Suchet immediately moved by Perdillo, and in three forced marches with his infantry arrived in sight of Fort Balaguer; the English fleet defended the shore and commanded with their guns the high road. Making a détour through the mountains to avoid their fire,

Suchet carried a column of infantry in sight of Tarragona, at the moment when General Maurice Mathieu, from Barcelona, approached on the other side. Seeing his danger, Murray now blew up Fort Balaguer, abandoned his heavy artillery, reëmbarked his troops, and resigned the command to Lord Bentinck, who returned to Alicante. In the mean time the Spanish army of Alicante, under the Duke del Parque, attacked Generals Harispe and Habert on the Xucar, but was defeated. Suchet returned to Valencia in triumph.

But hardly had he arrived there, when he received news of the battle of Vittoria, and orders to approach the frontiers of France. The evacuation of Valencia commenced on the fifth of July. The retreat of this army was accompanied by the sincere regrets of a large number of the inhabitants. Good officers with well provisioned garrisons were left at Denia, Peniscola, and Saguntum; the last of these places contained six months' supplies for the whole army. Tortosa, Tarragona, Lerida, Mequinenza, and Monzon, were also provided for. More than twenty thousand men were thus sacrificed to the vain hope of still holding the Peninsula, when their presence on the Rhine, and in Champagne, a few months later, might have saved France. Suchet was not to blame for this disposition; he had received positive orders. Our victory at Bautzen was known to him; as also the meeting of the congress of Prague; but he knew nothing of the defection of Austria, and hoped soon to receive orders to return to Valencia.

On reaching Barcelona, Suchet united with his own the army of Catalonia under General Decaen. Together they occupied the line of the Llobregat which they retained for several months. In the early part of August, General Bentinck threatened Tarragona. The French army crossed the Col de Santa Christiana and offered him battle, which he refused and retired toward Cambrils and the Col de Balaguer

Suchet now blew up the fortifications of Tarragona and removed the garrison to Barcelona. The enemy afterward established himself at Villa-Franca and the Col de Ordal. The latter place was attacked by the marshal on the night of the thirteenth of September, and carried, after an obstinate defense. We captured three field-pieces and three or four hundred men. The twenty-seventh English regiment of the line perished almost to a man. The next day our army reached Villa-Franca. General Bentinck prepared to retire on Tarragona, but our cavalry greatly harassed his retreat.

This victory secured us quiet cantonments between the Llobregat and Barcelona, and the winter passed away without any remarkable event, or any thing to disturb our forces, except the sad news of our disasters in Saxony. Our skirmishes with the Catalonians were regarded only as an everyday affair; they had become a matter of habit, and a daily routine.

CHAPTER XX.

AUTUMN CAMPAIGN OF 1813.

FROM THE CONGRESS OF PRAGUE, TO THE RETREAT BEHIND THE RHINE.

Renewal of Hostilities—Immense Efforts of the Coalition—Organization of the Allied forces—Organization of the French Army—Relative Position of the opposing Forces—Different Combinations of the Theatre of War—Preliminary Movements—Plan of Operations—Napoleon marches against Blucher—His Instructions to Macdonald—The Command of the Allied Forces—March of the Allies on Dresden—Their singular Dispositions for Attack—Napoleon's Project to cut them off at Königstein—Battle of Dresden—The Allies retreat—Operations of Vandamme near Königstein—His Disaster at Culm—Oudinot defeated at Gros-Beeren—Macdonald's Disaster at the Katzbach—Napoleon marches to his Assistance—Ney's defeat at Dennewitz—Remarks on this Battle—Remarks on Napoleon's Plan of Campaign—His Demonstrations on Bohemia—Third Attempt against Blucher—New Plans of the Allies—They assume the Offensive—Napoleon marches against Blucher and Bernadotte—Napoleon's Project of Manœuvering against Berlin—It is defeated by the Defection of Bavaria—The Allies concentrate on Leipsic—Singular Project of Schwartzenberg—First Day of Leipsic—Napoleon proposes an Armistice which is refused—The Allies receive Reënforcements—Second Day of Leipsic—Third Day of Leipsic—Remarks on this Battle—Napoleon retreats on Erfurth—Pursuit of the Allies—Departure of Murat—Threatening March of the Bavarians—Their Defeat at Hanau—The French retire behind the Rhine—Capitulation of Dresden—Operations before Hamburg—Capitulation of Dantzic—Siege and Blockade of the other Fortresses—Operations of Eugene in Italy—Soult's Operations in Spain.

Renewal of Hostilities.—Although the overthrow of my brother's throne had no immediate influence on the military operations in Germany, nevertheless, it greatly complicated my affairs. I had always supposed that I could at any time draw fifty thousand men from beyond the Pyrenees to the Elbe; but the unfortunate defeat of Vittoria not only destroyed these hopes, but on the contrary caused me alarm for the safety of my own territory. These events probably had their influence in the negotiations of Prague, and contributed to their unfortunate issue. Some future statesman may think that this failure, by destroying all further hopes of success in the Peninsula and drawing all my efforts to the continent, should have been an additional inducement for Austria to unite with me; but the cabinet of Vienna thought differently, and only rejoiced at the increase of my embarrassment and the probability of my fall. The congress of Prague having been dissolved on the tenth of August, as has already been said, the armistice expired on the fifteenth and hostilities recommenced the next day.

Immense Efforts of the Coalition.—The efforts of the coalition were almost incredible; I regarded the accounts of them which reached me as ridiculously exaggerated. Prussia alone had put in the line two hundred and forty thousand men, of which thirty-two thousand were cavalry. I had never thought her forces one-half that number. The Russians, besides the corps of Sacken and Langeron, received near one hundred thousand veterans from the hospitals and recruits from the depôts; they were the remainder of the levies of 1812, who, on account of their distance from the theatre of war, had not been able to arrive in time to take part in the campaign of 1812. The whole number of the troops of the first line put in motion against me, amounted to six hundred and fifty thousand men with eighteen hundred pieces of cannon, all included. The reserves and garrisons amounted to one hundred and sixty thousand, making a grand total of eight hundred and ten* thousand men against

* This number must be intended to represent the strength of the allied forces at the renewal of hostilities, for in September, as is stated immediately after, they numbered eight hundred and eighty-nine thousand three hundred and twenty men, and one thousand nine hundred and sixty-six pieces of artillery, and in December, their force was increased to one million one hundred thousand men.

me, in the north and in Italy, exclusive of the English, Spaniards, Portuguese, and Sicilians, in the Peninsula. It is true that some of these were militia and irregular troops; but if they did not serve in the line, they did us still more injury by their partisan warfare.

The English aided these efforts by subsidies and supplies of arms and artillery; they sent to Prussia, and to the Prince of Sweden, field-batteries and men to manage them, several companies of Congreve-rocketeers, and a siege-equipage which served in the attack of Glogau. They also carried four hundred thousand muskets, and one hundred thousand sabres to the continent, to assist in the armament of Germany.

Organization of the Allied Forces.—The following table exhibits the detailed organization of the allied armies in September, 1813:

Armies and Siege-Corps.	Nations.	Corps.	Battalions.	Squadrons.	Cossacks.	Men.	Artillery.
Barclay	Russians	Wittgenstein	30	36	4	23,000	60
	Prussians	Kleist	41	44	—	43,500	128
	Russians	Platoff	—	—	12	6,000	—
	"	Constantine	58	80	—	36,000	250
			183	160	16	108,500	438
Schwartzenberg	Austrians	Lichtenstein	4	18			12
	"	Bubna	7	18			12
	"	Colloredo	24	12			48
	"	Murfield	21	12			48
	"	Giulay	21	12			48
	"	Klenau	24	18			48
	"	Hesse-Hombourg	20	36			42
			121*	126		130,860	258
Blucher	Russians	Sacken	24	20	11	16,200	60
	"	Langeron	48	14	8	29,000	156
	"	St. Priest	20	26	4	13,800	36
	Prussians	York	40	44	—	37,700	104
			132	104	23	96,700	356

* Previous to the battle of Dresden the Austrians had but one hundred and twelve battalions; they here lost ten which were replaced by nineteen others, making one hundred and twenty-one battalions. In addition to this number they had thirty-four battalions in garrison at Prague, Theresien-Stadt, and Joseph-Stadt.

Armies and Siege-Corps.	Nations.	Corps.	Battalions.	Squadrons.	Cossacks.	Men.	Artillery.
Bernadotte	Russians	Wintzingerode	11	8	8	9,100	56
	"	Woronzof	8	24	13	12,250	56
	Swedes	———	35	32	—	24,010	62
	Allies*	Walmoden	37	33	4	28,500	53
	Prussians	Bulow	40	45	4	41,300	104
	"	Tauenzien	55	52	—	38,900	56
			186	194	29	154,060	387
Benningsen	Russians	Markoff	14	25	9	16,500	38
	"	Doctoroff	29	25	—	26,500	120
	"	Paskiewitz					
	"	Tolstoy	30	17	2	17,000	40
			73	67	11	60,000	198
Corps before the places of Dantzic	Russ. and Pruss.	Duke of Wurtemberg	70	17	8	35,000	80
Stettin	"	Plötz	19	4	—	35,000	25
Custrin	"	Hinricks	10	2	—	14,600	8
Glogau	"	Rosen	44	4	—	8,600	30
Zamosc	Russians	———	21	5	3	29,000	36
			164	32	11	122,200	179

The Russians employed in these sieges were militia, except at Dantzic, where there were four battalions of the old regiments, and the militia of St. Petersburg, who had fought gloriously during the war.

Recapitulation of these Forces.

	Men.	Artillery
Grand army in Bohemia (Barclay and Schwartzenberg)	239,360	696
Army of Blucher	96,700	356
Army of Bernadotte	154,060	387
Army of Benningsen	60,000	108
Austrians and Bavarians under General Wrede	55,000	120
Army of General Hill in Italy	50,000	120
Siege-corps	102,200	179
Reserve of Landwehr in the interior of Austria	60,000	—
Prussian reserve and garrisons	32,000	—
Reserve under Prince Labanof	40,000	—
Total	889,320	1,966

If we add to this number one hundred and forty-five thousand regulars, and one hundred and forty-five thousand

* Walmoden's corps was composed of Russians, Germans, Swedes and English.

Landwehr raised by the Germanic Confederation in the month of December, we have a grand total of more than *one million one hundred thousand men,* armed against France, exclusive of the forces in the Peninsula.

Organization of the French Army.—I also had profited by the armistice to reënforce my army in Germany, and, by almost inconceivable activity on my own part, and that of my officers, we had increased its numbers to near four hundred thousand, and the artillery to one thousand two hundred and fifty pieces. It was organized as follows :

Infantry.	1st	corps under	Vandamme,............	3	divisions,
	2d	" "	Victor,................	3	"
	3d	" "	Ney (afterwards Souham)	5	"
	4th	" "	Bertrand..............	3	"
	5th	" "	Lauriston, ...	3	"
	6th	" "	Marmont,..............	3	"
	7th	" "	Reynier, ...	3	"
	8th	" "	Poniatowski,...........	2	"
	9th	" "	Augereau, ...	2	"
	10th	" "	Rapp, at Dantzic,		
	11th	" "	Macdonald,............	3	"
	12th	" "	Oudinot, ...	3	"
	13th	" "	Davoust................	3	"
	14th	" "	St. Cyr, ...	3	"
Cavalry.	1st	" "	Latour-Maubourg,......	4	"
	2d	" "	Sebastiani,............	3	"
	3th	" "	Arrighi,...............	4	"
	4th	" "	Kellerman Jr...........	3	"

Relative Positions of the opposing Forces.—The respective forces were distributed as follows : on my right, twenty-five thousand Bavarians, assembled at Munich, were in observation before an army of nearly equal force which Austria had collected in the environs of Lintz. They were sustained, or rather restrained, by a corps of twenty thousand men which Augereau had assembled in the environs of Wurtzburg and Bamberg. On my left, Davoust occupied Hamburg and Lubeck with thirty thousand French and Danes, forming the thirteenth corps. He had before him the corps of Walmoden, of equal force. Bernadotte, Prince-Royal of Sweden, commanded, in the environs of Berlin, an army of some hundred and twenty thousand Russians, Swedes, and Prussians ; I opposed to him Oudinot, who with seventy thousand men, placed himself at Dahme on the road from Torgau to Berlin. My grand army of two hundred and thirty thousand men were cantoned from Dresden to Liegnitz ; it was composed of eleven corps of infantry, and four of cavalry, including the forces under Oudinot. Murat, having returned from Naples after my victory at Bautzen in order to obtain, by his devotion, pardon for his conduct in the retreat from Russia, was charged with the command of the reserve. The Russo-Prussian army of two hundred thousand combatants was in the environs of Schweidnitz, and one hundred and thirty thousand Austrians had united in Bohemia.

I have been reproached for having employed Davoust with thirty thousand men at Hamburg. This position, they say, had no connection with the great question to be decided on the Elbe ; the strength of my position depended upon the right and not the left, and the enemy could not throw himself upon Hamburg, so long as I was victorious between Magdebourg and Dresden. All this is true ; but then the English might have thrown ten thousand men, arms and money into the north of Germany, have raised Hanover and Westphalia, and, by uniting with Walmoden, have brought sixty thousand men on my rear, and even drawn Denmark after them. The position of Davoust freed me from this apprehension and, moreover, gave occupation to an equal number of the enemy. If ever a detachment was indispensable and useful, this one was.

Different Combinations of the Theatre of War.—The new theatre upon which we were about to wage so terrible a war, was different from those which preceded it. In examining its various combinations I found four systems from which to choose.

The first was to make the Elbe the pivot of all my movements; I held all the fortified points, Königstein, Dresden, Torgau; Wittemberg, and Magdebourg made me master of the course of this river, as Stettin, Glogau and Custrin commanded the Oder. I was certain of having bridges for manœuvering at my pleasure between the two rivers, with great advantage against the enemy who did not possess a single fortified passage. My position, it is true, was taken in reverse by Bohemia; but if the enemy wished to manœuvre by the left bank of the Elbe against Saxony, I could paralyze all who remained on the right bank, and throw myself in mass on those debouching from Bohemia. Thanks to the situation of the little fort of Königstein, I could even operate in my turn against the communications of the enemy, if he should descend the Elbe to Dresden. I might even allow the mass of the allied forces to break their heads against my barrier of the Elbe, while I threw myself alternately on the armies of the north and of Silesia. In either case, the tactical advantage was on my side.

The second system was to profit by the places of Magdebourg, Torgau and Goerlitz on Yung-Bunzlau or Prague, to take in reverse the grand army of the sovereigns which was moving on the Eger. This would have entirely changed my line of operations and have based me on the Danube and Bavaria. The success of this plan would have produced immense results; but, in case of reverse, all my defenses on the Elbe and my depôts would have been abandoned to themselves; it is true that they were well provided and might have held out for some months. In order to execute this grand operation, it would have been necessary to draw my army of Silesia into Bohemia, and leave to Oudinot the care of throwing good garrisons in Torgau and Dresden to form my rear guard on Zittau. The union of three hundred thousand Frenchmen in Bohemia in the plains of Yung-Bunzlau would have greatly embarrassed the sovereigns, for, by beating their principal army near Laun, it would have been thrown back near Egra on the Boehmerwald or on the Voightland, and been cut off from its base, from Blucher, and from Bernadotte; finally, its magazines, collected at great expense, would have amply provided us with provisions. It can not be denied that this plan was manifestly superior to either of the others. It may be said, perhaps, that its execution required a knowledge of the march decided on by the sovereigns at Trachenberg, and which I did not know till the sixteenth; but that was of little importance. Whether I found Schwartzenberg with one hundred thousand Austrians, or encountered the grand allied army, I would become master of the southern side of the theatre of war and drive the enemy to the other side where the advantages were already in my favor. Nevertheless, this manœuvre had the inconvenience of requiring, at its commencement, a retrograde movement of the army of Macdonald before the army of Silesia which would have pursued and perhaps have cut up the French marshal. However, Macdonald had the advantage of disputing in his retreat the defile from Lauban to Reichenberg, ground favorable for defense. The want of practicable roads was the greatest obstacle to the adoption of this system; for we had, in order to execute it, only the road from Rombourg and Gabel, and that from Lauban on Reichenberg.

The third system was to face toward the western frontiers of Bohemia, by placing my left near Dresden and extending my line in the direction of Zwichau and Plauen, abandoning all the right bank of the Elbe. Although the advocate of defensive war would give this the preference, it did not at all suit me. I should have been destitute of common sense to abandon voluntarily all the advantages of the Elbe and enable three allied armies to unite, when I could divide their efforts. My left, abandoned at Dresden, would have had to contend alone against these three armies ; or, if I had wished to bring the rest of my forces to its assistance I should necessarily have been obliged to change my front, in order to place myself in battle on the Elbe. This would have been war without reason and without results.

The fourth system was to evacuate Germany and establish myself behind the Rhine ; several of my generals, who did not comprehend my position, were inclined to adopt this plan. It was an absurd idea. There was no necessity for such a measure ; it would have been better to subscribe at once to all the sacrifices imposed by the coalition. Such a course would have been more honorable and more advantageous than to retire of my own accord, and draw upon the frontiers of France all Europe in arms, without putting an end to the war. To retire behind the Rhine would have been to surrender the Confederation, Italy, Switzerland, and Holland. Moreover, what could we have done with only four hundred thousand men to defend the whole line from Amsterdam to Bale ? It would have required half of this force to garrison the fortifications, and we would have had only two hundred thousand men in the field to fight six hundred thousand allies who assailed us in Saxony and Franconia. Here we might at least oppose to them all our forces and preserve our own territory untouched. Instead of throwing one hundred and fifty thousand men into our fortresses and ruining the soil of France, we could here keep these forces active, augment their numbers still further by the contingents of the Confederation, and carry on the war at the expense of others.

Preliminary Movements.—Every thing being arranged for the new campaign I left Dresden on the fifteenth, and went to Zittau.* The hostilities were not to begin till the sixteenth, but the allies put themselves in motion on the twelfth, to execute the plan which had been agreed upon at Trachenberg. Barclay, with more than one hundred thousand men, filing by his left, crossed Bohemia. His junction with the Austrians formed a mass of two hundred and twenty thousand men, destined to march on Dresden by the left bank of

* The following note, put by Jomini in the mouth of Napoleon, contains the substance of Napoleon's own dictations at St. Helena, as given in his Memoirs by Montholon and Gourgaud.

"On arriving at Bautzen I learned that General Jomini, chief of Marshal Ney's staff, had gone over to the Russian army. Although this event has been generally misjudged by the historians of the campaign, it was, nevertheless, of a nature to greatly annoy me. Jomini was a susceptible man, violent, self-willed, but too frank to conduct any premeditated intrigue. Many circumstances contributed to induce him to take this step. He was a Swiss. Constantly maltreated by the Prince of Neufchatel, he had already, in 1810, wished to enter the Russian service where he had been in fact offered the rank of general in the suite of the Emperor Alexander. He had asked for his discharge, but I had refused it. After having recently distinguished himself at Bautzen, as has been shown in the preceding chapter, he was arrested on the charge of not having sent, in time, certain returns and information which he could not obtain, and under this futile pretext he was published to the army in an order of the day as guilty of neglect of duty. Twice during the armistice, Ney had proposed him for the grade of general of division to which he had just claims for recent and important services. Numerous promotions had been made in his *corps-d'armée*; he alone was excepted, and instead of being recompensed, was subjected to unmerited punishment. Exasperated at such injustice, and certain, from what had occurred in 1810, that I would not accept his resignation, he determined to join a prince who promised him a distinguished reception, and whose magnanimity has been greatly extolled.

"However violent this step, the attenuating circumstances which accompanied it render it excusable. It was the result of a very natural feeling,—that of submitting to no humiliation. This officer was not a Frenchman, and was bound to our flag by no feelings of patriotism, the only feelings which can enable one to submit to ill-treatment.

"Some ill-informed writers have attributed to this event the retreat of our troops behind the Bober, by accusing Jomini of having communicated my plans to the enemy. He was incapable of such an act; moreover, he did not know my plan, for it could not have been communicated to him till after the renewal of hostilities. Others have attributed Blucher's attack to information given him by Jomini; this is equally false; Blucher entered the neutral territory on the twelfth of August, whereas Jomini did not leave for Prague till the fourteenth, and had previously had no communication with the Prussian

the Elbe. Blucher, left in Silesia with about one hundred thousand men, inundated the neutral territory, took possession of Breslau, and advanced on the Katzbach. My corps in Silesia were obliged to raise their cantonments in haste, and retire behind the Bober. Until now, I had believed that the Russian and Prussian masses, forming the general centre of the allies in Silesia, would advance on the Bober, and that the Austrians would attack me in flank with one hundred thousand men. All my dispositions were made to observe, with eighty thousand men each of the masses of the enemy, and to throw myself with a suitable reënforcement upon either, as occasion required.

Plan of Operations.—I had pushed Poniatowski, the seventeenth of August, on Gabel, to ascertain what was passing in Bohemia; we there learned at the same time the march of the sovereigns and the grand army on Bohemia, and the retreat of my army of Silesia. These two events left me no further doubt as to the part I was to take. As Blucher was coming against the mass of my forces, it was necessary to begin by getting rid of him. It has been thought that I would have done better to push forward on Yung-Bunzlau, so as to fall on the grand army of the sovereigns. Perhaps I should have done so, if there had been time; but as the armies of Oudinot and Macdonald had not been prepared for such an enterprise, I thought it more safe to fall at once on

general. He proved, besides, that so far from compromising Ney, he himself had taken, in spite of the marshal, every precaution to cover his camps, ordering, on his own authority, the light cavalry of General Beurmann to Liegnitz to place it in advance of the Katzbach. This fact alone attests that Jomini was a slave to his duty, and that in taking this desperate step he had obeyed his head, rather than his heart. His loss was a serious one; for, of all my officers, he best understood my system of war, and had rendered me important services at Ulm, at Jena, in Poland, at Eylau, in Spain, at the Beresina, and at Bautzen."

The different views taken of Jomini's conduct by his friends and his enemies are briefly stated in the biographical sketch of the author at the beginning of the first volume of this translation.

Blucher, leaving the grand question to be afterward decided. Although my information announced that the sovereigns were advancing on Bohemia, yet there was nothing to indicate whether they would cross the Elbe, or place themselves at Gabel, Leypa and Reichenberg ; in the last supposition, the attack on Prague would be only a front attack.

Napoleon marches against Blucher.—Having resolved to march into Silesia, I left St. Cyr to guard Dresden ; Vandamme and Poniatowski remained in echelons on the road to Gabel ; Belluno remained at Zittau to sustain them ; these last three corps were to mask my rear and cover my communications with the Elbe. I advanced into Silesia at the head of one hundred and forty thousand men. Mortier, Marmont, the guards, and Murat's cavalry, followed the corps of Ney, Lauriston, and Macdonald. We passed the Bober on the twenty-first. Unfortunately for us, Blucher refused battle, as had been agreed upon at Trachenberg. If I had known this intention, I should have changed my plan, and not have hesitated to march on Prague. Blucher fell back on Jauer. I could not follow him without compromising the safety of Dresden, threatened as it was by the grand army of the allies ; this point was the more important as it was to serve as the pivot of all my operations, and to enable me to act at pleasure upon either side of the Elbe.

Instructions to Macdonald.—I left Macdonald in Silesia with eighty thousand men, and with the remaining sixty thousand took the road to Lusace ; and, after marching one hundred and twenty leagues with my best troops, returned to the place from which I started, without having accomplished any object. I had given Macdonald detailed instructions which should have avoided the disasters which he experienced. On the twenty-third of August, at my departure from Löwenberg, I directed Berthier to write to him : "That in the present state of our troops we could do nothing better than to march against the enemy, as soon as he should take the offensive ; in that case, the allies would undoubtedly move on several points at the same time ; that Macdonald, on the contrary, should concentrate his force on a single point, so as to debouch against them and immediately take the initiative. He was informed of my project of debouching from Zittau on Prague, in case the enemy did not seriously threaten the intrenched camp of Dresden, or of debouching by that camp, if the enemy presented himself before it with the mass of his forces. In case he should be attacked by superior numbers, to fall back behind the Quiess, hold Goerlitz, and keep open his communications with me, so as to form a junction in case of need. If he should be pressed, and I in full operation, he would, at the worst, retire on the intrenched camp of Dresden, while my first care would be to keep up our communications with him."

Never did I take more wise precautions, and never were they worse understood or worse executed. Having returned to my army, on the twenty-fourth of August, between Goerlitz and Zittau, I hesitated whether or not I should debouch on Prague ; but the fears manifested by St. Cyr for the fate of Dresden decided me : I directed myself on Stolpe, the twenty-fifth, and very soon had cause to applaud this resolution, when I learned that Oudinot had been beaten, on the twenty-third, in a partial engagement at Gross-Beeren near Berlin. Having decided to operate on the communications of the grand allied army, I left Poniatowski alone to guard the defiles of Gabel, and assembled my masses between Stolpe and Lohman ; but before relating these operations let us look for a moment at what the enemy was doing.

The Command of the allied Forces.—The allied sovereigns, at the head of their grand army, had, on the twenty-first, crossed the mountains which separate Bohemia from Saxony, and advanced on Dresden. This movement, very well conceived, was very badly executed. The information which I had received proved to me the advantage which I possessed over my adversaries in the unity of command and combinations. Never had an army so many chiefs. Louis XIV. had conducted war with his ministers, his courtiers, and the envoys of his allies; but in fact Louvois and Turenne had directed everything. The Emperor Alexander seemed the natural chief of the new league; being more distant from France than the others, he seemed the most disinterested of the monarchs. It is said that the chief command was offered to him, but that, distrusting his own abilities, he had modestly declined it, and that it was then decided to confer the command on one of the secondary generals, directed by the council of sovereigns. Alexander had even the generosity to divide his own army, and to distribute his troops among those of Bernadotte, Blucher, and Schwartzenberg.

It is said that afterwards, stimulated by Moreau and Jomini, the emperor of Russia offered to charge himself with the responsibility which he had at first declined, but that the emperor of Austria, appreciating the advantage which that command would give him, refused his assent. The Prince of Schwartzenberg was, therefore, invested with the title of generalissimo. This brave soldier was not a man capable of directing so complicated a machine; on the other hand, he was of a modest, yielding character, in a word, more fitted to obey than to command. Thus the appointment would not have been so objectionable, if they had given him a skillful major-general (chief of staff) and a couple of aides-major-generals (subordinate officers of staff) capable of forming under him good plans of operation; but this they neglected to do. General Radetski was a good lieutenant-general, and young Count Latour an officer of great promise; but neither had the experience necessary for such a command. To these were added General Languenau, a Saxon officer who owed to me his advancement, and who, at the epoch of the battle of Lutzen, had rejoined the Austrian army. He had never done anything to justify my confidence. He had more talent for intrigue than military ability; some verbose memoirs secured for him the favor of Prince Metternich.

It must not be inferred, however, from this whimsical selection of officers, that Austria had no good ones, or that her army was bad because it had been often defeated. That her troops should be imperfect, after twenty years of reverses, was natural, and that her generals should lose their confidence, was still more natural; however, both exhibited great firmness in their reverses, and the good qualities of Wurmser's soldiers proved what was to be expected of an Austrian army when ably commanded. The staff was well-instructed in all the accessary branches, as topography, fortification, tactics of detail, &c. But the habit of the Aulic Council of directing everything themselves, and of selecting court-favorites for commands, caused many misfortunes. Why was it that in a country that produced Prince Charles, Kray, Laudon, and Lichtenstein, more competent persons could not be found to direct their military operations, than those charged with those important duties in 1813? Why was it that Metternich could not find some more skillful person to direct his armies, or at least more able staff-officers as advisers to the Prince of Schwartzenberg?

As it was, the Aulic committee of the campaign had the important task of preparing and issuing all orders, after first submitting them to the sovereigns who formed a kind of council of revision. The Emperor Alexander, the King of Prussia, Lord Cathcart (the English Ambassador), Lowenhielm (the Swedish Ambassador), Prince Wolkonsky, Generals Moreau, Barclay, Diebitsch, Toll, Jomini, and Knesebeck, discussed the projected operations. As they had to give their opinions on the crude plans of the others, this council led to interminable debates. Either because Schwartzenberg wished to free himself from such leading strings, or because he found it impossible to wait for these long discussions before combining his operations, his orders were often sent to the different corps without being first submitted to the sovereigns for their approval; and it was soon found that the formation of plans of operation for the army was left to men who were utterly ignorant of the duty. Several generals who were capable of appreciating the sad results of such a state of things, now urged the league to choose an Agamemnon, and intrust to him their destinies. There being no monarch suited for this office, they proposed the Archduke Charles, who had given proof of his capacity: but private interests defeated this object. It was therefore necessary that the Emperor Alexander should act as a kind of mediator, and by his moderation and address have the indirect control of affairs, and, at least, avoid great evils, if he could not accomplish great objects.

March of the Allies on Dresden.—My march on Silesia had been made almost in musket-shot of the Austrian frontier, which was well-guarded by custom-house officers, gamekeepers, forest-guards, &c., yet, strange to say, Schwartzenberg knew nothing of it. He descended on Marienberg and Pirna by a slow march, supposing me still at Dresden, when I was at the distance of sixty leagues. St. Cyr threw himself into that city with the resolution to defend it to the uttermost, so that I might have time to come to his assistance. The allies seconded his plans admirably by the slowness of their march. They passed the mountains on the twenty-first of August, but it was not till the evening of the twenty-fifth that their right under Barclay appeared before Dresden, after beating Claparède at Pirna, and leaving Ostermann in observation near Königstein. The Austrians, who were amusing themselves at a grand review in the plains of Laun, and pushing their left to the environs of Egra, combined their movements so badly that they could not arrive till two days after the Russo-Prussian army, which had debouched from the mountains of Glatz.

On learning at Gabel, on the seventeenth, this movement of the allies on the Elbe, I foresaw this attempt against Dresden, but was not at all embarrassed by it, for I knew that the place could not well be carried by an assault, and that I was more advantageously situated than they were, for manœuvring on their communications. Their first plan had been to march on Leipsic, where Bernadotte would join them, by passing the Elbe at Dessau. If they had followed this project, and I had gained a great battle, their destruction would have been almost certain. By drawing to me the army of Oudinot, I should have had two hundred thousand men; and by passing the Elbe at Dresden on their rear, I should have got possession of their magazines, and their line of operations on Bohemia; I would have attacked them at Leipsic with the advantage of having in my power all the fortified debouches of the Elbe; I would also have held the issues of that river, of the Oder, and of Bohemia, so that the allies, if beaten, would have been thrown back on the Baltic, without the ability of regaining Austria.

The king of Saxony, under an exaggerated idea of the inconvenience of living in a fortified capital, had, since 1810, begun to demolish the defenses of the old city. But during the armistice I had employed numerous workmen in rebuilding them: the dismantled fronts had been made sufficiently strong to resist an assault, and the rich exterior faubourgs were covered by an enceinte of thirteen redoubts, of which eight were on the right, and five on the left bank of the Elbe. These were not strong enough to resist a siege, nor even an assault, if defended by only an ordinary garrison; but defended by an entire army, the post was impregnable.

The allies had two courses to pursue: 1st, to debouch by Peterswalde, Altenberg, and Marienberg; to occupy the heights of Dippodiswalde with their right reënforced towards Gieshubel, and to there await my attack; 2d, to march rapidly against Dresden with several thousand fascines and scaling-ladders, and, if I was not found there with the mass of my forces, to attempt against the faubourgs and old town what Bernadotte and Soult had done at Lubeck: they might have been repelled with the loss of several thousand men; but as the result of the campaign depended upon the success of this operation, it was well worth the attempt. As soon as my presence at Dresden announced that the mass of my forces was opposed to them, the question was changed, and the allies ought then to have held themselves in the imposing position between Gieshubel and Dippodiswalde. This place would have been to me what Taroutina was in 1812. Placed on my line of operation, they might have continually inundated it with partisans, and nothing but a decisive battle could have rid me of such troublesome neighbors. If beaten, the allies could have escaped behind the Eger; if conquerors, they would have driven me back into Dresden, where, under such circumstances, my position would have been far from secure. I should have been obliged to adopt the course which I pursued in October,—to file on Leipsic. But the Austrians, who were ignorant of my being on the Katzbach, the twenty-first of August, did not yet know, on the twenty-fifth, that I had returned to Stolpe. In fact they had received only a few hours before the dispatches of Blucher, saying that I was hotly pressing him near Goldberg. How then was it possible that I could be on the Elbe the next day with the same troops!

At ten o'clock on the morning of the twenty-fifth the

allied sovereigns had assembled on the heights of Roeknitz before Dresden, to decide upon the disposition of their forces. Two divisions of St. Cyr were in advance of the city, deployed between the Gros-Garten and the road to Dippodiswalde, with their rear supported on the intrenched camp. A Russian general proposed to attack, citing in support of this opinion our operation against Blucher at Lubeck. A vigorous *coup-de-main* might have decided the campaign, by rendering the allies masters of my base of operations.

All the allies who had passed through Dresden some months before, knew that this old town had been partly dismantled, and that I had only been able to secure the place by field-works. On the supposition that I was still in Silesia, there was no reason to hesitate : they must either risk an attack, or form in battle-array between Gieshubel and Dippodiswalde. They determined upon the former : the attempt could cost nothing, and never was there a project with more powerful motives for its adoption. But Schwartzenberg wished to wait for the arrival of his Austrians, who were marching from Marienberg by horrible roads, instead of taking the great road, or at least that which runs directly from Sayda to Dresden. He therefore postponed the attack till four o'clock P. M. on the twenty-sixth. This was a great error, because the hundred thousand Russians and Prussians under Barclay were sufficient for a *coup-de-main* against three divisions. Numbers here were of no consequence, but time was everything. It was not in contending with me that they could lose thirty hours with impunity.

Their singular Dispositions for Attack.—To this mistake they added another still greater in their manner of attack. The plan prepared by Schwartzenberg fell into my hands among the baggage which was captured. It was a chef-d'œuvre of its kind ; it ran thus : *a general reconnoissance will be attempted on the place of Dresden ;* the army will advance in five columns which will endeavor to carry the works, and to penetrate into the city! . . . . . Can anything more incoherent be imagined! He either wished to reconnoitre, or to make an assault; in the first case, why place one hundred and eighty thousand men in mass around a place, and make them fight? If, instead of a simple reconnoissance, he designed an assault, why not prescribe the precautions and preparations for such an attempt? Mack has been greatly decried, but he never imagined anything like this!

Project to cut off the Allies at Koenigstein.—As has already been said, I had returned to Stolpe, on the twenty-fifth, by a remarkable forced march. My project was at first to debouch with one hundred thousand men by Koenigstein and Pirna on the enemy's rear; I informed the Duke of Bassano of this at Dresden, by the following letter which I addressed to him from Goerlitz, on the twenty-fourth of August:

"It is my intention to march to Stolpe. My army will be assembled there to-morrow; I shall pass the twenty-sixth there, in making preparations, and in rallying my columns. On the night of the twenty-sixth, I shall move my columns by Koenigstein, and at day-break on the twenty-seventh, I will establish myself in the camp of Pirna with one hundred thousand men. By seven o'clock in the morning, I will commence an attack on Hollendorf, and by noon will be master of the place. I will then put myself in a commanding position on that communication. I will make myself master of Pirna, and have pontoons ready to establish two bridges at that place, if necessary. If the enemy has taken for his line of operation the road from Peterswalde to Dresden, I will be found on his rear with all my army united against his, which he cannot rally in less than four or five hours. If he has taken his line of operations by the road to

Komotaw, Dresden will be relieved ; I shall then be in Bohemia, nearer Prague than the enemy, and will march there. Marshal St. Cyr will follow the enemy as soon as he appears disconcerted.

"I will mask my movement by covering the bank of the Elbe with thirty thousand cavalry and light artillery, so that the enemy, seeing all the shore occupied, will think my army about Dresden ! Such is my project. It may, however, be modified by the operations of the enemy. I suppose that when I shall undertake my attack, Dresden will not be so assailed that she can not hold out for twenty-four hours.

"You may impart to the King of Saxony alone my projects, and say to him that if the enemy press Dresden, it may be more convenient for him to take a country house on the right bank. Send none but very vague news to Paris, giving it to be understood that they will hear at the same time my victory over the army of Silesia, the capture of Berlin, and of other events still more important. Write to Erfurth, Munich, and Wurtzbourg in cypher. The letter to Wurtzbourg will be imparted to the Duke of Castiglione. Write to General Margaron that if he is pressed at Leipsic, he ought to retire on Torgau. See the director of the estafette, and have it pass through Leipsic and Torgau.

"If Marshal St. Cyr has sufficient force to defend Dresden, and should not be pressed, let him send out to meet General Vandamme, so that the latter may take position with his divisions at Neustadt, seeing that any retrograde movement may be disadvantageous."

The success of this enterprise would have produced immense results. I should have cut off the allies' line of retreat ; and, in case of reverse, I could have taken refuge under the fort of Koenigstein and the camp of Pirna, where I could recross the Elbe in security ; these *têtes-de-pont* were of incalculable importance to me. But information which I received from St. Cyr made me fear that a strong attempt might be made to carry Dresden, and as the force of the enemy was rumored to be two hundred thousand men, I sent Gourgaud to reconnoitre St. Cyr's position; he returned in haste, and assured me that the enemy were strong enough to carry the city, if they attacked it with vigor. I, therefore, concluded my projected manœuvre would be too adventurous, and preferred to march directly on Dresden so as to debouch from there, throwing Vandamme on the decisive point of the road to Peterswalde. Under the circumstances I did not repent having formed this resolution; but God alone knows what would have been the result, if I had executed the plan which I dictated at Stolpe on the twenty-fifth. I could have drawn Poniatowski toward me, and have placed one hundred and thirty thousand men on the only communication of the allies! On the other hand, my troops were young and without experience, and I had but few old cavalry. The allies had a more numerous force, were better organized, and numbered at least forty thousand experienced cavalry. Moreover, time was wanting to rally the armies of Macdonald and Oudinot, from which I would have been separated, had I been defeated. The last of these two marshals had just experienced a check at Gros-Beeren, of little importance in itself, but calculated to effect the morale of the contending forces. All these motives combined to induce me to change my project, and to march on Dresden the morning of the twenty-seventh.

Battle of Dresden, August 26th and 27th.—I thought that at the sight of my columns which descended the Elbe and commanded the right of Wittgenstein, the allies would renounce their project of attacking the city. The head of my columns entered the town at two o'clock, and to my great astonishment, at precisely four o'clock, one hundred and twenty thousand men assailed the works. I have since learned that this assault was made through an inconceivable misunderstanding. The Emperor Alexander, learning my return from the reports of my cannon, now pronounced it ridiculous to make the projected attack; all agreed in this opinion, and Schwartzenberg started to revoke the orders. It was now one o'clock, and there was plenty of time to give the counter-order. It required no new dispositions, merely a verbal direction to the principal officers countermanding the attack; but no direction was given. It is not pretended that it was forgotten, but that the objections of Radetzki and Languerau prevented its being sent. The responsibility of this neglect is to be divided between the generalissimo and those who composed his staff.

The enemy's columns assaulted the works with great impetuosity; those of Colloredo and Lichtenstein penetrated into the city. The Russians and Prussians formed a lodgment in Gros-Garten and Strieseu; at the left, Bianchi got possession of Lobela and the houses near the gate of Freyberg; Giulay and Metzko pushed on nearly to Friedrichstadt. St. Cyr had taken care to draw in the divisions which had been deployed on the twenty-fifth; so that columns of attack were ready to debouch as soon as the fire of the intrenchments had staggered the enemy. He was everywhere repulsed. Ney debouched at the head of two divisions of the Young Guard and drove back the left of the Austrians on Lobela; two other divisions made a sortie by the gate of Pinar and repulsed Kleist; St. Cyr, at the centre, drove back Chasteller and Colloredo. During the night I was rejoined by the remainder of my troops from Silesia, and now found myself at the head of one hundred and ten thousand men, independent of the corps of Vandamme; but the allies had one hundred and eighty thousand men besides those against Vandamme. Nevertheless, I did not hesitate to attack them; I required a complete victory to clear my communications.

On the morning of the twenty-seventh, we debouched from Dresden, while Vandamme took the enemy in reverse by Koenigstein. The allied army, drawn up in a semi-circle before Dresden, supported its right on the Elbe, its centre on the heights of Roekniz ; but its left was paralyzed by being placed beyond the defile of Tharandt, which it could not cross. Under the pretext of facilitating its junction, Schwartzenberg had insisted, against all advice, in placing three Austrian divisions beyond this precipice. This exposed them without necessity. It is true that it was advantageous to seize it ; but Klenau was there already ; there was no objection to his remaining at a distance, and it would even have been better if he had been left at Freyberg, instead of drawing him to Dresden, since the first of these points was two days' march nearer my base of operations, and from it he could have anticipated me if I had decided to regain the Saal.

In profiting by this error, I accomplished the double object of overthrowing their isolated divisions, and opening my own communication. I therefore threw the King of Naples against them with the cavalry of Latour-Maubourg and the corps of Belluno. A very warm combat was engaged between Lobela and Corbitz. The weather was frightful, torrents of rain had been falling since midnight ; the few Austrian cavalry could not resist our cuirassiers ; and the infantry, soaked with rain and not being able to fire their pieces, were broken at the centre near Corbitz. Giulay having been driven into the defile of Tharandt near Potschapel, Murat attacked the three brigades of the extreme right under Metzko, which, being isolated, turned, and defeated, laid down their arms, after useless efforts to escape. More than ten thousand prisoners were the fruit of this brilliant feat of arms. In the mean time the left of Belluno established itself in the village of Plauen, which constitutes the key of the defile of Tharandt, and the only point by which it was possible to succor the three compromitted divisions.

Marmont and St. Cyr, supporting themselves on the intrenched camp, had limited their operations to cannonading the enemy and repelling the charges of the Austrians and Prussians; the latter had made a lodgment in the Gros-Garten and rested on the village of Strehlen, which Kleist had at first been ordered to evacuate, and which he had afterward vainly attempted to recapture. The enormous masses of the allies at the centre on the heights of Roeknitz, did not allow us to undertake any thing on that point. I, however, caused it to be cannonaded by the artillery of the guard and that of the Duke of Ragusa. It was here that Moreau had his legs carried away by a French ball. This general, who had been deemed, by my enemies, capable of balancing my fortune, had returned from America to enter the Russian service. He soon perceived his error; for the Austrians allowed him no part in the command. He died the next day at Laun, worthy perhaps of a better fate.*

On our left, Ney, having united four divisions of the Young Guard between Gros-Garton and the Elbe, debouched from Gruna against Wittgenstein. It was now the more easy to push on to Reich, as the allies had determined during the night to concentrate on the heights of Leubnitz, and to

* The following remarks are copied from Thiers:

"Whilst these events were taking place on the allies' left, a strange accident occurred at the centre, where Napoleon was exchanging a vigorous cannonade with the Austrians, and where he himself directed the operations of his batteries in the very thickest of the fire. At the same time, the emperor was at a point exactly opposite, at Rackwitz, accompanied by General Moreau, who seeing the danger of his position, advised him to withdraw somewhat further back. This advice had barely been given, and was on the very point of being executed, when a bullet from the batteries of which Napoleon was personally directing the fire, struck the general on his legs, and hurled him and his horse to the ground. A strange stroke of fortune, this! which made the instrument of his death, a ball from a French cannon, fired, as it were, by Napoleon's own hand."

abandon the valley of the Elbe so as to fall on our flank if we ventured to engage ourselves there. The Russian general, Roth, nevertheless, made a glorious defense of the villages of Seidnitz and Gros-Dobritz, and regained in good order the right of Wittgenstein behind Reich.

In the meantime Kleist, Miloradowitch, the reserve of the Grand-duke Constantine, Colloredo, and the reserve of the Prince of Hesse-Homburg, had scarcely been engaged. The half of their masses accumulated on the centre might have attacked Ney by Strehlen, and have defeated him while extended too much to the left so as to form a line parallel to the Elbe. The project was approved by the Emperor Alexander, and the masses of Kleist and Miloradowitch were actually disposed for the purpose of striking this blow. Barclay was at the same time to descend from Leubnitz with the reserve and Gortschakof's corps; but he failed to give the signal for the others to act, and the thing was not attempted. If the movement had been executed with vigor and *ensemble*, it might have balanced the defeat of Giulay on the left.

The Austrians have only to attribute to their own chiefs this bloody defeat. Not satisfied with recommending to their left to hold all the space between Plauen and Priesnitz even to the Elbe, which was absurd, they attached to it only one division of cavalry, while the reserve of the Prince of Hesse-Homburg was concentrated on the centre and uselessly exposed to the fire of our artillery, from which it suffered as great losses as if it had been engaged. The ground here was unfavorable for the manœuvring of cavalry, and the Russian and Prussian horse would have been abundantly sufficient for the object in view, whereas three divisions of the Austrian cuirassiers on the left flank, might have decided the battle and saved their infantry.

The Allies determine to retreat.—It was now five o'clock, and beginning to grow dark; the rain was increasing, and the troops on both sides were drenched. The allies, or rather a majority of them, informed at the same time of the disaster of their left and of the passage of Vandamme at Koenigstein, were inclined to retreat. The Emperor of Russia was not pleased with the plan, and the King of Prussia was unwilling to hear it spoken of; but the Austrians declared that they had brought with them only half-supplies for their artillery, and had but a few more rounds to fire; that their parks of provisions had been unable to follow them through the narrow roads of the mountains; in a word, that it was necessary to regain Bohemia in order to prevent the dissolution of their army. Notwithstanding the constant opposition of the King of Prussia, they decided upon a retreat; two generals charged with drawing up the order of it, soon returned with a burlesque disposition for a retreat behind the Eger in five columns, each of which had its daily march marked out in regular stages as in time of peace and without any reference to what might occur to the other columns! Such combinations excited the ire of the enlightened critics, but time was pressing, and if they were to retire that night, not a moment was to be lost. The plan was, therefore, assented to through disgust rather than conviction. As a *chef-d'ouvre* of absurdity in this disposition, they feared to take, at the right, the good road to Pirna, because Vandamme occupied it with twenty-five thousand men, although there was no river or other obstacle to cross; Barclay, Kleist, and the Russian reserve might have taken this road without any great inconvenience. Vandamme, hemmed in between them and Ostermann's corps would have been happy to effect his own escape. They directed Barclay and Kleist by Dohna on Gieshubel; Klenau by Freyberg and Marienberg; the Austrians by Altenberg and Zinwald. This ill-planned order was still farther aggravated by Barclay, who, fearing to find the passage barred at Peterswalde or Dohna, threw himself with the Russians on the road to Dippodiswalde and Altenberg, where they became frightfully jammed in with the Austrians. This resolution was the more to be regretted as Ostermann, although left alone, succeeded in effecting a passage; and Barclay with fifty thousand men more could have found very little difficulty in doing the same thing.

The enemy lost much of their artillery and thirty thousand men *hors-de-combat*, including the ten thousand Austrians of the left wing who were taken prisoners. The trophies gained in the pursuit were scarcely less: we captured in the defiles two hundred pieces of artillery and caissons, a thousand waggons, and a multitude of wounded and stragglers. This was one of the most glorious victories I ever gained. We were but one to their two, nevertheless the victory was not for a moment doubtful at the points where I struck. It was the only battle where I operated at the same time on both wings; the position of Dresden at the centre enabled me to do so without danger. This circumstance was the more fortunate for me, as the principal communications of the allies were on the wings, and by getting possession of these I forced them to retreat in disorder through the defiles of the mountains.

Operations of Vandamme near Koenigstein.—The same day on which we gained these important successes, Vandamme, crossing the Elbe at Koenigstein with thirty thousand men, forced Count Ostermann, who masked this fort with the division of the old Russian guards and the corps of Prince Eugene of Wurtemberg, to retire, which he did by taking the road to Pirna, either because his right was turned or because he had been ordered to fall back in that direction. On the twenty-eighth of August he was forced, by the retrograde movement of the allies, to take the road to Peterswalde. Vandamme, having already turned him, cut the road, first at Gieshubel, and then at Hoellendorf. The Russian general was compelled to cut his way out, and our young soldiers, being obliged to defend too long a line, and assailed by veterans of the old guard, were driven back. Ostermann bivouacked at Peterswalde where he rallied his forces, and the next day defended the ground, foot by foot, with exemplary firmness as far as Culm: even one of his brigades which had been cut off succeeded in rejoining him. I had foreseen the advantage which was to be derived from Vandamme's position in case we were victorious at Dresden. I had ordered him to descend from the mountains, and push rapidly on Toeplitz, with the promise of his being sustained. If this movement had succeeded, it would have destroyed the greater part of the allies who were still engaged in retreat in the defiles of Altenberg. But fortune decided otherwise.

Disaster of Vandamme at Culm. — Ostermann and his troops also seeing the importance of the point of Toeplitz, fought on the twenty-ninth with an intrepidity above all praise, and finally succeeded in maintaining themselves behind Culm, notwithstanding the reiterated efforts of our troops. Towards evening they began to receive reënforcements which restored the equilibrium of the contending forces: the Grand-Duke Constantine carried there a part of the Russian reserve. This first contrariety was followed by a circumstance much more deplorable, which caused the ruin of Vandamme. No sooner was victory declared in our favor in the plains of Colditz and Dresden, than I devised the means of profiting by it. The king of Naples and Belluno followed the enemy on Sayda; Ragusa had taken the road to Altenberg; St. Cyr debouched on Dohna, Maxen, and Liebenau; Mortier, with the Young Guard, took the road to Pirna; and, on the morning of the twenty-eighth, I started with my head-quarters for that city. I was to leave there on the twenty-ninth to follow Vandamme: but a fatality which seemed to attach itself to all my enterprises, did not permit me to complete the movement. Having been exposed for fifteen hours on the twenty-seventh to a violent rain, I was seized the next day during my march to Pirna with so violent a fever as to compel me to return abruptly to Dresden. I had the project of joining the army of Oudinot with fifty thousand men, and taking possession of Berlin; this motive caused me to renounce the movement on Bohemia. I, at first, had reason to applaud this resolution; for, on returning to Dresden, I heard of Macdonald's bloody defeat on the Katzbach. The reënforcements intended to sustain Vandamme were then stopt at Pirna: but unfortunately he was not informed of this. Berthier probably neglected to take the proper means to communicate the information to him. The circumstances have never been explained.*

The allies descended with one hundred thousand men into the valley on the morning of the thirtieth, convinced that their safety depended upon the overthrow of Vandamme. A man less audacious would not have waited the attack, but would have effected his escape during the night or at break of day. But expecting my arrival he resolved to maintain his position. Although turned on the right and left, and assailed in front, he still refused to retreat, it being announced that a column was finally seen debouching on the mountains towards Hollendorf. But the joy caused by this news was of short duration; it was soon found that this column, instead of being one of mine, was the Prussian corps of Kleist, which the Emperor Alexander had ordered to descend on the flank of the French towards Kraupen, and

* Jomini, in a long note, contradicts the assertion of Fain that Vandamme descended from the mountains without orders. It appears that this order was given, and that Napoleon at first made his dispositions to sustain him; but when his illness forced him to return to Dresden, he either forgot to give counter-directions to Vandamme, or Berthier neglected to send the order.

which had taken the main road, instead of the path by the old castle, then encumbered with equipages. The cavalry of Vandamme threw itself on the first troops of Kleist and cut their way through: twelve thousand infantry had the good fortune to follow them, and to regain the army through the woods. All the others, and Vandamme himself, being surrounded, fought with desperation, but were taken in arms. This combat cost us at least fifteen thousand men and sixty pieces of artillery.

This defeat, so unexpected, was a double misfortune, for it might be imputed to a manifest forgetfulness of the principles of war. These principles required a hot pursuit of a beaten and broken army. On this depended the success of the war; all else was only accessory. If I had left Pirna to succor Macdonald, the resolution would have been excusable; but I did not then know of his defeat. If I had returned to Dresden for no other object than to prepare to march on Berlin, it would undoubtedly have been one of the gravest faults of my life. It is true that the consequences would have been less serious if Berthier had recalled Vandamme. Although this accident was not the result of my own intended dispositions, nevertheless, it not only prevented me from profiting by my victory, but also became the first cause of the defeat of my lieutenant.*

* The following is Thiers' account of this battle:

"Such was the unfortunate affair at Culm, which cost us five or six thousand men killed or wounded, seven thousand prisoners, forty-eight pieces of cannon, and two generals, and which, whilst costing the allies some six thousand men, relieved them from their position of defeat, reinspired them with the hope of victory, and effaced from their minds the remembrance of the disasters they had suffered on the twenty-sixth and twenty-seventh of August.

"Where can we look for the cause of this singular catastrophe? Shall we attribute it to Vandamme, saying that he ventured too much? Or to Mortier and St. Cyr, complaining that they failed to afford him timely succor? or to Napoleon, on the ground that he trusted too much to the favorable progress

Oudinot defeated at Gross-Beeren.—It was the more to be regretted as it tended to encourage the allied army at the moment of our misfortunes in Silesia and Brandenburg. I

of affairs? or shall we rather regard it as the legitimate consequence of the military skill displayed by the generals of the allied armies?

"The facts above narrated almost of themselves sufficiently answer these questions, and account for one of the greatest reverses of fortune of which the pages of history retain any record.

"Vandamme, whose many faults were counterbalanced by many fine qualities, is certainly not blamable for the unfortunate results of these days; for if, after having wisely established himself at Culm, it was General Kleist instead of Marshal Mortier who appeared in his rear, this was an extraordinary accident, to hold him responsible for which would be a crying injustice. During the catastrophe which followed, Vandamme preserved all his presence of mind, and took the only resolution which offered a chance of escape, namely, that of retracing his steps, and passing through the midst of the Prussian troops.

"He is not fairly open to reproach, and the supposition that he lost himself, in a too eager pursuit of that marshal's baton which, far more than others, he deserved for military services already performed, is a calumny upon a man whose misfortunes render him an object for pity rather than blame.

"If it be admitted, however, that Vandamme is not to be blamed, having been unfortunate only in the fact that a Prussian corps appeared in his rear instead of the French one which he expected, what are we to say of the French generals who might have supported him, and more particularly of Marshals Mortier and St. Cyr, the only ones posted within reach of Culm? Marshal Mortier, established at Pirna, liable to be dispatched thence either to Dresden, on the one hand, or to Toeplitz on the other, might certainly, had he acted with more self-reliance and vigilance, have hastened up to Vandamme's aid; but it was, at the same time, perfectly natural that, in the strict fulfilment of the orders he had received, he should await in complete immobility the expression of Napoleon's will; and with respect to the precise order given to him to aid Vandamme with two divisions, it is sufficient to state that this order did not reach him until the catastrophe had already taken place.

"It would be well if we could say as much with respect to Marshal St. Cyr; but the fact is that, that directed as he was to keep constantly on the track of Kleist's corps, he should never have lost sight of him for an instant, and had he fulfilled this positive duty the necessary result would have been, that when Kleist's corps fell upon Vandamme, it would itself have been attacked by a French corps in the rear, and would probably have been itself broken and routed instead of helping to break and rout the army of Vandamme.

"But unfortunately Marshal St. Cyr, never zealous for the success of any operations but those with the execution of which he was himself directly charged, and ever inclined rather to seek difficulties than to seek to overcome them, employed the twenty-eighth in moving to Maxen, and on the following day, the twenty-ninth, only advanced to Reinhard's Grimme, thus making a movement of no more than a league and a half on the very day when it was

have already said that Oudinot was left to fight at Gross-Beeren; this marshal who commanded about sixty-five thousand men, had received orders to take the initiative

important that the enemy should be pursued with the utmost vigor, and allowed Kleist to disappear from before him, and fall upon Vandamme's rear, whilst he employed himself in inquiring of the staff whether he should not follow Marmont on the Altenberg route.

"On the following day, the thirtieth, when he received the order directing him to endeavor to effect a junction with Vandamme by the lateral route, he at length aroused himself, and by the road which led Kleist upon Vandamme's rear, and which should have conducted himself upon Kleist's rear, arrived just in time to hear the cannon which announced our disaster. As for Marshal Marmont, he pushed the enemy as vigorously as he could, and engaged in several skirmishes which resulted to his advantage, but he was too far from Vandamme to be able to move up to his support. Posted decidedly on the right, he could not attempt to cross the mountains in advance of St. Cyr without exposing himself to falling alone amidst a crowd of enemies; and the catastrophe is not therefore, to be attributed to any error of his.

"With respect to Murat, it is sufficient to say that it was impossible that he should have had any share in the deplorable event, which took place at Culm, since he and his squadrons were traversing at the time the great Freyburg route.

"Of the persons who may be considered the responsible actors in this catastrophe, it remains, finally, to speak of Napoleon himself, who, by sedulously following his lieutenants, might have made them converge towards a common point, and by his presence would certainly have obtained what he hoped and expected. But he was turned aside, on the twenty-eighth, from this duty, by the news which reached him from the neighborhood of Lowenberg and Berlin, and also, it must be added, by the confidence he felt that the orders he had given were of themselves sufficient to secure the results he desired. Ever recurring to past experiences, Napoleon believed that he had done sufficient to render him certain of obtaining the most splendid triumphs.

"But unfortunately times were changed, and to have accomplished the destruction of the grand army of Bohemia would have required, at least, Napoleon's incessant superintendence of the execution of his designs. But now, distracted as he was by the passionate desire of obtaining all results at once, Berlin and Dantzic were as much means of leading him into error as Moscow had been during the previous year. Indeed, that he might strike a serious blow at Prussia and Germany, at Berlin, and be able to boast that his power extended from the Gulf of Tarentum to the Vistula, he had entertained the idea from the very commencement of this campaign of sending one of his corps to the Prussian capital, and keeping a garrison at Dantzic; and for the sake of these objects he had, as we have seen, allowed an error to creep into the finely conceived plan he had formed for the conduct of the campaign, giving an excessive extent to the circle of operations, the central point of which was to be against Bernadotte, to seek to beat him, and get possession of Berlin. In order to second him in this enterprise General Gerard had organized a flying corps of the best troops from

at Dresden, placing Macdonald at Lowenberg, instead of at Bautzen, and sending Oudinot against Berlin instead of establishing him at Wittenberg. And as the same cause continued to produce the same effects, he was anxious, on learning the misfortune which had happened to Macdonald, to succor him as soon as possible; and being also anxious to lead in person Oudinot's army to Berlin, he turned from Pirna and Culm, where he ought to have been with his guard, and neglected to achieve victories, the consequences of which would have been of the utmost advantage to him, for the purpose of running after others, and thus exposed himself to the danger of losing everything from an over-anxiety to obtain everything at once.

"But for this catastrophe at Culm alone must he be blamed, for in the details of the several manœuvres he had committed no fault. And at the same time it must be observed that the actual results were but little due to the merits of his enemies; a sentiment of despair rather than calculation having led them to carry into execution a combination which had the most unexpected and important consequences, and which was certainly due, not to the skill of the Emperor Alexander, to whom its merit has been attributed, but to the determination of the Prussian troops either to cut their way out of their perilous position or perish in the attempt.

"We must look, then, not so much to the military skill of the allies, although they were far from being deficient in this, as to the passionate spirit of patriotism which inspired them, and which rendered them comparatively indifferent to defeat, for the cause of their seizing with such promptitude the opportunity offered them at Culm.

"Another important moral lesson to be drawn from these great events is, that care should ever be taken not to drive men to despair, since to do this is to endow them with a supernatural strength which may enable them to overthrow the best calculations, and to frustrate the plans of the most consummate skill. The allies who, when they abandoned the battle-field of Dresden, regarded themselves as completely vanquished, and sadly questioned whether, in attempting to vanquish Napoleon, they had not undertaken an enterprise against destiny itself, suddenly, at the spectacle of the defeat and capture of Vandamme, regarded themselves as being once more in an excellent position, and believed that the balance of fortune between themselves and Napoleon was at least in equilibrium.

"It is true that the two days' fighting at Dresden, and the pursuit during the twenty-eighth and twenty-ninth, had cost them in killed, wounded, or prisoners, some forty thousand men, whilst the defeat of Vandamme had, at the most, cost us no more than twelve thousand.

"But, nevertheless, the result was that a feeling of confidence had re-entered their hearts, and they resolved to close with Napoleon at every opportunity, and leave him not a moment in repose. For the allies, not to be vanquished was almost to be victorious; whilst for Napoleon, on the contrary, to have

the garrisons of Magdebourg and Wittenberg. He was to debouch from the first of these places with six thousand men under General Lanusse, to act, in concert with Dombrowski's division from Wittenberg, on the right flank of the allies. Davoust on his side had received orders to ascend the Elbe and the Havel. This union of one hundred thousand men in the environs of Berlin seemed well calculated to secure to us immense results, both in a military and political point of view. I supposed that Bernadotte had but eighty thousand men, including Walmoden's corps, which was opposed to Davoust towards Hamburg. There remained, therefore, according to my calculation, only about fifty thousand combatants with Bernadotte; and Oudinot, superior in numbers, had only to gain one battle to accomplish his task. Unfortunately the enemy was much stronger than we supposed. Oudinot, after making some detachments of flankers and escorts, advanced with sixty thousand men on Trebbin and Berlin. Bernadotte, after making a feint of manœuvring against his left flank, took the position of Ruhlsdorf with ninety thousand men (of which twenty thousand were good cavalry), without counting the light corps of Generals Hirschfeld near Brandenburg, and that of Wobeser near Baruth. The left of the army under Tauenzien, was supported on the lake of Rangsdorf; the centre under Bulow, held the road to Berlin; the Russians and Swedes were on the right.

On the twenty-second of August, Oudinot passed the defile of Thyrow, after a warm combat against the advanced guard of Bulow. On the twenty-third, our army advanced in three columns; Bertrand and the fourth corps at the right on Johnsdorf; Reynier, with the Saxons, at the centre, by

failed to annihilate his adversaries was to have done nothing. On such extreme and almost impossible conditions had he based his hopes of safety."

the great road; Oudinot and the twelfth corps, by the road to Trebbin on Ahrensdorf. It would be difficult to say what the marshal intended by thus engaging his forces on ground cut up by woods and marshes, and without a single cross-road by which he could unite his columns; he himself marching in rear of his left? No preparations were made for a battle, and undoubtedly Oudinot did not expect one. Bertrand, at six o'clock in the morning, first encountered near Blankenfelde the corps of Tauenzien, who made a good defense of the debouch from the woods by means of that village. The combat was an obstinate one, and without result. It was already terminated when Reynier, at three o'clock in the afternoon, attacked, near Gross-Beeren, the advanced guard of Bulow which he dislodged. He was preparing to establish his bivouacs there, without thinking of the possibility of an attack, when Bulow fell upon him at the head of thirty-five thousand Prussians with one hundred pieces of artillery. Notwitstanding all that could be done by the Saxons and Durutte's division, they were forced to yield to so great a superiority; they effected their escape by favor of the woods, with the loss of three thousand men *hors-de-combat.* At the sound of the cannon, Generals Guilleminot and Fournier, who formed the head of the column of the twelfth corps, marched in all haste toward Neu-Beeren; they arrived at nightfall in time to protect the retreat, but too late to reëstablish the battle. The cavalry of General Fournier, in deploying at the left of this hamlet, was charged in flank by the enemy whom they had hardly perceived. A part of our squadrons, driving before them the Prussian platoons, advanced into the plain in sight of Hennersdorf when the enemy pursued them and drove them back more rapidly than they had advanced; they were very fortunate in effecting their escape.

Oudinot, on arriving at Wittskof, learned the defeat of his

centre and ordered a retreat on Wittenberg. Bernadotte committed the fault of allowing him to quietly take up his position, when his own vast superiority in number, and his formidable cavalry, gave him an opportunity to seriously cut him up during his retreat.

The first consequence of this check was the loss of Gérard's division which made a sortie from Magdebourg, and, while advancing alone in the midst of an army of one hundred thousand men, fell a certain prey to the enemy. General Hirschfeld, with the Cossacks of Czermischef, attacked him in front of Belzig, and forced him to retire again into Magdebourg with a loss of one thousand two hundred prisoners; it was fortunate that his whole command was not taken. Gérard himself was seriously wounded.

Although these two checks were unfortunate, there was nothing in them alarming; their worst result was to encourage the newly levied Prussian militia. But to the faults committed in the battle, Oudinot added that of falling back on Wittenberg and thus increased his distance from Luckau and Bautzen, which was the only suitable direction for acting in concert with me. I, therefore, sent Marshal Ney to take command of this army, informing him that I would immediately follow him at the head of my guard, two *corps-d'armée*, and my reserve of cavalry. I hoped, by means of these powerful reënforcements, to push Bernadotte hard, and to get possession of Berlin, which would have produced a powerful influence on the public opinion of Germany and of all Europe. As I hoped that Macdonald would, on his side, push Blucher on Breslau, my two secondary armies would thus find themselves in a good situation, my base would be enlarged, and I might return to strike a mortal blow at the grand allied army in Bohemia. But the sad disaster to my army in Silesia three days after, decided it otherwise.

Macdonald's Disaster at the Katzbach.—It will be remembered that I gave minute instructions to Macdonald on leaving Loewenberg. He was to profit by our joint superiority over Blucher, but it was recommended to him to allow the latter to come to him, then to take the initiative and fall on Blucher with all his corps united on a single point. Instead of waiting for the Prussian general to manifest his projects, Macdonald imagined, from false reports which he had received, that he had only to present himself to induce the enemy to retreat, and to gather the laurels of victory. He was severely punished for his excess of confidence. As the first of a series of unfortunate events, I had ordered Ney to follow me to Dresden, and the marshal, supposing that he was to march with the third corps, had conducted it to Bunzlau ; but learning here that I only wanted him personally and not his troops, he sent them back to the Katzbach, fatigued and worn out by this long and harassing march. Macdonald, still persuaded that he had only to advance to make Blucher fly before him, ordered, for the twenty-sixth of August, the passage of the Katzbach and the Wuthende-Neisse, then directed his three *corps-d'armée* in five columns from Schoenau to Liegnitz, on a front of from eight to ten leagues ;—a strange manner of applying the principles which I had marked out for him in my instructions ! In vain did Sebastiani represent to him the imprudence of engaging himself in the *coupe-gorge* of Crain, without first reconnoitering the enemy, who was reported to be concentrated on the opposite plateau. The marshal obstinately persisted in believing that Blucher was in full retreat on Breslau ; Lauriston directed, by his order, one division by Schoenau in the mountains, while the other two moved to the right against Langeron toward Hennesdorf. Macdonald himself advanced toward the mouth of the Wuthende-Neisse, and debouched on Weinberg at the head of the eleventh corps, while that of Sebastiani was to arrive by Crain on the same point. Souham, on the contrary, had instructions to direct himself on the left by Liegnitz at the distance of three leagues, to pass the Katzbach and fall on the enemy's right; a movement too extended, and which was to deprive him, during the whole battle, of the coöperation of that corps; it was the more to be regretted as there was an excellent ford at Schmoechwitz, very near the field of battle.

By a new fatality, Blucher, who had broken his line in order to cross the river and resume the offensive, now learned, on reaching the heights of Trebelwitz and Betzhof, that our troops were making the passage; his columns were already formed for an attack; from the plateau of Weinberg he discovered all that passed in our ranks and counted our battalions and squadrons as they debouched. In order to engage them to better advantage, he directed the advanced guard of York which formed his centre, to fall back. Thus every circumstance corresponded with the nature of the ground and combined to secure to Blucher immense advantages. As soon as the favorable moment had arrived, the signal was given. Hardly had the columns of the eleventh corps crowned the heights between Janowitz and Weinberg, and the light cavalry of Sebastiani formed toward Eichholz, when the enemy fell upon them from every direction. Our right rested on the deep ravine of the Neisse, but the left was without support; it was here that the Russians directed their efforts. Their cavalry under Wassiltschekof, assails and turns ours between Kleintintz and Eichholz. Sacken debouches from this last village with his infantry. The Prussians under York, who have drawn us forward, now face about and fall upon our line, which is soon driven back upon the deep ravine intended to cover its right. Our cavalry, attacked by superior numbers, falls back on the infantry or disperses to the left; all are now driven pell-mell into the gulf of the Wuthende-Neisse, a dangerous torrent which, in time of flood, becomes, as its name indicates, truly furious.* The disorder is so great that Sebastiani, not being able to regain Kroitsch where he has left his cuirassiers, descends this torrent to its junction with the Katzbach where the remount of his squadrons are saved as if by miracle. To increase the evil, Souham, hearing the cannonade, renounces his march on Liegnitz and falls back with the third corps on Kroitsch, too soon for the combat. The cuirassiers, which Sebastiani has left there in reserve, in ascending to the plateau encumber the passage which is now completely obstructed by the flying soldiers and the trains. On any other ground, this concentric manœuvre of Souham would have repaired everything, but in such a gulf it only tended to increase the confusion. Every effort to ascend this steep hill, crowned as it is by a superior and victorious enemy, proves disastrous. General Tarayre proposes to conduct two divisions by Schmoechwitz to attack the enemy in flank; they cross the Katzbach at night-fall; but Sacken and Wassiltschekof, having already rid themselves of Macdonald, march to meet them and drive them back to the left bank; this tardy movement only serves to compromise them.

During this horrible melée Lauriston fights, with doubtful success, the corps of Langeron about the village of Hennersdorf; the enemy, superior in numbers, is near making him experience the same fate as the centre; for, in addition to his inferiority, Lauriston is deprived of one of his divisions by extending it too far in the mountains toward Schoenau. For us the decisive point of battle was at Hennersdorf; here the ground rose in an insensible glacis to the plateau of Weinberg. If Macdonald, faithful to my instructions, had directed the cavalry of Sebastiani and the eleventh corps to sustain Lauriston, and had left Souham the care of debouch-

* *Wuthende*, signifies *furious*.

ing by Nieder-Crain or Schmoechwitz, the battle would probably have been won by bringing two-thirds of our force upon the decisive point. Blucher, cut off from Bohemia, would have been driven back on Breslau.

Every thing seemed to conspire against us in this unfortunate battle. The flood-gates of the heavens seemed opened, and it rained in perfect torrents, flooding the streams which flow from the mountains of Riesengebirg. The Neisse carried away all its bridges, and the affluents of the Bober so increased that stream as to render it a formidable obstacle. Macdonald, being forced to hasten his retreat, now saw that all the elements had combined to render it disastrous. Lauriston had difficulty in reaching Goldberg, hotly pursued by the corps of Langeron. He did not even venture to remain in this city long enough to rally the division of Puthod, which he had left compromitted in the mountains. The floods had only spared the bridge of Benzlow on the Bober; it was necessary to reach this in all haste, abandoning to the conqueror eighty pieces of artillery, the baggage, and several thousand prisoners. To increase our misfortune, Puthod's division, which had taken the right slope of the mountains, now found itself so engaged that it had not time to reach the main body, and the bridges in their rear were carried away by the flood. Not being able to pass at Hirschberg they descended again opposite Loewenberg, but were no more fortunate here. These delays enabled Langeron to surround them with twenty-five thousand men. They now saw no means of safety but in cutting a passage, sword in hand, on Bunzlau; but being soon surrounded on the heights of Plagwitz and forced back upon the torrent, they laid down their arms, after losing a large number killed in the battle or drowned in attempting to cross the Bober, which can ordinarily be passed without difficulty.

Macdonald returned behind the Queiss after having lost

twenty thousand men, the half of his artillery and a large part of his train. His troops, greatly discouraged and incapable of resistance, called loudly for reënforcements and for my presence to avenge their defeat. The marshal himself, not knowing what to do, begged that I would come in person to his assistance. I had hoped that he would hold out for some days at Goerlitz; but on the third of September, I learned that he had fallen back on Bautzen in frightful disorder.

Napoleon marches to Macdonald's Assistance.—It was, therefore, necessary that I should renounce going to sustain Ney against Berlin, and hasten to Macdonald's assistance. On the third of September, I left Dresden with the corps which I had brought with me from Silesia, and the next day I joined, at Hochkirch, the army of Macdonald, who was preparing to continue the retreat on Bautzen. I faced it about and immediately made it advance; but Blucher had the prudence to avoid an engagement and repassed the Neisse and the Queiss. I did not deem it proper to pursue him; as I still intended to march to the north in order to assist Ney. I, therefore, contented myself with restoring order and courage to Macdonald's army, and reënforcing it with the corps of Poniatowski, which was in observation in the environs of Zittau. I directed Marmont's corps on Hoyerswerda, and, on the sixth, returned in person to Dresden. The advanced guards of the grand allied army had crossed the mountains and now threatened to march on Pirna and Dresden. I deemed it necessary, in preference to everything else, to profit by the present occasion to wash out the affront of Culm and to bring down the presumption of that army. The sixty thousand men which I had left on the left of the Elbe being united in the camp of Dohna, I rejoined them there on the eighth, with my guards. The enemy fought in retreat; we pursued him to the mountains and occupied their summits. But, on the other side, Blucher had resumed the offensive and advanced to Bautzen, and Ney had suffered a bloody defeat at Dennewitz.

Ney's Defeat at Dennewitz.—It is an inconvenience inherent to vast theatres of war, that the general-in-chief can not be present every where; my lieutenants, very good under my own eyes, were wanting in judgment and self-confidence when left to themselves. I experienced a sad proof of this during the present campaign; all those whom I placed at the head of our secondary armies, proved themselves unequal to their command.

On the second of September, my instructions to Ney from Dresden were as follows: "We have just received news of the Duke of Reggio, who has deemed it proper to place himself beyond Wittenberg. The result of this untimely movement is that the corps of General Tauenzien and a strong body of Cossacks have gone in the direction of Luckau and Bautzen, and threaten the communications of the Duke of of Tarentum. *It is truly difficult for any one to have less head than the Duke of Reggio.*

"All here are in motion for Hoyerswerda, where the emperor will have his head-quarters on the fourth. It is necessary for you to march on the fourth, to be at Baruth on the sixth. The emperor will have, on the sixth, a corps at Luckau to form a junction. At Baruth you will be only three days' march from Berlin. Your communication with the emperor will be established, and the attack of Berlin may take place on the ninth or tenth. All this cloud of Cossacks and this mass of poor infantry of the landwehr will fall back on Berlin from every direction, as soon as your march becomes decided. You will see the necessity of manœuvring rapidly in order to profit by the disorder of the grand army in Bohemia, which may otherwise make some movements when it learns the departure of the emperor.

"The Duke of Reggio did not know how to attack the enemy; and he had the simplicity to expose one of his corps separately. If he had attacked the enemy properly he would have been every where victorious.

"Give us positive information of your march."

These instructions are perhaps a little too absolute, and less wise than those given to Macdonald:- it is, however, always understood that an order addressed to a commanding general of an army at a distance is to be taken in its spirit, and not literally; it must be subordinate to the position of the enemy. The slight advantage which the allies had gained over Oudinot confirmed my opinion of their inferiority, and induced me to believe that the defeat of the seventh corps at Gross-Beeren resulted from neglecting the rules of war. I also attached too little importance to the Russian militia, for I did not know their numbers. I had directed Ney to advance on Baruth, and this marshal, proud of our recent victory at Dresden, did not take suitable precautions to avoid a battle, or at least to be prepared for it. As I intended to sustain him in marching by Grossenhain on Luckau with fifty thousand men, in order to turn the army of Bernadotte, and throw it on the Elbe and Magdebourg, it was essential for Ney to base himself by Dahme on Torgau, without troubling himself about the road to Wittenberg. After having driven back the advanced guard of Tauenzien at Zahne and Seyda, he directed himself on Juterbogk. The fourth corps at the left advanced to Naundorf, the seventh at the centre to Tolmsdorf, the twelfth at the right to Seyda.

They were to break their line on the sixth at eight o'clock in the morning to pass Juterbogk. From the dispositions of Ney it would be impossible to imagine the object which he proposed to attain. He himself marched with the fourth corps by Dennewitz, where he arrived at ten o'clock in the morning, and encountered the corps of Tauenzien. Reynier, with the centre, advanced by the road to Rohrbeck; Oudinot and the twelfth corps had orders to march on Oehna, and wait till the seventh had filed past. Ney pretends that he wished to refuse his left; but there is nothing in his dispositions to indicate this, for he made it his turning and acting wing. He ought to have known that Bernadotte was on the great road from Wittenberg to Berlin by Potsdam, and that in this movement he would expose his left flank: no measures, however, were taken to prepare for an attack in that direction. If Ney was ignorant of the enemy's position, it was an inexcusable fault, for he had occupied it ever since the combat of Gross-Beeren, that is, for the last twelve days.

The marshal, debouching at ten o'clock from Dennewitz, engaged the fifteen thousand Prussians of Tauenzien: the fourth corps succeeded in getting possession of the first heights in rear of the wind-mill; but Tauenzien having been reënforced by the left of Bulow, Morand's division was turned, and the corps forced to refuse its left in order to pivot on Rohrbeck. Reynier, leaving later than he ought, finally arrived at Dennewitz; they could think no longer of the disposition of the morning, but were obliged to sustain the left of the fourth corps, threatened as it was by a superior enemy. It was now noon, and the twelfth corps had not even reached Oehna. The allied army, profiting by the information of the night before, made a natural movement to close up to the left; Bulow, placed with thirty-eight thousand Prussians near Kaltenborn, advanced to the assistance of Tauenzien as soon as he heard the sound of the cannon. Bernadotte, placed at Rabenstein, a distance of eight leagues, with seventy battalions and eighty squadrons of Russians and Swedes, united them first at Lobessen, and then advanced in second line towards Eckmonsdorf and Talichau;

he arrived there at three o'clock. It has been shown that Ney defiled with the fourth corps before the front of the Prussian army without knowing it, or suspecting the threatening storm that was about to fall on his left flank. Reynier was to carry, in all haste, Durutte's division in the direction of Nieder-Gersdorf to support Morand's division; as the enemy showed himself in force towards Gehlsdorf, the Saxons were obliged to form a crochet in order to face in that direction. General Thumen assailed Durutte's division at Gersdorf; Bulow turned upon the Saxons, and a serious contest took place on this point.

Oudinot, at the head of the twelfth corps, which was then marching towards Oehna at our extreme right, received orders to approach Dennewitz. Hearing the violent cannonade in the direction of Gehlsdorf, he marched towards that point. The enemy had already driven the Saxons from that village, when Guilleminot's division fortunately debouched, and restored our affairs. These two corps now vigorously repelled the attack of Bulow, and recaptured Gehlsdorf; the victory was doubtful, and, although Bernadotte had not yet engaged his Russians and Swedes, it might still be decided in our favor, or at least remain undecided. But Durutte's division, assailed at Nieder-Gersdorf by thirteen thousand Prussians of Bulow's corps, was driven back beyond Dennewitz, notwithstanding the most obstinate resistance. Ney, threatened by this attack on his left at the same time that Tauenzien forced Morand at the wind-mill, now drew back the fourth corps towards Rohrbeck. Durutte's retreat leaving the centre unsupported, and Bertrand exposed beyond the marshy ravine of Agerbach, Ney, who had not failed to perceive the danger of this state of things, reiterated his order to Oudinot to come and second him between Dennewitz and Rohrbeck. This movement, if it had been punctually executed, would have accelerated his destruction; for at the moment when he was stripping his left of its means of defense, Bernadotte was advancing at the head of forty thousand Russians and Swedes to assist Bulow on the same ground which Oudinot was ordered to leave. Guilleminot's left was threatened at the same instant by Borstel's brigade and four thousand horse, which turned the army by Seehausen. The Saxons, being left exposed to the blows of Bulow, were broken in their turn and driven back on Oehna. Guilleminot's division, being forced to engage itself, required support, and all the tenth corps thus entered into action without being able to reach its destination. The Prussians, who had driven back Durutte, now passed the stream between Dennewitz and Rohrbeck, and thus completed the defeat of the centre, at the same time that the cavalry pressed in the left. Ney vainly attempted to reëstablish his affairs by throwing the cavalry of Arrighi in the gap left by the enemy. Clouds of dust, driven by the wind into our faces, prevented us from making any dispositions, and for a time completely concealed the enemy from our view; besides, the allies had superior squadrons to oppose to his centre, and more than four thousand horse turned his right. As Oudinot found it impossible to assist the fourth corps, all the points were forced to yield. Ney could now do no better than to take the road to Dahme; Oudinot took the road to Schweidnitz and Annabourg; a part of the seventh corps accompanied the twelfth, and the remainder took the road to Hertzberg.

Here, as at Gross-Beeren, Bulow deserved all the honor of the victory. The only thing done by Bernadotte was to draw up a pompous bulletin complimenting those who, like himself, had been idle spectators of the event.

Remarks on this Battle.—The causes of this defeat have been much discussed; each one attributed them to others, whereas all were in some measure involved. Ney was here attacked while on the march, and when he least expected it; as was the case with Oudinot at Gross-Beeren. His right wing fought on the left and his left wing on the right—dispositions which plainly prove that the battle was entirely unexpected. There is a merit in gaining an unexpected battle; but here nothing was done to accomplish that result. Every thing goes to show that Ney mistook the secondary for the principal, in attaching himself exclusively to Tauenzien's corps which covered Juterbogk. His own report, instead of throwing light on his combinations, renders them still more incomprehensible; he wished, he said, to refuse his left, and yet he marched at its head and made it his advanced guard. He wished to manœuvre; and yet every thing indicates that he knew nothing of the enemy's positions. Ney's intellect shone only in the midst of a battle, when the balls were flying round him; there, his *coup-d'œil*, his coolness, and his vigor, were incomparable; but he was unable to combine his operations in the silence of the cabinet, while studying his maps. At the time when armies were encamped in each other's presence, Ney would have been the greatest fighting general of his age, for he could then always see his enemy before him; but in our times, when complicated movements are prepared in the cabinet, he was liable to fail, and he gave a sad proof of this at Dennewitz. The instructions which I gave him were not the best I must confess, but then he was on the spot and should have remedied any defects. His army returned in frightful disorder under the guns of Torgau; it had lost fifteen thousand men killed, wounded, prisoners and stragglers. This defeat was a fit companion to that of the Katzbach.

To defend the glory of this valiant warrior, some have pretended that Oudinot and Reynier did not obey him with zeal and the necessary punctuality. It is true that there was delay and a want of unity in the movements; but his orders were far from clear. Oudinot arrived too late, because he had been directed to wait till the seventh corps had filed past him. Admitting that he had arrived sooner, it proves nothing, for if Ney had beaten Tauenzien at Dennewitz, still the left would have been none the less exposed to all the efforts of Bulow and the Russo-Swedish corps. When Guilleminot was engaged at Gehlsdorf, Ney sent reiterated orders to Oudinot to fly to the support of Bertrand; if he had literally obeyed these orders, there would have been no doubt of the cause of the defeat, for the decisive point of the action was precisely that from which Ney called the twelfth corps. This order was one of the most unfortunate circumstances of the day, and, joined to the want of unity in the attacks made between ten and two o'clock, caused the loss of a battle which could only have been gained by well-combined manœuvres, and a concert of action in their execution. It has been insinuated that the Saxons failed in their duty; it is true that their disorder was complete; but without the assistance of the twelfth corps, how was it possible for them to hold out against at least fifteen thousand men in the first line and as many more in the second? The circumstance which compelled me to suspend my march on Luckau was certainly very unfortunate; but it had no influence whatever on Ney's reverses. I had immediately sent an officer to inform him of it, on the evening of the third, promising, nevertheless, that I would come to join him as soon as I could get rid of Blucher. Even if he had not received this message in time, it would have made no difference; for I could not have reached Dahme till the seventh, and he would, nevertheless, have been beaten on the sixth, from the very nature of the dispositions which he made.

Remarks on Napoleon's Plan of Campaign.—I have described at considerable length these three disasters of Gross-Beeren, the Katzbach, and Dennewitz, because they had a notable influence on the results of the campaign. These multiplied checks have induced some to doubt the wisdom of my plan and the solidity of the principles on which it was based. Nothing is more unjust. If I had had troops more warlike and more accustomed to the fatigues of a campaign, and a greater number of good cavalry, I should have succeeded. A plan based on the alternate employment of a superior mass on the decisive point, requires that the secondary armies which remain on the defensive should be so organized as to fight in retreat and prevent the enemy from cutting them up; but to do this requires good cavalry, especially if your infantry is inexperienced. To judge whether the system of central lines is defective, it is important to establish a parity of means, that is to know what I could have done between the Elbe and the Katzbach with the veteran armies and the eighty thousand horses of the allies.

I do not deny, however, that the system of central lines may be more advantageous with one hundred thousand men against three corps of thirty-three thousand each, than with a mass of four hundred thousand against three armies of one hundred and thirty thousand each. In the first place, it is so difficult to subsist a large force when concentrated in a narrow space; then again it is easier to manœuvre against fractions of thirty thousand men, and to give them mortal blows, than it is against one hundred and thirty thousand combatants. The greater the masses the more the efforts of genius are subjected to the caprice of accident, and the greater the reaction of secondary events. Nevertheless, in this case it was not the system that failed, but the measures for its execution. Could I anticipate that Macdonald would expose himself to so sanguinary a reverse, by acting contrary to my instructions? It would perhaps have been better if I had caused him to retire behind the Queiss, till after the result of the battle of Dresden. The same may be remarked of the operations of Oudinot and Ney against Bernadotte. I had no reason to anticipate their disasters. It, however, would have been better, if, while striking on the decisive point with the troops under my own command, I had merely placed my secondary armies in observation on the defensive. If I deviated from these maxims it was with the hope of diminishing the unfavorable chances which resulted from my inferiority in numbers, by everywhere taking the initiative; and the ill-success of the campaign probably resulted from an excess of confidence in the application of a rule so incontestable. The result would have been different if I could have been everywhere myself, for I could easily have remedied, by good manœuvres, any local and temporary inferiority. Frederic triumphed at Leuthen against triple numbers; and why could not Macdonald, at the Katzbach, with eighty thousand men, have contended with ninety-five thousand? In fact, what was mainly wanting to me in this campaign was two good lieutenants, who understood strategic war: I was certain of nothing where I could not be in person. If I ever had reason to feel the faulty system of my staff organization, it was in these memorable operations. I, of course, could not expect of my lieutenants all that I myself could have done: that was impossible. Arbiter of the reputations of my officers as a great captain, and master of their fortunes as a sovereign, I held in my hands the two most powerful motives which influence the actions of men; as soon as I appeared on any point, confidence, enthusiasm, ambition, fear,—all the passions were united around me, and I acted on my subordinates, making them perform prodigies. My lieutenants, on the contrary, everywhere encountered rivalries and distrust; with equal talent, they, therefore, could not have equaled me in their operations; and, for a still stronger reason, when the disparity of character and genius was greater than that of the means of action. Nevertheless, if the commanders of my secondary armies had understood strategic war, the campaign would certainly have taken a very different turn. Their faults rendered my position more critical every day. My armies were visibly melting away. I foresaw the time when it would be impossible to any longer sustain my defensive position. My marches on the Elbe, fatiguing as they were to our troops, produced no result, except to favor our enemies who were interested in temporizing, inasmuch as they were expecting considerable re-enforcements. General Benningsen, who had organized at Warsaw an army of sixty thousand Russians, was rapidly approaching the theatre of war.

Demonstrations on Bohemia.—Under these circumstances it was necessary to change the line of operations, drawing myself from the centre in order to operate on the extreme left of the allies; but the theatre of war, admirably suited for my first system, became more advantageous to my enemies as soon as I left the Elbe to approach the Saale. It only remained for me to try the offensive, at least to attempt to impose on the enemy. The vanguard of the grand army of the allies had again passed the mountains, and debouched in the plain of Pirna; I marched against it with forty thousand men. On the fifteenth of September we reoccupied Peterswalde, and the next day we dislodged the enemy from Hollendorf. On the seventeenth I made a feint of descending into the valley of Toeplitz; but my advanced guard, which had marched on Culm, being assailed in front and flank by forces infinitely superior, was driven back with considerable loss. Seeing that the enemy was prepared to receive us, I renounced my enterprise, and returned on Dresden.

Third Attempt against Blucher.—Not being able to do anything against the grand army, I hoped to take my revenge on Blucher, whom I knew to be weakened by a large body detached on Camentz. On the twenty-second I repaired to the army of Macdonald, and pushed it forward on Bautzen. After having crossed the forest of Goedau, we found ourselves, on the twenty-third of September, in the presence of Blucher's army, which occupied the position of Bautzen, while the corps which had been directed on Camentz, being now on its return, threatened our left and our communications with Dresden. A battle under such circumstances and against superior forces might produce the most disagreeable results. Being obliged to renounce all offensive projects, I felt the necessity of contracting the circle of my defense. I returned with the army of Macdonald into the position of Weissig, within two leagues of Dresden.

New Plans of the Allies.—While I was thus seeking to find an opportunity to strike some important blow, the sovereigns and the grand army remained at Toeplitz, waiting the arrival of Benningsen who had now crossed the Oder. Those who understood military operations, and appreciated the geographical position of Bohemia, advised that this new army be left to cover Silesia, and that Blucher should file by his left on Bohemia, so as to join the grand army, and, supporting his right wing near Koenigstein, debouch again on my communications with three hundred thousand men. The sovereigns approved this plan, and the order was issued. But Blucher was unwilling to act under Schwartzenberg, and preferred remaining on the opposite side to unite with Bernadotte. His pretext was that if the latter should be left alone before Berlin, that capital would be compromised; he thought it better to send Benningsen into Bohemia. This arrangement amounted to about the same thing; it was of little consequence whether Blucher or Benningsen was sent into Bohemia; the essential thing was to reënforce the decisive point against Dresden. The sovereigns approved this movement, leaving an open field for the ardor of Blucher, his staff and his army. From this time forward all the chances of the campaign turned against me; I had no opportunities to apply my system of war, for there was no longer any proportion between our means.

They assume the Offensive.—Benningsen arrived at Toeplitz near the end of September. The allies were merely waiting for his arrival to assume the offensive. Blucher filed by his right and marched by Elsterwerda and Hirtzberg on Elster where they passed the Elbe the thirtieth of October, after having defeated General Bertrand, who, with eighteen thousand men, opposed the irruption of the allies on the left of the river. In the mean time the Prince Royal of Sweden (Bernadotte) also crossed the Elbe at Acken and Roslau; and the grand army of the allies, which Benningsen had replaced in the valley of Toeplitz debouched by Sebastiansberg on Chemnitz.

Napoleon marches against Blucher and Bernadotte.—It was now evidently the intention of the allies to establish themselves in mass on my rear in order to cut off my retreat. My only chance was to throw myself between their armies and endeavor to fight them in detail. I first resolved to march against Blucher. As I still hoped to preserve the line of the Elbe I left St. Cyr at Dresden with twenty-seven thousand men, and detached the King of Naples to Freyburg with fifty thousand; these two corps were to hold the enemy in check on the side toward Bohemia. With the remainder of my forces I marched on Eilenbourg, where, on the ninth, I rallied Ney's army, which increased my force to one hundred and twenty-five thousand combatants.* I sup-

* Napoleon's army had at this time received a new organization in consequence of the losses sustained by several of his corps. The twelfth corps, (Oudinot) had been incorporated with the fourth. The third, (Ney's old corps, afterward Souham's) had been reduced to three divisions; Albert's division had reënforced Macdonald's corps (the eleventh) after the battle of the Katzbach, and Marchand's division had reënforced Reynier's corps (the seventh) after the disaster of Donnewitz.

posed Blucher at Duben, and the Prince of Sweden at Zoerbig; I learned too late that Sacken, who was at Mockrena, had been separated from the army of Silesia. Had I known this in time I would have pursued and destroyed him. But he again joined Blucher by a rapid march, which did him great credit. All my attention was turned in the direction of Dessau and Duben; if I had gained a decisive battle by destroying the bridge of Roslau and seizing that of Wurtembourg, I would have destroyed that army. The first condition of success was that Murat should be ready to join me without allowing himself to be cut up by the enemy. I recommended to the Prince of Neufchatel, at four o'clock P. M., of the tenth of October, to communicate to him my project, addressing to the former the following instructions: "You will write to the King of Naples that I have received his letter; that I have raised the blockade of Wittenberg; that I have separated Sacken's corps from the corps of Langeron and York; that I have ordered the Duke of Padua to send every thing that can embarrass his movements to Eulenbourg and to Wittenberg; that the Duke of Castiglione is at Lutzen or Leipsic this evening; that the Duke of Padua, having got rid of all that he can send away, will have at least fifteen thousand men, which, united with the Duke of Castiglione, will be to the king a reënforcement of thirty thousand; that one of the two following events will happen; that I will attack the enemy to-morrow and beat him; or that, if he retires, I will burn his bridges, by marching on the right bank. Therefore the King of Naples ought to manœuvre to preserve Leipsic, and give me time to fight the army of Silesia; but if he is obliged to leave Leipsic he ought to direct every thing on the Mulde; that the bridges of Eulenbourg and Duben are guarded; that my instruction in this case is to pass to the right of the Elbe and manœuvre between Magdebourg and Dresden, debouching by one of my four places to surprise the enemy. The King of Naples ought to manœuvre accordingly, etc."

It was important that St. Cyr should be informed at Dresden of the new direction which I intended giving to my operations. Berthier received orders to write to him in cypher, "that I was at Wittenberg, of which place I had raised the blockade; that the army of Silesia was retreating in all directions, on the left bank; that to-morrow I should oblige him to give battle, or to lose the bridges of Dessau and Wartenburg; that perhaps I should then decide to pass to the right bank with all my army; that it was by the right bank that I should move on Dresden."

I founded great hopes on the success of this plan, which might improve our affairs. I, in consequence, ordered Ney to push one corps from Wittenberg on both sides of the Elbe to Roslau, and another from Duben in the direction of Dessau, in the hopes of beating the enemy at the moment that I carried the bridge. But Blucher, being informed of his danger, agreed with Bernadotte to renounce his line of operations, to throw himself behind the Saale, and filed rapidly to the right on Zoerbig where the two armies effected a junction. On the eleventh, they combined their flank movement by the right and gained Halle, where they passed to the left bank of the Saale. This timely movement destroyed the finest opportunity that I had during the campaign; my best combined projects failed; my star was falling.

Project of manœuvring on the Right of the Elbe.—Seeing my operation fail from unforeseen accidents, I now formed one of the boldest projects of my whole life. Blucher and Bernadotte having escaped me, it was probable that the grand allied army would extend itself to the left to connect with them. By remaining between these masses, I no longer had sufficient space for operating, nor the means for striking decisive blows. I should run the risk of a sanguinary reverse;

on the contrary, the places of the Elbe and the Oder would permit me to make myself master of the country which the allies had left to throw themselves into Saxony. I would be established between the Elbe and the Oder, while they would concentrate in the plains of Leipsic. I would get possession of Berlin, and destroy the corps which they had left before Magdebourg, Torgau, Dresden, Glogau, Custrin and Stettin. Having no more bridges on the Elbe, they could do nothing against me, except by a forced passage of the river. I would make Prussia support the weight of the war, and thus prolong the contest.

The strategic theatre of the war on which we were now to decide the destinies of Europe was nearly a square: the Elbe and the Oder formed two sides of which I was master. The Baltic which corresponds to the third side, was alike an obstacle to both; by manœuvring so as to get possession of the fourth side, I would place the enemy between two lines of fortifications, the sea, and my army; I would have no further need of secondary armies: a single victory like that of Dresden would be sufficient to annihilate the enemy; and at the head of two hundred and fifty thousand men I felt certain of gaining it.

This plan appeared too adventurous to my marshals, who desired to fall back behind the Rhine; they, therefore, pressed me to renounce it. I hesitated all the day of the twenty-second. I confess that this plan required more experienced soldiers than those which I then had, and above all more cavalry. I required abundant supplies for my garrisons, and it was important to have allies in Westphalia and Bavaria, upon whom I could depend. If Germany had been as well disposed towards me as Poland, the chances of success would have been more favorable. But with five hundred thousand allies between me and the Rhine, and Germany insurgent, the chances were complicated. I might, however, have opened a road on the left of the Elbe, or if the allies pursued me on Berlin, I might rally on me the garrisons of the fortifications, and throw myself into Bohemia. With my old soldiers of Arcola, of Rivoli, and of Austerlitz, I should not have hesitated to adopt this plan. But now my situation was different. As an emperor I feared to undertake what as a general I should have unhesitatingly adopted.

The Defection of Bavaria renders it impracticable.—The news of the defection of Bavaria, which we received the same day, contributed not a little to shake my resolution. Since the commencement of the campaign this country had been acted upon by the suggestions of the Tugendbund and Austria. The king was sincerely attached to France, in whose service he had passed a part of his youth ; he was full of loyalty and gratitude for what I had done for him ; but he was too good-natured, and too easily influenced. A strong party pretended that Bavaria had lost in independence what she had gained in territory, and that the elector was more a king in 1804, than Maximilian Joseph, first sovereign of the Confederation of the Rhine. They painted me to him as insatiable of blood and power. They offered, on the one side, to guarantee to Bavaria the preservation of her territory, and the establishment of her independence, if she would pronounce against me ; on the other hand, they threatened her with invasion and the partition of her territory, if she took up arms against the coalition. Wrede, the ambitious Wrede, permitted himself to be seduced by this party, and soon became its principal leader. The presence of Augereau's little army towards Wurtzbourg, my first success, and the openly manifested sentiments of the king, had, for a time, imposed on the partisans of Austria. Maximilian had not left me ignorant of the intrigues of this party in his kingdom, nor of his own desire to remain faithful ; and after what he had written to the Prince of Neufchatel in July, I could not anticipate the possibility of his disaffection. His letter was dated Nymphenbourg, July 26th, 1813 ; it runs as follows :

"I profit, my dear Prince, by M. de Fonteville to inform you of my return ; I received yesterday, by two different conveyances, the news that seven thousand Austrians have arrived at Elferdingen ; that they are fortifying themselves ; that twenty-five thousand men are to arrive at Lintz ; and that in all there will be seventy thousand men between Wels and my frontiers. I immediately sent one of my aids-de-camp to learn exactly the state of things. As soon as I receive his report I will send it to you by an estafette. This ought, however, to show you how much I need troops to guard my frontiers, and to prevent in time of war the Tyrolese and the Voralberg from penetrating to the heart of my states . . . . I have not yet seen M. de Fonteville ; I expect him here in half an hour. I will give him all the information he may desire. *My attachment for the Emperor and for the cause of France has never varied for an instant.* You may, therefore, be certain that I will do all in my power to satisfy the desires of his imperial majesty. I only ask that he will not lose sight of the interests of my kingdom, and that he will come to my assistance in case of a war with Austria. However great the efforts which I may make, it will not be possible for me alone to resist for a long time, if the enemy attempt, with a corps of sixty thousand men, the passage of the Inn, I not being able to count on the Tyrol. Wrede is indefatigable. His *corps-d'armée* does wonders. I expect to review them in a few days ; would that it were twice as strong ! . . . . Be so kind as to present my homage to the Emperor : tell him that I am more attached to him than ever, and that if I do not make great efforts, it is because the moral and physical means are wanting. Old Bavaria is sound; also the circle of the upper Danube; a part of the circle of the Iller, the country of Anspach, and the greater part of Salzbourg. The Tyrol and the Bamberg, where there are many members of the old noblesse, Passau and Bayreuth, are partly unsound. It might be well that they should leave, and that I should countenance their departure. The entire loss of trade, and the wants that are the natural result of war, are the causes of this state of feeling. You see, my dear friend, that I have nothing to conceal from you, I am sure you will not abuse my confidence. I have just been in Baden, and have crossed Wurtemberg; the general cry is peace. If it is made, all will be well, and I promise that in less than two years the general feeling will become as favorable as can be desired, and that it will remain so. I am long and prosy, my dear nephew; but it is a month since I wrote to you. Adieu, I embrace you.

"MAX. JOSEPH."

The defeats of the Katzbach and Dennewitz had forced me to call Augereau's corps into Saxony, and it was impossible for the king and his minister, Montgelas, to resist the torrent; the leaders of the party carried their point even in opposition to the wishes of the king. A treaty of alliance was signed with Austria at Ried, and Bavaria acceded to the coalition. As the loss of so necessary an ally greatly diminished my chances of success, I renounced my project of manœuvring between the Elbe and the Oder, the success of which depended upon my being able to throw myself in mass by Magdebourg on Westphalia, or by Dresden into Bohemia, basing myself on Bavaria. Having no longer this alternative left, it would have been absurd to lead a French army between the Elbe and the Oder, leaving in its rear an army already double its numbers, and which the defection of Bavaria would infallibly increase by all the population to the Rhine.

March on Leipsic.—After renouncing this project it was dangerous to remain at Duben, and I was soon recalled in the direction of Leipsic, which place the grand army of the allies was approaching, notwithstanding the efforts of Murat to retard its march. In operating against Blucher I had hoped to conceal my movements for some days so as to have time to defeat and drive him into the Elbe and then return upon the grand army. If this army itself had not had the intention of taking the offensive my calculation would have been crowned with success; unfortunately, the allies, being stronger than I supposed, had resolved to debouch into Saxony even before knowing what course I intended to pursue. This incident and Blucher's march on Halle, deranged every thing. The advanced guards of the allies had already reached Borna and Pegau. I saw that all the forces of the allies were to unite on my rear. But it gave me no uneasiness; I hoped that the movement of Reynier on Roslau, and of Ney on Dessau, inspiring Bernadotte and Blucher with serious fears for Berlin, would decide them to return in all haste by Balbi on the right bank of the Elbe, which would have again separated them from the grand army. In fact the news of these movements alarmed the Prince of Sweden, who, on the thirteenth, fell back to Coethen; but Blucher held firm at Halle, and did not leave that place till he moved on Leipsic, after hearing of my return toward that city. It must be said in favor of the Prussians and Russians that they manœuvred well during this autumn campaign. The country people and the Cossacks informed them of all my movements, and they acted with promptitude.

The grand allied army was now nearly under the walls of Leipsic. It was very important for me not to be anticipated in my movements on this centre of all the communications of the country. I resolved to unite all my forces; knowing that some decisive blows were to be given here, I neglected no means of augmenting my strength by drawing in my detachments. I had already drawn to Leipsic fifteen thousand men of the little army assembled under the orders of Augereau at Wurtzbourg; they arrived there on the thirteenth of October, with a division of dragoons from Spain. In the present state of affairs, I could have desired to draw my troops from Dresden and Hambourg, for I felt that if I was not victorious, their loss would be inevitable, unless St. Cyr and Davoust should get timely notice and be skillful enough to effect their junction with Lemarrois and Narbonne, so as, in concert, to open a passage. I sent them orders to that effect, but they were intercepted.

The Allies concentrate about Leipsic.—I left Duben on the fourteenth, and arrived at Leipsic on the fifteenth; it was well that I did so; for Murat, not being able to contend against such a mass, had fallen back in good order on Leipsic; but he had terminated this honorable retreat by a grave fault. He was in position on the twelfth, in rear of the defile of Magdeborn (the Gozelbach), the right toward Crostewitz and the left at Stormthal. He there received my letter from Duben which informed him of the change in my plan of operations and of my immediate return to Leipsic. He assured me that he would hold Leipsic and a position in advance till the fourteenth, and threw up some intrenchments to cover the position which he occupied. Marmont had received orders to join him and ought to have been at Leipsic on the thirteenth. Murat was still further reënforced by Augereau's two divisions and some fine cavalry. He thus had with him five *corps-d'armée* and a numerous cavalry. Nevertheless, fearing to compromise so considerable a part of my army in a general engagement, and being full of the idea that I would first strike at the north of Leipsic against the combined armies, he suddenly determined to cross the Partha and to hold Leipsic only as a *tête-de-pont ;* the order which I had already sent to Marmont to turn back and observe the road to Halle at Spenditz, confirmed the King of Naples in this idea. His retreat was already begun on the thirteenth, when one of my officers informed him that I would be at Leipsic the next day ; he arrested his movement near Liebert-Wolkowitz, after having yielded to the allies the important defiles of Groebern and Goehren ; a circumstance which produced the most vexatious consequences.

Menaced on the fourteenth by the allies, Murat felt the necessity of repairing his fault. Encouraged still further by the information that I would arrive in the course of the day, he made a vigorous stand at Liebert-Wolkowitz, and threw himself between Wachau and Magdeborn on the numerous cavalry of Barclay who was closely pressing him. Our dragoons, who had just returned from Spain, burning to distinguish themselves, performed wonders. Notwithstanding the talents and bravery of Pahlen, and the charges of a part of the Russian reserves, we were on the point of gaining the victory, when a charge of Prussian cuirassiers on our scattered and harassed soldiers restored the combat in the enemy's favor.

It being urgent to scatter the tempest which was gathering against us from all points of the horizon, I had accelerated, as much as was in my power, the return of the force engaged between Duben and Dessau. It would have been advantageous to give battle on the fifteenth ; but the thing was physically impossible ; the mass of my forces were still too far off. Bertrand and the Young Guard arrived in the night of the fourteenth, toward Euterisch ; Macdonald passed Duben ; Souham, with the third corps, did not arrive till midnight ; he was obliged the next day to take the road to Eulenbourg in order to avoid the blocking up of the road.

Seeing here that the bridge was burned, he ascended the Mulde to find a passage, and on the night of the fifteenth, only reached Rothenhahn on the road to Leipsic. Reynier's corps which had descended the Elbe to Roslau, attempted to reëstablish the batteau-bridge of Bernadotte, so as to return directly, but the difficulty and slowness of the operation forced him to fall back on Wittenberg which retarded him by two days' march. All these incidents forced me to defer my attack till the sixteenth.

The sovereigns, on their side, being informed of my return to Leipsic, and fearing that I might overthrow Blucher, determined to attack me the same day. Proud of their success on the fourteenth, they deemed it advisable not to wait the arrival of Benningsen and Colloredo who could not enter the line before the seventeenth, for fear that I might have leisure in the interval to strike at the army of Silesia. It was, therefore, resolved to attack me on the sixteenth, not so much with the hope of gaining a decisive victory as to gain time for the arrival of all the forces of the coalition on the field of battle where was to be decided the fate of the civilized world.

Singular Project of Schwartzenberg.—Schwartzenberg at first had the singular idea of throwing his reserve and the mass of his army into the *cul-de-sac* between the Pleisse and the Elster, from which he could debouch only by a narrow bridge in the middle of my army; while the right, under the orders of Barclay, composed of the corps of Kleist, Wittgenstein, and Klenau, would advance between Liebert-Wolkowitz, and the Pleisse. If this arrangement had been followed the total defeat of the grand allied army would have been certain. But the Emperor Alexander, after having vainly demonstrated to Schwartzenberg the foolishness of his project, positively declared that his troops and those of the King of Prussia should remain on the right of the

Pleisse. Thus the grenadiers, the guards, and the reserves, —thirty-five thousand men of the *élite*, were retained at the decisive point by the firmness of the Emperor Alexander. The Austrian generalissimo persisted, on his side, in carrying his own forces into the *cul-de-sac* of Connewitz. Giulay's corps was still detached by Zwenkau to turn Leipsic and get possession of the great road to Lindenau. This position of the allies was too extended; Blucher and Bernadotte being then at Halle, it would perhaps have been better for the grand army to direct itself on Zeitz, so as to establish two hundred and fifty thousand men on my communications. Benningsen should have been directed from Coldiz on Altenbourg, to cover the road to Bohemia during this movement. Nevertheless, it is just to agree, that, as the march of Blucher and Bernadotte on the Saale was not the consequence of a plan concerted with the sovereigns, and as the latter had at Altenbourg only a vague notion of what the two armies of the north were doing, they could not form any plan of operations on such data. It was, therefore, natural that they should adopt the plan of marching directly against me, at the same time seeking to trouble my line of retreat. For this purpose it was agreed that the grand army of Bohemia should advance on Leipsic by the right bank of the Pleisse, carrying on my communications only the force necessary to get possession of the defiles and arrest the heads of my columns in retreat. Giulay's corps was sufficient for this; but it would have been well to give it three or four thousand more horse, for the allies had plenty of cavalry. The remainder of the allied troops should then have followed the main army, throwing only a light division into the space between Rotha and Zwenkau, in order to keep up the communication with Giulay; to place forty thousand men in this funnel was a ridiculous idea.

First Day of Leipsic, October 16th.—I did not at first perceive the exact bearing of the allies' movement; but I felt that whatever course they might take, a vigorous effort on Wachau could alone gain me the victory. I had given to Ney the command of all the forces north of Leipsic, *i. e.*, the corps of Bertrand, Marmont, Souham. There was every reason to suppose that Blucher, filing from Halle by his right, would come to attack us by the road to Mersebourg, in order the better to connect himself with the grand army. Nevertheless it was possible that he would carry his right on Leipsic by Skeuditz, and it, therefore, became necessary for me to prepare for either case. My first project had been to draw to me two of Ney's corps near Wachau, in order there to strike the necessary blow for restoring our affairs; the third corps, arriving from Duben, would relieve Marmont toward Moeckern, where he had observed a position very favorable for resisting a superior force, and where he had thrown up some intrenchments to strengthen it. If this first disposition had been executed I should have had forty thousand more men at Wachau, and the army of Bohemia would have been exposed to a defeat the more complete as Schwartzenberg accumulated fault upon fault. But while the allies were preparing to attack me only partially, fortune opposed me by a series of accidents which deranged all my plans.

I had expected that the duke of Padua would be sufficient with seven or eight thousand men for the defense of Leipsic: on the approach of Giulay's entire corps, threatening the passage of Lindenau (the only one which remained in case of retreat), Ney thought he ought to direct Bertrand there; and at six o'clock this general was already in motion on Liebert-Wolkwitz. Marmont, on his side, had not yet been relieved by the third corps, when, being delayed, as has been said, at the passage of the Mulde, he was informed of the approach of Blucher's advanced guard. His situation was critical; to retire without fighting would draw the enemy on Leipsic, and prevent Marmont from assisting me at Wachau. He prepared to hold on between Moeckern and Euterisch, so as not to lose Leipsic. Ney, thinking that this marshal was already acquainted with the localities, and that it would be as well to leave him on this point, resolved to replace him towards Wachau by the three divisions of the third corps which were to arrive at two o'clock. The result of these different contrarieties was that the forty thousand which I expected to reënforce me in order to assail the army of Bohemia, did not arrive.

If the victory had been certain, Ney might have thrown only one division of Bertrand at Lindenau, and the other on the northern faubourg of Leipsic, while Marmont and the third corps marched to Wachau; it is probable that Giulay and Blucher would not have been ready to make a serious attack on Leipsic on the sixteenth. Reënforced in time by Marmont and Souham, I might have turned the right of the allies, and have thrown Barclay into the Pleisse, while Schwartzenberg so foolishly shut himself up in the *cul-de-sac* of Connewitz; I would have collected immense trophies, and, pursuing the enemy to Zeitz, I would have opened a new line of retreat on Naumbourg, without troubling myself about Blucher's temporary occupation of Leipsic. But in truth this disposition would only have given me another victory, without, however, destroying or disabling my enemy; for Blucher and Bernadotte united could have followed in my rear, while Schwartzenberg, reënforced by Benningsen and Colloredo with sixty thousand men, would still have had one hundred and fifty thousand combatants to oppose me. I should still have been in the midst of two hundred and forty thousand enemies. The parks of my army, united at Eulenbourg, as well as Reynier's corps which was on the march to that city, would have been cut off, and forced to throw themselves on Torgau. It would be difficult to decide what change in the respective situation of the parties a more complete victory at Wachau would have produced. What combinations could affect an enemy who in a single day received reënforcements of one hundred thousand men? It was the disorganization which such a defeat would have produced at the head-quarters of Schwartzenberg which alone could rescue me, and prove whether the abandonment of Leipsic by Marmont had been a prudent measure. In the uncertainty of the event, it would have been playing a hazardous game.

The battle began on the sixteenth of October, at nine o'clock in the morning, that is, two hours sooner than I desired. I had intended to take the initiative, but the enemy first attacked us. Klenau on the right debouched in force by the woods of the university on Liebert-Wolkwitz and the Kohlberg. Wittgenstein moved on Wachau, and Kleist on Mark-Kleeberg. This first effort was sustained by Murat's forces. Lauriston vigorously defended Liebert-Wolkwitz; Belluno repulsed the enemy's attempts on Wachau; but Poniatowski had to abandon Mark-Kleeberg for a moment to the Prussians. I had just arrived from Reudnitz, near Liebert-Wolkwitz; the Young and Old Guards followed me; but they had not yet debouched on my right. The movement of the enemy made it necessary for me to change my dispositions. I sent Augereau from my left to the right, to sustain Poniatowski. Two divisions of the Young Guard, under Mortier, manœuvred at the left of Lauriston against the right of Klenau; the other two, under Oudinot, marched to the support of Belluno at Wachau. A fine mass of cavalry established itself as a third line in rear of the centre; and my reserve of artillery, placed along the front, opened its fire upon the enemy. A heavy cannonade followed along the line, and the combat continued till near noon, with varied success. Klenau was repulsed by Mortier and Lauriston. Poniatowski, sustained by Augereau, recaptured Mark-Kleeberg. At the centre Oudinot and Belluno drove back Wittgenstein on Stoermthal and Gossa.

In the meantime Schwartzenberg presented himself in person with the main body of the Austrians at the defiles of Connewitz and Doelitz, where he could not debouch. Lefol's division defended the first, and Sémélé's division from Augereau's corps covered the second.

Standing on the heights of Meysdorf I was still full of hope ; everything authorized me to expect a decisive victory; for Macdonald was finally debouching from Halzhausen, while Ney informed me from Euterisch, at half past ten o'clock, that Marmont was about marching to join me, and that even the third corps might follow him if Blucher should not appear in force on the road to Halle ; finally, Bertrand's corps, which had bivouacked between Euterisch and Leipsic, would be sufficient to guard the town, and drive Giulay from Lindenau. I immediately make dispositions to act more vigorously on the offensive, and to strike a decisive blow. I order Latour-Maubourg to carry the positions of the Russian corps at the right and left of Gossa, and direct Victor and Lauriston to sustain him. The most brilliant success crowns this double charge, although Latour-Maubourg has his leg carried away by a ball, and a part of his corps somewhat thrown into confusion by this accident. Nevertheless Bordesoult's division of cuirassiers supplies its place ; they throw themselves on the left of Prince Eugene of Wurtemberg, carry a battery, charge upon the battalions, overthrow the division of light cavalry of the guard which makes a flank-movement against them, and push on to the Emperor Alexander. This prince immediately engages the Cossacks of the élite, who served him as an escort. In a moment the batteries of the reserve of the guard are unmasked, Barclay's cavalry hastens to the threatened point, and as the wound of Latour-Maubourg prevents him from making suitable arrangements for sustaining the charge of our cuirassiers, it does not produce the result which I expected: the enemy even resumes the offensive on Gossa, and our squadrons re-form in rear, at the moment when our infantry is advancing to occupy the conquered ground.

Schwartzenberg, deaf, until ten o'clock, to all the representations of the Russian officers, had finally become convinced of the exposed condition of his right and that it was necessary to return to its assistance. All the efforts of Merfeldt to debouch from Doelitz having been unsuccessful, the prince then decided to return by Baschewitz on the right bank of the Pleisse, which, for his own glory, he should never have left; he brought back with him two divisions of cuirassiers and two divisions of grenadiers of the Prince of Hesse-Hombourg. This resolution, although very tardy, had its effect. The divisions of Austrian cuirassiers passed the Pleisse at a ford, and debouched from Groebern, at the moment when Kleist was warmly pressed. They fell between Augereau's corps and the cavalry, overthrew the latter, and pushed on to the Young Guard, at the very moment when Latour-Maubourg was effecting so much against the guard of the sovereigns on the heights of Gossa.

This charge of the enemy, which penetrated almost to me, gave me some uneasiness; on the other side the sound of cannon was heard at the north of Leipsic; Marmont, so far from being able to second me, was himself strongly engaged. The divisions of Russian grenadiers had just given renewed strength to the centre of the allies; the earth seemed to be covered with enemy's battalions, in proportion as we extended our horizon. I did not venture to sustain the gap between Latour-Maubourg and Belluno with my Old Guard, and all the remainder of my forces was already engaged. Macdonald was engaged with Klenau whom he had driven far enough. The fine cavalry from Spain which sustained him had been paralyzed by the wound of General Pajol who commanded it. This state of things left me slight hopes of gaining a decisive victory. The Russians, rallied at Gossa, held there with savage obstinacy; the arrival of the guards and Austrian grenadiers who debouched on the right of the Pleisse, in returning toward Crostewitz, had changed the chances of victory. Our first success was glorious, but it had not changed the situation of affairs. It was important to obtain other results before the close of the day. This motive induced me to attempt toward six o'clock a final effort. I was preparing for a decisive attack on Stoermthal and Groebern, when my attention was drawn to the rear of my right where the enemy had just passed the Pleisse. Schwartzenberg, not wishing to give up his project of passing at Doelitz, and thinking that the arrival of the Austrian grenadiers at Mark-Kleeberg would facilitate the passage of Merfeldt, had directed him to renew his attempts. Five or six Austrian battalions, having gained possession of Doelitz, now sought to debouch, followed by the whole *corps-d'armée.* Séméle's exhausted division could no longer resist them. I threw against them the Old Guard under General Curial, the only troops which remained disposable. Poniatowski also sent there his reserve; in an instant the head of Merfeldt's column was surrounded and captured; he himself was made prisoner with a thousand men; the remainder were driven into the Pleisse. The arrival of Brayer's division of the third corps completed the security of this point. However, the concentration of so many forces between Kluberg and the farm of Auenheim enabled the enemy to take Oudinot obliquely; and our centre instead of continuing its progress, deemed itself fortunate in maintaining its position against the masses which were opposed to it. Night scarcely terminated the protracted carnage.

Our affairs at the north of Leipsic had not been so successful. Marmont had just received orders to join me, when Blucher, anxious only for a fight, appeared in pursuit and forced him into an engagement; although this prevented him from arriving on the point where I expected to decide the combat, it would not have been so important if the divisions of the third corps, which were to relieve him had arrived in time; they could either have taken his place, or have fought at his side. They, however, did not make their appearance, till very late, toward Schoenfeld, and Ney, who wished to leave the defense of Lindenthal to Marmont, carried the third corps to the right and left of Wachau when the battle was about terminated. Marmont, left to himself, had too strong a party against him. To increase the misfortune, Delmas's division, which was returning by the road from Duben with the artillery of the third corps, would have been compromised if the enemy had known how to profit by his superiority. Dombrowski's division which was to hold Wetteritz until his arrival, sustained the efforts of Langeron's corps, but could not preserve the village. Fortunately, the enemy's patrols mistook Delmas's long column for a considerable corps, and were thus imposed upon. This general arrived at Wetteritz in the night, greatly harassed but without any important losses. Ney, on being informed of Marmont's check and of the danger of Delmas, was obliged to fall back in order to favor the retreat of Delmas, as well as that of the sixth corps. If the seven divisions of Ney, Marmont, and Dombrowski had been united, Blucher would no doubt have been beaten; but as the third corps lost the whole day in marches and countermarches, it was impossible for Marmont's twenty thousand men to contend with sixty thousand. His troops, nevertheless, defended with rare valor the village of Moeckern, where our soldiers of the marine covered themselves with glory. They were driven back on Eutritsch and

Gohlis with the loss of twenty pieces of artillery and four thousand men *hors-de-combat.* An additional park of thirty pieces was captured in the night bivouac by the Cossacks.

This check was the more unfortunate for us, as it was important to preserve the possession of Taucha on account of Reynier's corps, which was returning from Wittenberg by Eulenbourg. The fine defense of the sixth corps, and the return of the divisions of the third corps during the night, enabled us to accomplish this object.

Napoleon proposes an Armistice, which is refused.— It was truly unfortunate for us that we had not gained a decisive victory on the sixteenth. Although the last reports from St. Cyr made me doubt the near arrival of Benningsen, I knew that the Prince of Sweden would soon join Blucher. I would then be obliged to evacuate Leipsic, or to fight a new battle with all the chances against me. I was well aware that the loss of this city would render our position very precarious; with the few men that remained I could only hope to defend, foot by foot, the space that separated me from the Rhine; and as the loss of a battle could produce no other consequence, I determined to accept it. I, however, hesitated whether I should receive it before Leipsic or behind the Saale: my bad fortune prevailed. Nevertheless, before coming to blows again, I resolved to attempt to open negotiations. On the seventeenth I sent to the allies General Merfeldt who had been taken prisoner the day before, with proposals for an armistice, and the evacuation of all the places of the Vistula, and the Oder; and even those of the Elbe. Under the pretext of referring the matter to the emperor of Austria, Schwartzenberg did not reply; and the allies, being reënforced in the evening by more than one hundred thousand men, resolved to crush me on the morning of the eighteenth. I, however, did not sleep in the hope of a favorable answer; I waited for Reynier's corps and my head-quarters which were to join me from Eulenbourg on the evening of the seventeenth. If I should receive no satisfactory answer to Merfeldt's mission during the day, it was my intention to draw in my lines towards Leipsic during the night so as to retreat on the eighteenth. This delay was the more unfortunate as Giulay had just fallen back on Zwenkau, and nothing opposed my commencing the retreat on the seventeenth, immediately after the arrival of Reynier.

In fact, Schwartzenberg, like all pusillanimous generals, continually went from one extreme to another. Not content with being reënforced by two entire armies, he thought to draw Giulay into the narrow space between the Pleisse and the Elbe, in order to replace there the Austrian troops which had been withdrawn on the sixteenth to reënforce the centre at Wachau; this measure, which opened to me the road to Erfurt, was without justification; for after the arrival of a reënforcement of one hundred thousand men, it would have been much better to reënforce Giulay's corps, which was admirably placed for operating on our communications. I thus permitted to escape the only occasion which offered for effecting a safe retreat. I was influenced by the fear that this premature retreat might prevent the conclusion of the proposed armistice, and by the good augury for Merfeldt's mission which I derived from the absolute calm which reigned in the allied army. I was deceived: the allies were only waiting for the arrival of all their forces for a general attack.

The Allies re-enforced by Bernadotte, Benningsen, and Colloredo.—Bernadotte approached by the road to Landsberg; Benningsen, after leaving twenty thousand men before Dresden, marched with forty thousand men by Colditz on Leipsic; finally, Colloredo also rejoined the grand army with two Austrian divisions; all these corps arrived on the evening of the seventeenth. This gave the allies an additional force of near one hundred and twenty thousand men. Seeing on the night of the seventeenth and eighteenth, that Merfeldt did not return, I began to feel uneasy, and made preliminary dispositions for the evacuation of Leipsic; but the material was so considerable, and the defiles so long and numerous, that it required twenty-four hours to effect it with order in the presence of the enemy. However, as I had, at Wagram, in twelve hours in the night, constructed six bridges, and deployed an army on the Marchfeld, I hoped to succeed here. I, therefore, resolved to maintain a firm attitude on the eighteenth, in order to approach Leipsic in the evening: but the enemy did not give me time.

Second Day of Leipsic, October 18th.—The great battle which was to decide the fate of Europe took place on the eighteenth of October. While still waiting for Merfeldt's reply, I was informed of the approach of the enemy's columns on all sides. I had but one hundred and fifty thousand men to oppose three hundred thousand. To avoid being turned I placed my army in a semi-circular position with the wings resting on the Pleisse and the Partha. Bertrand's corps remained at the left of the Elster to defend the road to Naumbourg. The enemy attacked us on all the points of this semi-circle. The first positions of Holzhausen and Wachau were disputed only to give time to take a definitive position towards Probsthayde and Stoetteritz. Here was fought the real *battle of the giants.*

This second battle of Leipsic, although the most important of the age in its results, offers but little of interest in its relation to the military art. Three hundred thousand allies, crowded in a semi-circle of three or four leagues, offered no weak point; however much I might manœuvre, I was certain to find an impenetrable line, equally strong throughout. The battles of Fleurus, Friedland, and Essling are the only battles in our last wars that bear any resemblance to it. In all three, it was an army attacked by concentric columns, with a river in its rear. In the first, Jourdan was placed like myself in a semi-circle, with the Sambre behind him; but he was attacked with equal forces, and Cobourg occupied a line of ten leagues with less than eighty thousand men, so that it was not difficult to make a successful effort against any point of this too extended line. At Friedland the Russians, too much concentrated around the city, with the Alle behind them, were assailed by my four *corps-d'armée* in a circular and well-sustained line: their front being separated by a stream and a lake, enabled me to break their left separately, which exposed their right to inevitable destruction. But I had none of these favorable chances in the second battle of Leipsic. The only hope of victory which remained, was in the isolation of Blucher and Bernadotte on the right of the Partha, which enabled me to paralyze them the whole day by a weak corps of observation. But even this hope was not of long duration. These ninety thousand men, leaving Sacken's corps to attack the gate of Halle, passed the river in the morning between Taucha and Schoenfeld, and assailed Ney. There was now no means of supplying by good combinations my inferiority in numbers and material: it had become a butchery with no other object than to await the approach of night, in order to commence our retreat.

Notwithstanding our extreme inferiority in numbers, and the defection of the Saxon and Wurtemberg troops, who in the middle of the battle turned their arms against us, my army sustained itself admirably. I was myself surprised at the bravery and devotion of my young soldiers; a thousand pieces of cannon carried death into their ranks without breaking them; yet these were the same soldiers who had fought at the Katzbach and Dennewitz! Why this difference?

At break of day we begin our movement of concentration, at the moment when the enemy's masses are preparing to assail us on all sides. Belluno and Lauriston leave Wachau to take position, the first to the west of Probsthayde, and the second to the left of that village in the direction of Stoetteritz. They are followed foot by foot by the enemy, who assails their rear-guard, but without cutting it up. Poniatowski places himself to their right; Augereau closes the line between Loessnig and Connewitz. Oudinot, with two divisions of the Young Guard, serves as a reserve to this right wing. I place myself at the centre behind Belluno at a quarter of a league from Probsthayde, with Mortier's Young Guard, the Old Guard of Curial, and the reserve of cavalry. Macdonald, who has yielded Holzhausen to the masses of Klenau and Benningsen, draws in the eleventh corps and Sebastiani's cavalry from Stoetteritz and Molkau, to connect with Lauriston. Ney commanded the left, which extended from Paunsdorf to Schoenfeld. Our line formed a kind of obtuse angle with the vertex at Probsthayde.

Blucher, leaving Sacken to assail the faubourg of Leipsic on the side of Gohlis and the intrenchments of the gate of Halle, attacks Schoenfeld with the Russian corps of Langeron and St. Priest. Bernadotte assails Sellerhausen with Bulow and the Swedes. General Benningsen attacks Paunsdorf by his right and Zweinaundorf by his left, seconded by Klenau's corps. Kleist and Wittgenstein's corps, followed by the reserves, advance from Wachau on Probsthayde. The Austrians of Colloredo and Bianchi close the line to the Pleisse toward Connewitz. The interval between these two rivers was at this time abandoned to a light division; and Giulay receives orders, although too late, to carry himself again on Zwenkau so as to threaten the great road to Lutzen.

The enemy's masses employed a part of the morning in taking their positions. Toward noon the engagement becomes general; Colloredo, Bianchi, and the Prince of Hesse-Hombourg attack our right along the Pleisse. The weak divisions of Augereau and Poniatowski heroically defend the approaches to Loessnig and Connewitz. At the point of yielding to an overwhelming superiority, they are sustained by Oudinot's two divisions of the Young Guard, which restores the combat and enables them to maintain themselves with great firmness in these two villages and the broken ground that separates them from the Pleisse. At the centre the allied sovereigns seem to wish to strike a decisive blow on the salient point of our line at Probsthayde; on this point the army of Bohemia directs its efforts. Wittgenstein and Kleist, sustained by the Russian reserves, throw themselves with audacity on this village. Fortunately I had foreseen this; in addition to the corps of Belluno and Lauriston, I had assembled on this point the Old Guard, Mortier's Young Guard, and two corps of cavalry under the King of Naples. I also brought into line Drouet's artillery of reserve. The enemy advanced in very deep columns because the space becomes narrower as they approach, and there is no room to deploy. The movement is effected with such rapidity that only a part of the artillery can follow. Prince Augustus of Prussia forms the head of Kleist's column: Prince Gortschakof sustains him, and also the rest of Wittgenstein's corps. Their first battalions have already reached Probsthayde, when the second and third corps charge them with vigor and drive them back. Exposed to the fire of the sharp-shooters who occupy the gardens and the village, and the one hundred pieces of cannon which pour grape into their ranks, and menaced by our columns, they halt in the space which separates the lines, and reply with a murderous cannonade which is continued till dark. Further to the left, Kleist and Benningsen concentrate their march on Holzhausen and Zweinaundorf, from which they afterward debouch against the heights of Stoetteritz and Molkau, defended by Macdonald and the cavalry of Sebastiani; these troops maintain themselves in their position with the same success as on the right.

My left wing, under the orders of Ney, was not so fortunate as the centre. Blucher and Bernadotte, having passed the Partha at Taucha with ninety thousand men, directed themselves on Schoenfeld and Paunsdorf, where they connected with the corps of Benningsen. This last village was occupied by the Saxons under Reynier. Marmont guarded the space from there to Schoenfeld; Souham, with the third corps, served as a reserve. Marmont defends with much vigor the approaches and the village of Schoenfeld against Langeron. Reynier, menaced by Bubna at the right and by Bulow at the left, retires on Sellerhausen. Ney, who sees all the danger of a retrograde movement, runs to the threatened places and brings Durutte's division on Paunsdorf. The Saxons, being left to themselves, advance toward the enemy; this movement is at first attributed to an excess of audacity; but all at once their artillery is turned against us, and our brave and astonished troops witness the most odious defection ever recorded in the pages of history. Reynier, being now reduced to only the single division of Durutte, threatened on the right by Bubna and on the left by Bulow, is fortunate in finding a refuge at Sellerhausen. Marshal Ney sustains him with Delmas's division; Marmont draws in his right to maintain himself in line, and continues to defend Schoenfeld with his left. The combat is continued with animosity on this part of the line; and it is not difficult for Bulow's corps, seconded by Bubna, the Saxons, and the Swedes, to penetrate to Sellerhausen, notwithstanding the defense of the handful of brave men under Durutte and Delmas. Ney's right is thus forced back in the direction of Reudnitz. Being informed at Probsthayde of the defection of my allies and the retreat of the seventh corps, and fully appreciating the evil results of permitting the enemy to penetrate to the faubourg of Leipsic, I fly with the cuirassiers of Nansouty on the threatened point. I find Ney occupied in rallying his right near Strassenhoeuser. He throws himself on Bulow, whom I attack in flank with the cuirassiers of Nansouty from the direction of Moelkou, and drive back the head of his column on Sellerhausen. Being now more safe on this point, I return to my centre, which requires all my care. The combat near Strassenhoeuser degenerates into a murderous cannonade, as at Probsthayde. Bernadotte brings on this point the Saxon and Swedish artillery, and the English rocket batteries, with which he overwhelms the brave soldiers of Delmas and Durutte; the first of these two generals, the intrepid and republican Delmas, falls under this murderous fire; his troops, again forced to yield to an overwhelming superiority, return to Strassenhoeuser.

But if the enemy's artillery had a superiority over that of Delmas, ours had an equal advantage at Probsthayde over the deep masses of the enemy, who obstinately refused to retire. In vain did some of the Russian generals, certain that we would be obliged to retreat on the nineteenth, propose to stop this useless carnage, and to carry the reserves of cavalry and Giulay's corps on the road to Lutzen. This advice shared the fate of most other advice of the same character, and was not followed. The allies, like Kutusof at Krasnoe, were satisfied with a half success which rendered certain our retreat beyond the Rhine. They, however, withdrew some of their masses, after leaving them for a long time uselessly exposed to our fire.

Blucher and Langeron had not encountered less obstacles in attacking Schoenfeld, which was defended with great valor by Lagrange, Campans and Frederick; it was many times lost and retaken. These troops of Marmont, weakened by the battle of the sixteenth, and by this bloody contest, were on the point of yielding, in spite of the most glorious efforts. Campans was wounded; Frederick killed; Marmont saw his chief of staff and his aids-de-camp fall by his side; a few moments longer and the sixth corps would have been destroyed, when Ney threw upon the enemy the two divisions of the third corps, which had remained in reserve. Schoenfeld, lost and taken for the seventh time, remained in our possession, when the retrograde movements of the right and the approach of Langeron's reserve induced Ney to retire his left to within pistol shot of that village.

At the north of Leipsic, the corps of Sacken and York had made an unsuccessful attempt to carry the faubourg of Halle, which had been secured from a *coup-de-main*, and defended by Dombrowski's division and the cavalry of the Duke of Padua. In the direction of Lindenau, Bertrand, having received reënforcements, easily drove away Lichtenstein's division of Giulay's corps and opened the road to Weissenfels.

It will be seen by this narrative that we lost very little ground on the left, while the rest of the line maintained its position, and none of our corps were broken, thanks to the little use which the enemy made of his cavalry. This was much for glory; but it could have no influence on the success of the campaign; for, in the desperate situation of our affairs, a half-success was equivalent to a defeat.

Third Day of Leipsic, October 19th.—The battle, being continued till after dark, and the troops being worn out with fatigue and hunger, it was very difficult to effect a retreat in the night. To accomplish this with convenience required seventeen secondary bridges on the Pleisse and the Elster. The equipages should have filed on the eighteenth, under the protection of Bertrand's corps: on the contrary they were left heaped up between the army and Leipsic; not only had

Berthier done nothing himself to prepare for this retreat, but he had countermanded all the prudent measures taken by his staff officers, lest the preparations for retreat might discourage our troops. Nor had the chief of engineers supplied the necessary means for bridges; his park, it is true, had been left with the heavy equipages of the head-quarters at Eulenbourg; but there were sappers in the second *corps-d'armée*, and tools and carpenters in the city of Leipsic. I had ordered three supplementary bridges to be thrown across the Pleisse; but this order, given in haste and a little too late, was not well executed. The bridges were badly constructed and gave way. In fact, every thing in the army now seemed to depend on me alone; it was necessary for me to attend to every thing.

We had crossed the Danube in eight hours at Wagram at night with one hundred and fifty thousand men; but it was on six fine bridges, where each corps had its debouch arranged beforehand, and where the baggage did not pass till long after the army. In retreat, through the streets of a city, by a single narrow bridge, the operation is very different; and there necessarily resulted great confusion and crowding: the cowardly always push first, and two or three broken wagons are sufficient to stop everything in such a narrow defile. All these evils happened to us.

The break of day on the nineteenth found us in all the frightful embarrassments of a retreat. We were obliged to receive still another battle in order to effect it. The troops were ranged around the enceinte of the faubourgs which had previously been barricaded; they might easily be defended for twenty-four hours, if our troops should fight as at Dresden. We would thus gain time for the withdrawal of our forces, each corps passing successively from the combat into the line of retreat. Tactically speaking, our position was not bad, for Leipsic might be considered as a *tête-de-pont* covering the defile. There, however, was a lack of bridges to accelerate the retreat, and prevent accidents. There were required two bridges above, and two below the main road, covered with redans, connecting with the passage of Lindenau; and roads to these bridges should have been opened through the gardens. But we had returned from Duben only on the fifteenth; we had hoped to gain a battle on the sixteenth; and on the seventeenth had counted on an armistice; so that the necessary precautions for accelerating and securing a retreat had been neglected. The blame of this must rest on my major-general and the chief of engineers, rather than on me. I had passed the night in dictating such orders as were rendered necessary by our retreat upon the frontiers of France; I wrote to the council of the Regency, to Mayence, to Strasbourg, and to the whole line of the Rhine; to the lower Elbe, to Italy, to Spain, to Dantzic, to the Oder, to Dresden, to Torgau. I thought of all the great combinations which would be required in future: it was for Berthier, my chief of staff, to attend to the remainder. As soon as it was day, I went to see the king of Saxony, to advise him to trust his fate to the generosity of the kings who had recognized him, but reminding him that France had always been a better ally to the house of Saxony than either Austria or Prussia.

On leaving the king, I saw the horrible jam in all the streets of Leipsic, and moved towards the defile. The battle was continued along the whole circumference at any attempt made by the *corps-d'armée* to retire on the faubourgs of Leipsic. At the north, Sacken and Langeron attacked Pfaffendorf which was defended by Durutte; Woronzof and Bulow attacked the gates of Grimma and Hinterthor which were defended by Marmont and Ricard. At the south, Schwartzenberg pressed the Poles along the Pleisse; Barclay pushed Macdonald and Lauriston coming from Probsthayde by Strassenhoeuser. It was impossible for me to direct any movement. At nine o'clock I went to the gate of Ranstedt where the crowd and jam were frightful; I returned by the boulevards to gain the bridge. Belluno and Mortier had passed the defile; Souham and Marmont followed. Lauriston had formed his troops to pass in his turn.

But the successive evacuation weakened our lines, in proportion as the enemy's columns became more animated, and approached nearer to the city of Leipsic. They had already forced an entrance into the faubourgs, and had gained the western part of the boulevard which separates them from the old enceinte: the Badois had abandoned to them the gate of St. Peter, thus opening an access to the city, through which several columns of the allies precipitated themselves. The three *corps-d'armée* which had remained for its defense had no other course than to gain in haste the great road, and to defend themselves on the right and left by means of the houses of the faubourg of Ranstedt.

They succeeded in throwing themselves into this space; but the immense parks and equipages blocked up all the passages. Nevertheless the mass would have been gradually retired, had not the officer who was designated to destroy the bridges after the passage confided the important charge of blowing up the bridge of the mill on the great arm of the Elster, to a simple corporal of sappers. Langeron, following the boulevards from the north, extended himself in a parallel line to the west, and in order to gain our lines of retreat, his tirailleurs, being deployed in the gardens, succeeded in penetrating to the bridge. The corporal, on seeing the approach of the enemy, and thinking that only a few of our troops remained behind, put fire to the mines, and blew up the only means of retreat left to our rear-guard. These troops were now without hope. The boldest threw themselves into the Elster, and attempted to swim across; Macdonald saved himself, but Poniatowski was drowned.* A few thousand effected their escape; but near fifteen thousand, hemmed in by the enemy's masses, were obliged to lay down their

* The terrible losses sustained by the French in this evacuation of Leipsic shows the immense importance of having with such large armies a sufficient number of properly instructed engineer officers and engineer troops for the management of mines and pontoon bridges. The Russian campaign had destroyed the best part of this corps, and there had not been time to instruct others. The following is Thiers' account of this catastrophe:

"But whilst this terrible evacuation of Leipsic was thus taking place, a sudden catastrophe which might have been but too clearly foreseen, spread despair among the ranks of those who for the common safety had been intrusted with the defense of the Leipsic faubourgs. Colonel Montfort, of the engineers, had been ordered to prepare a mine under the first arch of the bridge, along which our troops were now effecting their retreat, and he had, accordingly, done so, and had posted at the spot some sappers with a corporal, who awaited, match in hand, the signal to fire the train. In the meantime, Colonel Montfort, in a state of the most anxious doubt as to what he ought to do, expecting every moment to see the enemy debouch *pêle-mêle* with our soldiers, and unable to obtain any accurate information with respect to the several corps still in the rear, determined to proceed to Lindenau, for the purpose of receiving further instructions from Napoleon's own mouth, and set out towards the other end of the bridge, having first directed the corporal of sappers to fire the mine only in case he should see the enemy approaching.

"Whilst Colonel Montfort was struggling in the midst of the mass which encumbered the bridge, unable either to advance or recede, some of Blucher's troops, in pursuit of the remnant of Reynier's corps, appearing close to the bridge *pêle-mêle* with the soldiers of the seventh corps, occasioned cries of 'Fire the mine! fire the mine!' and the corporal, believing that the right moment had come, applied the match, and thus in a moment condemned twenty thousand of our troops, who were still in the Leipsic faubourgs, either to perish, or to become the prisoners of an enemy whom the feelings of exasperation with which this war was conducted, had rendered inhuman.

"Believing that they had been betrayed, these men uttered shouts of indignation, and, swayed by the impulses of despair, now rushed upon the enemy, and now threw themselves into the Pleisse and the Elster, and endeavored to cross them by swimming.

"Poniatowski, who had been raised to the rank of marshal by Napoleon on the preceding evening, plunged with his horse into the Elster, and reached the other side, but there, weakened by many wounds, and unable to climb the steep bank, disappeared beneath the waters, buried in his glory beneath the ruins of our country and his own.

"Macdonald, making a similar attempt, was saved, but Reynier and Lauriston, surrounded by the enemy's troops before they had time to escape, were taken and carried before the allied sovereigns, when the Emperor Alexander, recognizing Lauriston as the wise embassador who had endeavored to prevent

arms, and surrender at discretion. Lauriston, Reynier, Prince Emile of Hesse, and some twenty other general officers were taken prisoners; and the enemy captured an immense booty in baggage, military stores, etc.

I was with the guard behind the last bridge of Lindenau when the bridge of the Elster was blown up; I formed it in line of battle, and stationed its batteries. We now found ourselves charged with protecting the retreat of the wrecks of the army to the Saale; and we fortunately succeeded in our object, although hemmed in by York on the side of Freyburg, and by Giulay on the side of Kosen. The most admirable order reigned in the entire passage of Weissenfels, where the staff-officers had redoubled their precautions, as if to repair their unpardonable neglect at Leipsic.

Remarks on this Battle.—The disaster of the bridge of Elster and the disorder in the retreat of the nineteenth of October, have been adduced by my detractors, with the retreat from Russia and the disasters of Waterloo, to prove that I lost my judgment in reverses; they have even pretended that I myself remained at the bridge with the match in hand!

I have but two things with which to reproach myself at

the war of 1812, took him by the hand, and had both him and his companion treated with the utmost courtesy;—a courtesy which he was far from displaying towards the unfortunate king of Saxony, who thrice during the morning sent officers to request an interview, which was refused, the only reply to his solicitations being, that he, the king of Saxony, had been taken with arms in his hands, and was, therefore, a prisoner of war; that the allied sovereigns would decide upon his fate, and would inform him of their decision.

"In the meantime, the broken ranks of the French army were continuing their retreat across the numerous arms of the Pleisse and the Elster, leaving twenty thousand of their soldiers either prisoners, or dying in the streets of Leipsic, or drowned in the blood-stained waters of the Pleisse and the Elster.

"This last of the four disastrous days of Leipsic raised the loss of the French army in killed, wounded, or prisoners, to the number of sixty thousand men.

"The enemy had lost an equal number in action, but their wounded had received all the grateful care that German patriotism could lavish on them, whilst ours had met with, alas! how different a treatment."

Leipsic. The first, in not having sent all our parks to Lindenau on the night of the seventeenth, and combined my battle on the eighteenth, so as to retreat during the night. The reason was that I still had some hopes of gaining the battle, and did not wish to precipitate the measures of evacuation. The second, in not having given a better organization to my staff, so as to provide, without express orders, for all such details. But this fault goes further back, and, as has already been remarked, resulted from a defective organization of my army.

It must, however, be confessed that when I renounced at Duben my march on Berlin to return to the plains of Leipsic, I ought to have regarded that place as our only anchor of safety. I should have said to myself, if I gain the great battle between the Pleisse and the Partha, I have no need of defensive measures; but if I lose it, it is necessary to provide for securing my retreat against the attacks of a superior force. Engineers, sappers and pontoniers, should have been employed from the fifteenth, in constructing a system of field-works connecting Lindenau with the faubourgs of Raustedt, and covering three or four bridges on which all the troops, the parks and the baggage could have passed without difficulty at any hour of the day or night.

Napoleon retreats on Erfurth.—We continued our retreat without delay to Erfurth, where we arrived on the twenty-third of October. The combats of Leipsic had cost me fifty thousand men, including the unfortunate loss of our rear-guard. With my remaining forces it was impossible to sustain myself beyond the Rhine. I, therefore, on the twenty-fifth resumed my march to pass that river.

Pursuit of the Allies.—The allies, satisfied with a victory far surpassing their hopes, remained two or three days at Leipsic to determine upon their future plan of operations. Klenau was detached on Dresden; Bernadotte and Benningsen on Hamburg; Blucher was to pursue me, turning Erfurth to the north and to redescend on Gotha; Bubna followed me in rear by Naumbourg. The grand army of the sovereigns threw itself to the south in the forest of Thuringen, to take a parallel line of march. A cloud of partisans annoyed our retreat on all sides. It was, however, effected at first without any remarkable event except the combat of Kosen where General Giulay was sharply repulsed by the fourth corps.

Departure of the King of Naples.—Murat left me at Erfurth to return to Naples. He had received overtures from Austria, promising to interest herself in the preservation of his throne, if, like Bernadotte, he would join the coalition. Metternich, by a refinement of revenge, applied all his address in sowing defection even in the ranks of my own family. The insinuation which failed with the virtuous King of Saxony, succeeded with Joachim. He made a mystery of these propositions, and excused his return to Naples on the pretended necessity of preparations for the defense of his kingdom. I, nevertheless, saw his object, for he had excited my distrust ever since his departure from Posen. I could easily have detained him, but I feared it might enable the English to effect the restoration of Ferdinand. Certain of the influence of my sister over her husband, I first represented to him the inevitable fall of his throne, if I should be compelled to yield, and then took my leave of him with deep emotion. I felt a sad presentiment of the fate which awaited him.

Threatening March of the Bavarians.—I learned at Erfurth that the Bavarians, having united with the Austrians, were already in full march on Wurtzbourg to intercept our retreat. Although I had known for the last ten days the treaty of alliance concluded at Ried, I did not expect so prompt an aggression on their part. But as soon as the alliance was ratified, the Austrian and Bavarian armies mingled their ranks, and marched against me. Perhaps I might have retained Bavaria by sending the divisions of Augereau to Ratisbon and Straubing; the king would then have been obliged to unite his army with mine; and these eight divisions of infantry, forming with the cavalry near sixty thousand men, might have invaded Bohemia at the moment of the victory of Dresden; this powerful diversion would have decided me to manœuvre on Prague by the right of Schwartzenberg, instead of uselessly marching, first on the Bober, then on Duben, and then in the mountains of Toeplitz.

By this union of the Bavarians and Austrians, the coalition had gained a new army of fifty-eight thousand men, of which Wrede took the command. On the fifteenth of October, he left Braunau, passed the Danube at Donawerth on the nineteenth, and reached Wurtzbourg on the twenty-fourth. On the twenty-seventh, he encamped at Aschaffenbourg, where he detached ten thousand Bavarians on Frankfort, and with the remainder of his army established himself at Hanau on the twenty-ninth, barring to us the passage of the Mayne; it was a parody of the Beresina.

I was sensibly affected by this defection; it was the most unjust of all; for I had heaped benefits on Bavaria. The Protectorate of the Confederation of the Rhine was no more an imposition than her vassalage to the Austrian Empire; and if she deemed it odious, she had only to substitute for it a simple defensive alliance. Her alliance with France was a natural one, and had existed ages before. In remembering the enthusiasm of the Bavarians in 1805 and at Abensberg, and the devotion which they showed in the glorious campaign of 1809, my heart swelled with emotion. . . . And were these the same men! I did not accuse the army, but the intrigues of courtiers, the facile and debonair character of the king, and the ambition of Wrede. In fact, the Bavarians had sacrificed me for their own preservation; Maurice of Saxony did still worse toward Charles V.; but there was something more noble in his opposing a victorious monarch. I should have said nothing, if Wrede had simply joined the enemy without thinking to cut off my retreat. I expected that he would annoy my flank and rear; but I did not suppose he would have the presumption to put me in irons!

We followed without obstruction the road from Erfurth by Gotha, Fulda, and Schluchtern. At this last place I first heard of Wrede's audacious manœuvre. We had no time to hesitate. It was necessary to cut our way through these new enemies before the arrival of those in our rear. Blucher, leaving the road to Eisenach, had gone north by Hersefeld towards the sources of the Nidda to fall on my left flank; Bubna followed me in rear, and the grand army was gaining my right by the mountains of Franconia. Raising myself to a level with the threatened danger, I was far from losing courage; I marched briskly on Hanau.

Their Defeat at Hanau.—We had still eighty thousand disposable men, exclusive of twenty-five thousand wounded and stragglers; but they formed a long procession extending to Fulda: I had but twenty thousand in hand. Wrede numbered fifty thousand. He placed himself audaciously, or rather imprudently, at the debouch of the forest of Lamboi, resting on the Kinzig. We attacked him on the thirtieth. While my tirailleurs, deployed in the forest, held in check the enemy's right and centre, my cavalry pierced their left and threw it partly into the Kinzig. With the assistance of the Cossacks who preceded Blucher's march towards Bergen, half of this broken wing regained Hanover, the rest were drowned or taken prisoners. Wrede, seeing the danger of his position, manœuvred by his right to change his front, and secure his retreat on Aschaffenbourg. My Old Guard under Friant drove him back. If I had had the corps of Bertrand, Ney, and Marmont about me, the Bavarian army would have been completely destroyed; I would have thrown it into the Mayne, by cutting off that road. But we had no time to lose; it was necessary to file on Frankfort immediately, for Blucher and Schwartzenberg might arrive at any moment. Our columns marched all night in order to reach that city.

But as my rear-guard of fourteen thousand men had not yet arrived at the height of Hanau, I left Marmont to hold this point, advising him to take the offensive in order to be more certain of his object. He accordingly attacked and carried the city of Hanau on the morning of the thirty-first, forced the bridge of Lamboi on the Kinzig, and drove back the enemy's right, thus gaining time for the arrival of the rear-guard. Now retreating in his turn, he left Bertrand to guard Hanau till all had passed. Wrede, wishing to wash out his defeat, again took the offensive, and penetrated into Hanau, where he was repulsed and seriously wounded. The Bavarian corps occupying Frankfort did not venture to await our arrival, but recrossed the Mayne, and destroyed the bridge.

The French retire behind the Rhine.—On the second of November I arrived at Mayence, and my army there crossed the Rhine. Guilleminot who brought up the rear, attempted to hold the heights of Hochheim, and was attacked by the Austrians with quadruple forces; but he had the good fortune to reach Cassel without suffering as much loss as might have been expected.

Our long retreat from Leipsic was not without disorder: fatigue and hunger carried off many of our troops, who also suffered much from a nervous epidemic fever. To old France this retreat was scarcely less fatal than that from Russia. Our losses for the last two years had been so great that the nation was in consternation; and if the allies had pursued their march, they might have entered Paris with our rear-guard. But the aspect of the military frontiers of France intimidated them. They wished to raise militia to blockade these fortresses before again engaging on a soil rich with the blood of the soldiers of the first coalition.

Capitulation of Dresden. — Before attempting anything further, the allies first occupied themselves in collecting the fruit of their great victory. The most important of all was the capitulation of Dresden, where I had unfortunately left twenty-five thousand men under St. Cyr. This great detachment has been the subject of much criticism. Certainly, if I had had no other object than the defense of Dresden, it would have been exceedingly foolish. But the object was to assist Murat in keeping the field as long as possible, in order to occupy the army of Bohemia, while I marched on Duben to crush Blucher. I expected to return by the right bank of the Elbe, after having captured Berlin. I have already shown what combination of circumstances forced me to renounce this project. I then, on the fourteenth of October, sent officers to St. Cyr directing him to descend the Elbe, and unite with the greater part of the garrisons of Torgau and Magdebourg. But none of them reached their destination. After the loss of Leipsic his fate was fixed. I hoped, however, that he would himself file on Torgau, draw to him some reënforcements from Wittenberg and Magdebourg, and unite with Davoust. The allies had left before Dresden only one good division and the Russian militia of Count Tolstoy. He would undoubtedly have succeeded if he had undertaken it in time. But after the battle of Leipsic, the allies sent Klenau at the head of twenty-five thousand Austrians to reënforce the blockading corps.

As his magazines were getting low, and our affairs seemed lost in Germany, St. Cyr agreed with the enemy to surrender the place on condition of a free passage for the garrison, which was afterward to be exchanged. The capitulation was agreed upon, and the troops had left the place, when the allied sovereigns disapproved of the arrangement and ordered his columns to return. But in the mean time the enemy had occupied the place and ascertained all its means of sustaining a siege. He, therefore, preferred to surrender as prisoners of war and throw upon the allies the odium of a violated capitulation. In this he was wrong. He should have remained in the place and required Klenau to furnish him with provisions till the return of the courier with the approbation of the allied sovereigns.

Operations before Hamburg.—On the other side the army of Bernadotte was broken up; Tauenzein's corps was blockading Wittenberg; Bulow was detached into Westphalia and the confines of Holland; and a part of the Russian troops under Wintzingerode took the same direction. Bernadotte united his Swedes with Benningsen's corps, and marched on the Lower Elbe to join Walmoden, detach Denmark, and capture Hamburg. Davoust, in concert with ten thousand Danes had kept the field in this vicinity with success. The Danes soon signed a peace; but that brave nation who had gathered nothing but thorns from our alliance, did not imitate the example of those who had reaped all the advantages; they limited themselves to a wise and honorable neutrality. Davoust, being left alone, prepared for a vigorous defense. The duties of a valiant governor who prefers to bury himself under the ruins of a city intrusted to his sword, rather than to surrender it, do not accord with the interests of the citizens; Davoust has left at Hamburg a name abhorred; and the extent of this hatred may be regarded as the measure of the praise actually due to him. To blockade and besiege a city like Hamburg, with Haarbourg and the islands, when it is defended by twenty-five thousand brave men and well provisioned, is no small task. Bernadotte and Benningsen spent five months without making much progress. Davoust defended the approaches with activity, and fought on the outside as long as he could. The place held out till after my abdication at Fontainebleau.

Capitulation of Dantzic.—Rapp was not quite so fortunate; he braved there for a year the attacks of the Duke of Wurtemberg. The means of the besiegers were not in proportion to the importance of the place and the strength of the garrison. The whole force there was twenty-five thousand men, of which five or six thousand were not capable of doing service; three or four thousand were equivocal Neapolitans; the Polish division of Granjean and that of Heudelet. After a blockade of six months, they attempted a siege, which would have been a long one, if the garrison had not capitulated for want of munitions and medicines. Rapp had the same fate as St. Cyr. He at first obtained a free sortie, which was not sanctioned. They, however, had reserved this sanction. Rapp had no other course than to surrender himself a prisoner of war.

Siege and Blockade of the other Places.—The Russians blockaded Wittenberg where General Lapoype made a very fine defense till 1814. Tauenzein's corps, with the Saxons who had joined the Russians, blockaded Torgau. This was followed by a *simulacrum* of a siege and a bombardment. The garrison was embarrassed with a mass of wounded men and equipages, which had taken refuge there at the battle of Leipsic; moreover, the troops had suffered greatly from the ravages of an epidemic fever. Narbonne who commanded the place was killed by a fall from his horse. He was succeeded by General Dutailles, having under him Brun de Villeret. The garrison, reduced to half its numbers and destitute of provisions, capitulated. Stettin, Modlin, Zamosc, and the citadel of Erfurth, also surrendered during the month of December, after having accomplished all that could be hoped from resignation and devotion. Glogau held out till the end of the war. Magdebourg, being defended by a strong garrison, was only blockaded, at first by Benningsen and then by the Russian militia. Custrin, defended by Fornier-d'Albe, was only invested; its position on an island of the Oder, rendered it as difficult of attack as it was easy of blockade. Moreover, the Prussians did not wish to destroy their places, being certain that in time they would be reduced by famine. For this reason the siege of Glogau was changed to a blockade, and the two places held out beyond all expectation, the first to the seventh of March, and the second to the tenth of April. This was the more honorable for Glogau, as of the five thousand men which formed its garrison, the governor was obliged to dismiss one-half, which was composed of German, Spanish and Illyrian troops, and he had to guard, with the few that remained, an enciente on both banks of the Oder.

Operations of Eugene in Italy.—In Italy there was nothing of a decisive character. The viceroy, who had been sent there after the battle of Lutzen, organized an army of forty-five thousand French and Italians. I hoped at one time to send Augereau to the valley of the Danube to act with the Bavarian army and Eugene against the gates of Vienna. This union of one hundred and twenty thousand men would have greatly embarrassed Austria. But the intrigues which paralyzed Bavaria from the commencement of the campaign, forced me to renounce this project. The Austrians, being thus relieved from danger from the Inn and the Tyrol, sent General Hiller against Eugene with a superior force, which was assisted by the violent inhabitants of the Tyrol and the Illyrian Croats. The viceroy occupied with the main body of his forces the famous passes of Tarvis and Laybach, while a detachment guarded the valley of the Adige to Prunecken.

Hiller, repulsed at Villach and Kraimbourg, had some success near Fiume; but the viceroy having carried there Pino's division, General Nugent was beaten like his chief. On being reënforced, Hiller passed the Drave on the nineteenth of September, and gained some advantages over the divisions of Verdier and Gratien. The viceroy maintained himself at Tarvis. The middle of October the Austrian general, certain of the accession of Bavaria, ascended the Drave with his main body on Prunecken to join his right in the valley of the Adige and carry the theatre of war by Trente on Verona; the left alone remained in the Friol. This movement was well conceived. The viceroy, being no longer able to hold in the mountains, fell back at first behind the Isonzo, then on the right bank of the Brenta, of which he destroyed the bridges.

Eugene might have fallen with all his forces on the left of the Austrians, and gained their rear by the Drave, as I had done against Wurmser by the gorges of the Brenta; he had the additional advantage of possessing Mantua. But to attempt such enterprises required an impetuous character and reliable troops, which Eugene had not. Weakened by the garrisons of Mantua and Venice, and the defection of Bavaria having opened the Tyrol to our enemies, he deemed it more wise to fall back on the Adige about Verona.

Hiller, not daring to debouch on his rear by forcing Rivoli, filed by the gorges of the Brenta, in order to join his left and to advance toward Vicenza. New contests took place in the so often disputed position of Caldiero. It was carried by the Austrians, for all the advantages of this celebrated post are against Verona and in favor of troops debouching from Vicenza. General Nugent blockaded Venice in concert with an English division, and got possession by water of the port of Ferrara. Istria, Dalmatia, Illyria, the Tyrol, and the States of Venice, fell into the power of the enemy in consequence of the battle of Leipsic and the unfortunate resolution of the court of Munich. The cabinet of Vienna, having decided upon the reconquest of Italy, sent there Marshal Bellegarde with a reënforcement of twenty-five thousand men under Klenau. Immediately after the fall of Dresden, this corps filed by Bavaria and the Tyrol on the Adige. We will describe their operations hereafter.

Soult's Operations in Spain.—In Spain our affairs were not more favorable. In order to give vigor to the army of Joseph, I had determined to recall him to Paris and give the general command to Soult. I ought to have done this in 1811. But although this resolution was rather too late, I still hoped that the marshal would be able at least to check the success of the British arms on the Pyrenees. He immediately resolved to advance to the assistance of Pampeluna. The project was well imagined; but the difficulty of the country and the situation of the respective parties rendered its success very difficult, if not problematical.

Soult descended from the Pyrenees by his left with forty thousand men in two columns, by Roncevaux and Maya. He himself marched by the first of these roads on Pampeluna, hoping to deliver the place and then turn against the centre of the allies. This manœuvre was good; but the asperity of the mountains, the length of the march, and the obstinate defense of the English right under General Picton, gave time for Wellington to approach with the main body. Reënforced by the Spanish troops from the siege of Pampeluna, he held Soult in check, while two English divisions under Hill and Dalhousie turned his right at the foot of the Col-d'Arrais, and threatened his communications by Lanz. Soult supported himself in his turn near Ostitz to rally on Drouet. This manœuvre has been the subject of ridiculous criticism. If he had permitted his right to be forced and turned between Ostitz and Lanz, he would have suffered the same fate as Joseph at Vittoria. He thought it prudent not to risk a general battle in a country so difficult, where, in fact, he had every thing to lose and little to gain. The enemies of the national glory of France have reproached me for having been too audacious, and attempt to criminate Soult for not having been more so! In fact, his movement, conceived on excellent principles, would have been more successful, if the road from Roncevaux had been better, and his first marches had been conducted with more activity, precision, and vigor; but as soon as the enemy had time to collect superior forces, with the advantage of ground and roads, the chances were against him. It must also be observed that, by turning the English right, he would have thrown Wellington back upon the sea: what would have caused the destruction of a continental army, would on the contrary have been a means of security to him. Soult returned to his positions after three successful combats, in which the enemy lost six or seven thousand men, while his own loss was much less.

The English general now warmly pushed the siege of St. Sebastian, which place had already been unsuccessfully assaulted by General Graham. The regular attack was renewed the twenty-eighth of August, with forty-five pieces of ordnance, a part of which were sixty-eight pound carronades: the breach was made practicable, and a second assault given on the thirty-first; it was more bloody than the first, and would also have failed, had not an explosion inside forced the garrison to retire to the castle. Wellington lost his two highest officers of engineers and three thousand men, and the English soiled their laurels by the excesses committed upon a friendly and allied city.

Soult made some efforts to succor this place, and passed the Bidassoa near the mountain of Haya and opposite St. Martial; but he found the enemy too strongly posted. The Spaniards especially distinguished themselves in the defense of St. Martial, where they rivaled the best English troops;—the miraculous effect of the influence on the valor of an army of a single chief who merits the full confidence of the soldier! After an engagement of some hours the three French columns recrossed the Bidassoa. The castle of St. Sebastian, being bombarded with heavy mortar batteries on the ninth of September, capitulated. The allies found here one thousand two hundred men and five hundred wounded; the siege had cost them four thousand.

Wellington, reënforced by his siege corps and a number of Spanish troops, resolved to possess himself of the central and salient position of the Rhune, which took in reverse all the upper valley of the Nivelle and the great road from St. Jean-de-Luz to Bayonne; its possession was calculated to secure from all surprise his right, which was posted at the Col-de-Maya, and could descend at will on Bayonne; he caused this post to be attacked by three strong Spanish columns and an English division. Soult, being greatly weakened by detachments, made but little defense of this advanced post, and concentrated his forces behind the Nivelle. Pampeluna fell a few days after, for want of provisions.

Nothing remarkable occurred in the east of Spain. Suchet continued to maintain his position in advance of Barcelona, without being seriously troubled by the enemy. He was waiting with impatience for orders to resume the offensive, and disengage the twenty thousand men whom he had unfortunately left to garrison the places in the interior. But the battle of Leipsic and the retreat behind the Rhine destroyed these vain hopes, and soon forced me to ask from him reënforcements for the defense of the Rhone.

CHAPTER XXI.

CAMPAIGN OF 1814.

FROM THE INVASION OF FRANCE, TO THE EXILE OF NAPOLEON TO ELBA.

General State of France—Change of the French Ministry—Propositions of the Allies—Dissolution of the Chamber—Preparations for Defense—Negotiations for the Restoration of Ferdinand—Situation of Affairs in Italy—Extraordinary Efforts of the Coalition—They resolve to invade France—Their Motives of Action—They pass the Rhine—Napoleon marches against them—He attacks Blucher—First Combat of Brienne—Battle of Brienne—Congress of Chatillon—Faults of Blucher—Position of the two Armies—Combat of Champ-Aubert—Combat of Montmirail—Affair of Chateau-Thierry—Defeat of Blucher at Vauchamps and Etoges—He rallies his Army at Chalons—Movement of the Allies on Nogent—Napoleon flies to the Seine—Slow March of Schwartzenberg—Combat of Nangis—Combat of Montereau—Schwartzenberg evacuates Troyes—Operations of Eugene and Augereau—Proposal of an Armistice—New Disposition of the Allied Forces—Blucher marches on Meaux—Operations of Mortier and Marmont—Napoleon marches against Blucher—Blucher repasses the Aisne—Battle of Craone—Ultimatum of Chatillon rejected—Battle of Laon—Affair of Reims—Schwartzenberg on the Aube—His Vanguard crosses the Seine—The Empress and Regency retire to Blois—Napoleon moves against the grand Allied Army—Battle of Arcis—Remarks on Napoleon's Position—Success of the Allies in the South—New Project of Manœuvring on the Enemy's Rear—Operations of Blucher—The Marshals are separated from Napoleon—Alexander decides to march on Paris—Efforts of Napoleon to communicate with his Marshals—The latter retire on Paris—Difficulties of Napoleon's Situation—He flies to the Defense of the Capital—Battle of Paris—Situation of France—Want of Public Spirit in Paris—Conduct of the Emperor of Russia—Intrigues of the Factions—Abdication of Fontainebleau—Battle of Toulouse—Napoleon retires to Elba—Evacuation of Italy—Concluding Remarks.

General State of France.—Notwithstanding our disasters on the Pyrenees, on the Adige, and on the Rhine, I still hoped to be able to defend, for a long time, the French soil. It is true that efforts to maintain ourselves on the Elbe, after the battle of Bautzen, had drawn from the interior of France every one capable of carrying a musket. I therefore had but few resources left. It was necessary to garrison our frontier places, but this was not a time when citizens, making it a point of honor and of duty to defend their ramparts, require only a good leader and a few soldiers to assist them. Unfortunately, our troops, in returning to France, had brought with them a fatal typhus fever which made cruel ravages in our ranks. Mayence was filled with the sick, and the contagion had extended even to Strasburg, and the people on both sides of the river were affected; and even the soldiers who escaped the fever, suffered a lassitude and loss of strength. This army presented a very different spectacle from that which passed the Rhine in 1805 to oppose Mack.

But what troubled me most was the general lukewarmness of public spirit in the interior. If I found France firm and resigned on my return from Moscow, I found her equally wavering and distrustful on my return from Leipsic. The reverses of Vittoria and Leipsic, and the approach of the masses of the coalition, had intimidated some, and revived the treasonable hopes of others. Intriguers, ever active in times of public danger, were exerting every means to overthrow my power, while others, who had lost their fortunes and privileges in the Revolution, forgot that they owed to me the preservation of their lives, and the restitution of a part of their property. They desired the triumph of the coalition, in hopes of regaining some ruined castles and portions of unalienated forests, or of living more at their ease in the restoration of feudal domination. Royalist committees were formed throughout the west of France and at Bordeaux. Perfidy and treason to the interests of France, were organized in the very salons of the capital, and spread from there in *Landes* and in the *Boccage.*

Change of Ministry.—Measuring the extent of the danger,

I had convoked the legislative body, in the hope that it would assist me with all the power of the laws. Being informed that Talleyrand's party had incited public opinion against the Duke of Bassano, whom they accused of being one of the principal instigators of the war, I determined to sacrifice my own affections, and remove this faithful servant from the portfolio of foreign affairs, and put Caulaincourt in his place. In this choice I was influenced by several motives: in the first place the Duke of Vicenza had always opposed the war with Russia; and, on account of the esteem in which he was held by the Emperor Alexander, he might now facilitate negotiations. No one knew better than I did, the unfounded character of the reports made against Maret, and I could not have given a stronger proof of my desire for peace than in displacing him from office. Caulaincourt was at the same time made minister of foreign relations and plenipotentiary.

Propositions of the Allies.—The coalition had just made some overtures by M. de St. Aignan, my envoy to Weymar, who, in passing at Frankfort, had had a conference with Metternich, Nesselrode, and Aberdeen. The first offered to treat, leaving us the line of the Rhine, the Alps, and the Pyrenees. I was ready to accept these conditions for myself and for France, but I wished at least to discuss what was to be done with Italy and Holland, which were still in our possession. To an empire like France, it was imposing on her the lowest of humiliations to refuse to treat with her respecting the fate of her nearest neighbors and allies.

Dissolution of the Chamber.—The legislative body did not answer my expectations. Instead of feeling that, in the face of three hundred thousand allies, it was the first duty of every patriot to assist, with every means in his power, in the defense of his threatened soil, they sought to discuss complaints against me, and to organize an untimely opposition.

At the opening of the chamber I had sent them a frank and unreserved communication on the state of affairs; presenting to them a sincere exposition of our dangers, and of the hopes which still remained of peace. I had even laid before a joint committee of the senate and legislative body, all my diplomatic correspondence, showing what I had offered the allied powers in order to obtain peace. Instead of responding to this confidence by providing the means of carrying on the negotiations, or of sustaining the national dignity and independence, the deputies charged with presenting to me the address of the chamber, spoke only of *future guarantees of the public liberty, and the exercise of political rights!* These words would have been honorable when I was victorious, but now, when all were bound to unite to save the state, they were of a factious character, tending to excite a schism in the government. I had but one of two courses to pursue: to yield to the factions, or to dissolve the legislative body. If I yielded, my throne was overthrown, my authority disputed, and France lost. The legislative body was dissolved, and I had recourse to the senate to give legality to the measures necessary for the safety of all. This was unfortunate, as it gave to my enemies a pretext for representing me to France as a despot, who no longer disguised his tyranny under rich harvests of laurels, and who was bringing all Europe upon France by the cruelty of his ambition. Those who thus excited discord under such circumstances are already judged. They connived with the conspirators who sought the restoration of the Bourbons. These fervent apostles of liberty were more desirous of power than of the welfare of the state.

Preparations for Defense.—Notwithstanding these contrarieties, I applied all my activity in reorganizing my little army. For the last twenty years our fortresses had neither been armed nor repaired, for they had not been threatened, and it now required the greatest efforts to place them in a state of defense. Neglecting all places of a secondary character, I directed my attention to the most important points. All our resources had been employed in reorganizing our army at Lutzen ; and we now required one hundred millions of francs, and two hundred thousand men to render our frontiers secure. If I had had a more provident ministry, and the nation had not been already impoverished, there would have been time enough to provide for the public security after the declaration of Austria. But the ministry could not venture upon such a measure after my disapproval of the levy of Fouché in 1809, and, moreover, France was not disposed for a levy *en masse.* I confess, nevertheless, that I ought to have organized the national guards immediately after the armistice of July ; this would have given me the means of garrisoning our fortresses, and, in case of reverse, would have enabled my army to keep the field. This organization had been decreed in 1805, and had partially been made on two occasions since ; but as the war had always been carried on beyond the frontiers of France, this measure had not received the extension of which it was susceptible. I remembered the thirteenth Vendemiaire, and desired to postpone the arming of the multitude as long as possible.

Some writers have asserted that *the only remaining means of saving France, was a grand national movement ; but that the loss of public liberty rendered the French indifferent to my fate.* History will decide upon the truth of these assertions ; it will ask of these great apostles of ideal liberty, whether the people ought not to regard the independence of their soil as the first of their liberties ; and if, in order to permit the declaimers of the tribune to censure the acts of the administration, it was necessary to admit foreign phalanxes into the heart of the state ; and to receive the laws of the Pandours, in order to have the pleasure of dictating to their own government! Woe to the people who become the dupes of such aberrations! Deceived by the results of the grand movement of 1793, of which they understood neither the cause nor the effects, these gentlemen suppose a tribune and public journals the only requisite to make a nation rise *en masse* against the enemy! Let them examine the archives of the war-office, and then say how many *volunteers* went to the frontier, from the flight of Dumouriez in April, 1792, to the taking of Valenciennes at the end of July? . . . Not one! The law of the requisition furnished only between eighty and ninety thousand men, instead of three hundred thousand; and it required the law of the fifth of September, that is, *terror, the guillotine, and all the attirail of the revolutionary army*, to raise five hundred thousand men, ill-armed and ill-equipped. Perhaps it may be asked, what was the liberty which these brave men were asked to defend?

With wise people, public liberty consists of equality before the law, freedom of the press, the right to vote on taxes and military levies, and individual freedom, where this does not tend to the overthrow of public order. All these rights were respected by the institutions which I created and by the acts of my administration. A committee of the Senate was directed to see that no arbitrary arrests were made by the police; and if this committee neglected their duty, it was their own fault, for that was the object for which it was instituted. I caused the arrest of some fifty bad characters, mostly military demagogues, who wished to play the part of Brutus, by boasting in public that they would treat me like Cæsar! I shut up in the state prisons some fifty turbulent characters of different parties, who were attempting to raise insurrections, and some twenty priests who sought to subject France to the ultramontane yoke. With the exception of these individuals, not a Frenchman who respected the laws was deprived of the enjoyment of his liberty.

I had preferred having the laws before the legislative body discussed by known and distinguished orators, in order to save France from the dangers of the tribune, after the commotions which had divided the French people into two nations. In doing this I rendered a service to the state; they have since seen the evils caused by a tribune occupied by unworthy or unknown orators. The vote by black and white balls, after the exposition of the motives of the proposed laws, was the most suitable mode of avoiding the return of anarchy or a dictatorship. In times of public tranquillity I should have been charmed at opening a field for the oratorical talent which distinguishes the French magistracy.

Negotiations for the Restoration of Ferdinand.—I have been reproached with too much indecision in my course toward Spain. It is certain that if I had sent back Ferdinand immediately after my return from Leipsic, and at the same time had recalled Suchet into Languedoc, I would have had disposable on the Rhone thirty or forty thousand men of the old bands by the middle of February, instead of leaving them to be invested in the fortifications of Catalonia. The propitious moment for effecting this restoration had passed; I have already remarked that I had refused to do it, at the beginning of 1813, on my return from Russia and previous to the battle of Vittoria, on account of the excess of my confidence in my resources, and from the fear of drawing Europe upon me by unveiling my weakness. But I ought certainly to have done it as soon as the rupture of the negotiations of Prague, the defeat of Joseph, and the defection of Austria, placed the grand question of the empire of the civilized world in the fields of Saxony and the mountains of Bohemia. Suchet might then have withdrawn all his garrisons which were uselessly compromitted in the fortifications of Spain and have appeared on the Rhine with forty thousand old troops. The half of Soult's army would have been sufficient to guard the chain of the Pyrenees.

On my return from Leipsic, I no longer hesitated on the course to be pursued; negotiations were immediately begun with the Duke of San Carlos, and a treaty signed at Valençay on the eleventh of December. But it would not do to restore Ferdinand, except upon conditions which would be recognized by Spain, and would be calculated to make him my friend. Even Francis I. could not force the fulfillment of the treaty signed with Charles V. at Madrid; and there was nothing to prove that Ferdinand would not act in the same way toward me. I would have accepted, whatever he desired, if I had been assured that the Spaniards would cease their hostilities and separate from the English; but if Wellington remained in arms on the Pyrenees, this return of the king would only add strength to my enemies, by placing Ferdinand at the side of the Duke d'Angoulême at the English head-quarters. The party which conspired against me, and especially Talleyrand, resorted to a thousand intrigues to retard this restoration and to intervene in the ratification of the treaty, in order to destroy the prestige of my superiority. Caulaincourt himself was a dupe to these intrigues. Too much accustomed to persevere in my enterprises, I the more easily gave an ear to these perfidious insinuations, and thus postponed a measure which I adopted when too late. I merely asked of Soult two divisions from his army, to be directed on the Seine, and ten thousand men of Suchet to be directed toward Lyons.

Situation of Affairs in Italy.—I had less hesitation in my course with Italy. I ordered Eugene to purchase, at the expense of Osoppo and Palma-Nova, an armistice of some days with Bellegarde, and to profit by it to echelon his army on Cremona and Milan, and then file by the Alps on Geneva.

I calculated that, being master of Alessandria and Mantua, I could in a few days plant my eagles on the Adige, if we obtained a decisive success in France. But to this success the coöperation of Eugene was necessary. In order to give more efficacy to this plan, Augereau was to form a corps of twenty-five thousand men at Lyons, of which the ten thousand soldiers of the élite from the army of Catalonia would form the nucleus. The union of these forces and Eugene, would enable me to recapture Switzerland, and thus throw sixty thousand men on the communications of the enemy, and to operate in concert with this mass, augmented by all the insurgent population of the Franche-Comté, Alsace, and Lorraine. I hoped that Bellegarde, blinded by the temporary conquest of Lombardy, would have sufficient occupation in investing Mantua and Alessandria, without thinking of following Eugene beyond the Alps. But nothing of all this was done ; some have attempted to attribute this to Eugene and his wife ; the accusation is false. Reflecting afterwards that even the French regiments of his army were recruited from the Piedmontese, Tuscan, and Roman conscripts, who would abandon their colors in crossing the Alps, I left it optional with him to remain in Italy, if he could maintain himself on the Mincio, or if he feared to draw after him another victorious army on France. He preferred to remain and fight it out on the Adige, which he did with glory, honor, and loyalty.

It will be seen from these dispositions that I appreciated the immensity of the task which I had to perform, but that I was not intimidated by the responsibility. If I had fortifications to guard, the allies had also to blockade Hamburg, Magdebourg, Stettin, Torgau, Wittenberg, Custrin, and Glogau ; if they passed the Rhine they would be obliged to invest Mayence and Strasbourg, which alone required an army. Making deductions of so many detachments, I calculated that the enemy would not have one hundred and fifty thousand men to advance to the Moselle. Here Metz and Thionville would require new corps for blockades. Not more than one hundred thousand allies could reach the Marne. I hoped in the course of a month to organize as large a force. But one hundred thousand Frenchmen fighting for their altars and firesides, under my direction, ought in a short time to clear the country; and if the viceroy had debouched by Geneva, the coalition would have paid dearly for their temerity in invading France.

Extraordinary Efforts of the Coalition.—But Europe had learned from us, from Spain, and from Russia, not to spare any sacrifice. The Confederation of the Rhine turned against me all the energy which I had impressed on it. Its contingent of troops of the line was fixed at one hundred and forty-five thousand men, including the Bavarians and Wurtembergers already in the army; and as many *landwehrs*. If we deduct from these the forty-eight thousand Bavarians and Wurtembergers, already with the enemy, there will be left more than two hundred thousand enemies which I had not expected.

The militia were left to blockade our garrisons, while the armed masses of Europe penetrated into France; they were more numerous than I supposed. If to the eight hundred and ten thousand men which we have before enumerated we add the two hundred thousand Germans, and the fifty thousand Russians of Labanof, we have a total of *One million, one hundred and fifty-two thousand men* thrown against me, between August and September!

The Allies resolve to invade France.—In the meantime the overtures of the coalition made through St. Aignan had not produced the immediate result which I had hoped. To choose a new minister, and to arrange his instructions respecting Italy and Holland, had occasioned a delay of some fifteen days, during which the allies changed their resolution, and prepared to invade France, without waiting for a final answer to their propositions.

Their Motives of Action.—But this was not strange, if we reflect upon their divergence of interests on approaching our frontiers. For whom and for what were they now to fight? Could Austria's wishes be the same as those of Russia? or could Russia consent to all that England desired? The emperor of Austria wished to offer me the line of the Rhine; but as soon as the question of Italy was discussed, the cabinet of Vienna feared they might lose their coveted prey. The allies had agreed not to treat separately. England had shown that Belgium and Antwerp interested her more than a continental monarchy; her plenipotentiaries protested against the offer made to St. Aignan; and the minister Castlereagh immediately departed from London to assist in the dissection of my empire. The Emperor of Russia wished to come to Paris to return my visit to Moscow, and to aid in the conquest of Antwerp, in order to obtain Warsaw. Austria espoused the maritime interests of England, because the preservation of my maritime establishments was of little importance to her; she consented to conquer Antwerp in order to be certain of regaining Milan and of retaining Venice!

The invasion, however, had some opponents who feared the influence of our fortifications and our national energy, and who saw the divergence in the political interests of the allies. The question was decided in the affirmative through the influence of a committee of intriguers in France, who encouraged the ruin of their country in order to satisfy personal ambition, and who sent secret agents to Frankfort to inform the allies of the facility of pushing on to Paris. In the mean time another committee of Bernese oligarchs came to offer the Swiss territory to serve as a bridge over the Rhine; for the Austrians, as usual, sought a distant passage when they could have made one almost anywhere. The invasion was then resolved upon.*

The Allies pass the Rhine.—Being aware that my Continental System had incited the opposition of the merchants of Amsterdam, and that many of our fortresses in Holland were deprived of all means of defense, the allies detached the corps of Bulow and Benkendorf against Holland. They took possession of all the country to the Waal without opposition, and Nimeguen and even Grave opened their gates, without making any defense.

Blucher passed the Rhine near Mayence, and leaving a corps at that place advanced on Nancy. Wittgenstein passed at Brisach and crossed the Vosge mountains; but they were met on the way by a crowd of armed country people who were prepared to dispute the invasion of their soil. In vain did the enemy pronounce death upon all villagers taken in arms, and burn to ashes every French village which attempted resistance: the plains of Alsace and the valleys of the Vosges threw out bands of laborers who made the isolated detachments of the armies of Prussia and Austria pay dearly for the excesses which they committed. They alone for a time suspended the march of the enemy. The inhabitants of Champagne and Franche-Comtè followed their example; the people of Burgundy rose in their turn, and for some days I ventured to hope that love of country would do, in 1814, as much as the system of terror in 1793.

* Jomini denies the charge made against him of having advised the invasion of his own country—Switzerland. He says he used every means in his power to prevent that invasion, by obtaining a promise from the Emperor of Russia to respect the neutrality of that country; but that this promise was broken by Austria on the solicitations of the Bernese oligarchs. Jomini also advised against the invasion of France in 1813, as contrary to the future interest of Russia, inasmuch as it would give to the English too great a preponderance, by depriving France of the means of opposing them. If the march on Paris was a memorable triumph, its fruits, he says, have been far from satisfactory. His opinions are fully sustained by reliable authorities.

Schwartzenberg had invaded Switzerland, pushing three columns on Geneva, in order to seize the road of Simplon and decide the evacuation of Italy. The grand allied army profited by the violation of the Swiss territory to cross Bâle, and advance on Bêfort and Vesoul. In conformity to my orders, our corps yielded to the enormous superiority of the enemy, to concentrate toward Chalons. The first engagement took place at Langres, where my Old Guard sustained a combat in order to give us a few days' repose.

Now began that ever memorable campaign which gives immortality to the handful of brave men who did not despair of their country. Their confidence animated mine; witnessing their patriotism, their devotion to my person, their valor, was I culpable in supposing that nothing was impossible for such soldiers?

Napoleon takes the Field against them.—The enemy was now within a few leagues of Paris. Notwithstanding the insufficiency of my means, it was necessary to do every thing in my power to prevent their arrival. On the twenty-fifth of January, after having assembled the chiefs of the National Guard of Paris, and received from them the oath of fidelity, I left the capital for Chalons. I had again confided the regency to the Empress Maria Louisa, and given the title of Lieutenant of the Empire to my brother Joseph, who was to preside in the council. On my departure I bid adieu to my wife and son. . . . My heart was bursting with emotion. . . . A sad presentiment agitated me. . . . I was bidding them an eternal farewell!

The allied sovereigns, with their grand army of one hundred and twenty thousand men, were advancing from Langres on Chaumont; Blucher with about fifty thousand men, had passed Nancy and directed his march towards Joinville and St. Dizier on the Marne. I had, to oppose these masses, only about seventy thousand men still scattered along an extensive line. Mortier, with fifteen thousand men, formed the right at Troyes; at the centre between Chalons and Vitry, Ney, Victor, and Marmont, had collected about forty-five thousand men; finally, Macdonald with nine thousand men coming from Namur, had passed Mézières and was approaching Rethèl.

He attacks Blucher.—I knew that the allies were advancing imprudently in separate corps; but as this usually happens in war, I had no exact data as to the precise positions of these corps or their strength. I knew, however, that by pushing rapidly with my centre from Vitry by St. Dizier and Joinville, cn Chaumont, I would succeed in placing myself between the army of Blucher and the grand allied army, and attack them before they could unite their forces On the twenty-seventh of January we marched on St. Dizier. This city was occupied by the Russian cavalry of Blucher's army, which was readily withdrawn. I here learned that Blucher with twenty-six thousand Russians had passed the Marne at Joinville, and already filed on Brienne, directing himself towards Troyes; but that General York with twenty thousand Prussians was still at St. Mihiel on the Meuse. We had thus cut in two the army of Silesia. I resolved to profit immediately by this circumstance to fall on Blucher before he could be joined by the grand allied army, which was in march from Chaumont on Bar-sur-Aube.

First Combat of Brienne.—On the twenty-eighth we reached Montierender; the twenty-ninth we marched on Brienne. Blucher was preparing to leave this city, to march on Troyes, and General Sacken with a corps of eighteen thousand men, already occupied Lesmont. Unfortunately an officer whom I had sent to Mortier with orders to approach me, was taken by a party of the enemy; from his dispatches Blucher learned that I was about to debouch on his rear; he recalled Sacken's corps in all haste. My infantry whose march was greatly retarded by the bad condition of the roads which are here almost impracticable in the winter, did not arrive before Brienne till about four o'clock in the afternoon. Blucher, reënforced by the Russian cavalry of the grand army, had collected there about twenty-eight thousand men. We attacked him. The Russians defended themselves at Brienne with obstinacy in order to cover the movement of their park on Lesmont. We carried the citadel, but the enemy held the city. This combat cost each party about three thousand men, without leading to any result. In the night Blucher retired, not by the road by which he came, but in the direction of Bar-sur-Aube, through which the grand army of the allies was to pass.

On the thirtieth I moved in advance. The enemy's cavalry covered the retreat of the army of Silesia, which occupied the position of Trannes. I established mine in that of Rothière. Prince Schwartzenberg, who commanded the grand army, transferred his head-quarters to Bar-sur-Aube. The greater part of his army concentrated on that place; but the corps of Wittgenstein and Wrede, making about forty thousand men, were thrown on Joinville, in order to secure the communication with York's corps, which arrived the same day at St. Dizier.

Battle of Brienne.—Being informed that Blucher was already in a position to be sustained by the grand army of the sovereigns, I did not venture to attack him at Trannes, for fear of encountering very superior forces. On the other side, it was important to unite with Mortier, so as to cover the road to Paris; and as the bridge of Lesmont had been destroyed, it was necessary to hold for twenty-four hours at Brienne in order to restore it. This was the only road which we could take, inasmuch as there was no direct road from Lesmont to Arcis, by the right bank of the Aube. It was therefore necessary at any price to gain one day, to march to Troyes, rally there Mortier and Macdonald, and wait to see more clearly the projects of the enemy. I hoped that they would pass the following day in uniting their forces, and combining an attack which would have given us time to effect my projects. I thought that, with the desire to profit by their superiority, they would make wide movements on my flanks, and enable me to fight them in detail. But unfortunately they had resolved at Chaumont to concentrate their masses, and give me battle, on the first of February.

The attack was begun at noon; my army sustained it admirably. On the right Gérard heroically disputed the bridge of Dienville with the Austrians of Giulay; at the centre, Sacken threw himself with impetuosity on Rothière which was defended by the Young Guard under Duhesme; our cavalry under Colbert, Pirè, and Guyot, charged most admirably upon the masses of the Russian infantry; it was on the point of breaking them, when Wassiltschikoff attacked and drove it back. Vainly did Nansouty and Grouchy present themselves on their flanks; it was too late: Sacken's infantry, emboldened by the success of the cavalry, attacked and carried Rothière. A good part of Duhesme's division and twenty-four pieces of artillery fell into the hands of the enemy.

But, notwithstanding this check, I should still have had hopes of victory, if Wrede had not debouched at the same instant from the woods of Soulaine, at the head of twenty-five thousand Austro-Bavarians, who threatened to crush our left. I went in person with a brigade of cavalry, one of infantry, and a battery, but this feeble reënforcement did not prevent Marmont's being driven from the heights of Marvilliers. I now resolved upon a retreat, but as it was necessary to gain time, I threw Oudinot, with a division of the Young Guard on Rothière, and charged Grouchy to second Belluno on the heights of La Giberie. Unfortunately the enemy was too strong; General Rotherbourg, penetrating to the middle of Rothière, was received there by Sacken and Blucher in person, who repelled him while the Russian grenadiers were near surrounding him. On the other side the Prince of Wurtemberg, also reënforced by two Russian divisions, had just carried the heights of La Giberie, driven back Belluno beyond Petit-Mesnil, and effected his junction with Wrede. Our danger was imminent; but night rescued us from embarrassment: the order for a retreat was given at eight o'clock, and executed in good order by means of the artillery of the guard which burned Rothière. We fell back on Brienne and Lesmont, abandoning fifty-four pieces of cannon, and three thousand prisoners; we lost, besides, four thousand killed and wounded. The loss of the enemy was not less than six thousand men.

This check at the beginning of operations in France, was the more to be regretted as it discouraged our own troops and raised the hopes of our foreign and domestic enemies. I, however, could not reproach myself for it, as the loss of the bridge of Lesmont and the want of a road from Brienne on Arcis left me no option but to fight. The next day I crossed the Aube at Lesmont and continued my retreat on Troyes. The Duke of Ragusa, left on the opposite bank of the river to favor our retreat, soon found himself surrounded by twenty-five thousand Bavarians. It required extraordinary coolness and intrepidity to effect his escape; but this marshal was equal to his task. At the head of his division he threw himself on the enemy, repulsed them, and, conqueror of the Bavarians, crossed the village of Rosnay, which opened to him a road to Arcis by the right bank of the Aube. Broken by this check, the enemy no longer thought of pursuit, which might easily have been continued as on the very night of the battle they had a heavy corps on the left of the river. On the third, we reached Troyes without loss. Nevertheless our affairs appeared desperate, since in engaging the greater part of my disposable forces I had not been able to gain a victory over a half of the allied army; for a stronger reason, could I hope for any greater success when they should unite all their forces? I, however, felt it our duty to defend the territory of France, foot by foot, and to the last drop of our blood. In such a disadvantageous contest, it was necessary, like Francis I., to resign ourselves to the loss of every thing save honor. But I still had great hopes on the arrival of Eugene's army at Geneva, the levy of the National Guards, and the troops of the *élite* from the army of Spain.

Congress of Chatillon.—The overtures made to St. Aignan finally led to a congress at Chatillon on the Seine. Lord Castlereagh landed in Holland, and, having first assisted in reënstalling the Prince of Orange, joined the head-quarters of the allied sovereigns at Langres. He there immediately made known the pretensions of England, and on his complaints the allies withdrew their offer of the limits of the Rhine, the Alps, and the Pyrenees, in which Antwerp was included. The representatives of the four great powers figured in this congress. Stadion represented Austria, and Count Razumousky represented Russia. Both were my sworn enemies. The latter, for a long time disconnected from public affairs, hated me with the most bitter animosity. Having taken part in producing the coalition of 1805, he had been severely handled in the articles of the *Moniteur*, which had excited his rancor. Moreover, he regarded me only as the conqueror of Friedland and Austerlitz, whom it was now necessary to humiliate. The interest of the Russian Empire was not his only motive of action. It is unfortunate when the destinies of nations are intrusted to men of violent personal animosities; however great their merit, their judgment is false. Russia only wished the Duchy of Warsaw. Prussia, her old possessions, or an equivalent of five millions of inhabitants; Austria desired Italy. I could agree to these sacrifices; it was also necessary to satisfy England; but without Antwerp she regarded peace as disadvantageous to her. I had then to resign the provinces which I had received from the Directory and dishonor my reign, or resolve to conquer or die.

The first overture to Caulaincourt, who represented me at Chatillon, was that it was necessary for me to return to the limits of 1792. This entirely changed the negotiation, for my instructions to him had been based on the propositions of Frankfort. The battle of Brienne and the arrival of the English minister had thus overthrown every thing. My minister asked for new instructions. He also asked of the allies to know what division was to be made of my spoils.

These new pretensions showed that I had nothing to hope from a congress which seemed more disposed to judge me, than to negotiate with me. I had, therefore, to trust only in my sword, and my affairs were daily becoming worse. In Italy Murat had thrown off the mask and decided against me, thus endangering the position of the viceroy. In Belgium, where General Maison had taken the command of a small corps of ten or twelve thousand men, Bulow's corps and Graham's English division had made preparations for the siege of Antwerp; Carnot commanded there, and the means at his disposal made me confident of a good defense. But the allied forces were accumulating with frightful rapidity. The Duke of Weymar was marching toward Belgium with a new corps of twenty-six thousand German confederates; this would enable the allies to withdraw Bulow's corps to reënforce the army of Blucher. There was not a moment to be lost; Europe in arms was pressing on me with all her force. Nevertheless, as I was expecting two divisions of good troops from the army of Spain, and some hastily organized battalions of National Guards, I determined to gain time. I communicated to my council the humiliating conditions of the allies. All, with the exception of Count Cessac (Lacuée), were of opinion that I should accept them in order to save France. The history of Carthage ought to have taught these pusillanimous councillors that a state is not to be saved by humiliating itself before implacable conquerors. I gave Caulaincourt *carte-blanche* to subscribe to all the sacrifices. I recommended to him to separate the question of Belgium from that of the left bank of the Rhine. In authorizing him to yield Belgium first, it was evident that on the first European war this province would return to us in a few days. At the worst, if they insisted on this double sacrifice, he could sign it, and as the power of confirming the treaty rested in me, I could refuse its ratification, or elude its execution; for I could never consent to save my throne at the expense of honor.

Faults of Blucher.—In the mean time, having united with Mortier, I resolved to profit by the nature of the country behind Troyes to arrest, at least for a few days, the progress of the allies; but a report received from Macdonald opened a new field for my hopes, and induced me to adopt other measures

After the battle of Rothière, if the allies had followed in mass the road to Paris by Troyes, they might have reached the gates of the capital. This was the opinion of the Emperor Alexander; but the allied generals wished to manœuvre: Schwartzenberg with the grand army crossed the Aube, and marched with slow and uncertain steps on Troyes, to act in the basin of the Seine. Blucher was to operate in the valley of the Marne by Epernay, Dormons, Chateau-Thierry, and La Ferté-sous-Jouarre; and the glory of preceding his colleague to Paris, drew him into a series of false movements. I received this information on the evening of the fifth, and immediately resolved to take advantage of these faults. I retired to Nogent where I could fall upon the left flank of Blucher, if he continued to march alone on Meaux.

Position of the two Armies.—I left Troyes on the sixth, and passed the Seine at Nogent on the seventh. Blucher continued to extend himself along the Marne, threatening Meaux. I saw that the moment had arrived to attack him: I left twenty thousand men with Oudinot and Victor to defend the course of the Seine, and the roads from Troyes to Paris, against the enterprises of the grand allied army, and with the remaining twenty-five thousand marched, on the ninth, from Nogent to Sezanne; on the tenth, I advanced on Champ-Aubert. Blucher had the gallantry to second my designs, by dividing his forces. Sacken with fifteen thousand Russians had already reached La Ferté-sous-Jouarre; York with twenty-thousand Prussians was in march on Chateau-Thierry; Champ-Aubert was occupied by the Russian division of Olsowzief, composed of five thousand infantry; finally the Prussian marshal himself was yet at Frère-Champenoise with the Prussian corps of Kleist, and the Russian corps of Kapzewicz, who had just joined his army, forming here a total of twenty thousand men. Thus this army of sixty thousand combatants could oppose to my blows only isolated divisions.

Combat of Champ-Aubert.—General Olsowzief was the first attacked; the combat commenced about nine o'clock in the morning. The Russians, although destitute of cavalry, defended their position for the whole day with valor; but, being overwhelmed by superior numbers and surrounded, they were entirely destroyed. Olsowzief himself was captured, with three thousand men and twenty pieces of artillery. Fifteen hundred Russians were killed. This affair, although important in itself as our first success, became still more so in its consequences. Our position at Champ-Aubert cut the army of Silesia in two, and Sacken's corps was greatly compromised. Not wishing to give him time to escape, I immediately marched against him. Leaving Marmont at Etoges to hold Blucher in check with eight or nine thousand men, I moved on the eleventh with the remainder of my forces from Champ-Aubert to Montmirail.

Combat of Montmirail.—I arrived here at ten o'clock in the morning. Blucher, seeing, when too late, the necessity of concentration, had ordered Sacken and York to fall back on Montmirail. These two generals deemed it their duty to execute this order; but Sacken had hardly reached Vieux-Maisons when he learned that we had anticipated him at Montmirail. On the other side, York informed him that, being delayed by the bad state of the roads, he could not reach that place before the close of the day. It would have now been prudent for the Russian general to file by his left to fall back on Chateau-Thierry, where the Prussians had guarded a bridge over the Marne; but Sacken deemed it his duty to obey the orders of his general, and to cut his way sword in hand by attacking us in the position which we occupied in advance of the city, a little above the branching of the streets to Chateau-Thierry and La Ferté. The affair was warm, and our victory complete. Night alone prevented the entire destruction of the enemy. As it was he lost twenty-six pieces of cannon, and four thousand men killed, wounded, and prisoners.

Affair of Chateau-Thierry.—The next day, reënforced by fifteen hundred horse, we pursued him to Chateau-Thierry, where he repassed the Marne in great disorder. The rear-guard of York, which was partly deployed on the road to this city, was pierced by the cavalry of Nansouty and thrown into the Marne. This affair cost the allies at least three thousand men. On the thirteenth, we passed the Marne at Chateau-Thierry. The enemy had continued their retreat on the road to Soissons. Mortier pursued them with a corps of four or five thousand men on Rocourt.

Defeat of Blucher at Vaux-Champs and Etoges. — To complete the defeat of the army of Silesia, I now had only to crush the corps of Kleist and Kapzewicz. Blucher admirably seconded my plans. The Prussian marshal, distinguished for his operations in Silesia and Saxony, seemed blinded by hatred and presumption. Not comprehending my manœuvre, he had remained for forty-eighty hours with his arms folded at Vertus, where he had gone from Frère-Champenoise on the morning of the eleventh. On the thirteenth, he marched in the direction of Montmirail. Marmont, being too weak to seriously engage him, fell back to Vaux-Champs. I saw with pleasure Blucher running blindly into my snare. Leaving Mortier at Rocourt to observe the remains of Sacken and York, I left Chateau-Thierry, with the remainder of my guard and the cavalry of Grouchy, for Montmirail, where I arrived at eight o'clock on the morning of the fourteenth. I here met Marmont and immediately ordered him to take the offensive against the enemy who had advanced to Vaux-Champs. We carried this village. Blucher, seeing himself attacked when he thought himself in pursuit, ordered a retreat; it was honorable but disastrous for the enemy. His columns, warmly pressed in rear and turned by the cavalry of Grouchy, experienced immense losses on their retrograde march on Etoges. This battle cost him an additional loss of ten colors, fifteen pieces of artillery, and about eight thousand men *hors-de-combat* or prisoners.

He rallies his Army on Chalons.—Blucher retired on Chalons, where he was joined by the corps of Sacken and York, who made a long detour by Rheims. The army of Silesia found itself weakened by the loss of twenty thousand men; but a reënforcement which it received at Chalons again increased its numbers to forty-five thousand combatants.

On the other side, the arrival of Wintzingerode's corps, which had finally got possession of Soissons by a *coup-de-main*, was calculated to lend him powerful aid. Notwithstanding this, the disorder was so great in his army when it reached Chalons that, if I had pushed it warmly, I should have annihilated it. But the danger of the capital called me in another direction. This was unfortunate, for in war as in smithery, it is necessary to strike while the iron is hot.

Movement of the Allies on Nogent.—While I was thus occupied on the Marne, Paris was threatened on the side of the Seine. The marshals whom I had left on the roads from Troyes to Paris were too weak to arrest the grand army of the allies, if it acted together and with vigor; but Schwartzenberg was tied down by the instructions of his cabinet which had ordered him not to pass the Seine. My father-in-law pretended to wish to spare the territory of his son-in-law, and to be willing to preserve for him the monarchy of Louis XIV., minus Lorraine and Alsace. All military dispositions were made subordinate to the political thermometer of the congress of Chatillon. The enemy had occupied Troyes on the seventh; he did not leave there till the tenth, and then advanced eccentrically on Nogent, Sens, and Auxerre. The Wurtembergers got possession of Sens on the eleventh. Generals Wittgenstein and Wrede were less fortunate before Nogent; the detachment left in this city by Marshal Victor, defended it with intrepidity. Despairing of being able to force this post, the enemy's generals determined to turn it. On the twelfth, Wittgenstein remained before Nogent while Wrede pushed on to Bray, which place he carried without opposition, the National Guards who were stationed there having fled without firing a shot! The loss of Bray forced Bourmont to evacuate Nogent. Oudinot and Victor attempted to oppose the progress of the allies across the Seine, but seeing it impossible, they fell back by Nangis on Guignes behind the Yères, where they were reënforced, on the fifteenth, by some detachments from the army of Spain and by the corps of Macdonald, which the victory of Montmirail had rendered disposable.

Napoleon flies to the Seine to save Paris.—Paris in the mean time was in alarm; they sent me courier after courier pressing me to come to their assistance. I was now ready to do so, as the army of Silesia, thrown back on Chalons gave me no more inquietude. I left Marmont with ten thousand men at Etoges to observe Blucher, and Grouchy with three thousand horse at Ferté-sous-Jouarre to serve as a reserve to Marmont and Mortier. With the remainder of my guard I left Montmirail on the fifteenth, and directed myself by Meaux on Guignes. The cavalry marched night and day and the infantry traveled *en-poste*. In this way we made three leagues in thirty-six hours and reached Guignes on the sixteenth, where we found the army of the marshals, which again gave me a force of thirty thousand combatants. I should have had less distance to march, if I had fallen by Sézanne on Nogent or Provins, supporting the marshals on this city in order to gain the right flank of Schwartzenberg and throw his line on Montereau, instead of establishing myself on his front; but the difficulty was to secure a junction with the three corps established behind the Yères, (Victor, Macdonald and Oudinot); and, bringing with me only the guard under the orders of Ney, it was necessary to begin by securing the means of attacking a superior army without compromising my troops in an isolated movement.

Slow March of Schwartzenberg.—Prince Schwartzenberg, hearing of Blucher's multiplied defeats, did not deem it his duty to cross the Seine with all his forces; he was content to throw on the right of the river the corps of the Prince of Wurtemberg, of Wrede, and of Wittgenstein, which established themselves at Montereau, Donemarie, and Provins.

Count Pahlen, with the vanguard of Wittgenstein, pushed on to Mormant.

Combat of Nangis.—Convinced that it was only by extreme activity that I could compensate for my inferiority in numbers, I took the offensive on the seventeenth, directing all my forces on Mormant. The advanced guard of Pahlen, being unexpectedly attacked, was almost all captured; the allies put themselves in retreat. Oudinot pursued them on Provins, Macdonald on Donemarie. Victor, being charged with gaining Montereau, encountered on the road a Bavarian division which he defeated; but this prevented him from reaching Montereau the same day. The enemy lost three thousand men, and fourteen pieces of cannon. This eccentric pursuit was a fault; I ought to have thrown all my forces on Provins or on Bray.

Combat of Montereau.—On the eighteenth we continued to advance to the Seine. Wittgenstein repassed the river at Nogent, and Wrede at Bray; but the Prince of Wurtemberg, fettered by the ill-conceived instructions of Schwartzenberg, had the temerity to accept an engagement before Montereau with the second corps. The position, covered by a numerous artillery, was good so long as they remained firm, but passing a *coup-gorge* in the rear, it was really a dangerous one. Victor attacked it first without success; but General Gérard carried himself there with his reserve which was composed of peasants; I gave him the command, and he threw all into the defile: I hastened to the place with some squadrons which completed the victory. Montereau and the bridge were carried by a charge, and the Wurtembergers driven to Marolles with the loss of six thousand killed, wounded, and prisoners. We lost two thousand and five hundred men, and the brave General Chateau, an officer of great hope; he was the son-in-law of the Duke of Belluno, and his chief of staff.

Schwartzenberg evacuates Troyes.—These checks discouraged the allies, and Schwartzenberg retired on Troyes, soliciting Blucher to fly to his assistance. I passed the Seine on the nineteenth at Montereau, and the following days marched on Troyes. On the twenty-second we arrived before that city. The grand army of the allies, concentrated at Troyes, occupied both banks of the Seine. Blucher coming from Chalons by Arcis, was at Méry, and in immediate connection with Schwartzenberg. This junction is the best proof that I had lost a part of my advantage in throwing myself on the left of the grand army. I should have produced greater results, and at least have had less ground to march over to turn and break its right: an operation which would have prevented any junction with Blucher. Be that as it may, I expected that the allies would profit by the union of such large forces to offer me a decisive battle. I was resolved to accept it, for we could not retreat without drawing the enemy on the capital; but to my great astonishment they did nothing, and continued their retreat. The events which had taken place in the south had redoubled the fears of Schwartzenberg, as they singularly opposed the views of his master on Italy.

These successes had revived my hopes, less by their positive results, than by the expectation that they would electrify France, and that a national movement would lead to the expulsion of the enemy from our territory. I only required fifty thousand National Guards to assist me in forcing the allies back into Germany; but these fifty thousand men were not raised! In my present victorious attitude the propositions made to Caulaincourt could not be accepted. I feared that he might use the unlimited powers which I had given him at the instance of my counselors, to accept these propositions; but fortunately he was in no haste to consummate my humiliation. These powers were now withdrawn.

Some men, very little versed in the diplomatic affairs of Europe, have accused him of having neglected these ten days, during which he had a *carte-blanche:* nothing can be more unjust. In doing this he might have saved my crown, but France would have gained nothing; instead of a brilliant monarchy she would have been only an abased empire. I felt grateful to him for sparing my glory by declining to sign any such propositions. At the moment when I withdrew his powers, he was required by the allies to submit a counter project, if he did not accept that which was presented to him as the *sine qua non* of the coalition. This gave place to new delays, at which I was not displeased; for I hoped everything from time, not thinking that every day would draw closer the bonds of an alliance justly regarded as monstrous. But before stating what took place at the diplomatic head-quarters of the sovereigns, I will briefly describe the events which had occurred in the south.

Operations of Eugene and Augereau.—The defection of Murat for a moment exalted the hopes of the cabinet of Vienna; but the slowness of his advance on the Po to operate in concert with Marshal Bellegarde, the mystery which covered his march, the relations maintained with the viceroy, made them suspect the fidelity of this new ally. On the other side, it was evident that the king of Naples delayed only to declare in favor of the successful party; and on the news of my first reverse in France Eugene would be assailed on all sides. The Austrians had already pushed detachments from Geneva on the communication of the Simplon. A storm was threatening Piedmont and Upper Italy. The English were preparing for a descent at Leghorn to join Murat. The viceroy, though surrounded by enemies, did not lose his courage: his first care was to evacuate the line of the Adige in order to concentrate his defense on the Mincio, with Mantua as his point of support. Bellegarde, attributing this retreat to fears inspired by Murat's approach to his communications, thought to profit by the circumstance to fall upon the viceroy, and made every preparation to pass the Mincio near Pozzolo on the seventh of February. Eugene, anticipating this manœuvre, had reënforced his right at Goito, and carried his guard, reserve, and head-quarters to Mantua, from which he debouched skillfully on the left flank of the Austrians, and drove it back to Valeggio. His numerical weakness prevented him from taking full advantage of this victory; but he so imposed on Bellegarde that that marshal, forced to return to the left bank of the Mincio, only made a feeble attempt to pass it, when he knew that one-third of the viceroy's army had been detached to Parma against Murat. The Austrian general, repulsed in this attempt, and in his ill-combined manœuvre by the mountains of Gavardo, remained on the defensive.

At this epoch, although rather late to effect the diversion which I had ordered on Geneva, it was still possible to obtain important results. Augereau had organized at Lyons a corps, composed principally of the veterans drawn from Catalonia. He was to advance on Geneva, raise Switzerland, reëstablish the communication of the Simplon, join the divisions which Eugene was to bring from Italy, and advance with that prince toward the upper Jura, in order to act in Burgundy in concert with me. Augereau did in part march on Geneva, but in detachments, and occupied himself for ten days with mere accessories; and the defection of Murat having prevented the army of Italy from joining him, the allied sovereigns had time to detach against him considerable forces. With one half of the energy and activity which he had shown at Castiglione, he might have overthrown Bubna, and organized our partisans in Switzerland; and God only knows what would have been the result.

Negotiations at Lusigny.—These events had caused no little sensation at the Austrian head-quarters, which were already considerably shaken by my success on the Seine. The allies, now become more yielding, had proposed to me an armistice which was negotiated at Lusigny. It was quite natural that my father-in-law should seek to direct the negotiations at Chatillon. By depriving me of Italy and securing to himself my influence in Germany, he would have no more points of difficulty with me, and could make a display of his generosity. In order the better to accomplish his purposes, Metternich exposed in a council the equivocal situation in which the allies were placed by these reverses on the Marne and the Seine, by the spirit manifested in the provinces which they occupied, and by the unexpected appearance of Augereau's corps toward Geneva. His object was too evident to be mistaken. The Emperor Alexander, disgusted at the manner in which they carried on the war, hesitated whether he should not unite his guards and Wittgenstein's corps to Blucher's army, and carry on his operations in a more military manner. As I have already said, this prince was anxious to go to Paris in order to return my visit to Moscow; he was excited against me, and had sworn my destruction. The choice which he made of Count Razumowsky, to represent him at Chatillon, was the best possible proof that he had no intention of treating with me.

On the other hand it appeared to him just that the acquisition of the Duchy of Warsaw should indemnify his empire for the great efforts which it had made; and to obtain this it was necessary to give Italy to Austria, a suitable indemnity to Prussia, and Antwerp to the English; but to accomplish this object it was necessary to reduce me to the last extremity. It was only the fear that the Austrians would formally separate from the coalition that prevented Alexander from uniting with Blucher and marching on Paris. But to remedy all the past evils, it was decided that the grand army should remain on the defensive at the centre, and carry the Austrian reserve and the new *corps-d'armée* of the Germanic Confederation on the Rhine, while Blucher, reënforced by the corps of Wintzingerode and Bulow, should operate with one hundred thousand men in the valley of the Marne. They flattered themselves by this *mezzo-termino* to neutralize the influence that state policy had had on the direction of military operations, and to strike decisive blows with Blucher's army, which would be under the more immediate direction of the Emperor of Russia and the King of Prussia. The conditions proposed at the armistice of Lusigny not being acceptable, it was necessary to resort again to the sword.

New Disposition of the Allied Forces.—In accordance with the system agreed upon at Vandœuvre, the grand army fell back to Chaumont; and Blucher prepared to advance on Meaux. We have just seen that he was to be reënforced by the troops of the old army of Bernadotte. Wintzingerode had just been joined by Woronzof's corps; and Bulow had been relieved in Belgium by the twenty-five thousand newly organized troops of the Germanic Confederation, under the orders of the Duke of Weymar. Finally, Count St. Priest was in march from the Rhine toward the Ardennes.

Blucher marches on Meaux.—Without waiting for all his reënforcements the Prussian marshal put himself in motion to march a second time on Meaux, with the hope of driving Marmont to the Marne, and of advancing on Paris by the right bank of that river. On the twenty-fourth of February, he passed the Aube at Baudemont and advanced on Sézanne where Marmont was encamped. The latter, in order not to expose himself to be cut up, retreated on Fertésous-Jouarre, where, on the twenty-sixth, he united with Mortier who had maintained his position between Soissons and Chateau-Thierry, against the new corps of the allies which had invaded France from the north. That of Wintzingerode was in the environs of Reims, and Bulow had just arrived at Laon.

Operations of Mortier and Marmont.—The marshals at Ferté-sous-Jouarre, weakened by the garrison which they had been obliged to throw into Soissons, had not over twelve thousand combatants of all arms. Hoping to destroy this handful of men, Blucher pushed from Rebais on Ferté-sous-Jouarre the corps of York and Kleist to occupy Marmont and Mortier, while the Russian corps belonging to his army marched on Meaux so as to turn their right and cut them off from Paris. Fortunately, the marshals saw the projects of the enemy. On the twenty-seventh, they moved from Ferté-sous-Jouarre to Meaux. They arrived there very *à propos;* Sacken's advanced guard was already in possession of the faubourg at the left of the Marne, and was about to penetrate into the city. The presence of our troops defeated his projects. Blucher, seeing himself anticipated at Meaux, resolved to operate by the left bank of the Marne. He withdrew the Russian corps to Ferté-sous-Jouarre where he passed the Marne with the mass of his army and directed his march on Lizy, leaving only York's corps on the left bank to cover his rear. The marshals, again divining his projects, prolonged their forces by their left to bar the passage, bordering the right bank of the Ourcq. On the twenty-eighth, they marched from Meaux on Lizy. The corps of Kleist, forming Blucher's advanced guard, was already beyond the Ourcq; but as the other corps of the army of Silesia were not in position to sustain him, he did not venture to engage alone, and fell back on Fullaines, after destroying the bridge of Lizy. Thus Blucher saw all his projects foiled; while on the other side, I was preparing to force him to give up the offensive and to think only of his own security.

Napoleon marches against Blucher.—I reëntered Troyes

on the twenty-fourth ; the grand army of the allies retired with so much precipitation that I could not pursue them without compromising the capital which was now seriously threatened by Blucher. I, therefore, only sent Marshal Macdonald in pursuit with thirty-five thousand men, while, with the remaining twenty-five thousand, I resolved to give the Prussian marshal another lesson of prudence by manœuvring on his rear. I left Troyes the twenty-seventh, and passing the Aube at Arcis, arrived at Herbisse. The next day I continued my march by Frère-Champenoise and Sézanne to Esternay. Blucher, checked in front by Marmont and Mortier, and threatened in rear by my army whose numbers were greatly exaggerated, found himself very much embarrassed. Thinking, however, to profit by the first day of March to defeat the marshals, he ordered Sacken to make demonstrations towards Lizy, while the corps of York and Kaptsewicz passed the Ourcy at Crouy to turn their left; but the bridge of Crouy being destroyed in time, the whole ended in an attempt by the Russians to force a passage at Gèvres, which was easily defeated by Marmont. The same day, towards evening, I arrived at Ferté-sous-Jouarre with the head of my column. We immediately commenced the construction of a bridge across the Marne. During the night the marshals were reënforced by six thousand men sent by my brother from Paris.

He forces Blucher to repass the Aisne.—Blucher now saw the necessity of a retreat : but this was no easy matter. I was in position to intercept the roads to Chalons and Reims. The only one which remained open was that to Soissons ; but that city, abandoned by Wintzingerode in consequence of my success at Montmirail, had been again occupied by our troops, and placed in a better state of defense. However, there was no alternative. On the second of March, the army of Silesia marched on Soissons, where

Blucher had directed Bulow and Wintzingerode to unite with his army. Marmont and Mortier pursued him on the road to Soissons, hotly pressing his rear-guard; while I manœuvred on his left to prevent him from throwing himself on Reims.

On the third I passed the Marne, and on the fourth arrived at Fismes. I had now strong hopes of destroying the army of Silesia, which having no permanent bridge on the Aisne, would be thrown upon that river, and exposed to infallible ruin. Unfortunately Soissons was commanded by General Moreau, an imbecile; not appreciating the importance of his post which was surrounded by Bulow and Wintzingerode, he thought he was doing wonders in obtaining the liberty of his garrison, and consented to capitulate on the third, without having exhausted his means of defense, and at the very moment when a distant cannonade announced to him the importance of holding out. Blucher, fortunate in escaping such imminent peril, passed the Aisne in the night of the third and fourth, and established himself on the right bank of this river, between Soissons and Craone. On the fifth, Mortier and Marmont attacked Soissons; but that city, defended by a garrison of eight thousand Russians, resisted with success. The loss of Soissons deranged my plan: I nevertheless determined to continue to manœuvre against the enemy's left, with the hope of cutting him off from Laon, and of throwing him into the angle formed by the Aisne and the Oise. On the sixth, we moved in mass on Berry-au-Bac, where I crossed the Aisne, and pushed on to Corbeny.

Battle of Craone.—I had thus succeeded in gaining the left of the enemy. It was now important to attack him before he could change his position. I resolved to make the attack instantly, although I had not yet been joined by Marmont's corps, which constituted my rear-guard. Accordingly on the seventh we debouched from Craone against the position which the enemy occupied in rear of this town between Ailles and Vassognes. I had with me only twenty-eight or thirty thousand men, while Blucher had three times as many; but he had engaged the greater part of his forces in a wide and ill-combined movement to the left of the Lette, with the intention of turning my right. It resulted from this that we had only to deal with the Russian corps of Sacken and Woronzof, which the Prussian marshal had left between the Aisne and the Lette to serve as a pivot for the movement of his army. Moreover the infantry of Sacken had received orders to retire, and the cavalry alone remained to protect the retreat of Woronzof. The latter, holding the most secure point of the plateau, chose to fight in a post where we could neither manœuvre nor bring our forces into action, and accordingly awaited us under the protection of a formidable artillery. His corps showed much tenacity in the defense of the strong position which he occupied. The combat was terrible. As Woronzof had his flanks protected by deep ravines, we could attack him only in front. He was on the point of being pierced, when Sacken's cavalry, thrown forward at the opportune moment, restored the equilibrium. It was only by redoubling their efforts, like Ney, that our young soldiers (who had been organized only fifteen days) succeeded in forcing the Russians to fall back on Chavignon where they were rejoined by the garrison of Soissons. We pursued them to Filain; the victory was ours; but our loss made it a dear one. On both sides there was a loss of more than six thousand men *hors-de-combat*. This was little for the allies, but much for us. Victor and Grouchy were seriously wounded.

Ultimatum of Chatillon rejected.—It was in the midst of the bloody and useless trophies of this battle that I received the news of the unfavorable issue of the negotiations of Chatillon. Instead of being disunited by my success, the allies had drawn closer the bonds of their union by a treaty signed at Chaumont, on the first of March. They bound themselves not to treat separately, and to redouble their efforts to carry on the war. In order to provide for the expenses of this war they issued in common a paper circulation under the guarantee of England. Thus, Europe lavished not only iron, soldiers, and gold, but all the resources of her credit, to crush that France who opposed to her only my genius, my activity, and the heroic devotion of a handful of brave men. The nation pressed down under the weight of my reverses, succumbed to the efforts of enemies to whom they had previously given an example of energy, devotion and patriotism.

Strengthened by this new alliance, the sovereigns had maintained their original pretensions without being troubled by my successes. They knew that victory would finally destroy my feeble resources, and that I must succumb sooner or later. But I could not believe that they would not eventually abate their demands. The attitude which they had assumed in consequence of my last victories, their demand for an armistice which they had several times before refused, the expected arrival of Augereau in Switzerland,—all these circumstances militated in my favor. I had already seen them, in consequence of my first victory, retreat on the Rhine, accusing each other of being the cause of the reverses which resulted only from the bad direction given to their masses by a tortuous policy. After this, how could I accept what the allies improperly called the limits of 1792? I would have asked nothing more, if they had given me the monarchy of Louis XVI.; for, as I have already had occasion to say, at no epoch of my greatest power was my relative situation as advantageous as that of France at the end of the American war. It was to deceive France and Europe, to publish that I refused the same territory which excited the pride of Louis XVI., and the envy of the civilized world. All was changed since 1792; and if these conditions had appeared to me intolerable in 1805, when Spain and Holland were yet in our alliance, under what aspect ought I to regard them when these countries, in the hands of our enemies, were to augment with all their strength and resources, the fearful preponderance of England? The France of 1792, without the family alliance of Austria, Naples, and Spain, without the alliance of Tippo-Saeb, without its navy and its colonies, was to the England of 1814, not one-quarter what the France of Louis XVI., was to the England of 1792. It was not the same on the continent; for France had lost all her ancient allies; Poland, who had formally sought her kings in the family of ours, was partitioned out, and her weight now cast into the balance of our new enemies. Isolated in the midst of Europe and hemmed in on all sides, France would be but the shadow of her former greatness. It was evident to those most blind, that, even with the limits of the Rhine, the Alps, and the Pyrenees, she would be not only below the relative state of Campo-Formio, but still much below her relative grandeur after the sad termination of the Seven Years War. Indignant at such harsh conditions, I ordered Caulaincourt to reply by a counter project equally exaggerated. Thenceforth, there was not the least hope of an understanding. In order to cut the Gordian knot, I determined to again attack Blucher.

Battle of Laon.—On the eighth of March, the Prussian marshal had assembled all his army at Laon; it numbered about one hundred thousand men. I had but thirty-five thousand combatants, even including Marmont's corps. But we were in a situation not to count our enemies. If I did not attack, the allies would take the initiative; it was better to profit by the temporary moral effect of our victory at Craone, in attacking the enemy, than to lose that effect by allowing him to attack us. I advanced toward Laon by the road to Soissons; Marmont directed himself by that of Bery-au-Bac. On the ninth, I attacked the enemy's position; the combat continued all day without any thing decisive. The allies preserved their position; and we maintained ours in the villages before their front. Blucher, having had time to reconnoitre the state of our forces, determined to make a night attack upon Marmont, who had not yet effected his junction with me. The corps of York and Kleist debouched from Athies and marched against him. The marshal's troops thinking only of repose, were completely surprised; they fled to Bery-au-Bac, leaving in the hands of the enemy two thousand five hundred prisoners and forty pieces of artillery. Being deprived by this disaster of the coöperation of Marmont, I had only twenty thousand men left; I nevertheless determined to make the most of a bad game. I calculated that the enemy, in order to secure the defeat of Marmont, had probably moved the mass of his forces on his left leaving Laon but feebly secured. He had in fact directed toward Bery-au-Bac about sixty thousand men, but near forty thousand yet remained at Laon, a sufficient force to repel our reiterated efforts, on the tenth, to force their position. However, we thereby gained time for Marmont to secure his retreat, for Blucher, alarmed at our obstinacy, ordered back on Laon the corps which had filed on Bery-au-Bac. This new concentration of all the enemy's forces, left us not the least chance of success. By attempting any longer, with my little army, to resist the quadruple forces of the allies, I would risk being enveloped. On the eleventh, I fell back on Soissons where I repassed the Aisne; Marmont fell back from Bery-au-Bac to Fismes. Some reenforcements received from the depôts again increased the total force of my army to thirty-five thousand men.*

* The following comments on Marmont's conduct on this occasion are copied from Thiers:

Affair of Reims.—Success was now absolutely necessary to remove the bad impression of my retreat from Laon. Fortune, or rather the fault of the Russian general, soon

"Marmont, unprotected at the village of Athies, in the midst of the plain, awaited Napoleon's instructions, which he had sent Colonel Fabrier, at the head of five hundred men, to learn. Was it well of Marmont to remain stationary, or ought he not rather, after having during the day caught a sight of the immense masses of the enemy's cavalry, to have taken up a position for the night in the rear, towards Festieux for example, a kind of little hillock by which he had debouched into the plain, and where he would have been in perfect safety. But the mistaken fear of abandoning the spot he had conquered in the afternoon, restrained him, and deterred him from making the retrograde movement that prudence would have suggested. What was still less excusable, as he did remain amidst hordes of enemies, was the not multiplying precautions against a night attack.

"With a characteristic thoughtlessness that detracted from his good qualities, Marmont deputed to his lieutenants the duty of providing for the common safety. The latter allowed the young tired soldiers to scatter themselves in the neighboring farms; they did not even think of protecting the battery of forty pieces that had cannonaded Athies with so much success. It was young marine-gunners, little accustomed to land service, that tended these cannon, and they had not taken the precaution to limber up their guns, so that they might be able to remove them at the first appearance of danger.

"Everybody, commander and officers, trusted to the darkness of night, of which they ought, on the contrary, to have entertained the deepest distrust.

"There were, alas! only too many reasons for distrusting this fatal night, for Blucher, as soon as he heard Marmont's cannon, believed that the attack by the Reims route was the true attack, and that the other, which had occupied the day on the Soissons route, was only a feint. He consequently decided to bring down the mass of his army on the Reims route. He immediately put into motion Sacken and Langeron, who had remained in reserve behind Laon. They had orders to make a circuitous march round the city, and join Kleist and York; Blucher, besides, sent part of his cavalry, which on that side could not fail to be useful.

"The day was far advanced when this movement was terminated; still the Prussian general was not willing to bind himself to preparatory arrangements, and conceived the design of profiting by the darkness to effect a night surprise by leading on his cavalry *en masse*.

"Towards midnight in fact, when Marmont's soldiers least expected it, a mass of horsemen dashed upon them, uttering terrific cries. Old soldiers accustomed to the vicissitudes of war would have been less surprised, and sooner rallied; but a sudden panic spread through the ranks of this young infantry, that took flight in every direction. The artillerymen, who had not thought of arranging their pieces so that they might be easily removed, fled without thinking of them. The enemy, amid the darkness, become mixed with us, furnished me an occasion. Count St. Priest, who commanded a new corps of twelve thousand men belonging to the army of Silesia, had arrived at Chalons, from whence he

and make part of the tumult; while their horsed artillery pursue us, firing grape, at the risk of killing Prussians as well as French.

"All hurry on in indescribable disorder, not knowing what to do, and Marmont is carried away at the same pace as the rest. Fortunately the sixth corps, which formed the nucleus of Marmont's troops, recover a little of their *sang-froid*, and stop at the heights of Festieux, where it would have been so easy to find a secure position during the night. The enemy, not daring to advance farther, suspend the pursuit, and our soldiers, delivered from their presence, rally at length from their disorder.

"This accident, one of the most vexatious that could befall a general, particularly on account of the consequences it involved, cost us materially only some pieces of cannon, two or three hundred men put *hors-de-combat*, and about a thousand prisoners; the greater number of whom returned next day; but our enterprise, already so difficult and complicated, was defeated. On learning during the night this deplorable skirmish, Napoleon gave way to the most violent anger against Marshal Marmont; but giving away to anger would not repair the mischief, and he immediately began to think what was best to be done. To give up the attack and retire would be to commence a retreat that must lead to the ruin of France and his own.

"To attack, when the movement confided to Marmont was no longer possible, and when he could be confronted by masses of the enemy assembled between Laon and the Soissons *chaussée*, to attack under such circumstances would have been rash. Either course seemed to lead to destruction.

"Listening only to the promptings of his own energetic soul, Napoleon determined to make a desperate attempt on Laon, and see whether chance, so fruitful of events of war, might not do for him what the most skillfully-laid plans had not been able to effect.

"Napoleon was about to throw himself on Laon when Blucher anticipated him. The latter had first thought of sending half his army against Marmont, believing his to be our principal column.

"But in his staff numerous voices were raised against this project, and it was proved to him that, above all things, he ought to oppose Napoleon in front of the city of Laon. Blucher, who was ill that day, and more inclined than usual to yield to the advice of his lieutenants, had, therefore, suspended the prescribed movement, and determined to direct his efforts straight before him, that is to say, on Clacy, whence Napoleon threatened to turn his position.

"At the very moment that Napoleon was putting his troops in motion to renew the attack, three divisions of Woronzof's infantry, advancing on our left, deployed around the village of Clacy, intending to carry the place. General Charpentier, who had replaced Victor, was at Clacy with his own division of the Young Guard and that of General Boyer, but very much reduced in number by the late engagements. Ney had on his side advanced to the left to

moved on Reims, which was carried without difficulty, the little garrison having no great means of defense. After this exploit, St. Priest remained at Reims intermediary between

support General Charpentier; he placed his artillery a little in the rear and diagonally, so that he could take the Russian masses *en écharpe* that were about to fall on Clacy. At nine in the morning an obstinate engagement commenced around this unfortunate village, whose site, happily for us, was slightly elevated. General Charpentier, who during the past days had displayed, as much energy as skill, allowed the Russian infantry to advance within musket shot, and then received them with a terrible *fusillade*. The officers and sub-officers exposed themselves incessantly, seeking to compensate for the want of training in their young soldiers, who in every respect, exhibited an unexampled devotedness. The first Russian division was received with so destructive a fire that it was driven back to the foot of the position, and immediately replaced by another that received like treatment. The assailing troops were exposed, not only to the fire from Clacy, but to that of Marshal Ney's artillery, which, happily posted as we have just related, committed fearful ravages in the enemy's ranks. In truth, some of the projectiles from this artillery knocked off some of our soldiers at Clacy, but in the enthusiasm that prevailed we only thought of checking the enemy, and destroying them, no matter at what price.

"The same attack, renewed five times by the Russians, failed five times through the heroism of General Charpentier and his soldiers. The Russians, repulsed, fell back on Laon. Napoleon, again conceiving some slight hopes, and flattering himself with having, perhaps, tired out the tenacity of Blucher, ordered Ney's two divisions (Meunier and Curial) to advance straight on Laon, through the Semilly suburb, which we had not evacuated. Our young soldiers, led by Ney to the hillock, overturned everything before them, ascended one side of the triangular peak of Laon, and taking advantage of the conformation of the land, which here was hollowed and receding, they succeeded in attaining the walls of the city. But Bulow's infantry stopped them at the foot of the ramparts, then pouring forth showers of grape, forced them to redescend this fatal height, before which our good fortune deserted us. Napoleon, however, who did not yet abandon the hope of driving Blucher from his position, sent Drouot at the head of a detachment to a great distance on our left, to try whether it would not be possible to advance along the route of La Fére, and annoy the enemy sufficiently to make him let go his hold.

"Drouot, whose sincerity was never called in question, having after a daring reconnoissance, pronounced this last attempt impracticable, Napoleon was obliged to admit the belief that Blucher's position was impregnable.

"The position of each had been so during the last twenty-four hours; Blucher had been as powerless against Clacy and Semilly as Napoleon against Laon. But Napoleon's position would not continue impregnable twenty-four hours longer, should Blucher execute his project of marching *en masse* by the route from Laon to Reims, to drive Marmont back on Berry-au-Bac, and cross the Aisne on our right. It was therefore impossible for Napoleon to remain

the grand army of the allies and that of Blucher I saw that it would be easy to defeat this corps alone; and, on the thirteenth, put myself in march on Reims, leaving Mortier at Soissons with twelve thousand men. At four o'clock in the afternoon we arrived before that city; the enemy, surprised at our abrupt appearance, had scarcely time to take position in front of that city on the road to Fismes. We attacked him, and threw him beyond the Vesle. Count St. Priest was mortally wounded; his troops were thrown into disorder. While their rear-guard defended themselves in Reims, I turned the city by forcing the passage of the Vesle at St. Brice. The rout of the enemy was decided; the mass of his corps gained Bery-au-Bac; the troops of the rear-guard scattered, and directed their flight by the roads to Neufchatel, Rethel, and Chalons. The enemy lost eleven pieces of cannon, two thousand and five hundred prisoners, one thousand and five hundred wounded, and seven hundred killed; we lost less than a thousand men *hors-de-combat.* I remained three days at Reims to give some repose to my troops before carrying them on the Aube and Seine, where the grand army of the allies had taken the offensive.

where he was; he was obliged to retrace his steps, and fall back on Soissons. However painful this determination might be, still, as it was indispensable, Napoleon made up his mind without hesitation, and the next morning, the eleventh of March, he repassed the defile of Chivy and Estouvelles, to fall back on Soissons, whilst Marmont, posted on the bridge of Berry-au-Bac, defended the Aisne above him.

"The enemy took especial care not to pursue this angry lion, the thought of whose return made even a victorious enemy tremble. Napoleon could therefore return to Soissons without disquietude.

"These three terrible days—the seventh at Craonne, the ninth and tenth at Laon—had cost Napoleon about twelve thousand men; and if they cost the enemy fifteen thousand, that was a poor consolation, because our adversaries had still ninety thousand soldiers, whilst we had little more than forty thousand, including even the small division of the Duke of Padua, who had come to reënforce Marshal Marmont.

"But the worst of all was, not the numerical, but the moral loss, and the military consequences of the last operations."

Operations of Schwartzenberg on the Aube.—After the evacuation of Troyes, Prince Schwartzenberg had continued his retreat to Chaumont, where he established his general head-quarters and his reserves. The other corps of his army still remained on the right bank of the Aube, having before them Marshals Macdonald, and Oudinot, the former occupying Ferté-sur-Aube and the second Bar-sur-Aube. Having learned that I had turned my efforts against Blucher, the allies, after consultation, took the initiative. On the twenty-seventh of February, Wittgenstein and Wrede attacked Oudinot and dislodged him from Bar-sur-Aube, after an obstinate combat which cost abeut three thousand men on each side. The next day the Prince of Wurtemberg and Giulay forced Macdonald to abandon Ferté-sur-Aube. The following day the allies slowly advanced on Troyes, where Macdonald had concentrated his army; but as this army, weakened by detachments, did not amount to more than twenty-five thousand men, Macdonald did not dare run the chance of a battle; he evacuated Troyes on the fourth of March, and retreated to Nogent where he repassed to the right bank of the Seine.

His Vanguard passes the Seine at Pont.—Prince Schwartzenberg, satisfied with his return to Troyes, remained there ten days with his arms folded, waiting with patience for news from Blucher. On the evening of the fourteenth, he learned that I had been repulsed before Laon. This good news excited his ardor and determined him to resume the offensive; nevertheless, this was done with the greatest caution, and only the corps of Wrede and Wittgenstein crossed the Seine at Pont. On the sixteenth, the latter attacked the left of Macdonald, who evacuated Provins and established himself near Maison-Rouge, on the road from Provins to Nangis; the allies did not advance any further. At the report of my return, Schwartzenberg gave himself up again to his habitual perplexities; fearing to be taken in flank or rear by my handful of men, he resolved to fall back on Brienne in order to cover his communications and the ground between the Aube and the Marne. On the seventeenth, the different corps of the grand army put themselves in retreat, ascending the Aube and the Seine. The same day I began my operations in the direction of Troyes.

The Empress and Regency remove to Blois. — As Paris continued to be the objective point of the enemy, I deemed it best to provide for the safety of my family. Joseph had received orders to remove with the council of ministers to the Loire, as soon as the danger became pressing. It would have been better, without doubt, in the month of February, when the capital was threatened, to send the regency, the senate, and administrative authorities to Nevers or Clermont. Then probably affairs would have taken a different turn, and the occupation of Paris by the Russians and Prussians would not have had the same importance, as in that case there would have been no legal authorities there to betray my interests and those of France. But I feared at that epoch to alarm the capital, and I had then but little confidence in the National Guards; it was, however, the senate and high functionaries whom I ought to have distrusted.

Operations of Napoleon against the Grand Allied Army. —Being forced to leave Marmont and Mortier on the Aisne with twenty thousand men to hold the army of Blucher in check, I could, therefore, take with me only eighteen thousand, notwithstanding the several reënforcements received from Reims; but I expected to be joined on the Aube by the army of Macdonald and by six thousand men whom General Lefebvre-Desnouettes was to bring me from Paris. Moreover, I had already seen what terror was inspired by my name alone at the head-quarters of Schwartzenberg. My first march was from Reims to Epernay. On the eighteenth,

I arrived at Frère-Champenoise, and on the nineteenth, at Plancy. My light cavalry passed the Aube and advanced on one side to Bessy and on the other to Méry. The allies were in full retreat in the direction of Troyes and Lesmont. If I had supposed that they would give me battle between the Seine and the Aube I would have waited at Plancy for Lefebvre-Desnouettes and Macdonald, without risking my feeble corps in the midst of their army; but as nothing on their part indicated such a resolution, I determined to push them warmly with what troops I had in hand, without giving them time to reconnoitre.

Battle of Arcis.—On the twentieth, I marched from Plancy on Arcis; my cavalry ascended the left bank of the Aube, and the infantry the right bank. We found Arcis evacuated, and established ourselves in front of that city on the roads to Troyes and Lesmont. The cavalry formed the right, and the half of the infantry, which had already passed the Aube, established itself on the left. The remainder of this arm was still on the march from Plancy to Arcis. I had regarded this place only as a point of departure for the pursuit of the enemy; on the contrary, we were obliged to sustain here a decisive combat.

The Emperor Alexander began to be wearied with the indecisive movements which political policy had assigned to the allied armies; it seemed to him disgraceful that the most formidable armies of Europe, commanded by their soveieigns in person, should be continually repulsed by a mere handful of men. He had at last declared in a council that they must unite with Blucher and act in a single mass on Paris to dictate there a peace which they could not impose on me at Chatillon. In accordance with the deliberations of this council, the allied army concentrated its forces on Arcis; Wrede's corps, which was nearest to this city, received orders to reoccupy it. At two o'clock P. M. the Bavarian general commenced his attack; my infantry maintained its position and defended with success the village of Grand-Torcy; but my cavalry was defeated by that of the allies. The stragglers threw themselves on the bridges of Arcis; the moment was critical. If the enemy should carry these bridges, my left, deprived of all means of retreat, would be destroyed. Seeing the importance of the moment, I made every effort to rally my right, and succeeded only by placing myself at their head, sword in hand; the bridges were preserved and my infantry took advantage of them to pass to the left of the Aube. The combat was continued till midnight: We experienced sensible losses, but kept our position. Thinking that Schwartzenberg had fought only to cover his retreat, I determined to pursue the enemy with my troops now considerably reënforced. On the night of the twentieth, I had been joined by the corps of Lefebvre-Desnouttes, and on the morning of the twenty-first, by twelve thousand men from the army of Macdonald. The remainder of Macdonald's troops had not yet passed Plancy. But the enemy, instead of retiring, had united all his army, and was preparing to give battle. My advanced guard discovered this army drawn up in several lines from Chaudrey-sur-Aube to the rivulet of Barbuisse. The enemy had near one hundred thousand men, and I not thirty-five thousand. To accept a battle with so great a disparity of forces, in a vast plain with a miry river behind me, would expose my last resources to infallible ruin. Imperious necessity imposed a retreat, and I resigned myself to it.

This retreat, executed in the presence of the enemy, might have been disastrous; but fortunately, Schwartzenberg, preoccupied with the idea of our attacking him, did not think to pursue us till two o'clock P. M. The greater part of my army had already passed the Aube. Oudinot's corps alone remained on the left bank in the city of Arcis to cover my march. This rear-guard was rudely assaulted; the allies penetrated into the city and obliged Oudinot to recross the river.

Remarks on Napoleon's Position.—My situation was now eminently perilous. On the very day of the battle of Arcis, the congress of Chatillon had dissolved. The allied sovereigns, having determined to overthrow my throne, were about to give free play to their military force; and my father-in-law, wearied with the course which he had adopted, less from his attachments for me than for the interests of his daughter, promised to offer no obstacles to this plan. Count d'Artois was at Vesoul, and the Duke d'Angoulême at Bordeaux; La Vendée was rising. Hemmed in by the enemy's two masses on the Aisne and Aube, the weakest of which was incomparably stronger than all my disposable forces on the theatre of war, it was now impossible for me to undertake anything serious against either of them. I had yet a small army in Italy, and strong garrisons in the north. I had finally sent back Ferdinand into Spain, and directed Suchet to restore to him the places which we still occupied on the Ebro; but it had become impossible for the armies of Spain to come to my assistance, for they were now strongly engaged against Wellington who, the middle of February, had resumed the offensive and invaded Gascony.

Success of the Allies in the South.—On the arrival of the Duke d'Angoulême, who gave him hopes of a *point-d'appui* in the provinces in the south, and hearing of the departure of two of Soult's divisions, Wellington resolved to pass the Adour and the Gaves, as soon as the roads became practicable. Soult, having only forty thousand men, and half of these conscripts, with which to oppose seventy-five thousand combatants, and being turned by his left, was obliged to retreat. He wisely resolved not to direct himself on the interior of France, but in a line parallel to the frontier of the

Pyrenees; he reached Orthès, where he decided to give battle. This action in which the English gained nothing but the field of battle, nevertheless obliged Soult to continue his movement on Toulouse. Wellington, solicited by the royalists to detach a corps on Bordeaux had sent Beresford to that place. This city, once so celebrated for its patriotism, received the English as the Romans received their triumphant legions, and France had the misfortune to see her own citizens the first to welcome the invaders.

Bold Project of Napoleon.—It will be seen from this brief review of my situation, that I was now obliged to resort to the most desperate means, as nothing less than extreme measures could afford me any chance of safety. The fate of France now depended on me alone; and no place was of importance except made so by my presence. As ten victories in Champagne had not softened the hatred of the enemy, it was necessary to remove the theatre of operations on a point where my success would obtain more important results. To make peace and save the Empire, it was necessary to replant our eagles on the banks of the Rhine. This object could not be accomplished by combats. We were too weak for that. I had no other resource than to manœuvre on the enemy's communications, at the risk of losing my own. I do not deny that the chance was hazardous, but it was the only hope of safety left.

I resolved to run this chance, throwing myself in mass by St. Dizier toward the Upper Meuse; I there expected strong reënforcements drawn from the garrisons of Lorraine and Alsace; and by raising the departments which had been overrun by the enemy, I would threaten the line of operations of the grand army, which would be seriously compromised. By thus compelling the enemy to retrace his steps, I would have the advantage of drawing him on ground singularly favorable for my strategic operations. A partial victory might destroy the armed force of the enemy, while, in case of a check, I could have time to recruit under the protection of our fortresses. I would leave Paris exposed; but this was of little importance for me whose capital was at my own head-quarters. As this plan of operations has not been justified by success, there are not wanting critics who regard it as absurd; for parlor generals, like the vulgar, judge every thing by the results. These same critics would have praised my combinations to the skies, if Schwartzenberg had fallen back on Bâle, as there was every reason to suppose he would. But what better could I do? I had no option. It was necessary to attempt this operation which, I confess, accelerated my fall before it was carried into execution, or to remain between the Seine and the Marne before the immense superiority of the enemy, and exposed to a more slow but more certain destruction. What impartial man will venture to blame my decision? If I had attempted it immediately after the victory of Montereau, and at the same time recalled Suchet to Lyons, who will say that I could not have obtained important results?

On the evening of the twenty-first of March, I pushed my advanced guard to Sommepuis; the remainder of my army echeloned from this town to the Aube. On the twenty-second, I passed the Marne at the ford of Frignicourt, and marched on Faremont. Macdonald came to Dosnon. The allies had thrown a garrison into Vitry; I summoned the place to surrender; it refused. It not being my intention to amuse myself with a siege, I passed on and reached St. Dizier on the twenty-third; Macdonald passed the Marne at Frignicourt, and arrived at Villotte. On the twenty-third I reached Doulevent.

The news of my retreat from Arcis had not produced the effect on the enemy which I had hoped. Schwartzenberg, stimulated by the Emperor Alexander, and by the partial success gained over my rear-guard at Arcis, and ignorant of my projects upon his communications, did not fall back on Chaumont as I had hoped. On the contrary, he had passed the Aube to follow me towards Vitry, as much to watch my movements as to protect his line of operations, and connect himself with Blucher. On the twenty-second, the grand army passed the Aube at Ramerupt, Songy, and Lesmont, pushing forwards parties as far as Vitry.

Operations of Blucher.—Blucher, on his side, unable to believe that he had gained a victory at Laon, intimidated by the defeat of St. Priest's corps, and remembering the rude blows which I had given him the month before, had remained inactive for ten entire days behind the Aisne. However, when he learned that I had left Reims, he prepared to cross that river, and resolved to detach Wintzingerode with eight thousand horse to restore his communications with Schwartzenberg. For this purpose a heavy body of Russian cavalry passed the Aisne on the right of Marmont, and threatened to cut off his retreat. This marshal who, with nine thousand men, found himself exposed to eighty thousand, had reason to fear being surrounded at Bery-au-Bac; he decided to blow up the bridge, and fall back on Fismes, where Mortier joined him after having evacuated Reims, which Wintzingerode occupied on the twentieth without opposition. The concentration of the two marshals at Fismes was very well, on the supposition that my enterprise on Arcis had been crowned with success; but was unfortunate for the execution of my new project. I could not blame them as they could not have known my present plan, and heretofore it had been their task to cover my communications with Paris.

Freed from the presence of Marmont at Bery-au-Bac, Blucher threw bridges over the Aisne, and sent the corps of Kleist and York in pursuit of our columns, while Wintzingerode took the road to Reims for the object already mentioned.

Everything seemed to combine, as if by enchantment to destroy my project; for, at the moment when Schwartzenberg approached the north, leaving the road to Chaumont exposed, Blucher, who before had resolved to march direct to Paris, took, by chance, the resolution to move to the south towards the army of Bohemia. *Thus, the two grand armies of the enemy, instead of pursuing diverging lines, concentrated their forces towards a single line, at the very moment that my two little masses separated from each other.*

Marmont and Mortier are separated from Napoleon.—The order to join me at Vitry, it is said, did not reach the marshals till the evening of the twenty-first, after their arrival at Fère-en-Tardenois. On this point must rest the judgment that will be given of their march. In addition to this unfortunate delay in receiving my orders, a still greater *contre-temps* now occurred. The Cossacks, on the twenty-second, captured a courier with my letter to the Empress communicating my project. Blucher immediately resolved to push the corps of Sacken and Langeron on Reims and Chalons, in order to connect himself with Schwartzenberg who, he learned, had marched in the direction of Vitry. This circumstance rendered the situation of the two marshals very critical. From Fère-en-Tardenois they could no longer return to Reims, as that city was in the possession of the enemy, and the corps of York and Kleist had followed them on Fismes. They could not expect to reach Chalons by Epernay, for Wintzingerode was already master of that road. They therefore resolved to march on Chateau-Thierry, in order to gain the road to Montmirail, and thus reach Vatry, an intermediate point between Chalons and Vitry. This circumspection, very natural for a corps of seventeen thousand men before two large armies, destroyed all my hopes.

Many writers have imputed blame to my lieutenants: but I confess that it was difficult for them to act otherwise than they did. Blucher marched on the twenty-third to Reims, and on the twenty-fourth to Chalons. If Marmont had received my order at Fismes, as has been said by some, it is certain that he might have forced his passage on the twenty-second through the cavalry of Wintzingerode, which could not have disputed Reims. But if that marshal received the order only at Fère-en-Tardenois, he is blameless; it was difficult to precede Blucher at Chalons. By marching on the twenty-second from Fère on Epernay, it was not physically impossible to reach Chalons on the twenty-third, but Wintzingerode was already there, and, being certain to be sustained by Blucher, he would not have abandoned the city. Moreover the road from Fère-en-Tardenois to Epernay is very difficult, and it would have required two hard days' march to reach Chalons.

The Emperor Alexander decides to march on Paris.—At the very moment when mere chance had given a concentric direction to the enemy's masses, the Emperor Alexander, having learned my project by an intercepted letter, and certain of the approach of Blucher, assembled at Sommepuis those of his generals in whom he had most confidence, and proposed to them the question, *whether it was most advisable to advance on Paris, without troubling himself about my movement on Lorraine, or whether he should fall back on the Rhine.* All agreed with him that the first was the preferable course. Even Schwartzenberg, who had been left free by my new project, in separating from the cabinet of the emperor of Austria who had retired from Bar-sur-Aube to Dijon, decided for this bold march. The information was immediately communicated to Blucher, and as soon as the allied sovereigns were certain that the junction of their armies was fully consummated, they prepared to march on Paris by the roads from Vitry to Sézanne, and from Chalons to Montmirail. General Wintzingerode with eight thousand horse and more than forty pieces of cannon, marched from Vitry on St. Dizier to cover their movements, and make us believe he was followed by the whole army. On the twenty-fifth, he occupied St. Dizier, and pushed his advanced guard to Eclaron on the left of the Marne.

This determination of the sovereigns was without doubt the best which they could have adopted. But I had no reason to expect so fundamental a change in the principles upon which they had acted for the last two months.

Efforts of Napoleon to communicate with Mortier and Marmont.—I had been joined at St. Dizier by Caulaincourt, but I could receive no news of Marmont and Mortier. The return of my negotiator had redoubled the audacity of the malcontents at my headquarters: seeing my fall approaching, they began to ask themselves whether it was necessary for them to share my fate by exposing themselves to the same chances. It seemed that the honor and the independence of France were of no account in this conflict where each thought only of his own preservation.

The army alone manifested true devotion.

In the mean time, to profit by my new situation, I pushed Oudinot to Bar-sur-Ornain. This was his native country, and he was to raise Lorraine. My light cavalry threw itself by Joinville on Chaumont, from which the Emperor of Austria was obliged to decamp in all haste on Dijon. I had been at Doulevent for twenty-four hours in a painful state of uncertainty, when, on the twenty-sixth, a considerable force of the enemy was discovered approaching from the direction of St. Dizier. I could not doubt its being the army of Schwartzenberg, and that its unexpected appearance had alone caused the delay of my marshals. How could I imagine that it was the army of Blucher, which I had left at Soissons behind the Aisne, separated by the corps of Marmont and Mortier. I had no time to hesitate, and marched against the enemy to defeat him, and open the road to Chalons, thinking that I was at last to join my marshals. Sebastiani and Milhaud drove back the squadrons of Wintzingerode to Bar and St. Mihiel, and inflicted on them a loss of twelve hundred men *hors-de-combat*. What was my astonishment when I learned from the prisoners that it was the army of Silesia that I had before me! They even spoke of the march of two armies on Paris: but I could not credit such a complication of unfortunate circumstances. I stopped at St. Dizier, and, the twenty-seventh, made a forced reconnoissance on Vitry. Here all my misfortunes were confirmed. The junction of the enemy's armies had been effected on the twenty-third, and the report of their march on Paris was but too well founded. A powerful party in the capital had invited them there; besides, they had just gained a victory at Frère-Champenoise. Notwithstanding this thunderbolt, I still hesitated to renounce my plan. But to execute it with any hope of success required the assistance of the twenty-five thousand men which Marmont, Mortier, and Pacthod were to bring me. But instead of adding to the force of my army which was to decide the fate of the Empire, they were likely to be surrounded and compromised in the midst of two powerful armies of the enemy. Moreover, all my generals exclaimed against the imprudence of abandoning Paris. For a time I resisted all their clamors. I feared less for my own fate, than that of my old companions in arms, and finally yielded to these importunate and pusillanimous representations. But before speaking of my return to the capital, let me describe the operations of the marshals.

These Marshals retire on Paris.—Marmont and Mortier, on leaving Chateau-Thierry had taken two different roads. The first arrived, on the evening of the twenty-fourth, at Sommesous and soon perceived that it was now impossible to join me, for his reconnoitring parties discovered the presence of an immense army on the plains between Chalons and Vitry, and the approach of the numerous columns that marched against me. He was obliged to wait the junction of Mortier, who had taken the road from Villeseneux and Chaintrix, ignorant of the vicinity of a formidable army. Marmont, however, began his retreat on Frère-Champenoise where he waited for Mortier's columns.

The allies, having received information of the presence of these two corps, commenced their movement, on the twenty-fifth, to crush them,—Blucher from the road from Montmirail, and Susanne, and the grand army by that from Vitry to Frère-Champenoise. The last brigade of Mortier's corps, retarded in its march, was overtaken at Frère-Champenoise by the cavalry of the allies; and after having received in square several charges sustained by artillery, it left the remains of six battalions in the hands of the enemy.

The corps of eight thousand National Guards which left Montmirail with a grand convoy of artillery, had just arrived on the Soude, without the marshals having received timely notice of their march, the orders for which were issued directly from my staff. Being attacked near Frécon by the Russian cavalry of the army of Silesia under the orders of Wassitsckof, it reached Frère-Champenoise in the hope of here joining the marshals. But, it was now attacked by the Emperor Alexander who had pushed the rear guard of Marmont at the head of the reserve of the Grand-duke Constantine. Our squares repulsed repeated charges of the enemy; but in resuming the march they fell into disorder. Two squares were separated and broken; the three others reduced to a single mass, and exposed to the fire of sixty pieces of artillery, were pierced and captured, notwithstanding a resistance very honorable for militia, who, perhaps, were here under fire for the first time.

This unfortunate check not only cost me ten thousand men and eighty pieces of cannon, so maladroitly sacrificed, but, deprived me of twenty-five thousand combatants upon whom I had counted to reënforce the army which was to deliver Alsace and Lorraine.

The marshals had no other course but to retire on Paris in all haste, and it was very far from certain that they could even reach there, for the Prussian corps of Kleist and York, at Chateau-Thierry, might easily prevent them. Fortunately, these Prussians had pushed forward only their infantry on Ferté-Goucher, having sent their cavalry in the direction of Sézanne to communicate with Blucher. The embarrassment of the marshals was, nevertheless, very great, when on their arrival at Ferté-Goucher, on the twenty-sixth, they found that city in the hands of the Prussians, who barred to them the great road from Sézanne to Paris. Being too weak to force a passage, sword in hand, they turned off to Provins where they arrived on the twenty-seventh ; the next day Mortier marched on Guignes, and Marmont to Melun. The same day the allies entered Meaux, and their advanced guard pushed on to Ville-Parisis. These events, so disastrous in themselves, became still more so by the consternation which they caused in the capital. The dispatches which I received proved that the approach of danger, instead of electrifying all minds, seemed to completely discourage them.

Difficulties of Napoleon's Situation.—This news plunged me into new perplexities ; wherever I cast my eyes all was disaster. I first thought to fall on the rear of the allies' columns ; I might undoubtedly turn Vitry by the ford of Frignicourt ; but further information proved that we could scarcely reach them before they passed the Marne at Meaux or Lagny ; they were sufficiently strong to dispute with me the passage of this river with a part of their forces, while the remainder attacked Paris. There seemed then no means of saving the capital. It was possible, however, that by directing my march on the left of the Seine, Paris would hold out till I could arrive. To increase my misfortune, my small army was now scattered. The main body was with me at Vitry; a considerable corps had pursued Wintzingerode to Bar-le-Duc. All my light cavalry had been pushed on Chaumont, to intercept the enemy's line of operations. The Emperor of Austria, who was there with his diplomatic and administrative head-quarters, saved himself in all haste at Dijon, hotly pursued by our partisans. I designated Troyes as the point of concentration for all my corps. I myself returned to St. Dizier, on the evening of the twenty-seventh, and on the twenty-eighth, went to Montierender.

He flies to Defend the Capital.—I had not yet lost all hope; I thought that the sight of the Cossacks at the foot of Montmartre would move all hearts, and that the Parisians, forgetting for the moment their ill-founded distrust, would make it a point of honor to repulse the enemy and defend, to the last extremity, the walls of the capital. This populous city might easily put on foot twenty thousand National Guards, who, with the depôt of the troops of the line in the place, could form an army of forty thousand men to defend the strong position which covered Paris on the right of the Seine; positions for the establishment of batteries had been marked out, and with proper activity they might have been armed with two hundred guns. The occupation of the capital being, therefore, not an affair of a day, I flattered myself that I might yet arrive in time to revive its defense by my presence and the troops who followed me. I took the post, and traveling all night, reached La Cour-de-France. What was my surprise at here meeting General Belliard with Mortier's cavalry! The army of the marshals was following near by; Paris then had fallen!

Battle of Paris.—During the day of the twenty-ninth, the allies had continued their march on Paris by the left bank of the Marne, leaving the corps of Sacken and Wrede at Meaux to cover their rear. The same night Mortier and Marmont had reached Charenton, and, on the morning of the thirtieth, occupied the heights which command Paris from the north. Reënforced by all the recruits of the depôts of the guard, they had twenty thousand men under arms; but the National Guards furnished only five thousand men to sustain the troops of the line, and they put in battery only a small part of the disposable garrison-artillery; with this exception, they employed all the resources of the place. The brilliant youth of the Polytechnic School and of the Veterinary School of Alfort, the hope of an entire generation, volunteered to serve the artillery, which had only mutilated invalids to point the guns. If we compare this conduct with that of the inhabitants of Vienna and Berlin when we entered these cities, we shall find that Paris exhibited still more patriotism than they. The allies had one hundred and twenty thousand men; their grand army attacked the heights of Belleville, while Blucher assailed Montmartre. The combat began with the day; my troops, notwithstanding their extreme inferiority in number, justified their ancient fame; they firmly disputed their last battle-field. Campans covered himself with glory at Romainville; old Marshal Moncey bravely fought at the head of the National Guard which assisted Mortier in the defense from Montmartre to the Seine. It was not till four o'clock P. M., that the enemy succeeded in crowning the heights of Belleville and Montmartre, from which they threw their projectiles on the faubourgs. There was now no resource but to defend foot by foot the streets; but this could not be done without the hearty coöperation of the inhabitants, and the marshals were doubtful whether they were disposed to make this effort. Moreover there was no one among these chiefs of sufficient head to conceive and execute such energetic measures. My brother Joseph, to whom I had given the command-in-chief, at Paris, was the first to leave. The marshals, with his authorization, entered into a treaty with the enemy. The capital opened its gates, and the troops of the line who had defended the approaches profited by the night to fall back on Essonne.

Situation of France.—I returned to Fontainebleau, my soul weighed down to death. By rallying all my troops, I could yet dispose of fifty thousand men; but this force, which would have been sufficient to prevent the entrance of the allies into Paris, was not sufficient to drive them out. The news from the south was far from favorable; the English were in possession of Bordeaux, and the Austrians of Lyons. The Anglo-Sicilian army of Bentinck, disposable in Catalonia, came to attack Genoa; my empire was falling on all sides. No human force could retard its overthrow, after France refused to unite her fate with mine. The French people had not displayed the energy which I expected in the defense of their soil; the small number of men who took up arms covered themselves with glory; the rest well merited the fate which befell them.

Want of Public Spirit in Paris.—I must confess that twenty years of war, the conscription, anticipated for two years, the cohorts of the bans levied in 1812, had exhausted the class which furnishes the best soldiers. Since the year 1800, the word *Patrie* was no longer heard in the streets, nor in the salons of Paris. Nevertheless, the word *honor*, which made to vibrate every heart in France, supplied its place. The remembrance of the grand movement of 1793, was still fresh in my memory; the independence of France was so closely connected with the integrity of the soil that I was unable to conceive the apathy of the nation at such a decisive crisis.

The orators of the tribune seized the moment of peril to

declaim and excite discord, when all resentments should have been stifled. Public scribblers with whom Paris swarmed and whom I had subjected to salutary restraint, now applied their pens to compose political pamphlets. The salons, filled with fops and old women who wished to guide the state, opened upon me their noisy batteries. In a word, the same nation, which in 1793 had condemned to death the young girls who went to Verdun to compliment the King of Prussia, in 1814, represented the defenders of their country as freebooters, and the soldiers of the coalition as heroes! They did not blush to deck themselves in bonnets *à la Blucher* eight days before his cannon thundered on Paris. The brave men who covered themselves with glory in defending the capital against a force ten times their own, exhausted with hunger, found no merited succor in traversing the city; but the shops, which had been closed to them, were thrown open to the Pandours! All heads were turned. Bordeaux even excelled Paris, and the English were there received as liberators! Lyons alone went into mourning at the appearance of the Austrians!*

* After describing the sudden change of opinion in Paris against Napoleon, Thiers says:

"Such was the fierce explosion of anger to which, by a terrible reaction in sublunary things, Napoleon was exposed; he who during twenty years had been so servilely flattered, he whose deeds had excited the admiration of the astonished world.

"But he was too great not to remain unmoved by such indignities, whilst he was at the same time conscious that his own acts had produced this revulsion of public feeling. And the flatteries lavished at the same time on the allied sovereigns made the picture of humanity still more pitiable.

"Alexander, undoubtedly, by his own conduct and the example he gave his allies, deserved the thanks of the French people. But if ingratitude can not be sanctioned under any circumstances, gratitude ought to be measured in expression when addressed to the conqerors of our native land. Yet it was not so, and the Royalists went so far as to say that the allied sovereigns, who had suffered so much from the French, displayed great magnanimity, in taking so gentle a vengeance. The flames of Moscow were every day recalled, not by Russian but by French writers. They were not content with praising Marshal Blucher and General Sacken, brave men, whose praise was natural and well-

Conduct of the Emperor of Russia in Paris.—But I will render unto Cæsar the things that are Cæsar's: and I must confess that the sojourn of Alexander at Paris contrasted with my treatment of Moscow and of Smolensko at my departure from these places; his conduct was noble and generous: it is true that it was for his interest to seek to gain the good will of the Parisians, and that France has paid dear for that generosity. But as it sprung from the heart, it is none the less worthy of eulogy. His entrance into Paris was more like that of Henry IV., than that of a conqueror who came to avenge the explosion of the Kremlin, and the ravage of his empire. An immense crowd saluted him with acclamation, and crowded to see him pass. They believed that, satisfied with my fall, he would not enrich himself with the spoils of the empire.

Intrigues of the Factions.—My reign had been no field for the intrigues of women. With the exception of the wives and families of my army whom I loaded with favors, they loved me not: mothers reproached me with the conscription, as though that had been my work; women of gallantry reproached my severity; dowagers of the faubourg St. Germain treated me as a parvenu soldier, and they never could pardon me for eclipsing the old régime. They received the allies with acclamations, and waved their handkerchiefs from

deserved from Prussian and Russian lips, but these writers sought out a French emigrant, General Langeron, who served in the army of the Czar, and related with complacency how he had distinguished himself in the attack on Montmartre, and with what well-merited reward he had been loaded by the Russian monarch. Thus, amongst the many changes of our great and terrible revolution, patriotism, like liberty, were doomed to reverses; and just as liberty, the idol of every heart in 1789, became in 1793, the object of universal execration, in like manner patriotism had now fallen into such disrepute, that the act of bearing arms against the natal soil, an act condemned in every age, now met laudation. Weary days of reaction, when the public mind, losing its primary notions of right and wrong, rejects what it had adored and adores what it had rejected, and esteems the most shameful contradictions a happy reconversion to truth."

all the windows of the boulevards through which the cortège passed. Intriguers presented this fortuitous circumstance as a manifestation of public opinion. To believe them, France was sighing for the princes which the same generation had refused to recognize: they pretended that these handkerchiefs were the oriflamme of the Valois, the flag of Philip Augustus!!! It was a fine theme for the poetic heads of demagogues, and for the machinations of the Talleyrands, the Dalbergs, the Fouchés, the Duponts, the Vitrolles, &c. The club of these gentlemen, directed by the ex-bishop of Autun, after having moved heaven and earth to bring the allies from Frankfort and Chaumont to Paris, easily acquired credit with the sovereigns; it persuaded them that the nation wished me no longer; and, certain of finding support among the old men of the senate, with whose conduct I had not always been satisfied, they hastened to obtain from this mutilated body a vote conformable to their designs. The second of April, the senate, which I had created and loaded with benefits, declared me dethroned, and instituted a provisional government. It must, however, be remarked that this resolution was passed by a factious minority; for of the one hundred and forty members composing that body only sixty-six took part in it, and these were not the men for whom I had done the least. They were presided over by Talleyrand, whose name will pass to posterity as the synonym of an apostate and a sycophant.*

* The following is Thiers' account of some of Talleyrand's intrigues at this epoch:

"The man destined soon to fill this void—M. de Talleyrand, whom by a secret instinct Napoleon had foreseen as the author of his fall, and whom the public, by an instinct as correct, looked upon as the necessary author of an approaching revolution,—M. de Talleyrand found himself at this moment in a state of extreme perplexity. In virtue of his rank as Grand Dignitary, he ought to follow the Regent; but by leaving, he rejected the great part that awaited his acceptance; and by not leaving, he exposed himself to be taken in an overt act of treason, which might involve serious consequences, if Napo-

Abdication of Fontainebleau.—The troops who surrounded me at Fontainebleau, although few in number, were so devoted, and capable of so much heroism that I might still

leon, by a sudden stroke of good fortune—always possible in his case—should re-appear as conqueror before the gates of the capital. To extricate himself from this embarrassment, he sought an interview with the Duke of Rovigo to obtain permission to remain at Paris, saying, that in the absence of the entire government, he would be able to render important services.

"The Duke of Rovigo, suspecting that these services would be rendered to some other than to Napoleon, refused the desired permission, which, in fact, he had not power to accord. M. de Talleyrand sought the prefects, but could not obtain what he desired; and not knowing how to cover with a specious pretext his prolonged stay at Paris, he took the resolution of stepping into a carriage, and affect at least a willingness to follow the Regent. Towards the close of the day, as the battle ceased to rage, he presented himself, without passport and with great traveling pomp, at the barrier leading to the Orleans route.

"The barrier was occupied by the National Guards, highly irritated against those who, during the past two days, had deserted the city. A kind of tumult was raised about M. de Talleyrand's carriage; some contemporaries regard this as a national outburst, others believe it to have been pre-arranged.

"His passport was demanded; he had none; a murmur was raised against this neglect of an essential formality; and then, with an affected deference to the opinion of the brave defenders of Paris, he retraced his steps and returned to his mansion.

"The greater part of those who contributed to detain him, and who were not desirous of a revolution, little suspected they had detained the man who was about to effect one.

"Not being fully satisfied as to the formality of his conduct, M. de Talleyrand repassed to the house of Marshal Marmont, who, the battle now over, had hastened to his dwelling, situate in the faubourg Poissonnière. People of every class flocked thither, seeking, on some side, a government, and crowding round the man who, at this moment, seemed to represent one, since he was head of the only force existing in the capital. Marshal Mortier was subordinate to him on all important occasions.

"The two prefects, a portion of the municipal body, and several distinguished personages were present. Every one spoke of the late events with emotion, and according to his individual sentiments. Seeing the marshal, whose face was blackened with powder, and his coat rent by balls, the assembly felicitated him on his courageous defense of Paris, and then proceeded to talk of the situation of affairs.

"There was a species of unanimity in condemning what they called the cowardly desertion of those that Napoleon had left in the capital to defend it, and against Napoleon himself, whose mad policy had brought the armies of Europe to the foot of Montmartre. The royalists—and there was a considerable number present—did not hesitate to say that the French ought to throw

have attempted some feat of arms. I, at first, thought of doing this, as, in the impossibility of conquering, every combat, whatever its issue, would at least add to the eclat of my

off an insupportable yoke, and boldly named the Bourbons. Two influential bankers, M.M. Peregaux and Lafitte, the one connected by the ties of blood, the other by those of friendship, with the Duke of Ragusa, attracted attention by the vivacity of their language. The second especially, whose secular success had just commenced, and whose versatile and brilliant talents had attracted general attention, spoke strongly, and went as far as to exclaim, on hearing the name of the Bourbons pronounced: 'Well, be it so, give us the Bourbons, if you wish, but with a Constitution that will guarantee us against a fearful despotism, and with peace, of which we have been so long deprived.' This unanimity of feeling against the imperial despotism, carried so far as to make the upper bourgeoisie consider the Bourbons, with whom they had never come in contact, very acceptable, produced an extraordinary impression on all present.

"It was suggested in the assembly that they ought not to think exclusively of the army, that the capital, too, ought to engage their attention. Marshal Marmont replied that he was not empowered to treat for the capital; it was therefore thought proper that the prefects, with a deputation from the Municipal Council and the National Guards, should be deputed to wait on the allied sovereigns, and demand from them that treatment to which Paris had a right from civilized princes, who, since the passage of the Rhine, had announced themselves as the liberators, and not the conquerors of France.

"Whilst these discussions were at the height, M. de Talleyrand arrived. He had a private conversation with Marshal Marmont. He wished at first to obtain something resembling an authorization of his stay at Paris, the which no person was less in a position to grant than the marshal, but he began to set less value on this permission when he saw what was passing around him.

"He instantly conceived the idea of making this visit facilitate a denouement which he now began to regard as inevitable, and which should, of necessity, be accomplished by him. No man was more open to flattery than Marshal Marmont, and none knew better than M. de Talleyrand how to administer the draught. The marshal had, during this campaign, committed serious errors, but discoverable only by military men, whilst he had, at the same time, displayed heroic bravery. On this very day especially, the thirtieth of March, he had acquired lasting claims on the gratitude of his country. His face, his hands, his dress, bore testimony to what he had done. M. de Talleyrand praised his courage, his talents, and especially his understanding, very much superior, as he affirmed, to that of other marshals. The Duke of Ragusa, as usual, became very much elated when told that he was endowed with high intelligence, in which his fellow-commanders were deficient, and it must be acknowledged, that in this respect, he possessed what they could lay no claim to.

"He listened, consequently, with a sentiment of profound satisfaction to what the arch-tempter, who was preparing his ruin, told him. M. de Talley-

fall. Besides who knows what would have been the result of a retrograde step of the allies? If we could not drive the enemy from Paris, it was easy to fall back behind the Loire, to rally Soult, Suchet, and Augereau, forming together a mass of one hundred and twenty or one hundred and thirty thousand men, throw them into our frontier line of fortresses, and fight as the Romans did in Spain when Hannibal was threatening the heart of the republic. The marshals,* wearied

rand took some trouble to point out the serious position of affairs, and the necessity of extricating France from the hands that had destroyed her; he gave the marshal to understand that under existing circumstances, a soldier who had defended Paris so gloriously, and who had still under his command the men at whose head he had fought, possessed the means of saving his country, which had now no master. M. de Talleyrand went no farther, for he knew that no person is seduced at the first attempt. He took his departure, and left the unfortunate Marmont intoxicated with vanity; and now, amid the disasters of France he sketched for himself, in imagination, the most brilliant destiny, whilst the simple-minded and upright soldier, who had been his colleague, on this same thirtieth March, Mortier, whose face, too, was blackened with powder, devoured his grief in the loneliness to which his modesty and uprightness consigned him."

* Thiers thus speaks of the conduct of Napoleon to his officers at this time:

"He thought it very natural that people should quit him, for these officers, who had always obeyed his commands, except on the last day, were naturally anxious to rally round the Bourbons, in order to preserve the rank which was the just reward of the labors of their life.

"He only wished they had been a little more frank, and to encourage, he addressed them in the following noble language:—'Serve the Bourbons,' he said to them, 'serve them faithfully; no other course remains to you. If they act wisely, France, under their rule, may be happy and respected. I resisted M. de Caulaincourt's earnest entreaties to make me accept the peace of Chatillon. I was right. For me these conditions were humiliating; they are not so for the Bourbons. They find France as they left her, and may accept her ancient limits without compromising their dignity. Such as she is, France will still be powerful, and though geographically diminished, she will be still as morally great as before, by her courage, her arts, and her intellectual influence over the rest of the world. If her territorial extent is diminished, her glory is not. The memories of our victories will remain to her as a monument of imperishable greatness, and which will always have immense weight in the councils of Europe.

Serve France under the princes who bring back at this moment fortune, so fickle in times of revolution. Serve France under them as you have done under me. Do not make the task too difficult for them, and leave me, but give me a place in your memory.'

* * * * * * * * *

with the war, thought differently; they demanded to know what were my hopes, my resources, and the term of their sacrifices. They spoke to me of abdication as the means of

Napoleon told M. de Caulaincourt how much he was pleased with the conduct of Marshal Macdonald, who, though so long antagonistic to him, acted in this trying moment like a devoted friend; he took an indulgent view of Marshal Ney's nobility, and speaking of the conduct of his lieutenants with a slightly disdainful gentleness, said to M. de Caulaincourt: 'Ah! Caulaincourt, men, men!

"'My marshals would blush to act as Marmont has done, for they express the strongest indignation at his conduct, but they are very sorry that he has so far outstripped them on the road to fortune.

"'They would be very glad, without dishonoring themselves, to do as he has done, to acquire the same rights to the favor of the Bourbons.'

"He afterward spoke of Marmont with vexation, but without bitterness. 'I treated him,' he said, 'as if he were my own child. I have often had to defend him against his colleagues, who did not appreciate his intellectual advantages, and who, judging him only by what he appears on the field of battle, made no account of his military talents.

"'I created him marshal and duke through personal affection and regard for the recollections of childhood, and, I may well say, that I reckoned on his fidelity. He is, perhaps, the only man whose desertion I was not prepared for; but vanity, weakness of mind, and ambition have misled him. The unhappy man does not know what awaits him; his name will be forever dishonored. Believe me, I have no longer a thought about myself—my career is finished, or, very nearly so. Besides, what desire could I now have to reign over hearts that have grown weary of me, and are eager to offer their allegiance to another? I think only of France, which it is frightful to leave in this state—clipped, crippled, after having had frontiers so vast! Oh, Caulaincourt, that is the most poignant of the many humiliations heaped on my head! Oh, if these dolts had not abandoned me, I would have rebuilt the fabric of her greatness; for, be assured, the allies, maintaining their actual position, having Paris behind them and me in front, would have been destroyed. Had they left Paris to escape the danger, they should never have entered it again. The very fact of their leaving the city, at my approach, would be in itself a signal defeat. That unfortunate Marmont has frustrated this glorious result. Ah, Caulaincourt, what joy it would have been to restore the greatness of France in a few hours! Now, what is to be done? I would have about one hundred and fifty thousand men, with those I have here, and the troops Eugene, Augereau, Suchet, and Soult could bring; but I would be obliged to retire behind the Loire, entice the enemy to follow, and thus extend indefinitely the ravages to which France has been so long exposed, and try the fidelity of many, who, perhaps, would not bear the test better than Marmont,—and I should make all these efforts to prolong a reign, which, I clearly see, is drawing to a close. I do not feel sufficient energy to make such efforts.

"'Undoubtedly, in prolonging the war, we should find means of improving our position.

saving France; I felt that I owed to my country this sacrifice of self-love, and was resigned to the measure. I, however, did not deceive myself as to the results of this abdication; but as this form might some day be of use to my son, I no longer hesitated. A numerous party was in favor of placing this child on the throne, as the means of preserving the revolution with my dynasty; I for a moment participated in this hope, and charged Caulaincourt and Ney to offer to the Emperor Alexander to treat on this basis. This prince hesitated: he had had time to see that the mad acclamations of a population of women, and of a few thousand malcontents of all colors, were at least very equivocal signs of the national spirit. Many parties besieged him with their fears and their hopes. He judged that if the army received reënforcements from the National Guards, and pronounced strongly in my favor, the position of the allies in Paris would become precarious. He was deliberating what course to pursue, when it was announced to him that Marmont and his *corps-d'armée* had abandoned me. This incident determined his course; he thought my cause had now become desperate in the eyes even of the army. He did that

"'I am informed, on all sides, that the peasants of Lorraine, Champagne, and Burgundy, cut down isolated parties of the enemy. Within a short time the people will conceive a horror of the enemy; the Parisians will tire of Alexander's magnanimity. This prince is gracious in his manner,—he pleases women; but so much graciousness in a conqueror soon becomes revolting to the national pride of the conquered. Moreover, the Bourbons are coming, and who can foresee the consequences.

"'To-day they reconcile France with Europe; but to-morrow in what state will she be in relation to herself? They represent external peace, but internal war. You will see what they will have done with the country in a year. They will not keep Talleyrand six months. There would be many chances of success in a prolonged struggle,—chances both political and military,—but at the price of fearful calamities. Besides, at this moment, something more is needed than myself. My name, my statue, my sword, all cause alarm. I must yield. I am going to recall the marshals, and you will see their delight, when I extricate them from their difficulties, and authorize them to do as Marmont has done, without compromising their honor.'"

army injustice. The brave men who composed it were attached to me for life or death. Their hearts told them that after my fall, there would be no glory, or prosperity, or integrity of territory, for France. I was in their eyes the tutelary angel of their country. They had never seen it so beautiful and flourishing as during my reign. If, at other epochs, I had delivered it from the furies of anarchy, and the odious presence of foreign troops, why might I not eventually come out victorious from this new contest? The hope of saving France inflamed their noble courage. They counted for nothing the fatigues and dangers which I had shared with them, and whose reward should be an immortal glory. But intriguers and royalists, compromised by their first steps towards the conquerors, hastened to present the dishonorable act of two ungrateful generals as the opinion of the army; but so far were the troops from participating in this defection, that it was necessary to employ a *ruse* to get them to Versailles, where they rose up against the treason of their own generals. But whatever weight was thrown into the scale in favor of my dynasty by the energetic protestations of Marmont's corps, the senate destroyed all by recalling to the throne the brother of Louis XVI. All was now lost for my son as well as for myself. Not deeming the crown worth the consequences of a civil war, as a sequel to the existing foreign war, I now signed an unreserved abdication.*

It has been pretended that the allies had no choice, and that they would have been greatly embarrassed at repelling

* The following is the formal abdication of Napoleon at Fontainebleau, dated April, 6th, 1814:

"The allied powers having declared that the Emperor Napoleon is the sole obstacle to the reëstablishment of peace in Europe, the Emperor, faithful to his oath, declares that he renounces, for himself and his heirs, the thrones of France and Italy, and that there is no personal sacrifice, not even that of life itself, which he is not willing to make for the interests of France.

"NAPOLEON."

the lieutenant of the kingdom who had already arrived at Nancy, by trampling under foot the principles for which they had been fighting for the last twenty years. Such arguments are too absurd; if Russia, Austria, and Prussia, had consented to treat of my abdication on condition of recognizing my dynasty, and of discussing the conditions of a definitive peace with a council of regency, the *mouchoirs blancs* would certainly not have prevented their doing so. They yielded less to necessity and the intrigues of some personages, than to their own views of convenience and of a durable peace.

In taking the crown I had sheltered thrones from the people; in restoring it to the Bourbons they thought to secure them from successful soldiers. The impartial statesman will say that in the universal shipwreck of France, the return of the Bourbons seemed favorable for the country. Without that return, the kingdom, abandoned to the government of a regency, would have been exposed to the horrors of civil war, and the country placed in a situation, perhaps, still more delicate than on my return from Egypt. The recall of the legitimate princes seemed calculated to save France from anarchy. It was to be supposed that twenty years of misfortune had taught these princes some salutary lessons; that they had forgotten much and learned much; they were better situated than any one else to reconcile old France with new France; they required only the head and heart of Henry IV.

I felt, when too late, that I had committed an error in not putting a difference of religion between my dynasty and that of the Bourbons. It was not the mediocrity of talent, nor the political faults of James and of Charles II. which a second time hurled the race of the Stuarts from the throne of England, but the opposition of religious opinion. If, at the epoch of the concordat, I had embraced the reformed religion with all the men attached to the public administration, all France would have imitated my example, and my son would probably have succeeded me on the throne.

Russia was not inclined to favor my dynasty: in the first place, personal animosity had succeeded to the sentiments which Alexander had entertained for me in 1807; in the second place, he reflected that my son, as a minor, with Maria-Louisa as regent, would be under the influence of Metternich, and thus add to the power of Austria. England, flattering herself that she would be able to exercise an ascendency over the Bourbon refugees, and wishing to give a triumph to the principles which Pitt had always alleged as a pretext for all his wars, was the more interested in the overthrow of my family, not from affection for the princes whose restoration she had more than once opposed, but because, by their return now, she could accomplish her own views.

A general peace followed the recall of the Bourbons; but its results were hard; France lost everything. It was a treaty in which each one demanded ample indemnifications for his sacrifices and his expenses; but Louis XVIII. had expended nothing, and could not ask, with a good grace, for anything in the partition of my spoils. Carnot has reproached the Bourbons for having so easily yielded Belgium; but this was a *sine qua non*, without which England would not treat with them; and their return without a maritime peace, would have led to a war still worse than that to which they were putting an end. Moreover, what means had they left to refuse this cession? The battle of Toulouse had just completed the ruin of our affairs.

Battle of Toulouse.—Soult was making every preparation to defend this city, when Wellington presented himself to attack it, six days after my abdication. A confused report of the events which had occurred at Paris was not sufficient to deter this marshal from defending a French city when it was attacked by the English; but party spirit, always ready to misrepresent circumstances and pronounce men guilty, has not failed to accuse Soult of crime in making this defense. They have compared him to the celebrated William of Orange, who fought the battle of Mons after a treaty of peace had been signed, and out of pure animosity to Louis XIV. The comparison is unjust; for the Prince of Orange knew that peace was signed; whereas Soult had received only vague rumors of the entrance of the allies into Paris; there was still a state of war, and he repelled a hostile aggression.* He was beaten. It is true that his left and centre

* Napier says:

"Marshal Soult and General Thouvenot have been accused of fighting with a full knowledge of Napoleon's abdication. This charge circulated originally by the Bourbon party is utterly unfounded. The extent of the information conveyed to Thouvenot through the advanced posts has been already noticed; it was not sufficiently authentic to induce Sir John Hope to make a formal communication, and the governor could only treat it as an idle story to insult or to deceive him, and baffle his defense by retarding his counter-operations while the works for the siege were advancing.

"For, how unlikely, nay impossible, must it not have appeared, that the Emperor Napoleon, whose victories at Montmirail and Champ-Aubert were known before the close investment of Bayonne, should have been deprived of his crown in the space of a few weeks, and the stupendous event be only hinted at the outposts without any relaxation in the preparations for the siege.

"As false and unsubstantial is the charge against Soult.

"The acute remarks of an English military writer, that if the Duke of Dalmatia had known of the peace before he fought, he would certainly have announced it after the battle, were it only to maintain himself in that city, and claim a victory, is unanswerable; but there are direct proofs of the falsehood of the accusation. How was the intelligence to reach him? It was not until the seventh that the provisional government wrote to him from Paris, and the bearer could not have reached Toulouse under three days, even by the most direct way, which was through Montauban. Now the allies were in possession of that road on the fourth, and on the ninth the French army was actually invested. The intelligence from Paris must therefore have reached the allies first, as in fact it did, and it was not Soult, it was Lord Wellington who commenced the battle.

"The charge would therefore bear more against the English general, who would yet have been the most insane as well as the wickedest of men to have risked his army and his fame in a battle where so many obstacles seemed to deny success. He also was the person of all others, called upon by honor,

had repelled all the attacks of the enemy on Toulouse. His right, resting on the rivulet of Ers was turned by Beresford at the head of the divisions of Cole and Clinton. This general had marched with the first of these between the rivulet and our redoubts in a parallel, and, to say the least, an auda-

gratitude, justice, and patriotism, to avenge the useless slaughter of his soldiers to proclaim the infamy and seek the punishment of his inhuman adversary.

"Did he ever, by word or deed, countenance the calumny?

"Lord Aberdeen, after the passing of the English Reform bill, repeated the accusation in the House of Lords, and reviled the minister for being on amicable terms with a man capable of such a crime. Lord Wellington rose on the instant, and emphatically declared that Marshal Soult did not know, and that it was impossible he could know of the emperor's abdication when he fought the battle. The detestable distinction of sporting with men's lives by wholesale attaches to no general on the records of history save the Orange William, the murderer of Glencoe.

"And though Marshal Soult had known of the emperor's abdication, he could not, for that, have been justly placed beside that cold-blooded prince who fought at St. Denis with the peace of Nimeguen in his pocket, because he "would not deny himself a safe lesson in his trade."

"The French marshal was at the head of a brave army, and it was impossible to know whether Napoleon had abdicated voluntarily or been constrained. The authority of such men as Talleyrand, Fouché, and other intriguers, forming a provisional government, self-instituted, and under the protection of foreign bayonets, demanded no respect from Soult. He had even the right of denying the emperor's legal power to abdicate.

"He had the right, if he thought himself strong enough, to declare that he would not suffer the throne to become the plaything of foreign invaders, and that he would rescue France even though Napoleon yielded the crown. In fine, it was a question of patriotism and of calculation, a national question which the general of an army had a right to decide for himself, having reference, always, to the real will and desire of the people at large.

"It was in this light that Soult viewed the matter, even after the battle, and when he had seen Colonel St. Simon.

"Writing to Talleyrand on the 22nd, he says, 'The circumstances which preceded my act of adhesion are so extraordinary as to create astonishment. The 7th, the provisional government informed me of the events which had happened since the 1st of April. The 6th and 7th, Count Dupont wrote to me on the same subject. On the 8th the duke of Feltre, in his quality of war minister, gave me notice that, having left the military cypher at Paris, he would immediately forward to me another. The 9th the prince Berthier, vice-constable and major-general, wrote to me from Fontainebleau, transmitting the copy of a convention and armistice which had been arranged at Paris with the allied powers; he demanded, at the same time, a state of the force and condition of my army; but neither the prince nor the duke of Feltre mentioned events; we

cious movement. Soult, who had watched this movement, threw upon them the reserve under Taupin, in two columns. Imitating my example at Rivoli when Lusignan prolonged himself on my rear, he cried out to his soldiers: *These English are ours, I give them to you;* but fortune cruelly deceived his expectation, and turned against him the manœuvre on which he founded his hopes of victory. Taupin leads his troops to the charge by battalion; he is killed; his troops hesitate: they are exposed to a murderous fire, and suffer terrible losses without inflicting any injury on the enemy; finally, they recoil and retire in disorder. Soult, frustrated by the result of an attack which he thought infallible, hastened to leave Toulouse in order to save his line of retreat. The events at the capital rendered these movements superfluous, and this battle, lost by one of my lieutenants, reconciled me in some degree to my abdication.

Napoleon retires to Elba.—Either out of respect for an old warrior, or to make a parade of their generosity, the allies allowed me to select my place of retreat; I chose Elba, as being near Corsica, where I was born, and touching Italy, the first theatre of my glory. They accorded to me the title which afterward seemed to give them so much offense.* Finally they permitted me to take with me a small number of my old soldiers with whom I had run so many hazards,—men whom misfortune had not discouraged. Little did they think that one year later, the emperor of the Island of Elba, with this mere handful of brave men, would again make the conquest of France!

had then only knowledge of a proclamation of the empress, dated the 3d, which forbade us to recognize anything coming from Paris.

"'The 10th I was attacked near Toulouse by the whole allied army under the orders of Lord Wellington. This vigorous action, where the French army, the weakest by half, shewed all its worth, cost the allies from eight to ten thousand men. Lord Wellington might, perhaps, have dispensed with it.'"

* The conduct of England in 1815, on this subject, exhibited a petty meanness unworthy of a great nation.

I set out accompanied by the commissioners of the allied powers. In crossing France in order to reach my place of exile, I had occasion to observe the difference of opinion respecting me. If I was cherished and regretted in the environs of Paris and in the East, I was equally hated in the South. They did not even respect my misfortune, and it was necessary to put myself under foreign protection to preserve my life against the very people who had so often been intoxicated with my triumphs. A year afterward I compared myself to Themistocles; and I believe I shall not be accused of wanting in modesty, in putting myself on a parallel with that illustrious Athenian.

Evacuation of Italy.—While *en route*, I received news which it was natural to expect; the Kingdom of Italy could not survive the empire. Threatened by the defection of Murat, and by his march on the Po; by the appearance of the English at Genoa, and of Bubna on the Simplon, Eugene still kept up his courage. A fanatical revolution excited at Milan by partisans of Austria, and still worse, by the news of my fall, finally induced him to conclude an arrangement for the evacuation of Italy by the handful of French who remained with him. In political commotions there is always a class of men who suffer; those who had had the confidence of Austria before 1796 and during the reaction of 1799, did not possess mine, and they now aspired to a change which would restore their influence. Making a pretext of the heavy taxes imposed, they excited the populace of Milan to rise against the minister of finances, Pirna, whom they inhumanely massacred. This movement gave me great pain. Italy owed every thing to me, and I had conceived, for her future, projects the most generous; her ingratitude revolted me, although I had already had plenty of occasions to know the human heart.

Concluding Remarks.—However great my fall, it does not

destroy all my works. I leave it for connoisseurs to judge of my campaign of 1814; if they are honest, they will regard it, with those of 1805 and 1809, as the most memorable and the most scientific of modern times. Even making proper deductions for the influence of state policy on the operations of the allies, they will not deny that my movements are models of activity, energy, and strategic *coup-d'œil.* With seventy thousand men in the field, I held my way against more than three hundred thousand, and was oftenest victorious. The devotion of my brave soldiers in these alternate marches against Blucher and Schwartzenberg, where we had every day to march ten leagues, and every day to fight new masses of fresh troops, confident and proud of their victories; this devotion, I say, is not less worthy of attention. The present generation has attempted to tarnish their laurels; posterity will avenge them; already it begins to render them justice, for their worst enemies no longer dare to separate their glory from that of France. Manes of the brave men of Montmirail, of Champ-Aubert, of Montereau,—repose in peace! Your glory is unfading; your exploits will incite the enthusiasm and respect of ages the most remote.

I must, however, say that the demoralization had, at Brienne, begun to reach my head-quarters. Berthier and his hangers-on seemed no longer able to conceal their fatigue and disgust. Instead of submitting without murmur to the sacrifices imposed on their rank, they were continually discussing, in my antechambers, the words *peace* and *repose*; as though these had been appropriate words when France was inundated with enemies, and when we owed to the nation the example of enthusiasm and the most absolute devotion. The conduct of my marshals at Fontainebleau was not the result of a spontaneous despair, but the natural consequence of the lamentations with which they had continually beseiged me after the battle of Dresden. I had put them, it is true, to severe tests, after the fatal passage of the Niemen in 1812; but from that time there was not a moment in which I had power to arrest, as has been pretended, the course of events. The Emperor of Russia had resolved not to treat with me without receiving guarantees which had been for me so many humiliations. If at Prague the mediation of Austria had been in my favor, that prince would have retired behind the Vistula, but would not have concluded peace, or would have inserted such conditions that I could not have accepted it. Nor did England then desire peace; for she even demanded of me Antwerp, when I still held Dantzic and Hamburg. Austria made a semblance of proposing peace, because she well knew that after being driven behind the Rhine, I could no longer defend Italy, and she coveted Lombardy. The contest between Europe and myself could only be decided by my fall, or by victories which would enable me to dictate peace to Germany.

The detractors of my glory have not hesitated to compare my defense of France with that of Henry II. against Charles V., and of Louis XIV. against Eugene and Marlborough, and to give me all the disadvantage of this ridiculous parallel. Charles V. attacked Metz with fifty thousand men; the place was defended by fifteen thousand under Guise-le-Balafré; the peasants of Champagne were sufficient to save it. Louis XIV. saw the power of the emperor and of England waste itself, for six months, before Lille, and three more before the little fort of Landrecies; it was not an army of seventy thousand men that could subjugate an empire like France, with such a system of operations. It is absurd to compare such events with the *invasion of a million and a half of men*, with all Europe to sustain them. This invasion, executed with rapidity and in a few weeks' time, at an epoch when no active army could be raised in France to oppose them, was, nevertheless, several times on the point of failing from the astonishing activity of our defense. It would, in fact, have utterly failed, if, instead of intrigues and intestine divisions, we had opposed to the enemy, *union, patriotism*, and *devotion*.

CHAPTER XXII.

CAMPAIGN OF 1815.

FROM NAPOLEON'S RETURN FROM ELBA TO HIS EXILE TO ST. HELENA.

Napoleon at Elba—Division of Parties in France—Course pursued by Louis XVIII.—Different Forms of Government—Defects of the Charter of Louis XVIII.—Errors in its Administration—Napoleon's Reasons for returning to France—His Departure from Elba—His Reception in France and March on Lyons—The Bourbons prepare for Defense—Decrees of Lyons—Ney declares for the Emperor—Napoleon resumes his Authority as Emperor—Composition of his Ministry—His Position towards Europe—General Coalition against him—Declaration of the Congress of Vienna—Operations of the Duke d'Angoulême in the South of France—Troubles in La Vendée—Affairs of Naples—Preparations to repel Aggression upon France—Motives of Napoleon's defensive Attitude—He refuses to adopt revolutionary Measures—The Champ de Mai—Opening of the Chambers—Their Addresses—Dogmatic Controversies of the Deputies—Napoleon's Reply—Military Preparations of Napoleon—Preparations of the Allies—Napoleon's general Plan of Campaign—He joins his Army—Plan of Operations—Opening of the Campaign—Passage of the Sambre, June 15th—Measures of the Allies—Decisive Movement prescribed to Ney—He delays its Execution—His Delay in marching on Quatre-Bras—Reconnoissance of the Position of the Prussians—Dispositions for forcing their Position—Battle of Ligny—Ney repulsed at Quatre-Bras—Position of Affairs on the Morning of the Seventeenth—Grouchy sent in Pursuit of the Prussians—The Reserves and Left Wing march against the English—Commencement of the Battle of Waterloo—First Appearance of the Prussians—Napoleon hastens the Attack on the English—Ney's first Attack on the Centre—Attack of the Left on Hougomont—Ney's second Attack—Bulow debouches on Planchenois—General Charge of the French Cavalry—Arrival of Blucher and Bulow—Wellington's Dispositions—Defeat of the French Right—Last Efforts and Rout of the French Army—Operations of Grouchy—Manœuvres of the Allies The French retreat on Avesnes—Napoleon's Return to Paris—Military Resources of France—Conspiracies of Napoleon's Adversaries—Dispositions of the Populace—Napoleon's second Abdication—He retires from France—He is exiled to St. Helena—His Death.

Napoleon at Elba.—Europe, familiar for the last twenty years, with my victories and gigantic enterprises, was quite astounded at the rapid fall of my empire, and unable to conceive that six months could be sufficient to bring the allies from the Elbe to the banks of the Seine, and to enable them to dictate to France the disgraceful treaty of Paris. The Congress of Vienna endeavored to reconcile the numerous claims, urged on all sides, for a share of the spoils of that bold conqueror, who, two years before, had dared to put one foot upon Cadiz, and the other upon Moscow. The task was a difficult one; for this congress was expected to re-establish the political equilibrium so strongly shaken, and to regulate the international relations of Europe, so completely overthrown by the storms of the French Revolution. Fallen from the throne of the most powerful empire to the petty sovereignty of the island of Elba, in consequence of my abdication of Fontainebleau, and separated from my wife and son in a manner disgraceful to the house of Austria, and for which history will one day justly reproach my enemies, I retired in a kind of exile, to Porto-Ferrajo, like Scipio in his asylum at Linternum, more displeased with the desertion of friends than with the persecution of enemies. Although condemned to be but a passive spectator of the great events of the world which I had directed for fifteen years by the superiority of my genius, I, nevertheless, felt a presentiment that sooner or later, I should be called to re-appear upon the stage; I understood men and the times too well to be deceived as to the extent of the embarrassment in which the Bourbons would be involved when they resumed the government of a country so much changed since they had left it, and so deeply humiliated by the disastrous circumstances attending their restoration to power. I was therefore confident that, so soon as the first intoxication occasioned by the general peace had partially subsided, the most energetic portion of the French nation, so deeply humiliated by the conditions of the restoration, would regret my abdication, and desire my return. But the uncertainty of the time when this would take place, and my utter inability to control events, prevented me from forming any definite plans. In the meantime I found some consolation in projecting a history of my life, and in animating the drooping hopes of my partisans. But important events followed each other in such rapid succession, that I was drawn from my retirement much sooner than I had anticipated.

Division of Parties in France.—Independently of the private information which I received from Queen Hortense and others of my faithful friends, the newspapers furnished me sufficient information concerning the general state of affairs; for, notwithstanding the strict censorship of the press, and in spite of the falsehoods usually circulated in the public journals, the different passions, of which they were the interpreters, were apparent to the least observing, and the excitement which raged in the kingdom was made known to the world.

It seemed that Louis XVIII. had at first fully appreciated the spirit of the age, and persuaded himself that the majority of France desired to consolidate the results of the revolution. This prince judged, after twenty years of experience, that his party was too weak to resist the wishes of the great mass of the middle classes, who, in a country stripped of aristocratic institutions, finish always by dictating law to the nation. To maintain himself upon the throne, he felt it necessary to reign with this majority, that is, in compliance with the principles of the Revolution: *Henry IV. had said that Paris was well worth a mass; Louis XVIII. thought the crown of France well worth a constitution.* It was evident that he could not govern by the ancient magistracies of the kingdom;—no vestige of them remained; nor could he hope to rule the France of 1814 by the defunct *états* of Brittany, Languedoc, or Burgundy. It was necessary, therefore, to reconstruct the government on an entirely new basis, and, if he did not submit to the revolutionary principle, he must take the alternative of doing over again the work of the revolution by virtue of the *divine right* upon which he founded his claim to the throne. He decreed a charter. Many have blamed Louis XVIII. for this measure; and, judging of the act by its effects, we are compelled to admit that it imperfectly accomplished its object. If it had been possible to seize the supreme power with a vigorous hand, and to govern by means of royal ordinances, it is incontestable that, for him, it would have been the safest course; but this being impracticable, it was left for the king to decide what form of government should be substituted for the one which had just been overthrown by the combined European powers. To revive the *parlements* or provincial *états*, was utterly impossible. To substitute for my glorious and energetic empire the absolute power of a *camarilla d'émigrés*, was the dream of some wiseacres;—if this course had been adopted the restoration would not have continued six months. A lady, exhibiting a superiority of genius and penetration when discoursing on any subject other than politics, has asserted that the Bourbons could have taken the empire just as they found it. "The bed was so well made," said she, "that it was only necessary to lie down in it." This saying of Madame de Staël, which received so much applause in the salons of Paris, was mere nonsense. How could the brother and successor of Louis XVI. acknowledge a senate which had betrayed its own founder, and had twice disposed of the throne in less than ten years! A legislative body which had raised its voice only when the country was invaded by a million of foreign enemies, and had become a turbulent arena of party passions, at a time when all patriots should have rallied around the head of the government, no matter what its character, was utterly unworthy of public confidence, and its reëstablishment could not have been acceptable to the French people. Moreover, the imperial institutions were so little pleasing to the visionary advocates of liberalism that these factious leaders of the senate, who had overthrown my empire were eager to force upon the Bourbons a charter of their own; but Louis XVIII., having decided to reject this illegal act, owed it to the ruling opinions to grant another which would guarantee the threatened interests of community.

Course to be pursued by the King.—The king had only to choose between two courses of action; the first, to grant a charter, as he actually did; the second, to govern provisionally as dictator, and to convoke a constituent assembly to form, in concert with his ministers, a national compact which, being sanctioned by the notables of France, should become irrevocable, and thus offer the double advantage of securing the interests of the throne as well as those of the nation. The first plan appeared to him the more prudent, as it was a voluntary concession and implied no acknowledgement of the principles of national sovereignty—principles specious in theory, but readily degenerating into an elective monarchy. Moreover, it was doubtful, to say the least, whether any complete, strong and well-matured system of government could emanate from a French constituent assembly, no matter how restricted in numbers. If, instead of an elective assembly, a commission of some forty or fifty members had been selected by the provisional government, to draw up and decide upon the terms of the national compact, as was done after the eighteenth Brumaire, what guarantee would such authority have presented, or what force could such a charter have had? A king has always a right to give laws where none exist, but what right has an assembly of fifty lawyers, stripped of all legitimate authority, to impose a contract upon the king, on the one side, and upon the entire nation, on the other, without submitting it to the vote of the primary assemblies, or, at least, to notables especially appointed for that purpose by the nation? But these two means were both inconsistent with the principles of the Bourbon monarchy and the interests of the crown. Holding all my power from popular election, I could not establish my government upon any other basis; but the case of the Bourbons was entirely different.*

Different Forms of Government.—When, in the course of events, the government of a country is destroyed, and a new one is to be substituted in its place, we are at liberty to select either of the following: first, an hereditary absolute monarchy, second, an hereditary monarchy of limited powers, third, an elective monarchy, fourth, an aristocratic or oligarchic republic, and fifth, a democratic republic. Much may be said both for and against each of these forms in the abstract, but in truth their advantages and disadvantages result rather from the particular circumstances of their application than from any thing belonging intrinsically to the forms themselves. A government suited to America, or to the petty Swiss cantons, would be utterly absurd for one of the large European States.

Defects of the Charter of Louis XVIII.—We have shown that, a new form of government being necessary, Louis XVIII. granted a charter to the nation in order to prevent their forming one for themselves. This charter should have been a kind of indissoluble compact, connecting the interests of the throne and the interests of the nation, forming, in short, a kind of brief declaration of rights. Unfortunately, it was so framed as to satisfy neither party. The royalists,

* The author explains, in a later edition of this chapter, that his political remarks have reference solely to monarchal governments of limited powers, like that of France, and that they are entirely inapplicable to republican governments like that of the United States of America, or to despotisms like those of Russia and Austria.

like the Spanish priests, wished a new master who would permit them to govern the country according to their own pleasure. The returned *émigrés* could see in the restoration of the Bourbons only the means of recovering their lost property and privileges. The clergy hoped to recover the ancient wealth and influence of the Church. The *noblesse* had been created anew, but it had no prerogatives or power; it was too exclusive to be democratic, and too pusillanimous to be aristocratic; highly offensive to the nation in its character, without even the means of self-defense. All these parties were ready to tear in pieces the charter at the earliest opportunity, because some of its clauses were favorable to the nation. On the other hand, the stipulations for a national legislative power were accompanied with so many restrictions as to afford good grounds for doubting the sincerity of the new government on this and other points connected with popular rights. If Louis had not too much feared the establishment of bad precedents in admitting dogmas looking toward an elective system, he could have increased the strength of his new edifice by giving it the sanction, if not of the whole country, at least of the new chambers. For this purpose it would have been sufficient for the king to arrange a royal *séance*, declaring the compact binding upon himself and his descendants, and upon the nation and its deputies; all swearing to maintain in its integrity the charter which ever afterward was to be equally obligatory upon the monarchy and its subjects, and to form a basis of public rights entirely new.

Errors in its Administration.—But instead of acting in this frank and open manner, the king let it be plainly seen that he was merely yielding to present necessity, and that an opportunity only was wanting to impose a more despotic rule. Surrounded by twenty thousand *émigrés*, who were clamorous for office, old imperial employees, who wished to retain office, Jacobins, equally avaricious of the spoils of place, *doctrinaires*, who believed themselves the only men in France capable of conducting the affairs of state, old royalists and high clergy, who opposed both the constitution and those holding office under it;—under such circumstances the only safety for Louis XVIII. was to pursue a firm and straightforward course, regardless of party influences. But this the king was incapable of doing. He intrusted the administration of affairs to a ministry which was without credit and entirely influenced by the coteries of the Tuileries. There was nothing but contradictions and inconsistencies in the system of government; words and deeds were without correspondence, for at heart the government was far from wishing to carry out the measures it had promised in writing. The *émigrés* demanded back their sequestered property, and to calm their importunities they were promised ultimate satisfaction, though in utter violation of the charter. Instead of putting down new pretensions and confirming the existing state of affairs, they pursued directly the opposite course. The purchasers of the national property were threatened with projects of restitution; brochures, attributed to Chancellor Dambray, opposed the legality of these sales and demonstrated the justice of restitution. The factious leaders of parties,—the men who had surrendered Toulon to the English, and those who had recovered it, the defenders of the divine rights of the throne, and those who had led Louis XVI. to the scaffold—were soon involved in the most virulent disputes. Fearing the consequence of such discussions, the government abolished the liberty of the press and of the tribune. In order to quiet public feeling and to soften down the violent party spirit springing from the excesses of the revolution, I had established a public censorship. This was not done through any interest of personal power, but for the good of the country. The evils resulting from it were due to its bad administration, rather than to its principle, for, on account of the deadly feuds engendered by the revolution, a limited censorship will be necessary for a time in order to harmonize contending factions. But the government of Louis XVIII., instead of confining it to the factious partisan newspapers of the day, made the restriction far too general; and as this censorship seemed contrary to the promises of the declaration of Saint Ouen, and to the spirit of the modified charter, the liberals, republicans, and *doctrinaires* raised incessant clamors and cried out despotism and deception! To other causes of agitation is to be added the dissatisfaction produced by the onerous treaties with foreign powers. Every one truly French at heart, and who retained a particle of national pride and patriotism, was indignant at the readiness with which Count d'Artois, even before having stipulated any of the conditions of peace, signed an order to surrender to the allies a hundred fortresses still occupied by French troops. The treaties of Paris, made by the point of the sword with a rigor justifiable, perhaps, in certain cases, were in this instance too severe even for the interests of the powers imposing them, for they implanted the seeds of bitterness in the hearts of all friends of the empire and of the revolution. All believed, whether with reason or not, that the Bourbons might have preserved at least a part of Belgium, Savoy, and the line of the Rhine as far as Coblentz, if they had not been too eager to get possession of the Tuileries.

The minister Ferrand, in a discourse from the tribune, classed all Frenchmen in two categories:—those who had pursued the *right line*, that is, who had fought with the *émigrés*, and in La Vendée; and those who had pursued the *curved line*, that is, who had admitted the Revolution and the Empire: a strange apostrophe to a whole nation; a singular means of supporting a law for restoring the unsold property of the *émigrés!* The government had retained the soldiers of the empire, because it feared them, and had no others to oppose to their influence; and, in passing them in review, heightened the glory of their enemies; crowds of *émigré* and Vendéan officers demanded the confirmation of their rank in the very army which they had opposed, thus encumbering the *cadres* of the army and staff, to the detriment of the veterans of a hundred battles. Thus military dissatisfaction was added to civil discontent. No one could confide in the existing state of affairs, for all things seemed unstable; there was no security of party interests, for all seemed compromised; nor of opinions, for they were stifled; nor was there any refuge in the strength of government, for it was without head, or arm, or will. A new contest seemed inevitable, and in the clash of interests and shock of factions, I again might become the arbiter of the destinies of France.

Napoleon's Reason for returning to France.—The state of affairs in France inspired me with the desire and hope of returning there, and the information which I received of the proceedings at the congress of Vienna was greatly calculated to strengthen this feeling. The congress had much difficulty in effecting a satisfactory division of the spoils; Austria, France, and England had agreed in the eventual treaties to guarantee Saxony against the pretensions of Prussia; Russia supported these pretensions, and the dissatisfied sovereigns of these last two countries already spoke of returning to their own capitals; even the day of their departure was said to be fixed. In return for the support promised by the Bourbons to Austria and England, they demanded the expulsion of Murat from the throne of Naples, and the restoration of that branch of their own family This demand was supported by the personal interest of the venal Talleyrand, because the restoration of the legitimate government of the Two-Sicilies would secure to him the incomes of the rich principality of Benevento. Moreover, I learned that the ministers of Louis XVIII. had proposed to the congress to remove me from the Isle of Elba, and to exile me to St. Helena. This was a gratuitous violation of the treaty of Fontainebleau, for I had then done nothing to expose me to the wrath of these sovereigns.* My feeble means of defense were not sufficient to resist the execution of this scheme, and resolving not to await their attack, I conceived the audacious project of re-ascending the throne of France. Small as was the number of my forces, they were stronger than those of the Bourbons, *because they were allied to the honor of their country*, and although that honor may sometimes slumber, it never dies in the hearts of Frenchmen. Fully trusting to the strength of this support, I passed in review the little army which was to second me in this great and hazardous enterprise. These soldiers were ill-clad and ill-supplied, for I had not the means even of equipping them. Our preparations were brief, for we carried only our swords.

His Departure from Elba.—Favored by the fortuitous absence of the English commissioner and the English fleet stationed to watch the Isle of Elba, our little flotilla set sail and, experiencing no accident, accomplished the voyage in five days. On the first of March I again saw the coast of France at Cannes, near the same beach of Frejus where I had landed fifteen years before on my return from Egypt. Fortune seemed again to smile upon me, as I returned a second time to my country, to raise again its fallen colors, and to restore its independence. In again touching the

* Jomini says that the French government did not pay the two millions stipulated to be annually paid by the treaty of Fontainebleau, but made the exile of Napoleon from Europe a condition for its fulfillment. Napoleon was informed of these facts by the Empress Maria-Louisa, and this circumstance, together with the false information which he received of the dissolution of the congress of Vienna, decided him to return immediately to France.

French soil I could not but experience the most lively emotions. I saluted it as the parent of heroism, and the home of genius. We debarked without obstacle. I had as yet formed no definite plans, for I had not sufficient information of the actual state of the southern departments upon which to base them. I was, therefore, to be guided by circumstances. But it was necessary to act promptly, and to secure at the outset some strong point of support. Grenoble was the nearest fortified town of importance, and one well suited to my purpose; I therefore marched as rapidly as possible in that direction, for I well knew that my ultimate success depended very much upon the possession of this fortress. At length my little army reached this point of destination, having marched eighty-four leagues in six days!

Reception in France and March upon Lyons.—My reception on the way answered my most sanguine hopes, and seemed to double the chances of my ultimate success, by giving me the assurance that the mass of the people, uncorrupted by passion or interest, had still preserved their pristine character, though wounded by the national humiliation. On the sixth of March I discovered at Vizille the first troops sent out to oppose me: they refused to parley with my officers. Certain that everything depended upon this first *rencontre*, and accustomed to take a prompt and decided part, I advanced fearlessly in front of these troops, and laid bare my breast to receive their fire. This act of rash confidence strongly moved the feelings of these old soldiers; far from seeing in me the audacious rebel and exciter of civil wars, as had been represented by the royalists, they could only distinguish their emperor marching at the head of his old warriors who had so often traced the road to victory. They did not long hesitate. This detachment of the fifth regiment of infantry was soon followed by the entire seventh, commanded by Labédoyère, who voluntarily ran forward to meet me.

The people and soldiers now welcomed me with shouts of joy; Grenoble opened its gates, and I advanced towards Lyons with five thousand men.

The Bourbons prepare for Defense.—At the first news of my debarkation the Bourbons were struck with astonishment; nevertheless, they hoped to intercept my progress; they offered a reward for my head, and proceeded against me as against a rebellious subject in arms against the state. The Count d'Artois and Macdonald set out immediately for Lyons; the Duke d'Angoulême left Bordeaux to establish a centre of royal authority at Toulouse; Ney, recalled to Paris, was sent into the east; and finally the chambers were hastily convoked in extraordinary session. It is even said that the most fiery of the ministers of the restoration (M. de Blacas), wishing to employ against me means more certain than the sword, hired a man named B * * * to assassinate me. This individual has since published an account of his exploits, but I prefer to believe it untrue, or at least greatly exaggerated.* Certain of having glory and France on my side, I felt confident of success. No sooner were the royal troops brought in presence of my own, than they ran together, and embraced each other with cries of *Vive l'empereur!* Macdonald escaped with difficulty, and the Count d'Artois had barely time to take post and return to Paris. The Lyonnaise received me with even greater enthusiasm than on my return from Marengo. This reception very much affected my feelings, and redoubled my courage and confidence in the future.

Celebrated Decrees of Lyons.—At Lyons I issued several decrees calculated to affect public opinion. Much complaint had been made by the *tiers-état* against the restriction of the

* See the brochure published by Moronval, Quai des Augustins, in 1816, which contains an account of this project, and the causes of its failure.

press and the privileges of the nobility. The condition of the country immediately after a revolution unexampled in history rendered this restriction necessary for public repose. I knew well the benefits of a free press, and I appreciated the advantages of the tribune; and I also knew the evils resulting from these same sources. But I hoped that the present circumstances were such as to enable France to profit by their advantages, and to avoid their evils. At any rate, I determined to make the experiment. I therefore proclaimed the abolition of all privileged *noblesse*, the freedom of the press,* and the sovereignty of the nation.

Ney declares for the Emperor.—Preceded by these memorable decrees, I continued to advance upon Chalons, where I was joined by the troops which Ney had assembled for the purpose of opposing me. This marshal was no statesman, and all his political religion consisted in avoiding civil war created for private interests. This was his motive at Fontainebleau when he contributed to provoke my first abdication. "*Tout pour France, rien pour un homme;*' was his motto; a dogma very respectable in appearance, but which, when carried too far, may cause great faults, and induce one to forget the most sacred duties. At the first news of my return Ney thought only of the scenes at Fontainebleau, and the dangers of civil war; he, therefore, accepted in good faith the appointment to repel me by force of arms, and so far forgot himself as to utter imprudent and unsuitable menaces against his ancient chief. But he was soon convinced, by his journey in Burgundy and in Franche-Comté, of the unanimity of popular sentiment in my favor; his own

* Jomini thinks that the reëstablishment of the unrestricted liberty of the daily press is a fault, and one of which Napoleon was the first victim. The periodical press and books, he says, ought generally to be exempt from the censure, but the daily press, he thinks, cannot be so in France without danger, at least in times of great political excitement.

soldiers unfurled the national colors in his presence; two officers sent secretly to him assured him of my wish to forget the past. Placed in the same alternative as Marlborough between James II. and William, he did not hesitate to throw himself into the ranks rendered illustrious by his many brilliant feats of arms. Yielding to a single dominant idea, he acted with impetuous haste, without reflecting that he might thereby violate other sacred duties, from which he might so easily have relieved himself by retiring to Besançon till after my entrance into the capital. The striking contrast between his proclamation at Sous-le-Saulnier, and his promises to Louis XVIII., will remain as an unfortunate blot in the history of his glorious career, because it gives a false idea of his character by having all the appearance of premeditated treason,—a crime of which he was utterly incapable.

Nothing could now arrest my progress, as I pursued my triumphal march at the head of ten thousand men. My adversaries had no other resource than the camp hastily assembled at Melun; but the soldiers of this camp, brothers of those of Grenoble, Lyons, and Chalons, were more disposed to rejoin their eagles than to fight against them. Astonished at the rapidity of my progress, the Bourbons knew not what course to take. It is impossible to describe the agitation and confusion which now reigned in Paris, and particularly in the palace of the Tuileries. Louis XVIII. preserved his usual calmness and resignation; but yielding to the advice of those around him he allowed himself to be drawn into resolutions the most opposite, and measures the most contradictory. On the one side he threw himself into the arms of the *doctrinaires*, and intrusted Benjamin Constant to draw up royal proclamations that should gain for him the confidence and love of the French! Placing himself under the ægis of the National Guards and revolutionary partisans, he made an appeal to all loyal royalists, and to the army which he had so ill-treated! Even Fouché was on the point of being ordered to the palace to be consulted, when it was decided to arrest him; but the wily sycophant made a timely escape from his hotel, and reached through a garden the house of Queen Hortense, where he found a refuge. Then followed a partial change of ministers; the police was confided to Bourrienne, formerly my private secretary and the friend of my youth, and now my calumniator and declared enemy; all received in turn caresses and promises; the National Guard and Royal Volunteers were appealed to; such were the measures resorted to by MM. Blacas, Ferrand, and Dambray, to repel or capture the conqueror of so many people! The chambers which had been convoked in so much haste, met in time to exhibit to the world the utter worthlessness of public assemblies deliberating in the presence of real danger, and to prove to Europe that the time had passed for ever when senators awaited death in their curule chairs. This meeting of the chambers had no other result than to give some speakers an opportunity of repeating the declamations against the imperial despotism inserted by Benjamin Constant in the *Journal des Debats*, and to give the king an occasion to present himself in state to the chambers, with his brother and nephews, to take there to the charter an oath of fidelity which would have been much more appropriate at the time of its promulgation;—an oath which, on the part of Count d'Artois, was generally suspected to be insincere.—Two days after this sentimental but tardy homily, the troops of the camp of Melun came over to join mine *en masse*, and the next day, March 20th, I entered the Tuileries. The Bourbons had barely time to escape to Belgium; the Duke d'Angoulême alone kept up a contest for some days in the south.

Napoleon reascends the Throne.—Thus was this astonishing revolution terminated in twenty days, without having cost a single drop of blood. France had now changed her aspect; the nation restored to itself had resumed its ancient bearing. It was free from the yoke imposed by the foreigner, for it had just performed the highest act of free will of which any people can be capable. The grandeur of my enterprise effaced the recollection of my reverses; it restored to me the confidence of the French people; I was again the man of their choice.

Composition of the new Ministry.—While awaiting the formation of definitive institutions of government, it was necessary to organize a temporary administration, by placing men at the head of the several ministerial departments. The war department was confided to Davoust, the marine to Decrès, the finances to Gaudin, foreign affairs to Caulaincourt, whose pacific views were well known to the allies, the seals to Cambacérès, the interior to Carnot, and the police to Fouché. The selection of these last two—old adepts in Jacobinism—was a sufficient pledge to the mass of the people against all cries of despotism. Carnot I knew well. This stern old republican had refused me the empire in 1815. His mind was stamped with a probity that no circumstances could change, but to this honest and energetic will there was added a love of opposition and of Utopian theories. His military arrangements in 1793 and 1794, had given him a reputation for talent in military defense, and his republican notions and stern integrity made him another Cato in the eyes of the multitude. It was now necessary to animate the courage of the people for self-defense, and no one was better calculated than Carnot to accomplish this object. Fouché had a most decided character for intrigue; he mistook craft and roguery for great talent for business. He was an Utopian demagogue, and yet he knew the shallowness of such theories. He wished a strong government, and yet opposed every measure calculated to give it strength. He was popular with a certain class, and I hoped to turn that popularity to account. I knew his character well, and was perfectly aware that he was unworthy of confidence. But I knew also that he would not remain a silent spectator of coming events. I must, therefore, either use or destroy him. If I locked him up at Vincennes or exiled him without judgment, there would have been good grounds for suspecting me of despotism. I, therefore, determined to run the risk of using him, and to counteract his intrigues by keeping him under the strictest watch. My leniency cost me dear. The clients of these old ex-conventionals, and those that ranged themselves under the Utopian banners of the Lafayettes, Lanjuinais, and the Benjamin Constants, proved more dangerous as friends than as enemies.

Napoleon's Position toward Europe.—Having thus attended to the formation of my council, I felt how urgent it was to look at the aspect of foreign affairs. I had refused the peace offered me at Chatillon with the limits of 1792, because I was then on the throne of France, and the conditions were too humiliating; but now there was nothing to prevent me from abiding by the conditions imposed on the Bourbons; returning from the Isle of Elba, I could not be responsible, either in the eyes of France or of posterity, for what had been done by others in my absence. In informing Murat of my departure, I had charged him to send a courier to Vienna to carry there my engagement to abide by the treaties of Paris, and to occupy myself only with the interior of France. Unfortunately, I then had no suitable person to send to the Emperor Alexander to demonstrate to this prince how much the rivalry of England would one day annoy him, and how important it was for Russia that France should have a government strong, national, and opposed to the interests of England. As I could no longer occupy myself with my former projects on the Vistula, and as France and Russia could no longer be rivals, it is difficult to say what effect such a mission might have produced on the mind of the Russian monarch; but it is unfortunate that the trial was not made. At any rate it is very natural to suppose that the positive assurances given by me to the sovereigns of Europe would have had some influence: for Europe, astonished at my return and at the energy of the French people, must have expected a repetition of the scenes of the revolution, if this people were again provoked to employ all their resources in propagandism. Success would have been quite certain if the congress had been dissolved, as I was erroneously informed, so that I could have treated with the cabinets separately.*

General Coalition against Him.—But the sovereigns being still assembled, they felt their self-love irritated; their interests had so clashed since the fall of my empire that they had found it difficult to continue negotiations; but the fear of losing all these rich spoils, again united the disputants, and all my efforts to preserve peace were unavailing. It was in vain that I protested my adhesion to the treaties; they refused to believe me. They dreaded the influence which the example of the French people might have upon their own subjects, and therefore were inclined to treat my return merely as a military revolt. Moreover, Austria, trembling lest I might dispute Italy with her, entirely forgot the connections which the events of 1814 had already broken. Russia, thinking that she could preserve Warsaw only by allying herself to her natural rivals, sacrificed every thing to secure this result. Prussia had been soliciting Austria to allow her

* The conduct of the European powers toward France in 1830, would seem to confirm the correctness of this assertion. Napoleon had left Elba on the faith of articles written from Vienna by Latour-Dupin, and inserted in the *Journal-des-Debats.* This paper announced the departure of the King of Prussia and of the Emperor Alexander as certain.

to extend her territory at the expense of Saxony, but she now eagerly accepted what had been offered her in lieu of this, lest she might lose all. England, governed at this time by mediocre men, thought she again saw my imperial eagles hovering over Boulogne, Antwerp and Egypt, and made lavish of her subsidies in order to sustain herself against an imaginary danger.

The Congress puts Napoleon under the Ban of Nations. —Thus all the interests of these sovereigns seemed opposed to my existence. The declaration of the thirteenth of March, declaring me an *outlaw*, sufficiently proves the fears inspired by my name. If we add to these motives the fear felt by Talleyrand lest my return might cause the sequestration of the ten millions of Bernese stocks held by him in England and lest his fortune in France might be compromitted by his banishment, it will be easy to understand the violence of that famous declaration which has generally been attributed to his pen. To quiet these powers it was necessary for me to assure Russia of Warsaw, and Austria of Italy; this I could have done if the negotiations had been conducted separately at St. Petersburg and at Vienna. But the declaration of the thirteenth of March, left little chance of success. Nevertheless, I at first hoped that this declaration was mainly intended to second the resistance of the Bourbons and to deter me from any ulterior projects against Europe. Nothing was more natural than that the powers who had placed Louis XVIII. on the throne of France, should wish to maintain him there; but since this prince had been so easily forced to a second emigration, the face of the question was entirely changed, and I had good reason to hope that the cabinets would be disposed to retrace their steps when they learned the rapidity of my triumph and the unheard-of success of my enterprise, and also of my pacific intentions. Unfortunately, the treaties of alliance, *offensive and defen-*

sive, signed the twenty-fifth of March, between the great powers, soon destroyed this illusion.

Operations of the Duke d'Angouleme.—But exterior embarrassments, resulting from the proceedings of the congress of Vienna, were not the only ones I now encountered. The Duke d'Angoulême, appointed by Louis XVIII. his lieutenant in the south, had organized the royal government at Toulouse, and, in concert with M. de Vitrolles and the Count Damas, had prepared to resist my empire. The mercantile population of Marseilles, whose love of lucre exceeded their love of liberty, and the fanatic inhabitants of Languedoc, whose religious dissensions were closely connected with their political quarrels, were easily induced to side with the royalists. The duke, with their aid and that of some regiments which yet remained faithful, formed three columns with which to ascend the Rhone and retake Lyons and Grenoble. But the greater part of his forces soon declared for my cause. Dauphiny declared against the Bourbons, and the tricolored flag again floated at Toulouse and at Montpellier, and the duke, surrounded on all sides, signed, on the ninth of April, at Pont-Saint-Esprit, a convention agreeing to evacuate France. Grouchy at first refused to ratify it, but I hastened to give it my sanction.

Troubles in La Vendee.—At the same time troubles broke out in La Vendée, and I was forced to send there fifteen thousand old soldiers. The skill and activity of Generals Lamarque and Fravot soon smothered the flames of civil war. Larochejacquelin was slain at the combat of Mathes, and signal victories were gained at Saint Gilles and Roche-Servières; but, on account of the peculiar localities and the obstinate character of the inhabitants, hostilities did not entirely cease for a long time.

Affairs in Naples.—While those events were taking place in France and at the congress of Vienna, Murat rendered my affairs still more complicated by his untimely commencement of hostilities in Italy—an enterprise worthy of his whimsical and adventurous character. Hearing of the negotiations between France and Austria for dethroning him, he demanded of the latter power a free passage through Italy, to take vengeance for the menaces of the minister of Louis XVIII.; of course this was refused. Hearing of my debarkation, he flattered himself that he could suddenly repair, in my eyes, his defection of 1814. He thought the moment had arrived when he was to play a great part, and, by promising the people of Italy a national insurrection, was to become the arbiter of great events. He debouches, on the twenty-second of March, from Ancona with forty thousand men, drives the Austrians from Cesena, and, favored by the population of Bologna and Modena, rapidly invades the country of the Po as far as Placentia, while another column invades the Roman states and Tuscany. He everywhere scatters proclamations, announcing that he comes to unite all Italy under the same flag; and takes formal possession of the provinces which he crosses; he even meditates the invasion of Lombardy across Piedmont, when he is arrested by the declaration of the English minister with threats of war. The Austrians soon assemble and throw against him General Bianchi, with twenty-five or thirty thousand men. Leaving Florence with the mass of his forces, this general marches by Foligno in order to cut off Murat's retreat, at the same time that Neipperg is to threaten him by the route of Ancona. The King of Naples, to avoid such a result, is obliged to retire in all haste; a decisive rencontre takes place at Tolentino on the second of May; the Neapolitan army is defeated and dispersed in all directions. Murat reaches his capital with only a small escort; he is now deserted by his warmest partisans, and compelled to fly from Naples to seek refuge in France; he debarks at Toulon. A convention signed at Capua, on the twentieth of May, restores Ferdinand IV. to the throne of the Two-Sicilies. Never was any thing more untimely than this operation of Murat. If Austria had had the least inclination to recede from the declaration of the thirteenth of March, this was to render the thing impossible; and even supposing that the cabinet of Vienna had resolved to persist in it, every thing should have been avoided that was calculated to strengthen the bonds of the coalition. In a military point of view, it was taking the initiative prematurely, for he commenced even before knowing whether or not I could second his operations. As a diversion, the King of Naples could have been of much avail; but in attempting to act the principal part in the war, he committed a great absurdity. Thus twice did Murat compromit the empire; the first time, (in 1814), by declaring for its enemies; the second, (in 1815), by taking arms *mal-à-propos* in its favor. He expiated, by a chivalric death, two faults that precipitated him from his throne; his memory as a soldier will ever be glorious.

Preparations to repel Aggression.—But the fatal result of this premature opening of hostilities by the King of Naples, the success of the Austrians, the reports which reached France of what was passing at Vienna and in the rest of Europe;—all these were of a nature to inspire a just fear in the least discerning. A formidable war was again about to threaten the national existence, and all hope of dissipating the storm was now gone; I had to decide either to brave it, or to fly from it like a coward; in such a dilemma could I hesitate? If personal honor had alone been at stake, I could have sacrificed it for the future welfare of France; but the honor of the nation was more involved than my own. A people of thirty millions, which had just raised one of its citizens to the highest power, could it, on a diplomatic declaration of a foreign congress, drive away this adopted chief, and submit to the yoke which these foreigners wished to impose ! ! ! Some have reproached me for continuing to occupy the throne after the reception of the declaration of Vienna. In their opinion I ought to have frankly exposed to France the position in which she would be placed toward Europe, alarmed and rushing to arms against myself, and then to have proposed to the nation to decide on one of the three following propositions :

1st. To submit without delay to the clemency of Louis XVIII. ;

2d. To proclaim for Napoleon II., with a regency, or some other form ;

3d. To declare the nullity of the abdication of Fontainebleau, and recognize anew the empire of Napoleon himself :

That, if the nation had adopted this last part, then the fate of France had been irrevocably connected with my own, and all desertions from me would have been cowardice or felony !

The fervent and unreflecting apostles of national sovereignty may find something specious in these ideas, but really they are without sagacity : in the first place, I did not despair of recalling Austria, and perhaps Russia, to sentiments more favorable to my cause ; I many times renewed the attempt, and even sent General Flahaut to Vienna with this intention : but if such hope had not existed, could I think of flying for ever from France, to which Louis XVIII. would have immediately returned with the allies, and all the men who had devoted themselves to my cause would have been given up to the fury of the *reactionnaires ?* Such a course would have been humiliating to the smallest prince in Europe ; how then could I submit to such a proscription ? Moreover, by abdicating in the early part of April, I should have left France without a government, at a moment when eight hundred thousand men were ready to fall upon her! There was no choice: it was necessary to fly, and to recall Louis XVIII., or to fight! This alternative was a hard one, and the chances were frightful, but there were no others. In adopting this alternative I felt certain that, if properly seconded, I should triumph over these enemies of myself and of France.

Other critics on my course at this time have been as rash as the above were weak:—these pretend that, instead of yielding to the approaching storm, I should have anticipated it, and profited by the first rising of the people to show, by invading Belgium, and proclaiming liberty throughout Europe, how redoubtable was the popular power; whereas my pacific attitude stifled the popular enthusiasm! Pitiful declamation! To throw a people in working blouses, and armed with pikes upon the warlike legions of all Europe! A large army was requisite, and to obtain this it was necessary to preserve, with all care, the precious nucleus then existing, and to form around this the people which were then being levied and organized.

The pacific attitude with which I have been reproached, consisted in working sixteen hours a day for three months to create this army. I increased the *cadres* of the regiments of the line from two to five battalions, and reënforced those of the cavalry by two squadrons. I organized two hundred battalions of movable National Guards, forty battalions of Old and Young Guards, twenty regiments of marines. The old disbanded soldiers were recalled to their colors; the conscriptions of 1814 and '15 were levied; even the old retired officers and soldiers were induced to return to the line. On the first of June, *i. e.*, in two months, the effective force of the French army had been increased from two hundred thousand to four hundred and fourteen thousand; by the month of September it would have numbered seven hundred thousand men; but for this time was wanting.*

Motives for Napoleon's defensive Attitude.—It would have been absurd, in the midst of these preparations, for me to think of invading Belgium in order to secure the line of the Rhine. This question was discussed immediately after my arrival in Paris, but more than one obstacle opposed it. At first I had in hand only forty thousand men, La Vendée was in insurrection, the Duke d'Angoulême was marching on Lyons, and the Marseillais on Grenoble. It is necessary to be master of one's own house, before attempting to rule in others. A still stronger reason opposed this invasion. How could I take such a step after writing the letter in which I had offered the sovereigns a sincere and lasting peace. It might have been rash to hope for the good will of the others, but there were still motives for trusting to that of my father-in-law. In 1814 the Emperor of Austria had sought to prevent my dethronement; at the moment of my return, the discussion was becoming warm with Russia on the partition of Galicia and the fate of Saxony. There was then every reason to hope that the cabinet of Vienna would consent, in 1815, to what its negotiator had proposed in 1814: to maintain me on the throne, if I would consent to relinquish Italy. I proposed this, and in spite of the famous declaration of the thirteenth of March, I might still flatter myself that I should yet see the father of Maria-Louisa return to his former sentiments. Moreover, the French had blamed in me a too great *penchant* for war; public opinion was in favor of peace, if it were possible, and would not have sanctioned a declaration of war, so long as there was any chance of maintaining peace. Even admitting that it was easy to foresee that these pacific measures would not prevent a war, there was but slight

* These details differ in some respects from those given by Napoleon in his St. Helena dictations.

chance of gaining anything by marching upon Brussels, guarded as it then was by the Germanic Confederation with an army of occupation; the fortresses of Luxembourg and Mayence no longer belonged to France, but, together with the places of Holland, secured to the allies several *débouches* on the left of the Rhine; under these circumstances it is not very certain that an invasion of Belgium would have been advantageous; it might have transferred the first battle-field from the Sambre to the Meuse or the Moselle, but it would have done nothing more. Supposing that Luxembourg and Antwerp could have been gained without a siege—a supposition altogether improbable—it would have been necessary to garrison them, and this the French were not then in a condition to do; if, on the contrary, these fortresses had remained in the enemy's hands, of what use would Brussels have been to us, surrounded as it was by Maestricht, Luxembourg, Berg-op-Zoom, and Antwerp? Was it not, under these circumstances, more wise to retain the old regiments, and so incorporate them into the new organization as to double its effective power, rather than to scatter them in Belgium?

Napoleon refuses to resort to revolutionary Means of Defense.—Some deemed it necessary to commence a new revolution in order to profit by the passions and blind devotion it might produce. Fouché advised this, and also Carnot, who still remained a Jacobin under the mantle of a count of the empire. I knew too well the difficulty of restraining popular storms within proper bounds, to again destroy the fabric of social order. To unchain the revolutionary tiger, is to drench the country with fraternal blood, and anarchy is far from infallible as a means of saving a nation; it succeeded in 1793, but it was by a combination of circumstances unexampled in history, and which probably may never again recur. In the coming contest I wished no other than legitimate passions,—the enthusiasm and energy naturally resulting from a popular conviction that my success was inseparably connected with the glory and honor of France. This point the nation itself was to decide, through its electors, at the Champ-de-Mai. If they should decide in favor of the new political organization and institutions, my own fate and that of France would become inseparable.

The Champ-de-Mai.—At length the so much desired first of June arrived; the ceremony took place with great pomp in the Champ-de-Mars. Clothed with the imperial mantle, surrounded by my dethroned brothers and the *doctrinaire* Lucien, the great state functionaries, marshals and prelates, I was seated on a superb throne, erected near the Ecole Militaire. Just around me were assembled twenty thousand electors seated in amphitheatre form; beyond these were the deputies of the armies; still further on, were fifty thousand men *en grande tenue;* and then an immense concourse of spectators, giving a magnificent aspect to this political solemnity. It was begun by divine service, after which M. Dubois d'Angers pronounced a fine discourse in the name of the electors of France, and proclaimed the acceptation of the additional act. I replied to this discourse in the following words:

"Gentlemen, electors of colleges, and of departments! Gentlemen, deputies from the army and navy to the Champ-de-Mai!

"Emperor, consul, soldier, I owe every thing to the French people. In prosperity, in adversity, in the field of battle, in the council, on the throne, in exile, France has been the only and constant object of all my thoughts and actions. Like the King of Athens, I sacrificed myself at Fontainebleau for the people, in the hope of seeing realized the promise of thereby securing to France her natural frontiers, her honors, and her rights. Indignation at beholding those sacred rights, the fruit of twenty-five years of victory, disregarded or forever lost; the cry of withered honor, the wishes of the nation, have brought me back to a throne which is dear to me, because it is the palladium of the independence, of the rights, and of the honor of the French people.

"Frenchmen! in traversing, amid the public rejoicing, the different provinces of the empire, I trusted that I could reckon on a long peace, for nations are bound by the treaties made by their governments, whatever they may be. My whole thoughts were then turned to the means of securing our liberty by a constitution resting on the wishes and interests of the people; and for this object have I called the assembly of the Champ-de-Mai. I soon learned, however, that the sovereigns, who resist all popular rights and disregard the wishes and interests of so many nations, were resolved on war. They intend to extend the kingdom of the Low Countries, by giving it for a barrier all our fortified places in the north, and to reconcile all differences by sharing among themselves Lorraine and Alsace. We must, therefore, prepare for war.

"Before personally exposing myself to the risks of the battle-field, I have made it my first care to establish the constitution of the nation. The people have accepted the act which I presented to them. When we shall have repelled these unjust aggressions; and Europe shall be convinced of what is due to the rights and independence of twenty-eight millions of Frenchmen, a solemn law, enacted according to the forms prescribed by the constitutional act, shall combine the different provisions of our constitutions, which are now scattered, into one body.

"Frenchmen! you are now about to return to your departments; tell your fellow-citizens that the times are perilous:—but that with union, energy, and perseverance, we shall emerge victorious out of this struggle of a great people against its oppressors ; tell them that future generations will severely scrutinize our conduct ; and that a nation has lost every thing, when it has lost its independence. Tell them that the foreign kings, whom I have raised to their thrones, or who are indebted to me for their crowns, and who in the days of my prosperity courted my alliance and the protection of the French people, are now aiming their blows at my person. Did I not know that it was really against our country that these blows are aimed, I would sacrifice myself to their hatred. But tell your fellow-citizens, also, that while they retain for me the sentiments of love, of which they give me so many proofs, this rage of our enemies will be impotent.

"Frenchmen ! my will is that of the people ; my rights are their rights ; my honor, my glory, my happiness, can never be distinct from the honor, the glory, and the happiness of France."

These words were pronounced with a firm and energetic voice, and produced the most lively enthusiasm. At their conclusion, I took the oath of fidelity to the charter, and Cambacérès, in the name of the electors, swore, *in the name of France*, the fidelity of the French people to the new government. This oath was repeated spontaneously by all the electors and deputies, and by the great majority of the spectators ; then followed the distribution of colors to the deputations of the army, to the troops present and to the National Guard. A few days after, the electors set out for their departments, having proclaimed the acceptation of the act additional, and appointed deputies for the new assembly.

Opening of the Chambers.—On the seventh of June, I opened the two chambers with the following discourse :

"Messieurs of the Chamber of Peers, and Messieurs of the Chamber of Representatives !—For the three months past, circumstances and the confidence of the people have invested me with unlimited power. At this moment the most anxious wish of my heart is accomplished; I have just commenced a constitutional monarchy. Men are too weak to secure the future; legal institutions alone can fix the destinies of nations. A monarchy is necessary to France, in order to secure the liberty, the independence, and the rights of the people. Our constitutions are scattered; one of our most important occupations will be to consolidate them into one body, and arrange them into one simple system. This labor will recommend the present epoch to the gratitude of future generations. It is my ambition to see France enjoy all possible liberty; I say *possible*, for unrestricted liberty leads to anarchy, and anarchy always resolves itself into absolute government.

"A formidable coalition of kings threatens our independence; their armies are approaching our frontiers. The English have attacked and taken one of our frigates in the Mediterranean. Blood has been shed in time of peace. Our enemies rely upon our internal divisions. They incite and foment civil war. * * * Legislative provisions are necessary to prevent this. I place unreserved confidence in your wisdom, your patriotism, and your attachment. The liberty of the press is inherent in the existing constitution, and no change in that respect can be made without changing all our political system; but it is necessary for the public good that there be some restrictions, especially at the present crisis. I recommend this subject to your special attention.

"The first duty of a prince may soon call me at the head of the children of the nation to fight for our country. The army and myself will do our duty; and you, Peers and Representatives, give to the nation the example of confidence, energy, and patriotism. Like the senate of the great people of antiquity, resolve to die rather than survive the degradation and dishonor of France. The sacred cause of the country shall be triumphant."

Addresses of the Chambers.—The chambers voted different addresses, both dwelt upon the necessity of submitting the absolute power to constitutional forms and rules. They promised, in case of reverses, to show perseverance and to redouble their attachment to the imperial cause, now become the cause of France. The peers assured Europe that with the new institutions, the seductions of victory could never draw the chief of the state beyond the bounds of prudence. To this recrimination on the past I replied :—" The contest in which we are now engaged is a serious one, the seduction of prosperity is not the danger that now threatens us : it is under the Caudine Forks that the foreigner would make us pass. The justice of our cause, the public spirit of the nation, and the courage of the army, are powerful reasons to hope for success. But should we experience reverses, then shall I expect to find in the Chamber of Peers proofs of attachment to the country and its chief. It is in difficult times that great nations, like great men, display all the energy of their character, and become objects of admiration to posterity."

Posterity will agree, in reading this discourse, that I, at least, foresaw all the dangers to which France was exposed, and neglected nothing calculated to prepare her for the contest. My answer to the Chamber of Deputies was still more pointed.

The Chamber of Deputies threatens to engage in dogmatic Controversies.—This chamber did not hesitate to exhibit its impatience to rush into the arena of constitutional debates. " Faithful," it said, " to its mission, it will fulfill the task devolving upon it in this noble work ; it asks, in order to satisfy the public will, that the national deliberation shall rectify as soon as possible, the defects in our institutions resulting from the urgency of our situation. *And while your majesty shall oppose to a most unjust aggression the honor of the national arms, and the force of genius, the Chamber of Representatives will endeavor to attain the same object by immediately drawing up a pact whose perfection shall cement still closer the union of the throne and the people, and fortify in the eyes of Europe the guarantee of our engagements for the amelioration of our institutions.*"

This was a clear annunciation that they intended to profit by the absence of the emperor to establish public controversies upon a constitution, without waiting for the initiation of the government, which still formed the fundamental basis of the existing legislation. This assumption of authority by the chamber was like that of the constituent assembly of 1789, but under circumstances still more dangerous; in a word, it was a revolutionary act, changing the entire face of the government. This address of the chamber indicated plainly enough that its main object would be to hamper the new government, and to reduce its sphere of action to a mere nullity:—an absurd and dangerous course of conduct, always indicating either national decay or approaching anarchy.

Napoleon's remarkable Reply.—I appreciated this address of the chamber at its full value, but preferred to show moderation in applauding the intentions of the *doctrinaires*, and at the same time calling their attention to the danger resulting from these untimely discussions. "In these grave circumstances," I replied, "my thoughts are absorbed by the impending war, on the success of which depend the independence and honor of France. I shall set out to-night to place myself at the head of my armies * * * During my absence I shall be pleased to hear that a committee appointed by each house maturely consider our institutions; the constitution is our rallying point, and it should be our polar-star in these moments of danger. But all public discussions tending to diminish directly or indirectly the confidence that should be reposed in the government and its dispositions, will be a national evil ; it will be placing the ship of state in the midst of rocks, without helm or compass. The present crisis is all-important ; let us not imitate the example of the Lower Empire which, surrounded on all sides by barbarians, became the jest of posterity by engaging in abstract discussions at the moment when the enemy's battering-ram was thundering at the gates of the capital."

I was truly grieved at the course pursued by the chamber, for I well knew that, instead of satisfying public opinion, these measures would tend to fatal results ; phrases being substituted for things, stormy debates for calm and firm administration, the arrogant assumption of authority by the chambers could lead to no other end than a division in the state. Factionists seized upon this error of the chambers to incite public opinion against the government, at the moment when it was absorbed in devising means to repel the invaders. Pamphlets of all descriptions, drawn up both by the Bourbonists and demagogues attacked every measure of government at the moment when all should have united in sustaining these measures ; this was not the moment to remedy political evils, whatever may have been their nature. To such an excess was the license of the press carried, that publications were issued promising *apotheosis to those who should deliver France by what means soever from the yoke of Napoleon, and that no jury could be found to condemn them!*

Military Preparations.—But notwithstanding the opposisition of the factions, the public excitement led to beneficial results. The National Guards were readily levied, and means were found to arm the inhabitants of the principal cities. Paris alone furnished twenty battalions of *tirailleurs-fédérés*, a force of little value in the open field, but which might supply the place of regulars in garrisoning the fortifications, aid the government in executing its measures, and assist in the defense of the cities. My thoughts were made sad at the unfortunate state of the political interior, but I hoped that the nation would appreciate its position, and exert all its energy to maintain its independence, and I redoubled my exertions in stimulating the ardor for military preparations. The armories, abandoned by my predecessor, resumed such an activity as to produce four thousand firearms per day; the movable National Guards were organized in all parts of the empire, at the same time that the conscription was levied. I have already said that the army of the line had been doubled in two months (from the first of April to the first of June), and that a vast system of defense secured its increase to seven hundred thousand by the first of September.

Preparations of the Allies.—The fate of French independence, therefore, depended in a great degree upon the possibility of postponing hostilities till the beginning of August. Far from allowing me this time, the allies, profiting by the lessons I had already taught them, marched post-haste towards the Rhine and the Meuse. The English and Prussians exhibited an unusual activity in their preparations, and the Russians marched in two months from Poland to the banks of the Rhine. The allies, who were disputing about Saxony and Cracovia, were still in arms, and with their numbers equal to the war complement; they had the match already lighted, and it did not require twenty minutes to dispatch from Vienna, on the same day, four orders of march, putting all Europe in motion. France had not retained the same formidable attitude as the rest of Europe: every thing tending to a national defense had been abandoned; on my arrival there were neither soldiers nor arms. Some have attempted to draw a parallel between the efforts of 1793 and

1815. In much less time I should have accomplished as much as the "committee of public safety" without having recourse to a "Revolutionary army," or to the twelve guillotines by which it was attended; but the allies of 1815 acted very differently from those of the first invasion; they did not, like Mack and Cobourg, pass three months before Valenciennes: the times had in all respects changed. The sea was everywhere covered with British convoys, bringing troops and siege-equipages. The wealth of India, seconded by the great progress of manufactures, had transformed England into an immense arsenal which forged, with wonderful activity, artillery, military munitions, and trains necessary for the allied armies. There was nothing like this in 1793.

At the end of May, Wellington and Blucher had united two hundred and twenty thousand English, Prussians, Belgians, Hanoverians and Brunswickers, between Liege and Courtray. The Bavarians, Wurtembergers, and Badois, assembled in the Black Forest and the Palatinate. The Austrians hastened to join them; their Italian army united with the Sardinians on the Alps. The Russians, by forced marches, had already crossed Franconia and Saxony. In fine, a million of men were ready to fall upon France; it might almost have been said of this coalition, that it had found the secret of Cadmus, to raise up men from the bosom of the earth.

Works for the Defense of Paris and Lyons.—However great my activity in organizing the army and frontier defenses, I still feared that the allied armies would be more numerous than my own, if hostilities should commence before August; in that case the destinies of the empire would be decided under the walls of Paris and Lyons. More than once had I thought of fortifying the heights of Paris; but the multiplicity of other engagements, and fear of exciting popular alarm, had prevented its execution. There were two modes of fortifying this capital; the first, by a system of detached forts connected by field works, and strengthened by properly manœuvring the waters of the Seine; the second, by an enciente of field-works strong enough to resist a *coup-de-main*. The last was adopted because it required less time than the other. The capital of a country contains the *élite* of the nation; it is the centre of public opinion, and the depôt of all its wealth and strength; to leave such an important point without defenses is national folly. In times of national misfortunes and great national calamities, states have often been in want of armies, but never of men capable of defending their walls. Fifty thousand National Guards with two or three thousand cannoneers, might defend a fortified capital against an army of two hundred thousand men. But these same fifty thousand undisciplined men commanded by inexperienced officers, would, in the open field, be put to rout by a mere handful of regular cavalry. Paris has many times owed its safety to its walls; if, in 1814, it had been capable of resisting only eight days, what a change might it not have produced in the affairs of the world! If, in 1805, Vienna had been well armed and better defended, the battle of Ulm would not have decided the war,—the battle of Austerlitz would never have taken place. If, in 1806, Berlin had been fortified, the army beaten at Jena would have rallied there, and have been rejoined by the Russian army. If, in 1808, Madrid had been fortified, the French armies, after the victories of Espinosa, Tudela, Burgos, and Sommo-Sierra, would never have ventured to march on that capital, with the English and Spanish armies at Salamanca and Valladolid. In fine, the fortifications of Vienna twice saved Europe from the Mussulman sabre.

I directed General Haxo to fortify Paris. This able engineer intrenched the heights at the north from Montmartre to Charonne, completed the canal of Ourcq, so as to cover the plain between Villette and Saint Denis. This city was to be intrenched and covered by the inundations of the Rouillon and the Crou. From the western base of Montmartre there was a line of intrenchments resting on the Seine above Clichy ; at the eastern extremity the park of Bercy, the spaces between Vincennes and Charonne were also covered. These works were armed with seven hundred pieces of cannon. On the south, the faubourgs between the Upper Seine and the Bièvre, and from the Bièvre to the Lower Seine, were also to have been defended ; the enciente here had already been marked out when the enemy appeared before Paris.

General Léry was charged with the defensive works at Lyons ; they were pushed on with vigor ; four hundred and fifty iron pieces of heavy calibre, brought from Toulon, and two hundred and fifty brass pieces, armed the ramparts, or formed the reserve. Every thing seemed to promise that the patriotic and brave inhabitants of this city, sustained by a *corps-d'armée*, would make a noble resistance to the enemy.

Besides these works I prepared to fortify Laon, Soissons, and the passes of the mountains, and had ordered immense works for placing the long neglected frontier fortresses in a state of defense. At the beginning of June these works were all in progress, but still very incomplete, and although the effective force had been increased, as has already been said, from two hundred to four hundred thousand men, a large number were still in the regimental depôts and in the frontier fortresses, so that I now had only one hundred and eighty thousand ready for the field ; by the middle of July this number would amount to three hundred thousand and the fortresses be garrisoned by National Guards and a few good regulars.

Napoleon decides to fall upon the Anglo-Prussians.—All attempts to prolong the negotiations proved vain, and I had now only two courses to pursue: the one, to march against the Anglo-Prussians at Brussels or Namur by the middle of June; the other, to await the allies under the walls of Paris and Lyons. The latter had the inconvenience of exposing the half of France to the ravages of the enemy; but it offered the advantage of gaining till the month of August to complete the levies, and finish the preparations, so as to fight, with united means, the allied armies when enfeebled by several corps detached for observation. On the contrary, by removing the theatre of war to Belgium, I might perhaps entirely save France from invasion; but I might also thus draw on the allies by the first of July, six weeks sooner than they would come of their own accord. The army of the *élite*, broken by reverses, was no longer capable of sustaining a too unequal combat, and the levies were incomplete. On the other hand, this course offered the hope of surprising the enemy, and was more conformable to the spirit of the French people. One can act the Fabius, like the Emperor of Russia, with a boundless empire, or like Wellington, on another's territory. But in a country like France with its capital at seventy leagues from the frontier, the case is very different. If there had been no political factions in France, and the entire nation had been ready to rally around its chief, and conquer with him, it would have been better to await the enemy at the foot of Montmartre. But when interests and opinions were divided, and political passions ran high, and a factious legislative body was exciting divisions and animosities in the capital, it would have been dangerous to there await an invasion. A victory beyond the frontiers would procure me time, and silence my political enemies in the interior. All things considered, it seemed advisable to attack Wellington and Blucher separately, and to endeavor to destroy successively the enemy's masses; and the courageous energy of the soldiers seemed to promise a certain victory;

moreover, at the beginning of the campaign a decisive blow might dissolve the coalition. To accomplish so desirable an object, it was important to collect a strong force, but I could not strip the other points of the frontier of all defense; small corps were necessary at Bordeaux, at Toulouse, on the Var, in Savoy, at Béfort, and at Strasbourg. These corps, though feeble in themselves, were important to check the enemy's advance, and to secure points of vast importance for levying the National Guards, and organizing other means of defense. Unfortunately La Vendée still remained in insurrection, in spite of the success of the movable columns. Civil war is a political cancer which must be extirpated in the germ, or the safety of the state is compromitted. I was, therefore, obliged to detach even a part of my Young Guard to reënforce the corps of General Lamarque. These several detachments, reduced to one hundred and twenty thousand combatants the force of the principal army which was to assemble between the Meuse and the Sambre, from Philippeville to Maubeurge. Although the enemy had at least two hundred thousand men in Belgium, I did not hesitate to attack them, for it was now necessary to act promptly, lest I should have all the allied armies on my hands at the same time.

Napoleon joins his Army and re-organizes it.—I left Paris on the twelfth of June, the next day I inspected the armament of Soissons and Laon, and on the fourteenth took up my head-quarters at Beaumont! The organization of the army was much modified; I gave the command of *corps-d'armée* to young generals who, having their marshal's *bâtons* to gain on the battle-field, would show more ardor for the triumph of my cause. This *bâton* was bestowed on Grouchy, who had shown talent and vigor in the campaign of 1814, and in the expedition against the Duke d'Angoulême. Soult was appointed major-general in the place of Berthier, who had abandoned his colors to follow the Bourbons, and who precipitated himself from the window of the palace of Bamberg, ashamed, it is said, to see himself in the midst of the enemy's columns, which were defiling below him to attack his country!* Davoust remained minister of war. Mortier was to have commanded the Guard, but he did not recover his health in time. Ney and Grouchy were to command the wings of the principal army, as my lieutenants. Suchet commanded the army of Italy; Rapp on the Rhine; Brune on the Var; Clausel and Decaen observed the Pyrenees.

Plan of Operations.—I had four lines of operations from which to select. I could unite my masses to the left towards Valenciennes, march by Mons on Brussels, fall upon the English army, and drive it back on Antwerp. At the centre I could march by Maubeurge on Charleroi, between the Sambre and Meuse, so as to strike the point of junction of the two armies of Blucher and Wellington. More to the right I might descend the Meuse towards Namur, fall upon the left of the Prussians, and cut them off from Coblentz and Cologne. Finally it was possible to descend between the Meuse and the Moselle, or between the Meuse and the Rhine, to fall upon the corps of Kleist, who covered the Ardennes and the communication of the Prussians with the Rhine.

This last operation would lead to nothing but menaces, and against a general like Blucher, it could produce no decided results; moreover, it led too far from the proposed object. An attack on the Meuse would have been more wise, but that would have thrown Blucher on Wellington, and effected a junction which it was important to prevent. The inverse manœuvre, by Mons, against Wellington, would have

* This is the generally received account of the death of Berthier. Some, however, have said that he fell by the hand of a personal enemy. His fate will serve as a warning to those who, led astray by political feeling, may be tempted to oppose their country's cause in time of war.

produced the same result in a different way, throwing the right of the allies upon their left. I therefore chose the centre where I could surprise Blucher *en flagrant délit*, and defeat him before Wellington could come to his rescue. To appreciate the nature of this plan, it must be remembered that I was not to attack a single army, under a single chief, and with a common interest, but, on the contrary, two armies, independent of each other, having two separate and divergent bases of operation; that of the English being on Ostend or Antwerp, and that of the Prussians on the Rhine and Cologne;—a decisive circumstance, greatly increasing the chances of success for a central operation which would divide them so that they could be fought separately.

Beginning of the Campaign.—The plan and commencement of this campaign form one of the most remarkable operations of my life. Nine corps of infantry or cavalry cantoned from Lille to Metz, by marches most skillfully concealed, concentrated before Charleroi, at the very instant that the guard arrived there from Paris! These movements were combined with so much precision that one hundred and twenty thousand men found themselves assembled, the fourteenth of June, on the Sambre, as if by enchantment. Wellington, occupied in giving *fêtes* at Brussels, thought me at Paris at the moment my columns presented themselves, on the morning of the fifteenth, to cross the river Sambre. My troops occupied, the night before, the following positions: the right of sixteen thousand men, under Count Gérard, at Philippeville; the centre, of about sixty thousand, under my own direction, near Beaumont; the left, of forty-five thousand men, at Ham-sur-Eur and Solre-sur-Sambre. So little idea had my enemies of these movements that their armies were not even assembled. Blucher had the first of his corps at Charleroi, the second at Namur, the third at Dinant, the fourth, under Bulow, at Liége, and the fifth, under

Kleist, covered Luxembourg. When I reached the army, I learned that Bourmont had just deserted, (on the fourteenth), from Philippeville to join Louis XVIII. and the allies. Blamable as was such a step, it is believed he did not aggravate it by divulging my plans of operation; on this subject even a common soldier, in such a case, should keep silence. Nevertheless, under the circumstances, the simple information of my arrival was an important matter, for it destroyed in part the effects of the surprise, Blucher having immediately ordered the concentration of his forces.* Wellington's forces were still in their cantonments between Oudenarde and Nivelle on the Scheldt, ready to move at the first signal. I did not know the precise composition and position of all the enemy's corps, but I was certain that the mass of the Prussians were cantoned between Charleroi and Liége, and that the Anglo-Belgians were between Ath and Brussels, with advanced guards towards Mons and Tournay. The road running from Charleroi to Brussels was, therefore, the point of junction of the two armies, and to this point I directed my operations, in order to scatter the enemy's forces, and fight them separately.†

* It has been said that a drummer, who deserted from the Old Guard, gave Blucher the first information of Napoleon's approach.

† The following table given by Jomini in his last work exhibits the strength and position of the hostile forces at the beginning of the campaign.

I.—THE ALLIES.

1.—*Prussians under Blucher.*

		STRENGTH.	POSITION.
1st corps, *Ziethen.*	4 divisions of infantry; Steinmetz, Pirch 2d, Jagow and Henkel.... Cavalry of Roder, 3,900..........	32,800	On the Sambre between Thuin and Auveloy.
2d corps, *Pirch.*	4 divisions of infantry: Tippels-Kirch, Krafft, Brause, and Langen. Cavalry of Jurgas, 4,000.........	31,800	about Namur.

June 15th, Passage of the Sambre. — Success depending on celerity, the French army passed the frontier on the fifteenth at break of day, and directed their march on Charleroi.

		STRENGTH.	POSITION.
3d corps, *Thielmann.*	4 divisions of infantry: Borcke, Kempfen, Luck and Stulpnagel... Cavalry of Hobe, 2,500..........	24,000	About Ciney and Dinant
4th corps, *Bulow.*	4 divisions of infantry; Haacke, Rysel, Lostyn, and Hiller....... Cavalry of Prince William of Prussia, 3,000..........................	30,300	Near Liége.
5th corps, *Kleist.*	about...........................	30,000	Luxembourg, and Bastogne.
	Total, not including Kleist, 136 battalions, 135 squadrons, 320 cannon....	118,900 combatants.	

2.—*Anglo-Netherlanders under Wellington.*

		STRENGTH.	POSITION.
1st corps, *Prince of Orange.*	2 English divisions, Guards and Alten.........................	10,800	About Eghein and Subise.
	Anglo-Belgians, Indian Brigade, Divisions Stedman, Perponcher and Chassé..................	24,300	From Oudenarde to Nivelle.
	Cavalry of Collaert.............	4,600	Braine-le-Comte.
2d corps, *Genl. Hill.*	5 Anglo-Hanoverians, divisions Clinton, Coleville, Picton, Lambert and Decken.........................	34,600	Ath, Renaix, Oudenarde, Leuze and Brussels.
	Cavalry of Lord Uxbridge.........	9,850	From Ghent to Mons.
Corps of Brunswick—Infantry and cavalry......		6,750	Brussels, Mechlin.
Contingent of Nassau........................		3.000	Brussels, Genappe.
Artillery..................................		6,000	Scattered.
Total 123 battalions, 114 squadrons, 240 cannon..................................		99,900 Combatants.	

3.—*Other troops of the Allies.*

The grand Austro-Russian army under Barclay de Tolly and Swartzenberg, more than	350,000
The Austro-Sardinian army in Italy..................................	100,000

To these must be added the Swiss, Spaniards and small German Contingents, making in all but little less than *a million of men* in arms against France.

The corps of General Rielle at Ham-sur-Eur, being nearest the enemy was to pass the Sambre at Marchiennes, and direct itself on Gosselies; that of Erlon, being more in rear, at

II.—THE FRENCH.

1.—*Active Army in Belgium.*

		STRENGTH.	POSITION.
1st corps. *D'Erlon.*	4 divisions of infantry: Guyot, Donzelot, Marcognet, and Durutte... 1 division of cavalry, Jaquenot.....	20,600	At Solre-sur-Sambre.
2d corps, *Reille.*	4 divisions of infantry: Bachelu Foy, Jerome Bonaparte and Girard. 1 divison of cavalry, Piré.........	22,800	Ham-sur-Eur.
3d corps, *Vandamme.*	3 divisions of infantry: Habert, Berthezène and Lefol.......... 1 division of cavalry, Morin.......	16,000	Beaumont.
4th corps, *Gérard.*	3 divisions of infantry: Vichey, Pecheux and Hulot............ 1 division of cavalry, Molin.......	14,600	Philippeville.
5th corps, *Lobau.*	3 divisions of infantry: Simmer, Jeannin and Teste............	12,600	Beaumont.
Guards.	2 divisions of the Old Guards, Friant and Morand....... 8,000 1 division of Young Guard, Duhesme.................... 4,000 Cavalry of the Guard, 19 squadrons of light, and 13 of heavy.. 4,000 Engineers and artillery....... 2,400	18,400	Beaumont.

2.—*Reserves of Cavalry.*

1st corps, *Pajol.*	Divisions of hussars and chasseurs, Soult and Subervic............	2,800	Beaumont.
2d corps, *Excelmans.*	Divisions of dragoons, Spraley and Chastel......................	3,000	"
3d corps, *Milhaud.*	Divisions of cuirassiers, Wotier and Delort....................	3,600	"
4th corps, *Kellerman.*	Divisions of cuirassiers, Sheritier and Roussel..................	3,700	"

This gives for the active French army in Belgium and the reserves of cavalry, a total of 167 incomplete battalions, 166 squadrons, 346 cannon, and 120,300 combatants.

3.—*Other French corps in Garrison or Observation,*

Rapp commanded the army of the Rhine.
Beliard " a corps at Metz.

Solre-sur-Sambre, was to follow in the same direction. The centre or corps of battle, with the reserves of cavalry under the orders of Grouchy,* marched from Beaumont on Charleroi, and the right from Philippeville on Catelet, where it was to cross the Sambre and prevent the Prussian division at Charleroi from retreating on Namur.

These movements, although unknown to the enemy, did not entirely accomplish their object. The corps of Reille crossed the Sambre with success and reached the road to Gosselies, preceded by the light cavalry of the guard; but that of Gérard, leaving Philippeville and having a longer march by the worst possible roads, arrived too late at Catelet, to reach the road to Gilly in time to accomplish its object. The centre also had very bad roads to travel over from Beaumont to Charleroi, and Vandamme, who was to form the head of this column, left his camp a little too late.† The Prussian generals whose divisions were scattered along the line, had on this account much more leisure than I intended, to collect their forces and abandon Charleroi; two or three battalions only were overthrown in partial combats. The first division of the corps of Ziethen wishing to retire from

Lecourbe commanded a small corps of observation at Belfort.
Suchet " the army of Italy in Savoy.
Brune " the corps of observation on the Var.
Decaen and Clausel commanded the corps of observation of the Pyrenees.
Lamarque commanded the corps of La Vendée.

It has already been shown in the text that these were mere skeletons of corps, possessing little strength in themselves, but available for observation, for assembling or organizing the new levies, and for securing important strategic points.

* Grouchy at first commanded all the cavalry, but when the army was completely organized, he took command of the right wing.

† Jomini thinks the delay of Vandamme caused by an error in the transmission of orders, for he was not a man likely to be tardy, and, indeed, at this time his ardor, excited by personal jealousy, needed restraint rather than stimulus.

Piéton by Gosselies, and finding this point already occupied by the advanced guard of Reille, sought to reach Heppignies. The second division re-united at Gilly on the road to Namur. The corps of Reille, having driven the Prussian division from Gosselies and seeing it direct its retreat by Heppignies on Fleurus, detached the division of Girard in pursuit, and with the other three divisions continued its march on Frasne. The light cavalry of the guard, which preceded it, drove from this town the advanced guard of the Prince of Weimar who now concentrated his brigade on Quatre-Bras. The light cavalry of Grouchy, having debouched from Charleroi on Gilly, found there the two divisions of Ziethen, and had to await the infantry of Vandamme, who was debouching with difficulty by the bridge of that city, which was greatly encumbered. In this position the two parties exchanged some cannon shot. While my columns were thus debouching from the bridges of the Sambre in search of the enemy, I established myself in advance of Charleroi at the branching of the roads to Gosselies and Fleurus, where I waited to receive the reports of my officers, and to determine upon the movements to be given to the masses which had been so suddenly and skillfully assembled.

Measures of the Allies.—It may be well, before going further, to briefly review the measures taken by the allies against the storm which was about to fall upon them. If their generals had allowed themselves to be surprised, it must be confessed that they made their preparations with skill. The Anglo-Prussians were to take the offensive on the first of July, and, in the mean time, every precaution was taken to prevent this plan from being counteracted. All partial and general rallying points were well indicated. To prevent me from manœuvring to separate their armies, Blucher was to rally his army on its right, in rear of Ligny, while Wellington was to rally his on its left, on Quatre-Bras; but, wise as were these dispositions, the celerity and impetuosity of my movements might, nevertheless, defeat them. In pursuance of the plan agreed upon by the allies, Blucher dispatched an order, on the fourteenth at midnight, to Ziethen to fall back, fighting, on Fleurus, and directed at the same instant the corps of Pirch to assemble at Sombref; he ordered Thielman to come in all haste from Dinant to Namur; while Bulow was to assemble at Hanut. These movements were evidently based on information received from deserters, but Blucher had not counted on my abrupt passage of the Sambre and on a decisive battle for the next day.

Decisive Movement prescribed to Ney.—I did not at this time know all the circumstances of the allies, or the details of their positions and movements; but I knew sufficiently well that Blucher would seek to collect his forces somewhere between Namur and the road from Charleroi* to Brussels so as to form a junction with the English. To anticipate this, I determined to seize upon Sombref on the one side, and the central point of Quatre-Bras on the other; master of these two points I could act, as occasion might require, upon either of the two hostile armies, and prevent their junction. I therefore gave to Grouchy a verbal order to push on the same evening as far as Sombref, if possible; Marshal Ney, who had just come from Paris by post, received orders to take command of the left wing formed of the corps of Reille and Erlon, and to march without delay on the road to Brussels in the direction of Quatre-Bras,†

* Those who now visit Charleroi may be surprised that so strong a place should be so readily abandoned by the allies, and so easily passed by Napoleon; but it must be remembered that in 1815 it was not defensible. The strong works that now partially surround this city have been built since the peace, and, it is said, with English money and under the direction of Wellington.

† Quatre-Bras is a small village named from the meeting of four roads; from Namur, Charleroi, Brussels, and Nivelles.

and to push forward his advanced guards on the three roads branching from that place, in order to collect correct information of the enemy. Having learned at the same moment that the cavalry of Grouchy had been checked near Gilly by a part of the corps of Ziethen, I hastened there to order an attack; the enemy, seeing the infantry of Vandamme arrive, retired fighting, and, at the end of a pretty warm cannonade, Excelmans and Vandamme dislodged him from the woods of Soleilmont and Lambusart, where the third division of Ziethen had collected.

Ney delays its Execution.—In the interval while this was passing on the right, Marshal Ney, having arrived between Gosselies and Frasne, and hearing the cannon thundering in the direction of Gilly, where Vandamme and Grouchy were attacking the second division of Ziethen, thought this combat might modify my projects, and, instead of pushing on rapidly as far as Quatre-Bras, established himself in front of Gosselies. I was a little vexed at this, but as night came on without the right wing having attained its object, I regarded the delay of the left the less objectionable as Quatre-Bras might be reached in time on the following morning. The troops of the corps of battle and the cavalry, bivouacked between the woods of Lambusart and the village of Heppignies, which was occupied by the division of Girard and the corps of Reille; the Guard and the corps of Lobau were in reserve about Charleroi; the forces of Count Gérard* remained near Châtelet; and the corps of Erlon had not passed Jumet. At ten o'clock in the evening I returned to Charleroi, where I was occupied with the vexatious news of the operations of the chambers and Jacobins at Paris, the organization of my army and the direction of movements

* This general should not be confounded with General *Girard;* the first commanded the fourth corps, and the other the fourth division of the second corps.

based on the further information gained of the enemy. The right wing of my army under Grouchy was composed of the corps of Vandamme and Gérard, and the cavalry of Pajol, Excelmans, and Milhaud; the left wing, under Ney, of the corps of Reille and Erlon, with the cavalry of Valmy and Lefèbre-Desnouettes; the reserve of about twenty-eight thousand men was formed of the corps of Lobau and the Guard. I myself was occupied at head-quarters early in the morning and left my lieutenants, Ney and Grouchy, to complete at sunrise the operations left incomplete on the night before,—to occupy Sombref and Quatre-Bras. To make more certain of these operations, I sent my aid-de-camp Flahaut to Marshal Ney at eight o'clock in the morning, with a written order to march rapidly on Quatre-Bras, to establish himself there strongly, to make an examination of the three roads, and then detach a good division of infantry with the light cavalry of the Guard upon Marbais, in order to connect himself with the right wing, which was about to establish itself at Sombref. This dispatch was to be preceded by a similar one given by the major-general. These orders reached Gosselies near eleven o'clock, but Ney had left to join the advanced guard of Reille near Frasne, so that he did not immediately receive them.

While these things were taking place at my head-quarters, the troops of Grouchy drove back the rear-guards of Ziethen from Fleurus; they retired upon the corps of battle, formed on the heights between Ligny and St. Amand, in the presence of which the French troops found themselves near eleven o'clock.

Ney again delays his March on Quatre-Bras.—I had just arrived near Ligny, and was about to observe the enemy's position, when I learned that Ney had again thought best, for several reasons, to delay his march on Quatre-Bras, and to wait where he was till he should learn my decision on the new information sent to me. Thwarted by this deplorable incident, I reiterated the order for Ney to push rapidly on to Quatre-Bras, it being understood that he was to detach the eight thousand men upon Marbais, as had already been directed through General Flahaut. I at the same time repeated, that Grouchy was about to occupy Sombref, and that he would certainly have to contend only against the troops coming from Brussels. Walewski, a Polish officer, was the bearer of this letter.

Reconnoissance of the Prussian Position.—While this officer was galloping on the road to Gosselies, I ascended the mill of Fleurus, to examine the Prussian corps. The position was a difficult one in front, covering the little stream of Ligny; the left extended to the environs of Sombref and Tongrines; the centre was near Ligny; the right behind St. Amand. This great town formed of three distinct villages (which were called St. Amand le Château, St. Amand la Haie, and St. Amand le Hameau), protected the right wing, the flank of which rested on Wagnèle. The second line and reserves were between Sombref and Bry. Thus six great villages, four of which were difficult to be taken, on account of the stream in front, covered like so many bastions, the enemy's line; his reserves and second line, placed in columns of attack by battalions between Sombref and Bry, could sustain it at all points.*

Dispositions for forcing this Position.—Having finished this reconnoissance, I had to chose between three plans of operation: 1st, to stop immediately the march of Ney's columns; order the cavalry of Kellerman to take position at

* The four divisions of Ziethen's corps formed the first line; those of Pirch's corps the second at Bry and Sombref. The left under Thielman, which arrived only at nine A. M., was near Tongrines. Gourgaud says this reconnoissance was made at about ten o'clock, but Jomini seems to think it was later. There is still some doubt respecting the details of these operations of the sixteenth. The main facts, however, are as related in the text.

Frasne so as to cover the line of retreat on Charleroi; then throw the seven divisions of Reille and Erlon, by the old Roman road, on Marbais, in order to turn Blucher and take him in reverse, while I attacked him in front. 2d. To prescribe this movement to the corps of Erlon only, leaving that of Reille with the cavalry of Kellerman defensively in the direction of Frasne and Quatre-Bras, in order to observe the enemy, and cover the road to Charleroi. 3d. To prescribe to Ney to fall with impetuosity on the enemy found at Quatre-Bras, and drive him on Genappe in the direction of Brussels, then fall back on Bry in the direction of Namur to coöperate in the attack upon Blucher.

Under ordinary circumstances, perhaps, the first project would have been most conformable to the rules of the art, but now it might endanger our natural line of retreat on Charleroi. Thinking that in all probability Ney, receiving the orders dispatched in the morning by Flahaut, had by this time rendered himself master of Quatre-Bras, and might, after having beaten the Anglo-Belgians, assist in the defeat of Blucher, I determined to adopt the second plan.*

Battle of Ligny.—I now made my dispositions to attack the Prussians. The corps of Count Lobau, left at first near Charleroi, was ordered to march in all haste to Fleurus. The left of the corps of battle under Vandamme presented

* In pursuance of this plan, it would seem, the following order was dispatched to Ney:

"IN BIVOUAC BEFORE FLEURUS, 2 o'clock P. M.

"M. LE MARSHAL.—The Emperor directs me to inform you that the enemy have united a body of troops between Sombref and Bry, and, that at half past two, Marshal Grouchy, with the third and fourth corps, will attack him.

"It is the intention of His Majesty that you also attack whatever is before you; *that after having pushed the enemy vigorously*, you fall back to assist in enveloping the corps just mentioned. If this corps were first beaten His Majesty would then manoeuvre in your direction to facilitate equally your operations. Inform the Emperor immediately of your dispositions, and of whatever shall take place on your front."

itself before the village of St. Amand; the centre, under Count Gérard, presented itself before Ligny; the Guard placed itself in rear of these two attacks; the cavalry of Grouchy deployed on the right to keep in check the left of the Prussians, just reënforced by the arrival of the entire corps of Thielman. The attack began between two and three o'clock at St. Amand, of which Vandamme got possession in spite of a vigorous resistance; but the Prussians, favored by the village of La Haie, and the heights commanding it, advanced their second line and retook it. Count Gérard experienced the same opposition at Ligny, of which he could occupy only a part. I knew from this opposition that the enemy was in stronger force than I had at first supposed, which rendered it still more important to manœuvre so as to turn his right flank, and prevent his falling back in that direction. I therefore dispatched another formal order to Ney,* directing him to manœuvre with his forces on Bry and St. Amand. I supposed that ere this he had occupied Quatre-Bras, and would be now on his way towards the flank of Blucher, so that the order would reach him in time; fearing, however, that, from the recent and unaccountable delays of the left wing in executing my orders, this also might be in some way thwarted, and knowing that the corps

* This order dispatched at a quarter past three o'clock, was as follows:

"IN BIVOUAC BEFORE FLEURUS, from a quarter to half past 3, P. M.

"M. MARSHAL NEY.—I wrote to you an hour since that the Emperor would attack the enemy in the position he had taken between the village of St. Amand and Bry; at this moment the forces are sharply engaged: His Majesty directs me to say that you are to manœuvre immediately so as to envelop the enemy's right, and to fall by main strength on his rear; his army is lost if you only act vigorously. The fate of France is in your hands; therefore do not hesitate a moment to make the movement ordered by the Emperor, and direct yourself on the heights of Bry and St. Amand to assist in a victory perhaps decisive: the enemy is taken *en flagrant délit* at the moment when he seeks to unite with the English.

"DUC DE DALMATIE."

of Erlon had not yet passed Frasne, I sent General Labedoyère to communicate to Count d'Erlon the order given to Marshal Ney, and to direct him to commence its execution.

In the meantime the battle was continued throughout the line with great fury. A second attack of Vandamme on St. Amand, favored by the division of Girard which had crossed the ravine, and turned the enemy, put us in possession of this village; but the brave Girard purchased with his life a success which was of short duration; for Blucher having carried there a part of his reserves, the village of St. Amand was retaken and disputed with great fury. They fought still more fiercely at Ligny, which place Gérard had several times carried without being able to retain it; forced to leave the division of Hulot in observation on his right, and thus reduced to ten thousand combatants, he maintained himself with a most brilliant valor against more than twenty-five thousand Prussians, in the lower part of the village where the little stream cuts it in two. The Guard placed in rear of these two attacks disposed itself to sustain either as occasion might require. At the extreme right, Excelmans manœuvred skillfully to prevent the left of the Prussians from debouching from Tongrenelle, while Pajol observed Boignée, and the cuirassiers of Milhaud sustained the right of Gérard. This was the state of the battle at half past five, and I was becoming impatient at hearing nothing of the movements prescribed to Ney, nor of his operations at Quatre-Bras (for the noise of a violent cannonade and the direction of the wind had prevented me from hearing his attack), and I was preparing to dispose of the Guard when Vandamme informed me that a strong column had appeared in the direction of Wagnèle, and that the division of Girard, deprived of its general, and at the same time attacked by superior forces, was obliged to retire towards St. Amand le Hameau. General Vandamme announced that he had at first taken this column for a detachment which Ney was to direct on Marbais; but as it was much longer, and as his scouts had reported it to belong to the enemy, he should fall back in retreat unless promptly sustained. Although I could not comprehend how a column could thus slip between me and Ney, nevertheless it was barely possible that it might be a reënforcement sent from Quatre-Bras to Blucher, or a corps of his own army sent around by the old Roman road beyond Wagnèle to turn the left of Vandamme; it was therefore necessary to ascertain definitely the state of the case, and accordingly I sent one of my aids-de-camp to reconnoitre. This officer reported in about an hour that it was the corps of Erlon, which, instead of marching to the north towards Bry or Marbais, had inclined too much to the south in the direction of Villers-Peruin, drawn there without doubt by the noise of two or three hundred pieces of cannon which were thundering in the direction of St. Amand. My main attack had already been too long delayed, but the appearance of the corps of Erlon was a sufficient indication that Ney himself could not be far off, and would now direct this portion of the left wing as had been ordered, and I therefore commenced the march on Ligny, for it being now half past six, no further time was to be lost. By this impetuous debouch from that village with a division of the Guard, the infantry, and the cuirassiers of Milhaud, the enemy's centre was pierced and a part of it thrown on Bry, and a part of it on Sombref.

The Prussians fought well during the whole day, and the battle was undecided when I advanced with a reserve; Blucher seeing the departure of the Guard from the environs of St. Amand, and thinking this movement the commencement of a retreat, attacked himself what remained on St. Amand, in the hope of pursuing the French. Being soon undeceived, he headed a charge with the few cavalry he could collect. But of what use was the courage of a general-in-chief in such a *melée?* His horse having been shot under him, he fell to the ground,* and for some ten minutes was in the hands of the French cuirassiers without its being known, and at last, through the presence of mind of his aid-de-camp, Nostitz, he regained Bry on the horse of a lancer. At night-fall our victory was complete. But before noticing its results, let us follow the operations of Ney on the left.

Ney repulsed at Quatre-Bras.—Ney, from the delays already mentioned, did not reach his position till two o'clock, with three incomplete divisions of Reille's corps, Pirch's division of light cavalry and a brigade of Kellerman's cuirassiers, and for the first hour engaged the enemy in skirmishes; but at three o'clock, hearing the cannonade at St. Amand he took the resolution to make a serious attack upon the allies. But things had here very much changed since morning. General Perponcher, seeing how important it was, for rallying the army of Wellington and effecting its junction with Blucher, to hold this place, took position here with his division and the brigade of the Prince of Weimar, in all nine thousand men. These forces, commanded by the Prince of Orange, might easily have been routed, had they been attacked with two *corps-d'armée* in the morning. At eleven o'clock Wellington had withdrawn to this place the advance posts from near Frasne, and, at the moment Ney brought the divisions of Reille to the attack, the enemy was reënforced by the English division of Picton from Brussels, and the division of the Duke of Brunswick. Nevertheless Ney fought with his usual vigor. The division of Foy on the left marched on Quatre-Bras and Germioncourt, while that of Bachelu attacked the village of Piermont. That of

* It is said that while Blucher was thus entangled with his horse, he was actually ridden over by two regiments of cavalry.

Prince Jerome attacked, a little later, the wood of Bossut on the extreme left. Everywhere the French troops pushed the enemy with vigor. Wellington, certain of being soon reënforced, received these attacks with his usual *sang-froid ;* nevertheless the troops of the Prince of Orange and Picton were driven from these posts with considerable loss. The arrival of Brunswick's corps restored the equilibrium, and the field was disputed with great fury ; Brunswick himself fell pierced with balls. Ney now received the order of the major-general and heard, at the same time, that Erlon's corps was directed on Bry. He had no reserve of infantry, and most of his cuirassiers had been left with Erlon near Frasne. Running to Kellerman, he said to him : "My dear general, the fate of France is here involved, and we must make an extraordinary effort ; take your cavalry, and plunge into the middle of the English army ; I will sustain you with Piré." At these words Kellerman unhesitatingly charged at the head of his brigade of brave men, overthrew the sixty-ninth regiment, carried the batteries, and, piercing through two lines, reached even to the farm of Quatre-Bras, where the reserve of English, Hanoverian, and Belgian infantry received him with so murderous a fire that his soldiers were forced to retreat. Kellerman's horse being slain under him, he remained dismounted in the midst of the English, and had great difficulty in escaping again to his own army. The French infantry, incited by so fine a charge, renewed its efforts on Quatre-Bras and the wood of Bossut, the greater part of which was occupied by the division of Prince Jerome. But at this critical moment, the division of English Guards and the division of General Alten, coming into line after a forced march, gave Wellington so great a superiority that Ney could have no further hope. He had sent to Erlon an imperative order to come to his assistance, instead of taking position on Bry, but this corps was now too far off to arrive in time, so that the marshal was obliged to fall back on Frasne, with a loss of four thousand men *hors-de-combat;* the allies, entering only successively into action, had lost five thousand. Wellington pursued Ney at first with some vigor, but Roussel's division of cuirassiers protected his retreat. Erlon, imperatively recalled by Ney when already beyond Villers-Peruin, marched to rejoin him with three divisions and the light cavalry of the Guard, leaving the division of Durutte between Villers-Peruin and St. Amand, to coöperate if necessary on Bry. This division remained here all night inactive on the flank of the rear-guard that had been left by Blucher in this village, which it occupied till one o'clock in the morning, while the corps of Ziethen retired, by favor of the darkness, on Gilly, that of Pirch on Gentinne, and the left, under Thielman, took the direction of Gemblaux.

A fatality seemed to have presided over all the operations of my left wing. If it had moved, as I directed, on Quatre-Bras, on the evening of the fifteenth, or the morning of the sixteenth, it could very easily have beaten the isolated division of Perponcher, have occupied the position, and detached two divisions on Marbais and Bry, to complete the overthrow of Blucher. But when Ney received the order in the afternoon to march on Bry, the thing was impossible, for he had just engaged a superior force at Quatre-Bras. As it was, he had better have remained at Frasnes, for no advantage was gained at Quatre-Bras, and his recall of Count Erlon rendered this corps utterly useless, at a time when it might have had an important influence on the fate of Blucher's army. Our victory at Ligny was a glorious one, for, with sixty thousand men, we had beaten ninety thousand. In two days the enemy had lost from eighteen to twenty thousand killed, wounded, and prisoners, and forty pieces of cannon. My army was full of enthusiasm and confidence, ready to fly to new victories. Under any other circumstances the battle of Ligny would have been decisive. But, for reasons already given, all my plans for the coöperation of my left wing failed. Nor did I know that Durutte passed the night on the flank of the Prussian line of retreat, so near that his advanced guards heard distinctly the noise caused by the march of their trains, and the confusion of their columns. Had I known this I should have pushed these troops forward to harass the retreat, and, in spite of the darkness of the night, and the failure of the intended coöperation, I might have gained much by a well-regulated night pursuit.

At break of day the rear-guard of Blucher had disappeared from Bry; that of Thielman was seen on the road from Sombref to Corroy-le-Chateau in the direction of Gemblaux intermediary between the road to Namur and that to Brussels by Wavre. Blucher had committed a great fault in accepting battle, and he now thought it necessary to remedy, as promptly as possible, the influence which this defeat would have upon his army; unable to reach Bousseval directly, he resolved to rally on Bulow, and seek to gain communication with the English by Wavre. Consequently Thielman was directed on Gemblaux, and Ziethen and Pirch fell back by Mont-St.-Guibert on Bierge and Aisemont; and the Prussian marshal dispatched his chief of staff to concert with Wellington some plan for forming a junction either in front or in rear of the forest of Soignies.

The Morning of the 17th.—On the morning of the seventeenth, I waited with equal anxiety for Ney's report of the operations on Quatre-Bras, and the news from Paris of the political operations of the chambers and the Jacobins. In the mean time I ordered the cavalry of Pajol to follow the Prussians on the road to Namur, which was their natural line of operations, Excelmans on the road to Gemblaux, and

Monthion in the direction of Tilly and Mont-St.-Guibert. I also regulated my affairs of administration and visited the field of battle to succor the wounded of both parties; this care was the more necessary as the moving hospitals (*ambulances*) had been unable to follow the armies in their forced marches.

Grouchy sent in Pursuit of the Prussians.—I at length received, by my aid-de-camp, Flahaut, the details of the unfortunate affair of Quatre-Bras, at the same time that Pajol announced the capture of some Prussian cannon at Mazy, on the road to Namur. I now resolved to turn against the English with my reserve and left wing, and sent Grouchy with his seven divisions of infantry and two corps of cavalry in close pursuit of the Prussians.

The Reserve and Left Wing march against the English.—My advanced guard marched for Quatre-Bras near ten o'clock, and the Guard at eleven. The weather was terrible; it rained as though the flood-gates of heaven were open; nevertheless, my troops showed themselves no less eager in the pursuit.

The English retreat.—On arriving at Genappe, I found only the English rear-guard. Wellington, hearing accidentally of Blucher's defeat at eight o'clock in the morning, (the officer sent with the dispatch lost his way and was killed), abandoned Quatre-Bras and hastened to put his *impedimenta* in retreat on the road to Brussels, covering it with the cavalry of Lord Uxbridge. The French followed in close pursuit as far as Maison-du-Roi and the heights of Planchenois, where the army arrived at nightfall. The enemy manifested an intention to maintain himself in front of the forest of Soignies, but we thought it was only the rear-guard covering the retreat of the army through the forest; however as it was too late to begin an attack that night, our different corps bivouacked near Planchenois. The rain continued to fall in torrents all night. At three o'clock in the morning, I went the rounds of the posts and assured myself that the enemy had not moved ; Wellington had therefore resolved to fight ; this was exactly what I wished ; to meet and attack the two armies separately was the main point considered in the plan of campaign. Blucher had already been defeated and forced to retreat on a line diverging from the other army, and I had detached after him a sufficient force to increase the distance of separation and effectually prevent a junction. The other army was now in the toils, and my only apprehension was that it would refuse battle.

Grouchy ordered to occupy the Defile of St. Lambert.—Nevertheless, to profit with security by this happy chance it was best to entirely prevent the junction of the allied armies. I, therefore, dispatched a courier, in the early part of the night of the sixteenth, to Grouchy at Wavre with an order to occupy without delay the defile of St. Lambert, so that if he did not take an active part in the coming battle by falling on the left of the English, he could at least give them some trouble, and at the same time cover my flank. But at midnight I received Grouchy's report, saying that he had arrrived at Gembloux at five o'clock in the evening and was passing the night there, having marched only *two leagues!!* This delay was exceedingly vexatious, as he might well have reached Wavre about the same time that I had La-Belle-Alliance, as the distance was but little greater. But as he could not have received the order which I had sent to Wavre, another was immediately despatched to Gembloux hoping that he would receive it in time.

Reasons for attacking the English.—My army had been much harrassed by rains, bad roads, and forced marches. Under ordinary circumstances it would have been best to allow it some repose, and afterward to dislodge Wellington by manœuvres. But other armies were about to invade France, and my presence would soon be needed elsewhere. Moreover, Blucher would soon rally, and, with reënforcements, again attempt to force a junction with the right of the allies; it was, therefore, necessary to end with the English as soon as possible.

Position of the Allied Army.—They occupied in front of Mont-St.-Jean, a fine plateau, the slope from which, like the glacis of a fort, was favorable for their fire and offered them a good view of our operations. The right extended to the rear of Braine-la-Leud, and a corps of Netherlanders of fifteen thousand men was still detached as far as Halle to cover the road from Mons to Brussels. The position in itself had great defensive advantages, the villages of Braine and Merbes, the chateau of Hougomont, La-Haie-Sainte, La-Haie, and Frichemont forming, as it were, advanced bastions which flanked and secured the whole line; but it was just on the brink of the vast forest of Soignies,* with no possible outlet for a great army, with its immense material and numerous cavalry.

Plan of Attack.—As the enemy had decided to await battle, it became necessary to determine the plan of attack. To manœuvre by the left to turn the enemy's right might cut off his retreat on that side of the forest, but it would separate me from the centre of operations, and throw Wellington in the direction of Blucher; moreover this wing was secured by the farm of Hougomont (now converted into a strong field-work) and the great bourgs of Braine-la-Leud and Merbe-Braine. To attack with the right to crush the enemy's left was preferable, inasmuch as it maintained a direct relation on an interior line with Grouchy. But as the ground in this direction was unfavorable, I, therefore, deter-

* The traveler will now find this forest much changed, and far more accessible for an army than it was in 1815. Much of the timber has been removed within the last few years.

mined to assail the left and pierce the centre. To attack the centre only, as at Montenotte, Rivoli, and Austerlitz, can be done when this point is left unsecured, which very seldom happens. In the present case the manœuvre of Wagram and Moskwa was preferable. The mass of my forces was directed on the centre; the extreme left was to be assailed only by the division forming the right of the corps of Erlon, which was to attack Papelotte and La-Haie;* Ney was to conduct the three other divisions to the right of La-Haie-Sainte;* the corps of Reille was to support this movement at the left of the road to Mont-St.-Jean; the divisions of Bachelu and Foy, between this road and the farm of Hougomont; that of Prince Jerome, conducted by Guilleminot, was to attack this farm which constituted the salient point of the enemy's line. Wellington had formed loop-holes in the walls of the chateau and garden, and secured the enclosure of the park, occupying the whole with the English Guards.† Count Lobau, with the sixth corps and a mass of cavalry, followed as a third and a fourth line to the centre, on the right and left of the road, so as to support Ney's attack upon La-Haie-Sainte; finally twenty-four battalions of the Guard and cuirassiers of the Duke of Valmy, forming the fifth and sixth lines, were ready to bear upon the decisive point.‡ I had purposed to begin the attack early in the morning, but the torrents of rain which had fallen during the night and previous day had so softened the ground that

* These two places must not be confounded; the first was at the left wing of the allies, and the other at the centre.

† The thick walls of the house, chapel, and garden, pierced with loop-holes and arranged for a double tier of fire, were almost impregnable; exterior to these was a ditch with a good embankment covered with a thick hedge; and the whole was surrounded by a thick woods, which have since been removed. The whole formed an excellent field fortification, which from its position produced a marked effect upon the operations of the battle.

‡ Jomini says that Napoleon may offer this plan of battle as a model to the masters of the art, for nothing can be better.

it would have been hardly possible for the artillery and cavalry to manœuvre. As the weather began to clear up, the attack was delayed in order that the ground might become more firm; in the meantime the several corps were placed in position.

Commencement of the Battle of La Belle-Alliance, or Waterloo.—At eleven o'clock the attack commenced with artillery and musketry against the farm of Hougomont, which Jerome endeavored to carry; a few moments after, Ney presented himself near Frichemont at the opposite extremity of the line. A few cannon-shot were exchanged, when it was ascertained that the stream, although narrow and shallow, was so very muddy, that it was necessary to turn to the west of Smouhen, it being difficult to pass lower down in face of the enemy's batteries. Ney, obliged thus to withdraw a part of his right to the centre, at length succeeded in forming these four divisions of the corps of Erlon, and it was only by herculean efforts that he could form his artillery in the soft ground where the carriages sunk to their hubs in the mud.

First Appearance of the Prussians.—The marshal soon began a violent cannonade against the enemy's left, merely waiting for my signal to fall upon it. I was about giving this signal a little after twelve o'clock, when strong columns were discovered on the right in the direction of Lasne and St. Lambert; these I supposed to be the detachment asked of Grouchy, though after his report received the night before from Gembloux, I had hardly expected him so soon; nevertheless, by setting out very early in the morning he might have reached here by noon. To promptly ascertain the true state of things in this direction, I dispatched General Homond with three thousand horse towards Pajeau, where they could either cover our flank, or open a communication with Grouchy, as the circumstances might require. They soon after brought in a Prussian hussar with an intercepted letter, announcing the approach of Bulow with a force estimated at thirty thousand men.

Napoleon determines to hasten the Attack upon the English.—Notwithstanding this vexatious *contre-temps*, my affairs were still far from desperate; if Grouchy had permitted Bulow to penetrate between us, he certainly must be near at hand in pursuit, and if so, the chances of the battle were still unchanged. I therefore ordered Ney to begin the attack, and, to secure the threatened flank, I moved the two divisions of Count Lobau in the direction of Planchenois where they could serve as a reserve to Ney or oppose Bulow, as the circumstances might require. The Prussian corps, if followed up by Grouchy as I had every reason to believe it was, would thus find itself between two fires in a *coup-gorge*, and would become an additional trophy to the conqueror. Nearly a hundred cannon were now thundering against the enemy's centre to the right and left of La-Haie-Sainte; it was here that the principal effort was to be made; and if Ney, seconded by Lobau and the Guard, should succeed in penetrating here as he did at Friedland, I would command the road through the forest of Soignes, which constituted the enemy's only chance of retreat.

Ney's first Attack on the Centre.—Near one o'clock, Ney threw himself at the head of the corps of Erlon, which deployed in columns by division in order to cross more rapidly the space between it and the enemy. This movement, executed with close and deep masses under a murderous fire, and in a horrible mud, caused a slight undulation in his columns; a part of his artillery remained behind, and continued a distant fire upon the enemy's batteries, while the infantry was passing the ravine. The extreme right division of this corps moved in the direction of Smouhen in concert with the light cavalry of Jaquinot. A brigade of the left attacked the farm-house of La-Haie-Sainte, where it met a strong resistance, and experienced considerable losses. The remainder of this corps, having all the difficulties of the deep mud and the formidable fire of the enemy's artillery, reached the part of the first line formed of the Belgian brigade of Bylant (division of Perponcher) and pierced it by a vigorous charge. But they were now suddenly assailed by the English division of Picton, placed in the second line, and lying hid behind a rise of ground favorable for their concealment. The combat now becomes furious; the English infantry are deployed and envelope, with their concentric fire, the compact corps of Ney. Picton falls dead; but his troops hold firm, and the French column, arrested by this murderous fire, begins to waver. At this instant Lord Uxbridge advances the English cavalry of General Ponsonby to charge it in flank: emboldened by success, they charge in the interval between the second and third columns, and precipitate themselves on Ney's reserve of artillery, a part of which remains in rear, on account of the mud; they sabre the soldiers of the train and the cannoneers, and carry away the horses, thus depriving the infantry of a part of its cannon. Seeing the operations of these horsemen, I throw out against them the cuirassiers of Milhaud and a brigade of lancers; in a few minutes they are completely destroyed, and Ponsonby is slain; but the French infantry has been broken, and a part of its cannon have been rendered immovable.

The Left attacks Hougomont.—While these things were taking place against the left and left centre of the allies, Jerome, seconded by Foy, had, with difficulty, dislodged the enemy from the park of Hougomont, but all efforts were vain against the embattled walls and chateau, where Wellington himself conducted the reënforcements to the English Guards who defended this important post with the most admirable valor. Wellington was waiting for the promised aid of Blucher, and he sought every means to prolong the contest. For him there was no hope of retreat; he must conquer or die. Seeing my efforts directed towards the centre he hastened to close his line, calling from Braine-la-Leud and Merbes twenty battalions of Belgians and Brunswickers, and placing them successively in reserve behind the right and centre. He himself then repaired to the defense of Hougomont. General Foy, on his side, wishing to second the attacks made on the chateau by the division of Jerome (conducted by Guilleminot), sought to pass this post, and fell upon the line of Lord Hill and the Brunswickers, who were formed in rear of a cross-road which ran along in front of the enemy's line from the Nivelle road to near Papelotte. But being wounded in the shoulder by a ball, and seeing his troops cut down by a murderous fire without hope of dislodging the enemy, Foy renounced his project, and the combat on this point degenerated into a cannonade and skirmishes without advantages to either side.

Ney's second Attack.—In this interval Ney applied all his energy and force of character to repair the check which he had received in his first attacks; his right, in possession of Smouhen, debouched on Papelotte, and the marshal himself directed a new attack on La-Haie-Sainte. The division of Donzelot, sustained on the left of the road by a brigade of Valmy's cuirassiers, and on the right by a brigade of Quinot's infantry, at last succeeded in routing the Scotch and Hanoverian battalions; and at four o'clock his troops, after the most glorious efforts, remained masters of these two points. During this contest I passed along the lines of Ney and Milhaud amid a shower of bullets; General Devaux, commandant of the artillery of the Guard and reserve, was killed at my side,—an irreparable loss at the moment when I was directing him to renew the decisive manœuvres of Wagram.

Bulow debouches on Planchenois.—At four o'clock the possession of La-Haie-Sainte and Papelotte gave us a decided superiority, and all the chances were in our favor, but at this moment I learned that Bulow had debouched from the wood of Frichemont, and attacked Count Lobau. I now feared that Grouchy had not followed this Prussian corps, and that I should be obliged, unassisted, to fight both armies. But Bulow was unsustained, and from my central position and the advantages already gained, I still felt confident of success, and resolved to fight them successively. Bulow had now advanced so far that his bullets reached the Charleroi road in rear of my centre; it was therefore necessary to force him to retreat. Accordingly, at five o'clock, I directed against him the Young Guard under the brave Duhesme, sustained by General Morand with a part of the Old Guard, intending afterwards to fall upon Wellington with the united reserves; in the meantime Ney was merely to sustain himself in possession of La-Haie-Sainte and Papelotte.

Grand Charge of the French Cavalry.—At this time, the marshal, finding himself too much isolated by the attack of the corps of Reille about the chateau of Hougomont, urgently asked for reënforcements. Having then no infantry at my disposal, I assigned to him the cuirassiers of Milhaud. Wellington, on his side, encouraged by the attack of Bulow, and reënforced by the troops of his extreme right, conceived the hope of regaining possession of the park of Hougomont and the farm-house of La-Haie-Sainte. For this purpose the Hanoverians were directed, at five o'clock, on the latter post, and at the same time the English under Lord Hill on the former. At this moment, Ney, whose troops were suffering terribly from the enemy's fire, seeing the light cavalry of his right forced by the English horse, sought to get possession at all hazards of the plateau of Mont-St.-Jean, and threw his brave cuirassiers on the centre of the allies. Unfortunately his infantry was not in condition to give it more than a feeble assistance. Nevertheless, these squadrons, encountering the Hanoverians in march on La-Haie-Sainte, fall upon them, sabre a regiment, capture the enemy's artillery, force the German legion which had formed in square, and even charge upon others; the enemy forms his troops in squares by regiments, rescues his cannoneers and artillery horses, and, by a well sustained fire, repels the efforts of this heroic cavalry*, which, charged in its turn by the English cavalry of Lord Somerset, rallied and resumed the attack even under the fire of the enemy's line.

This was a glorious operation, most heroically executed; but it was ill-timed; it should have been executed sooner, in concert with the first attack of Erlon, or have been deferred until the return of the Young Guard, so as to form a combined effort of the three arms united. But the plateau was crowned; and it was now necessary to sustain Ney where he was, or to allow his troops to be cut off. I therefore ordered Kellerman, after six o'clock, to advance with his cuirassiers to the left of the road to La-Haie-Sainte, and to overthrow everything before him. Unfortunately, and contrary to my intention, the heavy cavalry of the Guard followed this movement. Milhaud, seeing these reënforcements renews his attacks. These ten thousand horse cause great havoc in the enemy's line, capture sixty pieces of artillery, force two squares, and their progress is checked only by the infantry of the second line; the combined English, Belgian, Hanoverian, and Brunswick cavalry, under Lord Uxbridge, now charge upon the French; but these rally again at a little distance, and drive back the allies' horse upon their infantry. The repeated efforts of this cavalry are glorious

* Wellington himself assured the author, at the congress of Vienna, that he never saw anything more admirable than the ten or twelve reiterated charges of the French cuirassiers against troops of all arms.

beyond description, and the impassible perseverance of their adversaries is also deserving of the highest praise. But disorder now begins in the combined army, and the alarm even reaches Brussels, where we are every moment expected to appear. Bulow, attacked by Lobau, Duhesme, and a detachment of the Old Guard under Morand, is driven back on the road to Pajeau; finally Grouchy's cannon are now heard on the Dyle, and, in spite of all the *contre-temps*, victory seems certain. To give it the finishing stroke, I order, at half past seven, all the Guard to unite, and carry the position of Mont-St.-Jean. This effort must certainly incline the balance most decidedly in our favor.

Blucher debouches on Smouhen, and Pirch and Bulow on Planchenois.—But this illusion was of short duration; the French cavalry had hardly rallied its victorious squadrons, when new columns of the enemy were discovered from the plateau, coming from Ohain: it was Blucher himself, who had arrived with the corps of Ziethen in the direction of Papelotte. At the same time, the corps of Pirch, having debouched from Lasne, was already in action to second Bulow at Planchenois. I could not know the strength of these forces, but I feared that their arrival would snatch from me the victory. Nevertheless, I thought it possible to restore the equilibrium, and, perhaps, to force back the English, by refusing my right, which was now threatened by greatly superior numbers, and direct my principal efforts by my left on Hougomont and Mont-St.-Jean; this was a bold, and by some considered a rash measure, inasmuch as it changed my line of retreat from Charleroi to the causeway of Nivelle, and endangered my communication with Grouchy; but its character cannot be properly judged of, as circumstances at the time prevented its execution. Disorder began to reach the cavalry, and the division of Durutte was threatened by triple forces on the plateau between Smouhen and the *chaussée*; it was important to sustain Erlon without even waiting the return of the Guard commanded by Morand, and some other detachments. I put myself at the head of the division of Friant, which were the only troops disposable, and conducted it to La-Haie-Sainte, at the same time that I ordered Reille to make a new effort in the direction of Hougomont. This attack, led on by myself, restored courage to the French cavalry and to the remains of the corps of Erlon; if the whole division of Morand had been present, there would still have been some chances of success; but, forced to keep some battalions in hand towards Belle-Alliance, I could unite only four on the summit of the plateau in advance of La-Haie-Sainte. Ney, sword in hand, led them against the enemy.

Wellington's Dispositions.—In the mean time Wellington, certain of the near approach of Blucher on his left, thought to regain the park of Hougomont and La-Haie-Sainte; he threw the division of Brunswick and a Belgian brigade on the latter of these points at the moment that the few heroes of the guard charged bayonet upon the line of Anglo-Hanoverians. The Prince of Orange, seeing the importance of this movement, attacked them lively at the head of a regiment of Nassau, while the division of Brunswick attacked them on the other side; but the prince fell from a shot, while showing his men the road to victory. The brave soldiers of the Old Guard at first sustained the shock, but being unsupported in the midst of enemies who had just been reënforced by the Belgian brigade *de-chasse*, and exposed on all sides to a murderous fire, they fell back to the foot of the plateau which already had cost so much blood. In the mean time I succeeded in uniting six other battalions of the Old Guard which had been detached to different points, and I was making dispositions to second the efforts on Mont-Saint-Jean, when the disorder, which began to show itself on the right of the corps of Erlon, compelled me to form these battalions in squares to the right of La-Haie-Sainte.

Defeat of the French Right.—While these things were passing on the front of the French army, between the hours of eight and nine, the Young Guard and Lobau were fighting with rare bravery against the continually increasing forces of the Prussians. Seconded by the arrival of the corps of Pirch, Bulow succeeded in driving back these brave men who had been weakened by the withdrawal of the Old Guard, and were now overpowered by the double opposition of Blucher and Ziethen on their left flank. On the arrival of the latter, the cavalry of Wellington's left wing (brigades of Vivian and Vandeleur), which had suffered least during the combat, flew to the centre to second his efforts there. Ziethen, who had debouched at eight o'clock at the summit of the angle formed by the French line toward Frichemont, easily crushed Durutte, at the same time that he turned the left of the crochet formed by Lobau and the Young Guard. Pirch turned Planchenois and Bulow attacked it in front. All this part of the imperial army, broken and pierced by forces quadruple their own numbers, took refuge in flight. Duhesme and Barrois were severely wounded; Lobau was taken prisoner in the act of rallying his soldiers; Pelet forced his way with a handful of brave men which he drew about him. The heroic defense of these twelve or fifteen thousand French, against sixty thousand Prussians, who were favored by the nature of the ground, has drawn a tribute of admiration even from their enemies.*

Last Efforts and Rout of the French.—Wellington, seeing that the attack of Blucher is giving the decisive blow, collects his best troops, regains the park of Hougomont, and, at about nine o'clock, falls upon the Old Guard with an

* Vide report of General Gneisenau.

overwhelming superiority. The combat is most furious; General Friant and Michel are severely wounded; the remnant of the cuirassiers and the cavalry of the Guard do wonders; but all is in vain. Assailed by sixty thousand Prussians assembled on the left of Wellington, the entire French right is driven back in disorder on La-Belle-Alliance: the Guard is obliged to fight both to the front and rear; the cavalry of Wellington profits by this disorder and charges between the corps of Reille and the Guard which is formed in squares, at the same time that Blucher takes the line in reverse. These masses render it impossible to rally the troops of Count D'Erlon and Reille. The Prussian artillery have so far advanced as to reach with their fire the chaussée to Charleroi far in rear of the line; this contributes not a little to the disorder, and the darkness of the night finishes our overthrow. Infantry, cavalry, and artillery take pell-mell, the road to Genappe, some even seeking to gain the road to Nivelle, that to Charleroi now being occupied. I remain with a few brave men under Cambronne, on a piece of rising ground, endeavoring to stem the torrent of the enemy, and at last am obliged to effect my retreat across the fields, accompanied only by my staff, not having left even a battalion with which to check the enemy.

Operations of Grouchy.—Having related the fatal results of the appearance of the Prussians upon the field of Waterloo, it may be well to notice the circumstances under which this junction, so fortunate for the allies, was effected.

Grouchy, as has already been said, left Gembloux on the seventeenth at noon. It must also be remembered that the corps of Thielman had retired from Sombref in the same direction for the purpose, undoubtedly, of forming a junction with Bulow, who had just arrived there after a forced march of twelve leagues, while Blucher's right, composed of the corps of Ziethen and Pirch, had retired by Mont-Saint-Guibert on Bierge and Aisemont. Grouchy, on his arrival at Gembloux, learned, in the evening, that Bulow and Thielman had united there in the morning and had afterward marched in the direction of Wavre, forming together a mass of fifty-two thousand men. The corps of Gérard, on account of the violent storm which had drenched the troops and rendered the roads almost impassable, did not reach Gembloux till eleven o'clock in the evening, and Grouchy resolved to set out for Wavre at six o'clock the next morning, with the corps of Vandamme, leaving Gérard till eight o'clock to rest his troops.

Here was Grouchy's great fault. As soon as Blucher had renounced his natural base on the Meuse, it was evident that his object was to form a junction with Wellington, assume the offensive, and revenge himself for the defeat he had just sustained. Even admitting that my order to Grouchy was to follow on the heels of the Prussians, and that I had directed the pursuit on Namur (as has by some been alleged) the order had evidently become impossible of execution, and the marshal was now master of his own course of action. But the order afterwards transmitted by General Bertrand to march on Gembloux, sufficiently indicated the object which I wished him to accomplish. It was, most certainly, his duty to pursue the Prussians, but to do this, it was not necessary to follow in the trail of the retreating columns. To harass the enemy's rear-guards with light troops, while the main force is directed on the flank of the retreating columns,—or a lateral pursuit, as it is called,—was the method followed by the Russians in 1812 at Wiasma, Krasnoi, and on the Beresina. The same method has been adopted with similar success in other instances; but never have there been more favorable circumstances for such an operation than in the case of Grouchy. His principal object evidently was to keep the Prussians away from the left wing of our army; to harass them in their retreat was only a secondary object. By marching his infantry parallel to the Prussian columns, and at the same time harassing their rear with his light cavalry, he would have attained the double object of preventing any junction with the English, and have avoided the danger of fighting in defiles. He had the choice of three principal routes: that of the right by Sart-a-Walhain which Blucher had followed; that of the left by Mont-St.-Guibert, and along the Dyle to Wavre; or, by passing this river at Moustier, and reaching Wavre by the left, thus avoiding the defiles of the right bank. All these three routes were nearly of the same length, but the left brought Grouchy three leagues nearer the other wing of the French army, while the route on the right carried him three leagues in the other direction. The first, therefore, had the advantage of nearly an entire march, and in addition placed Grouchy between the two allied armies. There was no reason, then, why Grouchy should hesitate to march, on the eighteenth, at the break of day, in all haste, on Moustier with Excelmans, Vandamme, and Gérard, directing the cavalry of Pajol and the division of Teste on Wavre, in the pursuit of the enemy's rear-guard. He could reach Moustier by ten o'clock, and could then direct his infantry on Wavre by Limale, and the dragoons of Excelmans on Saint-Lambert, or march upon Lasne itself, when he heard the heavy cannonade of Waterloo. Instead of taking this wise resolution, Grouchy directed his forces on Sart-a-Walhain. The marshal was, apparently, induced to pursue this course through an obstinate desire to follow literally in the trail of the Prussians, and through ignorance that half of the Prussian army had passed by Gentines and Mont-St.-Guibert. To this fault is to be added that of a tardy departure in the morning, so that Vandamme did not pass Sart-a-Walhain, nor the head of Gérard's columns reach that village, till near noon. Grouchy had just been joined by this last general when the sound of a heavy and distant cannonade gave the signal of a serious battle: Gérard recommended to Grouchy to march immediately in the direction of the battle, persuaded that in marching to the cannon, as Ney had done at Eylau, he might decide the victory. "If Blucher," said he, "has effected a junction with Wellington, we will find him on the field of battle, and your order will be executed to the letter. If he should not be there, our arrival will decide the battle. In two hours we can take part in the engagement; and if we destroy the English, what will Blucher, already beaten, be able to do?"

This certainly was wise counsel, and, had it been followed, might have produced a decided influence on the event of the battle; but it must be confessed that it could not promise the same advantages as if this movement had been made at break of day from Gembloux. Considering the frightful state of the roads, the bad condition of the bridges, and the marshy defile of the Dyle, and above all, the presence of Thielman's corps extending from the heights of Bierge on Limale to oppose this passage, it may perhaps, at that hour of the day, have become impossible for Grouchy to reach Lasne or St.-Lambert before seven or eight o'clock in the evening. But even in that case, had he arrived too late to save the battle, he certainly could have made the defeat less disastrous. It is now impossible to say what course Blucher and his counselors would have pursued, if Grouchy had appeared in the direction of Moustier; but it is certain that this operation would have greatly embarrassed the Prussian general, and no one can decide what would have been the ultimate results of that embarrassment. But whatever may have been the result of the battle, no one can say that Grouchy would have run any risk in following the advice of Gérard; it was one of those operations that might have had a very beneficial influence, and could hardly have produced any evil results.

Manœuvres of the Allies.—While the army of Grouchy was committing these fatal errors, their adversaries executed a manœuvre both skillful and bold. The Prussian marshal, who bivouacked on the evening of the seventeenth about Wavre, sent his chief of staff, Gneisenau, to Wellington, to combine their ulterior operations. It was agreed that if the French should attack the English in front of the forest of Soignies, Blucher, favored by the Dyle and the direction of its course, would fall upon the French right; and if, on the contrary, the attack should be directed upon the Prussians at Wavre, Wellington would march to their assistance, falling upon the French left. Blucher seeing the false direction of Grouchy's march, and learning from his scouts that the main attack was directed against the English, determined to fly to their assistance. This he could now do without fear, Grouchy's error having left his operations in this direction unchecked. He, therefore, dispatched the corps of Bulow and Pirch, at four o'clock on the morning of the eighteenth, for Saint-Lambert, and marched himself with that of Ziethen on Ohain, in order to form a junction with the left of the English. Thielman was left with twenty-five thousand men at Wavre to defend the Dyle, with orders to follow the other corps if Grouchy should not appear. This plan was well conceived, and great praise is due to the allied generals who so skillfully took advantage of the error of my lieutenant.

In accordance with these wise dispositions Bulow was traversing Wavre between seven and eight o'clock in the morning when a violent fire broke out in the principal street which was the only passage through the town. The advanced guard having already passed this burning defile, continued its route; but the artillery could not immediately follow, the column being detained for a time to extinguish the fire. Towards twelve o'clock the advanced guard, formed at Saint-Lambert, awaited the arrival of the corps which debouched between three and four o'clock from the environs of Pijeau ; the corps of Pirch had passed Lasne between five and six o'clock ; Blucher with the corps of Ziethen, being delayed by counter-marches, did not reach Ohain before seven o'clock in the evening. The part taken in the battle by these sixty-five thousand Prussians has already been noticed ; at the same time the corps of Thielman, stationed on the heights of Bierge which command the valley of the Dyle, was watching for the approach of Grouchy. This marshal arrived at Wavre at four o'clock, and disposed his forces to attack the enemy's troops left there to dispute the passage of the Dyle. At five o'clock P. M. he received the order which had been sent to him at Gembloux in the morning ; he now directed Pajol with eight thousand men on Limale, and with the remainder of his forces attacked the detachment of Thielman. In this combat, which continued from Wavre to the Bierge mill, Gérard was wounded. The battle was very creditable to our arms, but what was passing at Mont-Saint-Jean rendered the success more injurious than useful.

The French Army retreats on Avesnes.—The wreck of my army reached Genappe in great disorder ; in vain did the staff-officers attempt to rally and form some of the corps ; all was pell-mell. It would be unjust for this to censure my brave troops ; never had they fought with greater valor ; but crossed by adverse circumstances and overwhelmed by a vast superiority of numbers, they yielded only when their strength and munitions were entirely exhausted. Owing to the darkness of the night, and the rapid pursuit of Blucher's able chief of staff, Gneisenau, it became impossible to make a successful stand for covering the retreat ; and the troops, being checked and confused in the barricaded avenues of the defile of Genappe, were subjected to heavy losses. In this way the disastrous retreat was continued till the fugitives were rallied under the cannon of Avesnes. From Quatre-Bras I dispatched several officers with orders for Grouchy to retreat upon Namur; I then went to Charleroi, directed the scattered troops, defiling through this place, upon Avesnes, and afterward repaired to Philippeville, in order to be in more direct communication with Grouchy, Rapp, and the forces on the Rhine. Grouchy with his remaining thirty-five thousand men fell back upon Namur in order to take the road of Givet and Meziers; Prince Jerome had rallied twenty-five thousand men with two hundred pieces of cannon behind Avesnes; he received orders to march them on Laon. It was also determined to direct upon the same point, the forces of Grouchy, and all that could be drawn from the interior, from Metz, and from the corps of Rapp, leaving in Lorraine and Alsace merely enough to garrison the fortifications.

We had, indeed, sustained severe losses, including the prisoners taken in the retreat, but still these losses were less than those sustained by the enemy. The imperial cause was shaken, but not yet lost. There was still every reason to hope, if all Frenchmen would unite in hurling back the invading armies of Europe with the same courage as the Spartans of Leonidas, the same energy as the Russians in 1812, or the Spaniards of Palafox. But, as unfortunately for them as for me, internal dissensions distracted their minds and blunted their patriotism.

Napoleon's Return to Paris.—While my forces were collecting at Laon, there was time enough for me to repair to Paris and there organize the means of national defense. The council of war, called at this time were divided in opinion on the policy of this step. The majority, however, of the members advised it, and accordingly I set out on the night of the twenty-first with the intention of being back by the twenty-fifth. In six days I could organize things in the capital for the great national crisis, complete the defenses of Paris, and collect the reserves that could be obtained from the depôts and the provinces. This return, so natural, to Paris, was misinterpreted by my enemies; they pretended to regard my departure from the army as an act of cowardice. I had shown at Arcole, at Eylau, at Ratisbon, at Arcis, and at Waterloo even, that a cannon ball had no terrors for me; and if I had despaired of the resources of France, I could have died at the head of the wreck of my army. If I had now left this army, it was only after it had retreated beyond the reach of the enemy, into positions from which the lowest general of the rear-guard could conduct them to Laon as safely as I could; but who could supply my place at the helm of state, which at this moment, unfortunately, was not at my head-quarters, but at the Tuileries!

Military Resources still left to France.—In eight or ten days, I hoped to return to Laon at the head of one hundred thousand men, and four hundred pieces of cannon, to punish the Anglo-Prussians for invading the soil of France. This force of course, would not enable me to disperse the armies which the allied sovereigns were leading toward the defiles of the Vosges, but it would give me time; and, with the three hundred thousand men to be assembled on the Loire in July, France might still conquer her independence and save her glory, for other nations have rescued themselves from still greater dangers. After the battle of Waterloo her condition was critical, but it was not desperate. All arrangements had been made on a supposition of a defeat in Belgium. The forces assembled between Laon and Paris, the troops of the depôts, and the twenty-five thousand select men under Rapp, might all be concentrated around Paris early in

July; by that time the artillery would be repaired and greatly increased. Independent of this, the capital had for its defense thirty-six thousand National Guards, thirty thousand riflemen, six thousand gunners, six hundred cannon in battery; it was formidably intrenched on the right bank of the Seine, and in a few days the engineers would render defensible the works on the left bank. The English and Prussian armies, weakened by their great losses, would cross the Somme with very reduced forces, and would be compelled to wait there for the coöperation of the Austrian and Russian armies which could not reach the Marne before the middle of July. Paris had, therefore, twenty days to prepare for defense, to complete her armaments, her supplies, her provisions, her fortifications, and to collect troops from all parts of France. Lyons also was well armed, provisioned and intrenched. The defense of all the fortified places was secured. They were commanded by select officers, and garrisoned by faithful troops. Every thing might be retrieved; but it required character, energy and firmness on the part of the officers, the government, the chambers, and the whole nation; it required them to be animated by sentiments of honor, of glory, and of national independence—to take, as a model, Rome after the battle of Cannae, and not Carthage after that of Zama. Should France assume this lofty tone, she would be invincible; her population was more military than that of any other nation. The means of carrying on the war were abundant, and fit for every purpose.

Without recurring to the ages of the Scipios, there are sufficient examples in modern history, such as Spain in 1808, and Russia in 1812. Some will say that the circumstances of France were different from Spain and Russia, and that she was too much exhausted in men and resources to hope for a similar result. Such reasons merit no answer: pusillanimous minds never want pretexts for submission, in preference to incurring the obligation of "victory or death." It is not given to all to think like Spartans.

Conspiracies of Napoleon's Adversaries.—Notwithstanding these unfounded fears of the faint-hearted, the army and the revolutionary party were in favor of resistance, without stopping to count the sacrifices it might require. But the factious leaders of radicalism sought to turn this feeling to their own account, and to separate the cause of France from that of her constituted rulers. Every thing was to be sacrificed to the selfish views and Utopian doctrines of these men. They thought to resist armed Europe with decrees! Even Lafayette had the credulity to believe that Europe was fighting only against my ambition, and that the allied sovereigns would lay down their arms before his Gallo-American doctrines; but he found, when too late, that it was precisely against these same doctrines that the sovereigns had declared war.

Great disasters, like volcanoes, are announced by a commotion in the subterranean elements. On the twentieth of June Paris was agitated by the most alarming reports. Fouché dispatched his secret agents through the capital to promulgate the opinion that my abdication was the only thing that could save the country, and at the same time assembled at his house his friends of the chambers,—Lafayette, Manuel, Dupont de l'Eure, Flauguergues, Dupin, and Henri Lacoste,—for the purpose of devising means to secure this abdication. Fearing lest the dissolution of the chambers might put an end to their own usurped authority, it was agreed in this conclave that Lafayette should propose the next day to the chamber to declare itself permanent, and to pronounce him a traitor to the country who should order its dissolution. As a reward for this the *grand citoyen* who had accompanied the people from Paris to Versailles in 1779, was anew to be decorated with his favorite title of commandant of the National Guards of the kingdom!

While the infamous Fouché and his friends were thus secretly planning my overthrow, and the usurpation of the reins of government by themselves, I arrived, at four o'clock in the morning, at the palace Elysée-Bourbon, where Caulaincourt was waiting for me with great impatience. Instead of speaking of dissolution, the first words spoken by me were to announce the project of convening the two chambers in extraordinary session, in order to lay before them the true state of the disasters of Waterloo, and to ask of them the means necessary to save France, after which I would hasten to rejoin the army. The ministers were immediately called together to deliberate on the measures to be taken to save the country. I expressed to them frankly my own views of the resources of the French, of their ability to repel the invaders, and of the necessity, in the present crisis, of establishing a dictatorial power. This power might be established either by the emperor or by the chambers. A majority of the ministers thought the latter the most efficacious and legal method of proceeding. But was there any confidence to be placed in this factious assembly, led on by traitors, demagogues, and men of Utopian and impracticable theories? Caulaincourt feared that the dissolution of the chambers would lead to the same frightful results as in 1814. Fouché, steeped in dissimulation and treason, based all his schemes of mischief and personal aggrandizement on the influence of his party in these assemblies. Decrès, on the contrary, reposed no confidence in them. Regnault de Saint-Jean d'Angely himself, that obsequious and complaisant orator, dared to suggest that the chambers would undoubtedly require a new abdication, and even insinuated that if it was not voluntarily given, they would demand it. Lucien, remembering the eighteenth Brumaire, was of opinion that the emperor should dissolve the assembly, and himself save France. Carnot, the old republican leader, best understood the nature of the crisis, and the means necessary for a desperate national defense. In his opinion the French soil was, at any price, to be freed from foreign invaders, and the best means of accomplishing this object, was to constitute a dictatorial power with all the energy of the committee of public safety in 1793. If Carnot was no great statesman, he at least possessed the energy of a real old Roman, and let it ever be remembered in his praise that in the darkest hour of French history he shook off the shackles of party prejudice, and thought only of his country's honor and glory.

While these grave questions were discussed at the palace of Elysée-Bourbon, and while every exertion was made to preserve harmony with the chambers, as the only plank of public safety, the partisans of Fouché were hatching their plots of revolution and treason in the assemblies. Rumors of dissolution were perfidiously circulated among the members, and in a moment of excitement, the deputies, influenced by jealousy or cowardice, voted the decree denouncing as a traitor whoever should dare to pronounce a dissolution! The dissolution of the chambers was one of the rights secured to the emperor by the constitution which these very men had adopted, and yet these pretended apostles of law and order, assumed a power over the constitution to condemn me in anticipation for the execution of this very law! To reach me, they did not hesitate to trample under foot the constitution and laws of their country, and to sacrifice to their own ambition the glory and honor of France.

This decree, in itself utterly illegal and revolutionary, directed the ministers to appear before the assembly; Lucien accompanied the ministers and demanded, in the name of the emperor, the appointment of a committee to take into consideration measures necessary to secure the public safety; a committee was appointed, it is true, but it was composed of my bitterest enemies, men of petty ambition, mediocre talent, and Utopian views,—Lanjuinais, Lafayette, Grenier, Flauguergues, and Dupont de l'Eure; this committee, instead of seeking to secure the national independence and save the national honor, talked of foreign treaties and republican principles, and, Nero-like, fiddled the tune of natural and constitutional rights, while the enemy was approaching the gates of the capital!!

The People side with Napoleon.—In the mean time the lower classes of the people, distrusting the factious and traitorous leaders of the chambers, assembled around the palace of Elysée-Bourbon, rending the air with cries of "Vive-l'Empereur!" and demanding arms. Lucien endeavored to persuade me to profit by this enthusiasm, and make another eighteenth Brumaire, much more legal than the first, by ordering a dissolution of the chambers in the legal forms, and, if necessary, compelling its execution. The idea of saving the country by arming the lower classes of the people against the first magistrates, was revolting to my mind. I was no admirer of insurrectionary movements. Moreover, this measure, more like that of the thirty-first of May, 1793, than the eighteenth Brumaire, would tend rather to divide than to unite public feeling. The crisis demanded a union of all classes, and this alone could save the country. It would not have been difficult for me to crush the opposition and destroy the weak and traitorous men who had conspired to overturn my throne. But in doing this, could I save France? While striving with internal enemies, could I oppose sufficient strength to check the million of armed men who were striking at the independence of my country? could I consent to overthrow the whole social fabric of France, to satisfy my own military vanity? The foolish and factious leaders of the chambers were insane enough to imagine that Europe would hasten to lay down its arms before their puny decrees; they thought to give a triumph to their Utopian doctrines by sacrificing the only man capable of guiding the nation gloriously through the gigantic contest; these men, and these alone, are responsible for the humiliations they prepared for their country.*

His second Abdication.—Seeing that these men had determined either to rule or ruin France, I had but one course to pursue—to resign; I, therefore, dictated to my brother Lucien the following abdication in favor of my son:

"Frenchmen! In commencing the war to sustain the national independence, I counted on the union of all efforts, of all wills, and of all the national authorities; I had good reason to hope for success, and I braved all the declarations of foreign powers against me. The circumstances seem changed, and I now offer myself as a sacrifice to the hatred of the enemies of France. May they be sincere in their declarations, and direct their hostilities only against my person. My political life is ended; and I proclaim my son, under the title of Napoleon II., Emperor of the French. The existing ministers will form the council of government. The interest which I feel in my son induces me to invite the

* There is no more painful picture in the history of nations than that of a people, in times of great public danger, governed by mediocre men, by Utopian theorists, and factious, selfish and profligate politicians. When great men are stricken down by party jealousies and party intrigues, and when good men shrink from office rather than come in contact with the rottenness with which it is too often surrounded, or expose themselves to the partisan abuse, increased and intensified by the license of the press, which is poured upon them if they repel this corruption, there is little hope for the nation. If it finally becomes virtuous and independent, it is only after long abasement and severe suffering.

France in 1814 and 1815, is not the only example in history. The fall of Rome is the most striking of all. This republic and empire was undermined and destroyed by factious intriguing politicians, who debauched the people for their votes, corrupted public virtue in pursuit of office, and drove into the retirement of private life all who were capable or willing to save the country. France, after great suffering, reconquered her independence, but Rome was utterly destroyed by the corruption of her own political rulers.

chambers to organize without delay the regency by law. Let all unite for the public safety, and the maintenance of the national independence ! !"

Determined to exile myself from Europe and go to America, I hoped that the allies would be satisfied with the hostage I had just placed at their discretion, and that they would leave the crown on the head of the son of Maria Louisa. This stipulation had been made on an understanding with the leaders of the chambers ; and I believed it the best means of fusing the old and new interests, and of preventing civil war. The republican leaders were utterly incapable of governing France ; the Bourbons, if again restored by foreign bayonets, would sooner or later be again hurled from their thrones, for this dynasty had become odious to the French people. To avoid a repetition of the scenes enacted between 1789 and 1804, it was necessary to avoid the extremes of ultra democracy, on the one hand, and old legitimacy on the other. No government that did not fuse together these separate interests could be of long duration.

Whatever may have been the views of the allied sovereigns on this point, all action on the subject was dispensed with by the singular course pursued by the leaders of the chambers, who still flattered themselves that they could dictate laws to France, and force Europe to observe them. Unwilling to acknowledge Napoleon II., or to establish a regency, they hastened to form a provisional government, in the hope of seizing upon the reins of state, treating for their existence with the allied sovereigns, and of receiving the Bourbon government only on such conditions as the chambers should impose ; an absurd dream, for could it be supposed that Louis XVIII. or the allied sovereigns, armed for the support of legitimate thrones, would consent to principles that struck at the root of the old dynasties ? But let us return to the military operations of the allies.

Informed by the traitor Fouché of my abdication, and of the anarchy existing at Paris, the Anglo-Prussians advanced upon the capital with a rapidity and carelessness that might readily have led to their own destruction. In seeking to turn the fortifications erected on the north of Paris, the Prussians passed the Seine alone near Pecq, while Wellington remained on the right bank, unable to sustain them. The French army, then commanded by Davoust, and encamped in the vicinity, might easily have fallen on them with seventy thousand men, and, driving them into the Seine, have utterly annihilated them. I proposed to the provisional government to take the command of the army, and to resign it when I had conquered; but base intrigues prevented me from washing out the stain of Waterloo, and of taking leave of France by a victory which would have enabled her to treat honorably with the allied sovereigns, instead of surrendering at discretion, as was done by the provisional government, to a British general and a Prussian marshal. Instead of accepting my offer, Fouché, who was in active correspondence with Wellington, resolved to secure my person, and in fact I was placed in a kind of captivity under the guard of General Becker, lest I might of my own accord place myself at the head of the army. Nevertheless, the enthusiasm of the troops was so great, that this miserable government had the greatest difficulty in suspending hostilities, and General Excelmans destroyed an entire brigade near Ville-d'Avray, at the moment that the authorities were exerting themselves to restrain the patriotism and courage of his comrades.

He retires from France.—I immediately afterwards departed for Rochefort. The minister, Decrès, proposed that I should repair to Havre where there was an American vessel ready to sail. But the position of this port on the English Channel was objectionable, and, moreover, it was now too late to reach the vessel in time. I purposed sailing from Bordeaux in a vessel belonging to my brother Joseph. I was deterred by my legal advisers from embarking in a commercial port, and Joseph, sailing without me, reached America in safety. It has been positively affirmed that Fouché informed Wellington of my place of embarkation, and organized the means of capturing me. Immediately on leaving Rochefort I was pursued by an English cruiser, and seeing that it would be difficult to escape, I made directly for the vessel, placing myself under the safeguard of British honor and British laws. I wrote to the Prince Regent the following letter, which I sent to the commander of the cruiser, and the next day embarked on board the Bellerophon, being received by Captain Maitland with a general's salute:

"YOUR ROYAL HIGHNESS,—

"Exposed to the factions which divide my country, and to the hostility of the great powers of Europe, I have terminated my political career. I come, like Themistocles, to seat myself at the hearth of the British people. I put myself under the protection of their laws, and I claim it from Your Royal Highness, as from the most powerful, the most constant, and the most generous of my enemies."

And is exiled to St. Helena.—On reaching the shores of England I found, to my disappointment, that I had made an erroneous estimate of British hospitality; I was received as a criminal, and sentenced to be imprisoned for life upon a lonely and desolate island. To this barbarous treatment I entered the following formal protest:

"I protest solemnly, in the face of heaven and of men, against the violation of my most sacred rights, by the forcible disposal of my person and of my liberty. I came freely on board the Bellerophon. I am not the prisoner; I am the guest of England. Once on board the Bellerophon, I was immediately entitled to the hospitality of the British people. If the government, by giving orders to the captain of the Bellerophon to receive me and my suite, intended merely to lay a snare for me, it has forfeited its honor, and sullied its flag. If this act be consummated, it will be in vain that the English will boast to Europe of their loyalty, of their laws, of their liberty. British faith will have been lost in the hospitality of the Bellerophon. I appeal therefore to history. It will say that an enemy who made war for twenty years on the people of England, came freely, in his misfortune, to seek an asylum under their laws. What more striking proof could he give of his esteem and of his confidence? But how did they answer it in England? They pretended to hold out an hospitable hand to this enemy, and when he had surrendered himself to them in good faith, they sacrificed him!"

His Death.—Posterity will decide upon the character of this act, and I leave to its judgment the treatment which I received from the English.*

A prisoner upon another hemisphere, I had no other occupation than to defend my reputation against the many slanders which the malignity of party spirit invented against me, and to prepare for history the memoirs of my life. Death

* Lord Holland and the Duke of Sussex both protested against the bill for detaining Napoleon. The following is the protest of the former:

"Because, without reference to the character or previous conduct of the person who is the object of the present bill, I disapprove of the measure which it sanctions and continues.

"To consign to distant exile and imprisonment a foreign and captive chief, who, after the abdication of his authority, relying on British generosity, had surrendered himself to us in preference to his other enemies, is unworthy of the magnanimity of a great country; and the treaties by which after his captivity, we have bound ourselves to detain him in custody, at the will of sovereigns, to whom he had never surrendered himself, appear to me repugnant to the principles of equity, and utterly uncalled for by expediency or necessity.

(signed) "Holland."

surprised me while thus engaged, and the work was necessarily left incomplete.* Nevertheless I am satisfied; I can now rest in peace; pigmies may rise up against me, but they

* Most readers are familiar with the history of Napoleon's exile in St. Helena, and the petty annoyances which he suffered from the governor,—a treatment as disgraceful to Sir Hudson Lowe personally as it was unworthy of the great nation which he represented.

The following narrative of Napoleon's death, by Thiers, is brief and interesting:

"The year 1821 came at last, that year that was to terminate the wondrous career of Napoleon. At the commencement of January his health improved, but only for a few days. 'It is a respite,' he said, 'of a week or two, and then the disease will resume its course.' He then dictated a few pages touching Cæsar to Marchand; they were the last he wrote. About the same time, he saw the death of his sister Eliza announced in the papers. It pained him deeply. She was the first person of his family that had died since he had attained the use of reason. 'She has shown me the way,' he said, 'I must follow.' The symptoms of his disease returned now with greater violence than ever. Napoleon's complexion became livid, his glance was expressive of as much power as ever, but his eyes were sunken, his legs swelled, his extremities became cold, and his stomach rejected every species of food, and these ejections were accompanied by a discharge of blackish matter. February brought no other change than an increased intensity of the symptoms. Not being able to digest any food, the august invalid became weaker every day. He was tormented by intense thirst, and his pulse, once so slow, beat with feverish rapidity. He wished for air, though he could not endure it when admitted. The light pained him, and he now never left the rooms in which were his two camp-beds, being removed occasionally from one to the other. He did not dictate any more, but had Homer read to him, and the account of Hannibal's war in Livy, not having been able to procure Polybius.

"His health became still worse in March, and on the seventeenth, thinking that during a short drive he could breathe more freely, he was put into a carriage, but when brought into the air, he very nearly fainted, and was borne back to the bed in which he was to die. 'I am no longer,' he said, 'that proud Napoleon whom the world has so often seen on horseback. The monarchs who persecute me may set their minds at rest, I shall soon remove every cause of fear.' Napoleon's faithful servants never left him. Montholon and Marchand remained day and night by his bedside, an attention for which he showed himself profoundly grateful. The grand-marshal told him that neither he nor his wife would leave, and Napoleon thanked him warmly. The grand-marshal asked permission for his wife to visit him. 'I am not fit to be seen,' he said; 'I shall receive Madame Bertrand when I am better. Tell her I thank her for the devotion that has kept her for six years in this desert.'

* * * * * * *

"Napoleon devoted several days to making these arrangements, and committing them to writing. His labor suffered frequent interruptions from pain

can never obscure my glory; I have gained in the victories of Montenotte, Castiglione, Rivoli, the Pyramids, Marengo, Ulm, Austerlitz, Jena, Friedland, Abensberg, Ratisbon,

and weariness. All was arranged at length, and with his usual love of order he had a legal document drawn up of the transfer of his will, and all that he possessed, to his testamentary executors, that there might be no cause of dispute after his death. He desired that the rites of the Catholic faith should be observed at his burial, and that the dining-room in which he was accustomed to hear mass, should be converted into a *chapelle ardente.* Dr. Antomarchi could not help smiling as he heard these orders given to the Abbé Vignale. Napoleon considered this as a want of respect to his authority, his genius, and his death. 'Young man,' he said in a severe tone, 'perhaps you are too clever to believe in God; I am not in that position, *a man can not become an atheist merely by wishing it.*' This severe lesson, spoken in terms worthy of a great man at the point of death, overwhelmed the young doctor with confusion; he made a thousand excuses, and made profession of the most satisfactory moral principles.

"These preparations for death weakened Napoleon, and perhaps, hastened his end. Still it was both a moral and physical relief to him to have arranged his affairs, and secured, as far as he could, the fate of his companions. Meeting death with a smile as dignified as it was grateful, he said to Montholon and Marchand who never left him: 'It would be a great pity not to die, now that I have arranged all my affairs so well.'

"The end of April had arrived, and every moment increased his danger and suffering. He had no relief from the spasms, vomitings, fever and burning thirst. Napoleon was relieved by occasionally drinking some drops of fresh water brought from the foot of the peak of Diana, the spot where he had wished to have a dwelling erected. 'I wish,' he said, 'if it is possible, that I should be buried on the banks of the Seine, or at Ajaccio in my family domain, or should my body be fated to continue a prisoner, at the foot of the fountain, whose waters have afforded me some relief.' This his friends promised with tears, for they no longer concealed from him a state he so well understood himself. 'You will return bearing with you the reflection of my glory, with the honor of your own fidelity. You will be esteemed and happy. I go to meet Kleber, Desaix, Lannes, Massena, Bessières, Duroc, Ney! They will come to meet me. They will experience once more the intoxication of human glory. We shall speak of what we have done. We shall talk of our profession with Frederick, Turenne, Condé, Cæsar, and Hannibal.' Then pausing, Napoleon added with a peculiar smile, 'Unless there should be as great an objection in the upper spheres, as there is here below to see a number of soldiers together.' This *badinage*, alternating with the most solemn discourse, produced a profound effect upon those present. On the first of May the agony seemed to commence, and he was in constant torture. On the second and third, Napoleon was in high fever, and suffered continual spasms. Whenever his sufferings abated his mind was as radiant as ever, and he spoke with clearness and serenity. During one of these intervals, he dictated under the title of first

Wagram, Dresden, Champ-Aubert, Montmirail, Ligny, glory enough to efface the disaster of Waterloo; my Five Codes, worthy of the approbation of the seven sages of Greece, will remain a monument to posterity not less creditable to my genius than are my military feats; the great works of improvement and of art which I have constructed in France and in Italy, will attest my greatness to the remotest ages. To the reproach of ambition, I will say with Mahomet:

> Je fus ambitieux * * *
> Mais jamais roi, pontife, ou chef ou citoyen
> Ne conçut un projet aussi grand que le mien."*

and second revery, two notes on the defense of France in case of an invasion. On the third he became delirious, and amid his ravings these words were distinguishable: 'My son. The army. Desaix.' It would seem as though he had a last vision of the battle of Marengo recovered by Desaix. The agony continued during the entire day of the fourth, and the noble countenance of the hero was terribly distorted. The weather was terrible, it was the bad season at St. Helena. Sudden gusts of wind tore up some of the planted trees. On the fifth of May there was no doubt but that the last day of his extraordinary life had dawned. All his servants kneeling round his bed watched the last flickerings of the vital flame. These were unfortunately attended with bitter sufferings. The English officers assembled outside, listened with respectful interest to the accounts the servants gave of his agony. Towards the decline of day, his life and sufferings decreased together; the cold extending from the extremities became general, and death seemed about to seize his glorious victim. The weather had become calm and serene. About twenty minutes past five, when the sun was setting in waves of light, and the English cannon gave the signal for retiring, those around the bed perceived that the patient did not breathe, and cried out that he was dead. They covered his hands with kisses, and Marchand who had brought to Saint-Helena the cloak the First Consul had worn at Marengo, laid it over his body, leaving only his noble head uncovered.

"The convulsions of the death agony, always so painful to witness, were succeeded by a majestic tranquillity of expression. That face so wondrously beautiful, now restored to the slenderness of youth, and the figure clad in the mantle of Marengo, seemed to present again to the witnesses of that touching scene, General Bonaparte in the meridian of his glory."

* Alison thus describes the removal of Napoleon's remains from St. Helena to France:

"Time rolled on, and brought its usual changes on its wings. The dynasty of the Restoration proved unequal to the arduous task of coercing the desires of the Revolution, weakened, but not extinguished, by the overthrow of Napoleon: a new generation arose, teeming with passions and forgetful of the sufferings of former times; and the revolt of the barricades restored the tri-

EPILOGUE.

No sooner had Napoleon ended his recital, than his illustrious auditors declared, with unanimous voice, that, although he had failed in the execution of his vast projects he surpassed them all in his force of genius and greatness of soul.

color flag, and established a semi-revolutionary dynasty on the French throne.

"England shared in the renewed convulsion consequent on these momentous events; a great organic change in the constitution placed the popular party for a course of years in power; a temporary alliance, founded on political passion, not national interest, for a time united its government with that of France; and under the auspices of M. Thiers' administration, a request was made to the British to restore the remains of their Great Emperor to the French people.

"This request, received in a worthy spirit by the English administration, was immediately complied with, in the hope, as it was eloquently, though fallaciously said at the time, 'that these two great nations would henceforth bury their discord in the tomb of Napoleon.'

"The solitary grave in St. Helena was disturbed; the lonely willow no longer wept over the remains of the emperor; the sepulchre was opened in presence of all the officers of the island, and many of his faithful followers; and the winding-sheet, rolled back with pious care, revealed to the entranced spectators the well-known features of the immortal hero, serene, undecayed, in his now canonized military dress, as when he stood on the fields of Austerlitz or Jena. The body was removed from its resting place with the highest military honors; the British army and navy in the island, with generous sympathy, vied with each other in doing honor to their great antagonist; and when it was lowered amidst the thunder of artillery into the French frigate, England felt that she had voluntarily, but in a right spirit, relinquished the proudest trophy of her national glory.

"The remains of the emperor were conveyed in safety to Europe on board the Belle Poule frigate, and landed, with appropriate honors, at Havre de Grace. From thence they were removed to Paris, with a view to their being interred, with the other illustrious warriors of France, in the Church of the Invalides. The re-interment, which awakened the deepest interest in France and over Europe, took place on the sixth of December, 1849.

"The day was fine, though piercingly cold; but such was the interest excited, that six hundred thousand persons were assembled to witness the ceremony. The procession approached Paris by the road from St. Cloud, so often traversed by the emperor in the days of his glory; it passed through the now finished and stupendous arch erected to the Grand Army at the barrier of

Each in particular eulogized those traits which most resembled his own :—Alexander praised Napoleon for his generosity to his conquered foes ; Cæsar admired his having built up an empire out of the scattered fragments of public liberty, and established his power with legions destined to defend that liberty ; Frederick applauded his spirit of order and economy, and was particularly pleased at seeing his own system of war receive such new and extensive developments.

From that moment the four heroes became inseparable, and their conversations form an inexhaustible source of political and military instruction, and constitutes the principal charm and delight of the illustrious shades who inhabit the fields of Elysium.

Neuilly; and slowly moving through the Elysian Fields, reached the Invalides by the bridge of La Concorde.

"Louis Philippe and all his court officiated at the august ceremony, which was performed with extraordinary pomp in the splendid church of the edifice; but nothing awakened such deep feeling as a band of the mutilated veterans of the Old Guard, who with mournful visages, but yet a military air, attended the remains of their beloved chief to his last resting place.

"An aged charger, once rode by the emperor on his fields of fame, survived to follow the colossal hearse to the grave. The place of interment was worthy of the hero who was now placed beneath its roof: it contained the remains of Turenne and Vauban, and the paladins of France; enchanting music thrilled every heart as the coffin was lowered into the tomb; the thunders of the artillery, so often vocal to his triumphs, now gave him the last honors of mortality; the genius of Marochatti was selected to erect a fitting monument to his memory; and the bones of Napoleon finally reposed on the banks of the Seine, amidst the 'people whom he had loved so well.'

"Yet will future ages perhaps regret the ocean-girt isle, the solitary stone, the willow tree. Napoleon will live when Paris is in ruins; his deeds will survive the dome of the Invalides;—no man can show the tomb of Alexander!"

GENERAL INDEX.

THE ROMAN NUMERALS REFER TO THE VOLUME AND THE FIGURES TO THE PAGE.

A.

C.

D.

F

G.

H.

I.

J.

L.

N.

O.

V.

CPSIA information can be obtained
at www.ICGtesting.com
Printed in the USA
LVHW022015120422
716028LV00006B/190

9 783752 592481